Rave Reviews for Recent Xanth Adventures

"The Xanth books constitute Anthony's longest and most successful series. . . . They are intended to be kind-spirited, fun reading, a series of wondrous beasts and beings, and, most of all, an endless succession of outrageous puns."
—Lee Killough, *The Wichita Eagle*

"Classic Xanthromancy! *Air Apparent* sends a company of adventurers on a quest through multiple Xanths, encountering absurdities, dancers, and romance but also finding themselves unwittingly involved in extremely complex intrigue."
—*Booklist*

"Prolific fantasy and SF author Anthony celebrates his thirtieth volume in the perpetually popular Xanth series with a tale of love's struggle to overcome adversity. Filled with the requisite puns and plays on words, *Stork Naked* features both old and new Xanth residents caught up in a series of whirlwind events." —*Library Journal*

"*Swell Foop* is a fantasy confection, full of puns, clever mathematical and grammatical lessons. . . . Xanth fans will rejoice at this fast-paced romp." —*Publishers Weekly*

TWO
TO THE
FIFTH

PIERS ANTHONY

TWO
TO THE
FIFTH

TOR®
fantasy

A TOM DOHERTY ASSOCIATES BOOK
NEW YORK

This is a work of fiction. All of the characters, organizations, and events portrayed in this novel are either products of the author's imagination or are used fictitiously.

TWO TO THE FIFTH

Copyright © by 2008 by Piers Anthony Jacob

A Tor Book
Published by Tom Doherty Associates, LLC
175 Fifth Avenue
New York, NY 10010

www.tor-forge.com

Tor® is a registered trademark of Tom Doherty Associates, LLC.

ISBN 978-0-7653-5894-3

First Edition: October 2008
First Mass Market Edition: October 2009

Printed in the United States of America

0 9 8 7 6 5 4 3 2 1

Contents

TWO
TO THE
FIFTH

CYRUS

G et the lead out of your ass."

Cyrus jumped, almost falling off his donkey. "Who said that?"

"Get thee to a nunnery."

This time he placed the source. "You're talking!" he said to the donkey.

"Who said that?" the animal said. "You're talking."

"You're repeating whatever you have heard most recently," Cyrus said, catching on. "That voice unit was supposed to be for braying. How can you speak words?"

"Defective workmanship," the donkey said. "You installed the wrong unit."

Cyrus sighed. So using lead instead of iron wasn't his only error when he constructed the donkey. When the mechanical animal was too heavy to function effectively, Cyrus's father Roland had given him blunt advice: remove the lead. So he had done so, and had a robot animal he could ride.

"Who said the other?" he asked. "About the nunnery. That's like a monastery, isn't it?"

"Your barbarian mother said it," the donkey answered. "You weren't paying attention. She was not referring to nuns."

"Not?"

"Not. According to my defective data bank, it's old Mundanian slang for a house of ill repute."

"What is that? I never heard of an ill house."

"Naturally you wouldn't know. You were created halfway innocent, for some obscure reason. But she thought it would make a man of you."

"I'm not a man," Cyrus protested. "I'm a cyborg. Half robot, half human. I will never be fully human."

"That's what comes of getting yourself delivered to a humanoid robot and a barbarian. If you wanted to be normal you should have selected a normal couple for parents."

"I didn't have a choice, you nutty and bolty contraption. They signaled the stork, not me."

"Neither did I have a choice, half-breed."

"Had you had one, you should have chosen a more competent builder," Cyrus said with a halfway metallic smile.

"Indubitably. But since I'm stuck with you, how about giving me a name?"

"You're an ass. An equine breed. So suppose I call you—"

"Forget it, cogbrain!"

Cyrus reconsidered. "Donkey won't do?"

"Let's abbreviate it. Don will do."

"Don Donkey. Not phenomenally original."

"Neither are you, cyborg."

"It will do," Cyrus agreed with resignation.

He rode on, careful not to remark on the animal's jerky gait, lest he get another sour reminder of his clumsiness in assembling it. The varied terrain of the Land of Xanth passed, becoming less familiar as they got farther away from home. They were following one of the enchanted paths, so there was no danger.

Cyrus got thirsty, so fished a can of tsoda pop from a saddlebag. He was about to open it when it slipped out of his hand, fell to the ground, and rolled off the enchanted path. "Bleep," he said. Because he had been assembled adult, he was able to use that term. It signaled spot disaffection with the situation.

There was a golden streak. Something zipped after the can, caught it in its mouth, and brought it back, holding it up. It was a dog made from pure gold.

"Thank you," Cyrus said, accepting the can. The dog zipped away again. "I wonder what kind of creature that was?"

"A golden retriever, dummy," Don said. "Check your memory bank."

The donkey was right: the information was there. Cyrus simply hadn't made the connection. "Thank you," he said again.

"I'm low on fuel," Don complained.

Cyrus considered. Chances of getting where they were going today were small, so there was no point in pushing it. "We'll stop at the next grazing area we see," he said.

"We'd better."

They came to a small glade strewn with sticks and tufts of old dry grass. "And this is it," Cyrus said, dismounting.

They stepped off the path. Don put his head down and picked up a stick with his mouth. He chewed, and the stick broke in two. He swallowed the pieces.

"Oh what a cute little horse!" a voice exclaimed. It was a rather young pretty girl, in fact almost nymphlike, but clothed. She had flouncing bark brown hair and sky blue eyes.

Don lifted his head to view her. "I'm not a horse," he said sourly. "I'm an ass."

She looked bemused. "A what?"

"A donkey," Cyrus said quickly, realizing that the Adult Conspiracy prevented her from knowing the other term. "A robot donkey. Call him Don."

"Hello, Don," she said shyly. "I'm Piper Nymph."

"I don't see a pipe," Don said.

"I don't have a pipe. It's my name. My parents are Hiatus Human and Desiree Dryad. They named me."

Cyrus's data bank oriented. He knew of them; Hiatus was the son of the late Zombie Master, with the talent of growing things like ears on walls. He had fallen in love with a tree nymph, a hamadryad, and finally married her after a seemingly hopeless quest. Cyrus was jealous; he had no romantic prospects at all. At any rate, that explained Piper's nymph-like appearance: she was half nymph.

"What good are you?" Don asked.

"He's an ass—I mean donkey," Cyrus said quickly. "He has barnyard manners. Ignore him."

"No, I'll answer," Piper said. "My talent is healing. That can be very useful. In fact I have a pet whirlwind I healed, Dusty."

"A useful whirlwind?" Don asked, his voice fairly rusting with sarcasm.

"Sure. I'll show you. What do you most need?"

"More dry wood. It's my fuel. I'm a wood-burning robot ass." Don obviously thought he had stifled her positive attitude.

Piper put two fingers to her mouth and made an ungirl-like whistle. In a moment a whirling cloud of dust cruised in toward them, tossing leaves and small twigs about. "This is Dusty," she said as the whirlwind hovered beside her. "Dusty Dust Devil."

"What an ill wind," Don said.

The wind coalesced into a small horned creature. "Why thank you, asinine junk," the little devil said.

Don took it in stride. "Can you bring me dry wood, you horny midget?"

"Please," Piper said. "I've got a feeling there's a bad word there."

The devil disappeared, becoming the dust devil. It whirled

all around the glade and into the surrounding forest. In a moment it returned, filled with brush, and faded. A pile of dead branches fell to the ground as the devil formed.

Don stared. "That will hold me for three days!" He started chomping wood.

"Say thank you," Cyrus murmured to the donkey.

"Why?" Don asked around a mouthful.

Cyrus realized that politeness was not part of the animal's program. So he gave a reason that would make sense to a selfish creature. "Because you want to encourage him to do it again some time, after you run out of fuel."

Don cocked an ear, understanding. "Thank you, Dusty."

The little devil blushed blue.

"Say you're welcome," Piper murmured.

"You're welcome."

Don paused in midchomp. He was coming to appreciate the possible benefits of common courtesy.

Piper smiled. She was pretty when she did that. "It's nice to see folk get along," she said.

Too bad she was only thirteen years old, according to Cyrus's data bank: too young to be a prospect for romance. Not that Cyrus knew anything about romance.

They had to wait while the donkey took in the pile of wood. "What are you doing here?" Cyrus asked the nymph.

"I'm just widening my horizons," she said. "Every year mother lets me wander farther from the tree. By the time I'm adult, I should be familiar with the whole area. Already today I met a man with the talent of selective friction: he can move anywhere, because if he's on slippery ice, he can make one foot have a lot of friction, and push with it, then change to the other foot."

"So what good is that?" Don asked. "There's no ice here."

"Maybe some day there'll be ice," Piper said. "Or something else that's slippery or soupy."

"What do you want to do when you are adult?" Cyrus asked,

partly to stop the donkey from being obnoxious. But also because he did not know what he wanted to do, and perhaps she would give him an idea.

"I'd like to be an actress, I think," she said. "To be in a play and have people watch me and applaud. I wouldn't even have to be famous. I'd just like to be on stage."

That seemed like a curious ambition, but Cyrus's caution-circuit prevented him from saying so. "I hope you find your play."

"I hope so too." Piper looked around. "I'd better get home; mother worries when I'm out alone too long. She's afraid I'll run afoul of some strange man or something."

Like a cyborg? That, too, was worth not saying. "Tell her you met a robot donkey with asinine manners."

"I will," she said. "Come on, Dusty; I'll race you to the tree."

The little devil became the whirlwind. Dust devil and girl took off into the forest, racing each other.

Meanwhile Don had finished the pile of wood. His belly was full; it would, as he said, burn for three days, keeping him hot and active.

They wended their way back to the enchanted path. "You know, I'd be able to eat faster and last longer if you'd designed me to burn coal," Don said.

"Coal has to be mined. Wood's easier to get. Anyway, I had to use parts of wrecked robots, and they were all wood-burning."

"That also explains where you got my warped brain chip."

It did indeed. Cyrus was beginning to regret raiding that old battleground. But there hadn't seemed to be much alternative if he wanted to ride.

As the day waned they came to a camping area. There were pie trees galore, and a nice caterpillar tent.

As they approached the tent, a young woman emerged. She looked lean and aggressive. Could she be barbarian?

"Who the bleep are you?" she demanded. "This tent is mine; I got here first. Go away."

Cyrus sifted through his data banks. "Enchanted Path Camping Sites are open to all legitimate travelers," he said. "We are legitimate."

"What, you and that dumb ass?"

"I'm an ass, but I'm not dumb," Don said. "I'm a smart ass. How smart is your ass, wench?" He eyed her posterior.

The woman stared, evidently taken aback, or at least paused in place. "You talk!"

"Let's exchange introductions," Cyrus said hastily. "I am Cyrus Cyborg, and this is Don, a robot donkey."

"He's got a bleeping potty mouth on him."

"Look who's talking, you bleeping tart."

Cyrus interposed again. "And you are?"

"Tess," she said aggressively. "Tess Tosterone. I have a problem."

Don opened his mouth. Cyrus hastily stuffed a scrounged piece of wood into it. "May we inquire what it is?"

"I'm too pushy. They tell me I need S Trojan to fix it. But I don't know who or where or what he is, so I'm irritable."

Cyrus's data bank sifted again. "Trojan is one name of the Night Stallion who runs the dream realm. The horse of a different color. But he doesn't have a first name."

"Then it must be someone else. What would I want with a horse? Your talking mule is bad enough. Now are you going to clear out of here and let me be?"

Don had chewed and swallowed the stick. "Listen, harridan—"

Cyrus made another effort to settle things politely, though her attitude was both annoying and intriguing. "We feel we have equal rights to camp here, so we won't be moving on tonight. Why do you object to sharing?"

"Because you're a man," Tess said bluntly. "All you men want only one thing."

This interested him. "What is that?"

"Don't pretend you don't know, you jerk!"

"I'm not pretending. I *don't* know. That's why I'm traveling to see the Good Magician. I hope he will tell me what I truly want."

Tess gazed at him, taking stock. "You're serious."

"I am a serious person, yes."

"And a cyborg."

"Yes."

"What's a cyborg?"

"I am a robot-human crossbreed, part alive, part machine. I am not sure in which category I best belong."

She studied him. "You look completely human."

"Yes, I am crafted to be, externally. But my bones are iron, and I have a memory bank and consciousness chip in my iron skull. I am programmed to have a human outlook. My parents assembled me carefully."

"Actually, you're one handsome male specimen, with a perfect rough-hewn face, fairly wild hair, and nice muscles."

"My mother is a barbarian. She likes that type."

"She has good taste in men. Your appearance is appealing to women."

"It is? I did not know."

"And you really don't know what all men want."

"True. The information may be in my data bank, but I need a more specific description to evoke it. If you know, I would appreciate it if you would tell me. It might save me a year's service with the Good Magician."

Tess laughed, surprising him. "It might indeed. Very well, I will share the tent with you, and maybe by morning you will figure it out for yourself."

"I doubt it. I'm sure it would be simpler if you just told me."

"Simpler, yes. More fun, no."

Was she teasing him? Teasing was another human thing Cyrus did not properly understand. There were a number of things like that, that it seemed only experience and new information could clarify. At any rate, Tess seemed to have mellowed, so he didn't question it. Maybe she would tell him in the morning.

"I'll fetch something to eat," Cyrus said. "Maybe some of those lichens."

"Don't," she said. "Those aren't like-ens, they're dislike-ens. Eat one, and you'll be unfriendly until you find and eat a like-en to cancel it. I found out the hard way."

He might have guessed. "Thank you."

"The effect wears off eventually. But why complicate things?"

They foraged for pies and had a nice dinner while Don snoozed beside the pond. Tess was companionable, now that she had accepted him as legitimate, but she seemed privately amused about something. Cyrus suppressed his annoyance.

As night closed, Tess took charge, in the aggressive way she had. "There are two bunks in the tent. You take the left one, I'll take the right one. We'll wash up first."

"As you wish," he agreed.

"Not as *you* wish?"

"I am amenable to whatever normal procedure is. I admit to having had little experience. It is my first journey away from home."

"What, away from your mommy?"

There was something in her tone, but it seemed a fair question. "Yes. Hannah Barbarian."

"Just how old are you, cyborg?"

"As much as two years."

"Two years! You look grown!"

"I *am* grown. I was delivered as a grown-man kit, in a small cat-shaped box, with some assembly required. I understand that effort drove both my parents to distraction, but in the course of the following year they managed to assemble me, and here I am."

She gazed at him assessingly. "So are you grown, or a baby? Are you familiar with the Adult Conspiracy?"

"Yes, of course. It is in my data bank. It concerns the things that children must be shielded from, such as bad words and stork summoning. Naturally I honor it to the letter; it's in my programming."

"Have you ever seen a bare woman?"

"Oh, yes, there are pictures in my data bank."

"A real one."

"No. But I'm sure I know the description."

She shook her head as if bemused. "This way." She walked to the pond.

He followed. "Actually my data indicates that strangers do not readily show their bodies in public, so perhaps I should wait in the tent until you are through."

"Stay."

"But then—" He paused, for she had hauled off her shirt. She was somewhat leaner than the picture in his data bank, but it was clear that she was female. "I see."

"I'll bet. Strip, Cyrus."

"As you wish." Carefully he removed his shoes, shirt, and trousers.

"Well, you look mostly human," she said.

"I am nevertheless a composite, as I said. My bones may be iron, but my flesh is alive. I am remarkably strong, but my vessels do bleed when punctured, and I feel pain."

"Look at me."

He had not looked since she removed her skirt, for some reason. Now he did as directed. Her lower half was also lean but definitely female, according to his stored images. That gave him an odd urge, but he was unable to define it. "I am looking."

"And not reacting. You definitely have had no experience." She waded into the pond.

"This is true." He followed her. Soon they were standing

chest deep (or whatever) in the water. Her chest was rather more curvaceous than his. He felt slightly guilty for being intrigued.

She stood beside him, eyeing him sidelong. Her glance angled off his shoulder and chest before striking the water beyond, raising an amused ripple. "You won't short out in the water or anything?"

"No, I'm proof against short-circuiting. I don't have wires as such. Thank you for your concern."

"That was irony, pun intended, not concern."

Now he was almost certain she was teasing him, but he didn't know how to react, so he didn't. "Thank you."

Tess shook her head. "You are a wonder! Come on, I'll wash your back." Before he could figure out how to respond, she came up behind him and splashed cool water across his neck and shoulders. Then her hands rubbed against his shoulder blades, and traveled down his back, under the water. "How's that feel?"

Actually it felt good. The flesh of his back was tight from traveling, and her touch made it relax. "Satisfactory."

"That so? How about this?" Her hands moved down and squeezed his bottom.

"That feels good in a different way," he said, surprised.

"Really?" She seemed to be stifling laughter. "Now it's your turn. Do me." She turned around.

He turned to face her back. He stroked her shoulders as she had stroked his, then moved down her back, and finally squeezed her bottom. It was considerably plumper than his, despite her general leanness. There was something really evocative about it. "You have a—a nice—posterior," he said haltingly.

Tess shook her head. "You really, truly, don't know," she said.

A bulb flashed over his head. "Does this relate to what every man wants?"

"Oh, yes, Cyrus."

"Please, won't you tell me? This is making me feel strange."

She sighed. "I thought you were just another man on the make. I see you are truly innocent. You have the information in your memory, but you don't know how to apply it to the real world. You haven't existed long enough. You are adult mainly in body, not experience."

"That seems to be true."

"And I've been teasing you, trying to make you reveal your real nature. I shouldn't have."

"Oh, I am sure you are without fault."

"Thank you." She considered half a moment more, then made a decision. "Since I teased you, I will untease you. I will show you what you need to know."

"I would really appreciate that."

"What men want is to seduce young women."

"Seduce?"

"Persuade them to assist in signaling the stork."

Cyrus was amazed. "But only married people do that."

Tess stood before him, her hands on his upper arms. "This is one of the differences between what goes into proper data banks and what exists in the real world. People can signal the stork without being married. Elders may frown on it, but it happens."

"I—didn't know."

"Precisely. But I will persuade you." She squeezed his arms. "Put your arms around me and bring me close to you. We will do it now."

"But we're standing in the water!"

"Another myth. It can be done anywhere, any way up. Embrace me. Do it."

He put his arms around her and drew her in until she was right up against him. She suddenly seemed twice as shapely as before, especially in front. "This is amazing."

"Indeed. Now let's say that you have captured me, and want to go farther. A kiss would be persuasive."

"It would?"

"Kiss me, idiot."

Oh. He brought his face down to hers, and hesitated. "On the—?"

She jammed her mouth against his, kissing him avidly. He felt as if his head were floating off his neck. This was a level of experience he had never imagined.

She drew back a little. "Now stroke my bottom, as before, but more firmly."

He obeyed. It was as though he were fondling a fine sculpture, evoking a strong yet loving reaction. "Oh, Tess, that makes me want to—" Again he ran out of concept.

"To summon the stork. Exactly as any man in this situation would. The next step is to—"

"BRA-A-AAY!"

They both jumped half out of the water, falling away from each other. Don was there by the shore, having awakened from his snooze.

"You silly ass!" Tess exclaimed angrily.

"He's not silly, he's a smart ass," Cyrus reminded her. "He told you."

"I just wanted to remind you it's getting late," the donkey said. "You need to get out of the water while you can still see your way."

The woman shook herself, evidently annoyed about something. Then she made some kind of internal decision. "He's right. I think you have the idea now. When you get a woman like that, that's what you do. You understand what to do with her."

"Yes, I do," Cyrus agreed. He was almost disappointed that Don had not waited to interrupt them a few minutes later. "Thank you."

"You're welcome." She seemed partly frustrated and partly relieved.

They emerged from the pool, dried off, and went to their separate beds. Cyrus's feelings were in turmoil. Tess was right: he did want what she had shown him. Yet he knew it was not customary on so brief an acquaintance. So surely it was best that the donkey had interrupted them.

"If you wish, I will join you on your bed," Tess said from the nearby darkness. "To keep you warm."

Cyrus knew that he would never be able to control himself if she did that. He did not want to antagonize her. It really wasn't cool enough to warrant such help. So he demurred. "Thank you, but I am warm enough."

"Okay." She sounded vaguely disappointed. That was surely his imperfect imagination. Why would a woman want to keep a cyborg warm?

"Don't let the tics bite you."

"The whats?"

"Bugs that hide in your bed and bite when you're asleep. Such as robot tics, that make you get all metal and jerky."

"Oh, that would not affect me. I am already part metal, but not, I hope, a jerk."

She laughed for some reason. "Or synthe tics, made of plastic and metal."

"Yes, of course."

"Or roman tics, bred in a love spring, that make you amorous."

Cyrus suspected that one of those had already gotten him, but he didn't want to admit that. "Thank you. I'll be careful."

That was all. Yet somehow he felt immensely frustrated. What was the matter with him? He had learned a lot, but realized that though he was indeed interested in summoning the stork, he still wasn't satisfied about the course of his life.

Well, tomorrow he would reach the Good Magician's Castle. The Good Magician would surely know. The GM knew everything.

Cyrus did not need a lot of sleep, but it was the human thing to do, so he lay still and turned his animation low.

In the morning they harvested fresh eggs from the eggplants, bread from the breadfruit tree, and grape and strawberry jellyfish from the pond. Tess showed him how to get fresh cups of hot tea from the T-Tree. It was very good.

It was time to resume traveling. "Thank you for your assistance," Cyrus told Tess. "It has been nice being with you."

"It could have been nicer."

"I don't understand."

She sighed. "Of course you don't. But next time you get bare with a woman, see that the donkey is nowhere near."

"I will try to do that," he agreed, perplexed.

"Let's get a move on," Don said impatiently. "We don't have all day."

"Which way are you going?" Tess asked.

"West, to the Good Magician's Castle."

"I'm going east."

"So we may not meet again."

"We may not," she agreed.

The exchange was somehow unsatisfactory, but Cyrus couldn't figure out how to correct it. He mounted Don and rode out of the campsite.

They almost collided with a slight man coming in. "Oops, my fault," the man said. "I wasn't watching where I was going."

"Neither was I," Cyrus said. Then, for want of anything else to say, he introduced himself. "I am Cyrus Cyborg, and this is Don Donkey, a robot ass."

"I am Trojan. S Trojan, a meek man."

Cyrus's memory bank whirred. That was the name Tess was looking for. "There is a woman you must meet."

"Oh, I would be too shy. I am considered effeminate. Women aren't much interested in me."

"This may be the exception. Come, I'll introduce you to her." He jumped off the donkey and led the way back.

Tess was packing her things into her backpack, about to depart. "What the bleep is this?" she demanded irritably. Perhaps she had eaten another dislike-en.

"This is Trojan," Cyrus said. "S Trojan."

She looked stricken. It was almost as if she would have preferred to use less coarse language in this instance.

"I really didn't mean to bother you," Trojan said apologetically. "I am on an unlikely quest to find my ideal Significant Other, assuming such a person exists."

Tess recovered. "Come here, Trojan."

"I beg your pardon?"

She strode forward, sweeping him up in a hearty embrace. "You are the one I have been looking for!"

"I don't understand. I'm just a nonentity."

"Shut up or I'll kiss you."

"You will what?"

She kissed him. "Never call my bluff."

"I confess that is heady stuff. But what would a fine woman like you want with a nothing like me?"

"I think he's grimy from travel," Cyrus said. "He'll need to wash up in the pond."

She shot him a look of naughty gratitude. "Yes. I'll join him there." She carried Trojan away.

Cyrus returned to the donkey, feeling elated. He had managed to do a good deed.

"I don't understand," Don said.

"Naturally not," Cyrus agreed smugly.

They had not gone far before they heard someone crying. It was a girl, staring wildly around. "Don't stop," Don muttered. "We can't let silly females slow us down. That pushy Tess was bad enough."

But Cyrus had another idea. "I'm trying to learn about women. I learned a lot last night, but I'm sure there's still more. Also, I have an empathy circuit that makes me want to help folk in need."

"Suit yourself, sucker. Fortunately I lack that silly-ass circuit. Chances are you won't be able to help her anyway."

They approached the girl. "May I help you?" Cyrus asked gallantly as he dismounted, still flush from his success with Tess.

"I don't think so," the girl said. "I'm Xina. I can change my hair at will." As she spoke her hair changed from short brown to flowing blond. "I'm supposed to join a play ensemble as an actress, but I can't find it."

"A play group?" Cyrus's data bank whirled. "Those are mainly organized by the Curse Fiends."

"No, this is supposed to be right around here," she insisted. "Only it isn't. I don't know what to do."

Cyrus had no idea what to do. "Neither do I. Maybe you should ask the Good Magician."

"I just came from him," she flared, her hair turning fiery red. "I asked him what was my destiny, and he said to act in this ensemble that is forming here. Only there's nothing. I owe a year's service for this?" She broke down in tears again.

"I told you," Don said.

"Oh, a talking mule!" Xina exclaimed.

"Ass."

"What?" She looked as if she had heard a bad word.

"Donkey," Cyrus said. "He is a robot."

"I love horses," Xina said, her grief evaporating. "He looks a lot like a small horse. May I pet him?"

Don eyed her assessingly. "Do you like asses?"

"Four-footed ones, yes. You're quite handsome, like your companion."

"Then you may pet me."

Xina did so. "You have such a nice metal mane."

"Yours is pretty nice too." Don was mellowing considerably, coincidentally.

"Could I ride you?"

"Hop on."

Cyrus was unable to help with her problem. There had to be some mistake. Then he thought of something. "Don can stay with you until I return, as the castle is surely close by. I'll try to ascertain where the ensemble is really supposed to be. It is surely a clerical error."

"Do you really think so?" she asked, brightening.

Cyrus was doubtful, but couldn't say that. "All I can do is ask."

"Oh, thank you," she said. She leaned down from the donkey and kissed him on the ear.

Cyrus was too startled to react. He stood there, the lingering impression of the kiss caressing his ear. He had had no idea that a woman could practice such magic.

Then Don moved away, carrying Xina, and Cyrus was alone. Well, it was time to get on to the Good Magician's Castle.

2

CHALLENGES

The Good Magician's Castle was a pretty sight, nestled within a circular moat in a lightly forested valley. There was a bird flying over the moat, a turtle dove. Then it dove into the water with a splash and swam away. Oh, not a bird, but a flying turtle that dived, or dove as the case might be.

He followed the path directly to it. But just before he got there, he found the way partly barred by an open shack beside the path. A placard perched on its roof said SAND WITCH SHOPPE.

Cyrus wasn't sure he wanted to mess with a witch, so he skirted the stand. But the Sand Witch appeared, an ugly old crone with a pointed black hat, calling out to him. "Buy a knuckle sandwich, stranger! It's a real bash in the mouth."

Could he avoid it? He tried. "Thank you, but I'm not hungry at the moment."

"Bleep! My shoppe is off the beaten path. I don't get much business."

"I regret that," he said, edging on by. If this was a Challenge, it did not seem to be much of one. He didn't trust that. His memory bank indicated that there were always three Challenges to querents seeking to enter the castle, and they were always devious. What was he missing?

"You'll be back, if you know what's good for you," the witch said wrathfully.

"I have little notion what's good for me," he said. It was truer than he liked.

"Would you change your mind if I looked like this?" She became a luscious young witch with restless brown hair and a prominent bosom trying to escape from an inadequate halter. He would hardly have recognized her, except that she wore the same conical hat.

He considered. "Are you of barbarian stock?"

"Of course not. I'm of witchly stock."

"Then I think I wouldn't change my mind."

She gazed at him a moment in perplexity. "You're an oddity."

"I'm a cyborg."

She sighed, putting a severe strain on the halter. "Maybe that explains it. Well, if you should get hungry for anything, I will still be here."

The mere sight of her made him hungry for something, but he was sure this was not the occasion for that. He regretted that Tess Tosterone had not managed to educate him further. "Thank you." He moved on, leaving her shaking her head.

The path shortly wended its way to another shop. This was an array of large colored stones. In fact they were boulders. The sign said ENUFF TUFF STUFF—ROCK & ROLL. The proprietor was snoozing behind a stone counter shaped like an upside-down funnel. He was a big tough-looking man who hardly seemed to need the softly shaped bed rock he lay on.

Cyrus paused, curious. Surely all this was here for a reason, but he couldn't fathom what it was.

The man woke and jumped off his rock bed. "Hi, stranger! I'm Tuff. What can I sell you? I have stone galore, from the very best volcanoes."

"I'm really not in the market for stone," Cyrus said. "Though what you have here is pretty."

"Are you sure? Any rock you buy, I roll into place for you. It makes excellent walls, foundations, statues. There's an island almost surrounded by tuff statues, a marvelous sight."

"Surely it is," Cyrus agreed. "But I'm not here to build anything. I just want to see the Good Magician."

"Suit yourself." Tuff settled back into his snooze.

Cyrus moved on. Surely all this made sense in some fashion. Maybe as a cyborg he just wasn't equipped to appreciate it.

He heard screaming and laughter ahead. A sign said BEWARE THE STRIP TIDE. He still didn't get the relevance.

Then the path ended in an inlet of water, maybe part of the moat. It was filled with swimming bare girls who were screaming and splashing each other. Were they nymphs?

One spied him. "Hi! Who are you?"

"I am Cyrus Cyborg. I want to see the Good Magician."

She laughed. "Don't we all! But we tried to swim across, and got caught by the strip tide. Don't try it yourself, unless you want to join us."

"Strip tide?" He remembered the warning sign.

"It's a wave that strips whoever it catches. We're all embarrassingly bare." She eyed him, not seeming much embarrassed. "Still, we might have some fun if you joined us." She glanced across the water, where some bare children played. "We'd have to banish the sea urchins for a while of course; Adult Conspiracy, you know."

But Cyrus remained a bit nervous about fun with women. Tess had shown him that he desired such contact, but he wanted to know more about it before getting bare with dozens of girls. Otherwise he would surely embarrass himself. "Thank you, but I think I can't afford such a diversion at this time. I need to see the Good Magician."

She shrugged, flashing some interesting wet flesh in the process. "Are you sure?"

"I am not at all sure. It's a judgment call."

She eyed him somewhat the way the Witch had. "You seem remarkably candid."

"I'm a cyborg," he reminded her. "I don't have much experience with human duplicity."

She nodded. "I like that. Most men are eager to deceive girls in my position." She took a deep breath so he could properly appreciate her position. "I am Acro Nymph. I came to ask the Good Magician what my talent might be, and he told me I'd find out in the course of my Service for the Answer. It seems it's somehow tied in with my name. I can quit any time I learn it, without completing my Service, since I won't need the Answer if I figure it out for myself. But so far I'm baffled. So here I am, trying to tempt you into the water." She frowned cutely. "Don't do it. It won't hurt you to be bare, but you will wash out of the Challenge and never get to see the Good Magician."

Cyrus hesitated. "As I said, I don't properly understand duplicity. Why would you tell me this, if it is your job to prevent me from passing?"

"I'm a sucker for honesty. It forces me to be honest in return."

Cyrus ran her name through his data bank, and came up with a near match. "Acronym!"

"What?"

"It means forming words from the first letters, or first few letters, of other words. Maybe that's your talent."

She frowned. "But can't anybody do that? Just take any words and use their first letters? How would that qualify as a magic talent?"

"I don't know. Maybe it's a bad idea."

"I'm not sure of that. Maybe I just need to figure out how it applies."

"I'll ponder further," Cyrus said. "Maybe it will come to me."

"But if it does, you'll be long gone from here and unable to tell me. What good would that do me?"

"None," Cyrus said regretfully. "I'm sorry I couldn't be more helpful."

"That's all right. I think you've given me part of the answer. I'll mull it over. Thank you so much."

"You're welcome." He gazed at the water, with its array of nymphs. "I thought there were supposed to be moat monsters."

"There are, normally. But Souffle and Sesame Serpent took Serendipity to visit the Castle Roogna moat, leaving this one temporarily vacant."

"Serendipity?" he asked, not finding that name in his data bank.

"Their new baby daughter, Serendipity Serpent. They found her in a gene pool, of course. Her talent is to spontaneously find things she's not looking for. She's really cute, if you like that type."

"I'm sure she is. I'm just not keen on encountering moat monsters. It has to do with my physical health."

She glanced at him again. "You're handsome. I'd like to kiss you. I promise not to drag you into the water. I'll come out of it for the moment." She swam to the bank and put her feet down, starting to lift her upper body out of the water. Much more flesh showed. Her chest was—

Cyrus's vision blurred. His eyes were locked on her, unable to look away. "Something's wrong," he said. "My eyes are corroding."

"Oh, bleep!" she said. "I forgot about that. Most men freak out at the sight of panties, but less experienced ones are susceptible to even bare flesh. Cover your eyes."

He put up a hand, cutting off the view. His eyes relaxed, though dangerous circular afterimages still stalked them. "That must have been it."

"I'll be there in a moment. Stay covered."

He heard water dripping from her bare body. The very thought of her touch got him all hot and nervous. "Please— I'm not sure I could—could handle your kiss. I need to proceed without such a distraction." He half hoped she would ignore his demurral.

She stopped. "I understand. Good luck." She splashed back into the water. "Bye, Cyrus."

"Bye, Acro." Yet he wondered: if this was a Challenge, why was she letting him go? In fact why had the Witch and Tuff the rock salesman been so ready to let him pass?

Cyrus uncovered his eyes and walked along the bank, seeking some way across. Wasn't there supposed to be a drawbridge? He found none. Instead he located the Wave, the strip tide, rippling restlessly as if seeking more victims. Whenever it passed a girl, she screamed and seemed to be another stage barer, if that was possible.

He raised his hand again to break the threatening lock on his gaze that the screaming girls generated. He was fortunate that none of them was wearing panties, because that would have finished him. As it was, their swimming and diving had him on the very verge of the brink of a freak, especially when their legs flashed up out of the water.

Could he plunge in and swim when the tide wasn't there? Maybe if he did it right behind the Wave, so it would take time to circle around and pass this way again. Then he saw the Wave abruptly reverse course. It was unpredictable. So that was no good.

He noticed that the girls were very similar in appearance. In fact they seemed identical. Were there really that many nymphs—or was there just one, replicated by illusion to fill the moat? Did it matter? One would be more than enough to embarrass him if she caught him naked in the water. Tess had clearly meant well, after her initial distrust of him; he had no guarantee the nymph did, despite her seeming candor. Maybe she was there not just to demonstrate the danger. Maybe she *was* the danger. The Challenge was to get across without being humiliated.

It was best not to risk it. He needed to find a way to get across without entering the water.

Then he thought of something. Enuff tuff stuff—sufficient to form a ramp or causeway across the moat, so that he could walk. That must be the key.

He returned to the stone shop. "I'd like a fair quantity of your wares, if you please. Enough to cross the moat."

"That's a big order," Tuff remarked.

"How may I obtain it?"

Tuff considered. "I'd trade it for one really good snack. I haven't eaten since dawn. But none of this bland nothing that passes for food; I want something with a kick."

Aha. "How about a knuckle sandwich? I understand it's a real bash in the mouth."

"That's the kind," Tuff agreed.

Cyrus walked back to the Sand Witch Shoppe. The witch was back in her old homely form. Maybe that was just as well. "Hello, Witch."

"You again? I thought you were doing a void dance."

"A what?"

"A void dance. It's what folk use to get out of trouble or avoid anything else, such as ugly old witches."

"Avoidance," he echoed. It was a pun.

"So what do you want?"

"I'll take a knuckle sandwich. What do you require in return?"

"I'm bored as bleep. I'd trade it for one good laugh."

What would make a witch laugh? That was a challenge indeed. His mind sifted through the humor section of his data bank.

And found something. He fetched a stick from beside the path, then used it to beat madly at the path.

"What are you doing?" the witch demanded.

"I'm beating the path," he explained. "So that you are truly off the beaten path."

"That's crazy!" But in half a moment her expression changed. "It's crazy enough to be funny. Oh, no—I think I'm going to laugh." She struggled with herself, but the laugh surged up and finally burst out, hurling her back against her shoppe wall. Piled sandwiches fell off the shelf, half burying her. "Ha-ha-ha! Ho-ho-ho!" Her form seemed to be changing back to young and full, as she lost control.

Cyrus doubted that it was really that funny, but this was a Challenge, and the witch was probably keyed to laugh at any reasonable attempt. "So if I may have that sandwich now . . ."

One foot lifted from the pile, bearing a sandwich. The foot was on a marvelously bare and well formed leg. He squinted to focus only on the sandwich and accepted it. "Thank you." He shut his eyes until he could turn away from the leg.

The sandwich was shaped like a big fist with protruding knuckles. Cyrus kept it well away from his face. He carried it back to Tuff's domain. "Here is your knuckle sandwich." He handed it over.

The man took it and lifted it to his mouth. The sandwich leaped forward and smashed into his face. "Hoo!" Tuff exclaimed, licking off a spot of blood from his lip. "This one's smashing."

"As represented," Cyrus agreed, bemused.

Tuff had at the sandwich. The next time it tried to smash him, he met it with open mouth, and chomped down on a knuckle. The sandwich didn't give up, but every time it jabbed, it encountered the stony teeth again, and lost another joint. Finally it was gone.

"Great stuff," Tuff said. "I haven't had one of those in years. Really punches me up."

"You're welcome," Cyrus said.

"Now you want stone for the moat," Tuff said, getting back to business. He bent forward, put his hands on an orange boulder, and heaved. The stone rolled onto the path. Tuff heaved again, keeping it going, until at last it rolled into the water of the moat with a satisfying splash.

"Eeeek!" the nymphs screamed cutely in unison.

"Sorry about that, Acro," Tuff said, looking at several of the nymphs without freaking out.

"Are not," they chorused. "Did it on purpose."

"Well, sure, but it's part of the Challenge." Tuff turned about and walked back to his shop.

The nearest nymph looked at Cyrus. "So you're figuring it out."

"I seem to be, yes," he agreed.

"I want to come with you. I think you'll figure out the rest of my riddle, in time."

Could she do that? "You'd freak me out."

"I'd put on new clothing, silly," she said. "I promise not to freak you out unless you ask me to. May I join you?"

Cyrus suspected he should say no, but it was difficult to do. "Yes, if you're sure."

"Thanks! I'll meet you at the far side." She and the other nymphs swam away.

Tuff returned with another boulder. "She's a nice girl," he remarked as the stone splashed into the water. "A man could do worse."

"All she wants is for me to figure out her magic talent."

"Well, sure, but she's still worthwhile. I'd have taken her, had she been interested. The nights get lonely. There must be something about you." He went back for another boulder.

Cyrus was afraid he was getting in trouble, without even meaning to. Tess had been attracted to him, and it seemed the Witch also, and now Acro. Sure, he had been created handsome, but was that all that women cared about? Could this have any bearing on his destiny? If so, he really needed to sort it out soon.

In due course the boulders formed a ramp across the moat. "There you are," Tuff said as the last one splashed into place. "Good luck."

"Thank you." Cyrus stepped carefully from boulder to boulder, crossing the moat without touching the water. The Wave hovered, as if hoping he would fall in so it could pounce, but he disappointed it. He had navigated the first Challenge.

"Congratulations," Acro said as he stepped onto the inner bank. She was now garbed in blouse, skirt, and slippers, none of which detracted from her appeal. However, it was now possible for him to look at her without his eyeballs locking up. "I'm not allowed to help you with the other Challenges, but I will cheer you on."

"Thank you."

"Are you sure you wouldn't like me to kiss you?"

"I am not sure. That's probably why you shouldn't do it."

"I don't think I quite understand."

"It might make my mind freak out, so I would not be able to pass the remaining Challenges."

"Oh. Yes, of course. That's very logical."

"Robots are supremely logical. I'm half robot."

"What's the other half?"

"Barbarian. That makes me ill-equipped to handle civilized things, especially women."

"You are fascinating."

He assumed that was a compliment. "Thank you."

He looked ahead. He was in a kind of garden swarming with ants. They were large and looked aggressive.

He stepped forward. Immediately the ants formed a line, lifting front legs with weapons: little spears, clubs, swords, and whips. "I don't like the look of this," he muttered.

"They won't let you pass," Acro said. She was standing near an ant, but it ignored her. "This is the next Challenge."

He had gathered as much. He suspected that the little weapons would be most painful to his ankles. In fact some ants had little buckets of fire. Those would be fire ants.

That gave him an idea. Were the others of individual types? Maybe if he identified them, they would let him by. It was the kind of intellectual challenge the Good Magician was known for.

He moved toward the closest ant.

"Halt!" its tiny voice cried. "I will defend my domain to the death!"

"You're a Warrior Ant," Cyrus said.

"True, and you shall not pass, intruder." The ant raised its spear threateningly.

He had identified it, but it still would not let him pass. Had he figured it out wrong? He sifted through his memory bank. Endless information was there, but he didn't know how to adapt it to this situation. He had to use the thinking portion of his brain.

What had he not done? Often in Xanth things had to be taken literally, and with a groaning admixture of puns. Was he supposed to make the ant laugh, as he had with the witch?

Then a bulb flashed. That always startled him, though it was a standard effect when someone got a sudden bright idea. There was a pun of sorts. "You're a Defend Ant," he said.

"O bleep, he got it," the ant swore. "I have to let him pass." It stepped aside. "Pass, jerk."

"Thank you." Cyrus stepped past.

But immediately there was another ant in the way. "Didn't you get the message, idiot? We don't want you here."

"What message was that?"

"I sent you an a-mail. You lacked the courtesy to answer. You shall not pass."

A-mail. That would be the ants' version of e-mail. But where was the pun? "I'm sorry, I didn't receive it."

"The bleep you didn't, rogue! It's right there in your pocket."

Cyrus looked. There was a small note tucked into his breast pocket. It must have gotten there magically; a-mail was surely like that. He took it out and read it. GO AWAY. FAILURE TO ACKNOWLEDGE THIS CORRESPONDENCE WILL NOT ALTER ITS IMPORT. YOU HAVE BEEN WARNED.

Correspondence. New he got it. "You're a Correspond Ant."

"Bleep," the ant said, as ungracious as the first. "Thought I had you." It stood aside.

But there was another ant. It seemed that ants came not single-spy, but in battalions. "Not so fast, ruffian," this one said. "I am going to keep after you until you quit. I will never give over."

And what ant word was this describing? Cyrus got belatedly smart and sifted through his vocabulary data bank, checking through definitions for words ending in ant. There it was. "Persist Ant."

"You're a real spoilsport, know that?" the ant complained, standing aside.

The next one was ready. "I am fully acquainted with your recent history, and know how to handle you, invader. Begone."

Fully acquainted, knowledgeable. He sifted again. "Convers ant."

"You're no fun at all," the ant griped, standing aside.

Then next ant was a squalling baby. Cyrus got it right away. "Inf Ant." The squalling increased, but the ant moved aside.

But the ants had just begun to fight. Another blocked his way. The mental energy was making Cyrus hot; he was getting sweaty. He looked for a cloth to wipe his forehead, but of course there was none.

"I can fix that," the ant said. "No sweat. Just depart."

No sweat? That was an odd phrase, since ants didn't sweat anyway. Which gave it away. "Antiperspir Ant."

"We are going to have to make a judgment here," the next ant said. "You have no—"

"Adjudic ant."

The next ant spit in disgust. "Go—"

"Expector Ant."

He continued on through Miscre, Disinfect, Mendic, Contest, Merch, Eleph, Inform, Flagr, Claim, and Consult. At last the last of them had been identified, and he was through the ant farm. The second Challenge was done.

Now he faced a barren waste. Dust was everywhere. It covered the ground, the cacti, the stones, even the resting animals. There was a dust-covered path wending its way onward through rocks and rills, the latter looking disgusted about the situation.

Cyrus paused. Was this all? Surely it couldn't be as easy as merely following the path to wherever it led. Yet what else was there to do?

He stepped onto the path. Dust billowed up in small clouds, settling on his legs and feet. Messy but harmless.

Then there was a stirring in the distance. A big dust cloud was whirling toward him, spreading so much dust that everything behind it was obscured. It came right up to him, and then he was in the middle of it, choking on it, unable to see anything. It was a small dust storm.

He stepped back. Then things cleared; he was technically outside the scene, which remained obscure.

This, then, was the Challenge: to follow the path through the scene—when he was unable to see anything. He might put on goggles, if he had them, to protect his eyes, and a mask to filter the air he breathed, but there would be no way to fathom the path. He was sure he would have to follow the path exactly, or he wouldn't find its end.

He pondered. First, he knew that there had to be some way through, if he could just figure it out. Second, something was stirring up the dust; if he could nullify that, he should be all right. What could it be, and how could he deal with it? It looked like a small dust storm.

He remembered something. "Dusty!" he exclaimed.

The whirlwind coalesced into a small female devil. She was pretty in a dusty outfit, with little horns. "That's Dusti," she said. "Get it right, dummy."

"Oh! I took you for someone else."

"My little brother Dusty, of course. He has no ambition. I do. That's why I'm here."

"Your purpose is to prevent me from crossing, by stirring up so much dust I can't see my way."

She eyed him sidelong. Somehow that glance made her seem fuller bodied than before. "You're pretty smart for a querent."

"So I have to figure out how to nullify you so I can get through."

"Duh."

"There has to be something here that will enable me to accomplish that."

"You know, you're sorta cute." She dissolved into whirling dust, then reformed, larger and fuller. "Maybe I'll kiss you. We can improvise from there."

Was she coming on to him? This was odd indeed. "What interest would a dust devil have in a mere cyborg?"

Her head dissolved into whirling dust as she considered, then reformed. "I don't know. But there's something about you that makes me want to impress you."

"I'm not very impressive."

"I didn't say you were. I said I want to impress you. That's different."

She was correct. But the larger mystery remained: what interest did any of these young women have in him? He didn't know, and none of them seemed to know either. "Well, I'm going to set about defeating you so that I can talk to the Good Magician."

"That would impress me." She dissolved into the whirlwind again, then lurched toward him. He felt the imprint of lips on his as the dust swirled around his head. She had, indeed, kissed him.

He focused on the Challenge. How could he get through, when he couldn't see anything? Could he get down on hands and knees and feel his way along the path under the dust?

He tried that. Immediately the dust devil enveloped him, forcing him to jam his eyes and mouth shut. He felt kisses on his ears and neck. She was indulging herself while keeping up with her business.

His strategy didn't work. There was so much dust that whatever was under it was indistinct. He could not tell what was path and what was ordinary land. He had to be wrong, because soon he banged into the trunk of a big tree.

What kind of tree was it? It hardly seemed to matter, but he was curious what variety would grow in perpetual dust. He felt the bark, and found it smooth. He tapped it, and there was a half-hollow sound. He sifted his memory, seeking to match sound to wood.

And got it. This was a beer-barrel tree, with a huge cylindrical trunk filled or partly filled with beer. Or was it? He tapped again, analyzing the sound. No, not beer, but ale; this was an ale tree. Its beverage would be a bit stronger.

That gave him a wicked idea. How much experience did Dusti have with strong ale? She was obviously of age to drink it if she wanted to, but might not have done so before. If he could get her to drink some, it might impair her judgment and make her forget to stir up so much dust.

He worked his way around the trunk until he found a spigot.

He turned it on and caught a little fluid in the palm of one hand. He sipped it.

"That's certainly, really, awfully good," he murmured. And paused, considering. Why had he chosen those superfluous words?

The question brought the answer. This was adverbi ale, that caused the drinker to use too many words ending in LY. He had taken only a sip, so only three had gotten out.

Unfortunately he didn't see how that would stop the dust devil. He might get her to drink some, but she would catch on the moment the LYs came spewing out. He needed a brew that would get her tipsy without side effects.

Still, there was hope. He crawled on, seeking another tree. There might be a better one for his purpose, as they tended to grow in groves.

He found one, and tried it—and went into a coughing fit. That was bronchi ale, and congested the lungs. That was no good.

Or was it? Maybe he could after all make it work.

He fetched the butter cup he kept in reserve. He had long since used up its butter, and saved the cup as a folded yellow sac. He opened it, held it under the spigot, and filled it with ale. Then he drew the petal flap over to seal it in. He was ready.

He stood up. "Dusti!" he called. "I have something for you."

The whirling wind coalesced into the she-devil. "What is it?"

"A cup of ale."

"Ale?"

"Bronchi Ale, from a local ale-barrel tree."

She made a face. "I don't drink that stuff. It interferes with my wind."

"Too bad." He opened the cup and dumped it on her head.

Immediately she went into a coughing fit. "You—cough— despicable—cough—scheming—cough—lout!"

"Maybe you shouldn't have kissed me," he remarked as the dust settled out of the air around them.

She changed to whirlwind form, but it too was racked by coughing. Its winds went yon and hither, randomly, unable to maintain a tight circle.

Cyrus walked along the path that was becoming visible again. Dusti resumed devil form and intercepted him. "You—cough—tricked—cough—me! I—cough—ought—cough—to—cough—kiss you—cough—into—cough—oblivion!"

"I'd like to see you try," he said amicably as he strode along.

She jammed up against him, bringing her face to his. But she was so wracked by coughs that she couldn't complete the act. "Bleep—cough—it!" she swore. "Bleep—cough—it—cough—to—cough—cough!" She was unable to finish.

"This way," he said, pausing. He caught her by her heaving shoulders, brought her in close, and kissed her on the forehead.

"COUGH you!" she said villainously. "If I—cough—could just—cough—get my breath—"

"To be sure." He let her go and stepped off the path into the castle proper. He had made it through the third Challenge.

3

ASSIGNMENT

A woman was waiting for him just within. "Welcome, Cyrus Cyborg," she said, looking him in the eye. "I am Wira, the Good Magician's daughter-in-law. He is busy at the moment, but Sofia and I will give you the necessary background."

"Background?"

"For your Assignment. Your Service. It is important."

"But I don't have my Answer yet."

"That relates. This way, please."

He followed her, two fifths bemused. He knew of Wira, of course; she was in his memory bank as Magician Humfrey's favorite daughter-in-law. But there was something odd about her. About the way she had looked him in the eye.

That was it. "You're not blind!" he exclaimed.

"Not any more," she agreed. "But I am not yet fully acclimatized to vision, so tend to close my eyes when navigating the castle. It's more comfortable."

"But how—?"

"It is a long and dull story. Nimby gave me sight."

Nimby. That was the donkey-headed dragon aspect of the Demon Xanth, another long story. Certainly he was capable of doing it, if he chose. "I see. As it were."

Wira smiled. She was an older woman, fifty-six chronologically, thirty-four physically, because she had been youthened to marry the Good Magician's son. But she was pretty when she smiled. "There is much to be seen," she agreed.

They came to what looked like an expanded closet. There was a drab woman sorting a huge pile of socks. "This is Sofia Socksorter, the Designated Wife for this month," Wira said. Then, to the woman: "Mother Sofia, this is Cyrus Cyborg, the querent. He needs background."

Sofia looked up. "Hello, Cyrus. I never met a cyborg before." She had a strong Mundane accent. "I must say, you are a handsome specimen."

He was beginning to regret being created handsome. It seemed that most of the women he encountered had inclinations to do something with him, regardless whether he properly understood the details of it. Even someone's wife? That made him nervous. "I believe I am the first cyborg in Xanth," Cyrus said. "Which relates to my Question for the Good Magician. I need to know whether there is any suitable woman for me, and if so, where I might find her."

She nodded wisely. "Of course you wouldn't be satisfied with just any young woman who is attracted to your face. You'll be looking for one who truly appreciates your nature. And for that Answer you will embark on a remarkable secret mission."

This was news. Evidently this woman did have information he wanted. He knew the Good Magician was apt to be very brief and taciturn—in simple terms, grumpy—so was unlikely to provide much beyond a technical response. It was surely worthwhile talking to Sofia.

"May I help you with your chore?" he inquired. "I see you have more socks to sort that can be done in a day. It must be uncomfortably dull."

She was surprised. "No one ever offered to help before, aside from Wira."

"It's my empathy circuit. Am I in error to offer? I am not fully acclimatized to pure human ways."

Both Sofia and Wira smiled. "Stay the way you are," Wira said. "Women prefer naïveté of that nature."

"They do?" It hadn't occurred to him that his very ignorance might be attractive.

"We do," Sofia agreed. "Most men are too certain of their masculinity to inquire after feminine preferences, let alone sort socks."

They settled down to help Sofia sort socks. They were of many types and colors. All were clean, having evidently been washed and dried, but were hopelessly jumbled together. Cyrus knew that the Good Magician had married Sofia because of her expertise in sorting socks, and that had solved his chronic problem. But she was in the castle only one month in five and a half, so the socks did accumulate in her absence. It had probably taken her a week to get them to this stage. Twos of a kind needed to be located and balled together for future use. It was easy to do, but tedious.

"Here is the situation," Sofia said. "There is a young male roc bird with a bad attitude and a dangerous talent. It may not yet be of Magician caliber, but it is close, and maturing, and all too soon is apt to be the strongest in Xanth. You have to understand that Xanth could suffer enormous damage if this is not promptly dealt with. But there are complications."

"Couldn't somebody talk to him?" Cyrus asked. "There are folk who speak animal dialects."

"The Roc is not interested in being talked to. All he wants is power and the rewards of power. He means to take over the whole of Xanth as its monarch. Anyone who objects is rendered null."

"Null? Do you mean killed?"

"Not exactly. His name is Ragna Roc, and his talent is to

render things illusory. No one dares question him, because any who have tried have been illusioned."

"Couldn't a Magician or Sorceress nullify him? I understand they have phenomenal powers."

"They could if they could get close enough. But not only does Ragna delete anyone he even suspects he might not like, he lives in a hidden fancy rock candy castle perched on the Rock of Ages, with a harem of winsome roc hens. Only his closest associates know exactly where it is."

"But there are folk who can magically fathom the direction of anything."

"Yes. So we do know where it is. But we must not let him know we know, lest we all be deleted and need to be disillusioned. So we must pretend we don't know."

"What about Com Pewter? Couldn't he change reality in that vicinity to nullify the Roc's power?"

"At the moment Pewter is tied up in a contest of his own with a Magnet Monster. He can't help."

"Then how can anyone go there to deal with him?"

"Only Himself knows."

"That is Good Magician Humfrey," Wira clarified. "Sofia's name for him."

"Anybody's name for him, by rights," Sofia said. "Because he's so full of himself."

She did not seem to have a lot of respect for the almost mythical figure of the Good Magician. Maybe that came of being buried in his stinky old socks. "Does this relate in some manner to my Service?"

"Yes. You are to be the one Ragna summons to meet him. You will bring along the Three Princesses, who will then deal with him."

"Do you mean the Princesses Melody, Harmony, and Rhythm? According to my information they are children, only twelve years old."

"They are not ordinary children," Sofia said seriously. "They are general-purpose Sorceresses. Any single one of them is a full Sorceress in her own right, able to perform almost any magic she chooses. Any two of them together square that power, increasing the effect enormously. The three of them together cube it, making them the most powerful practitioners in Xanth. Nothing can stand against their united magic. But they have to be within range to do it, and Ragna would illusion them from well beyond that range if he saw them coming. So caution is necessary."

"I see," Cyrus said, awed. "I will of course be glad to help, but I don't see how I can. I have no separate magic that I know; I think my magic is merely to exist as a composite living machine. Ragna would have no reason to summon me."

"Himself will see to that," Sofia said. "Wira, do you think he's ready now?"

"I will check," Wira said, hastening away.

"Such a dear girl," Sofia said. "Everyone likes her. That may not be surprising; her talent is to relate to animals. Human beings are merely another variety of animal."

"That makes sense," he agreed.

"Some time you must get her to tell you about her adventure with Princess Ida's Moons. It's amazing. But she's so modest she doesn't volunteer it."

"Modesty becomes a person," he agreed.

"Have some fruit." She proffered a bowl of pretty colored greens, reds, yellows, blues, and oranges.

"Thank you." He picked up an orange.

"Anchors aweigh!" the fruit sang.

He almost dropped it. "It sings!"

"Well, it's a Naval Orange."

A bell rang. "Battle stations!" the orange cried, rolling out of his hand. "All hands on deck!"

"It's still got its naval conditioning," Sofia said from the stove, where the bell had summoned her to turn off the oven. "Maybe you would be better off with a different fruit."

"Maybe so," Cyrus agreed, bemused. He saw there were also some berries in the bowl, purple, orange, green, black and blue. So he took a blue berry, though it looked rather sad. "I am curious. Is there some set protocol about which wife attends the Good Magician? I know you have to take turns, but who decides who is when?"

"We got together and voted on the order," Sofia said. "We wives get along well when we meet each other. We have a common complaint."

"Complaint?"

"Himself."

Oh. "I thought maybe it depended on the type of visitors anticipated."

"Not really. Well, we had to swap out once, when the Gorgon got annoyed. A querent had the talent of making mirrors appear. He flashed one in her face, thinking it would make her stone herself. It didn't, but she was so annoyed by the trick that she was ready to remove her veil and stone *him*. The Maiden Taiwan had to advance her schedule and finish the Gorgon's stint."

Cyrus smiled. "I appreciate the Gorgon's position. It was a dirty trick. I wonder what it would be like if all the wives somehow showed up together?"

Sofia laughed. "Chaos! Someone should write a story about that. It would amuse all of us no end."

Wira returned. "The Good Magician will see you now."

Cyrus followed her through gloomy passages and up a narrow circular flight of stone stairs. They came to a small room packed with books. A gnomishly small man sat on a high stool poring over a huge open tome. This was the fabled Good Magician.

"Father, this is Cyrus Cyborg, the querent," Wira said.

"Grumph."

"I need to know my true desire," Cyrus said nervously. "My parents differ on what I should do, and—" He stopped, realizing that he had just asked the wrong question. Could he take it back? He really wanted to know whether there was any cyborg woman he might marry. "That is—"

"You will be the master of thespians," Humfrey said.

This took Cyrus totally by surprise. "Actors?"

"Your desire is to become a playwright and direct your plays. You will form a troupe and do that. The Designated Wife, what's her name—"

"Sofia," Wira filled in.

"Will fill you in on your Service." The tired old eyes returned to the book. Cyrus had been answered and dismissed.

He had the Answer to the wrong Question.

The weird thing was that it was a good answer. Suddenly he knew that this was indeed his desire. To be creative in a literary manner. To write and produce plays. Somehow he had never thought of it before. The Good Magician had known.

But what would he do for a wife? He needed someone to truly understand and support him. Had he just doomed himself to become a successful bachelor playwright? Happy on the outside, lonely on the inside?

"Thank you," he said belatedly as Wira guided him away from the study.

"That wasn't the Question I had expected you to ask," Wira said as they walked.

"My mind got garbled," he admitted.

"Actually I think it was a better Question. You should be able to find a suitable woman on your own."

"If I only knew how," he said ruefully.

She laughed. "I can tell you that. Merely make a general announcement that you are interested in a relationship provided you find a suitable woman. Women will flock to demonstrate their suitability. Select the best one."

"I can't believe it's that easy."

"Actually it's easier. *She* will select *you*. Naturally she will pretend that you did the selecting."

"Naturally," he echoed weakly.

"Don't let on that I told you. It might be considered a violation of the Female Conspiracy."

"There's a Female Conspiracy?"

"Oops; men aren't supposed to know about that. About how we actually govern them. Don't tell."

"I won't," he agreed weakly. But his private respect for women was increasing significantly. He had seen the way his mother governed his father, but had assumed that was because she was barbarian and as a robot he lacked imagination. Evidently it was more than that.

Back in the sock-sorting chamber he confessed his amazement to Sofia. "He gave me my Answer, a better one than I perhaps deserved, and I will perform my Service. But it's hard to see how I qualify for the mission you have described."

"The Challenges took care of that," Sofia said matter-of-factly. She was a very matter-of-fact woman, just as Wira was a very understanding one. "You would never have gotten through had you not been qualified."

"But they consisted of seemingly random elements such as a knuckle sandwich, a Tuff guy, and a Strip Tide."

"Disparate elements," she agreed. "A good play director may have to understand and assemble similar elements to make his production work."

"Oh." She was right. "Then I had to identify opposing ants. How does that relate to a play production?"

"Identifying individuals by their salient qualities, so as to fairly understand their capacities. This is necessary for proper casting in roles."

He nodded. "So it is. And maybe I will have to relate at some point to ants. But the third Challenge had a nasty dust devil I had to squelch. I don't see how that relates."

"You will be dealing with actors," she said. "Creative, sensitive, emotive types who need to be carefully managed. Some will be obnoxious, especially when they don't get the lead roles they are sure they deserve. You will need to handle them, politely if possible, impolitely if necessary. Just as you handled Dusti. Who was, incidentally, playing a role herself; she's actually a nice person, for a devil."

Again she was right. "How it is that a smart woman like you is satisfied doing a menial chore like sorting socks?"

"I am good at it, and I love the magic ambiance, even though I have no magic of my own. There's something about Xanth that makes me glad to be here."

"And we are glad to have you here, Sofia," Wira said. "And not just because of the socks. You handle Magician Humfrey as competently as you do the socks."

"Well, they are two of a kind, socks and men," Sofia said, putting together two matching stockings. "All it requires is sufficient socks appeal."

Truly, Cyrus thought, women did manage men. "Maybe you could help me with something else, before we return to business. I am at best an ordinary person, only imperfectly human or machine. Yet full-human women seem to be attracted to me. Even part-human, like the witch and the dust devil. Why should this be? I am in doubt that most women are so foolish as to be guided only by appearance."

"It is similar to my situation," Sofia said. "The ambiance governs. They knew through some subtle foresight that you were about to become a play producer. All women want to be actresses, could they but confess it to themselves."

"All women *are* actresses," Wira said.

Sofia nodded. "Of course. They were playing up to you in the hope that you would cast them in nice roles."

"That must be it," he agreed. "But as yet I have no plays to cast anyone in, let alone a bevy of young women."

"So you will write plays to make suitable parts for them. Then you will be properly armed."

"I will," he said, amazed anew. "I am already getting ideas, thanks to your insights. But how can doing this enable me to be summoned by Ragna Roc?"

"This is the real challenge," Sofia said. "You must write and produce plays so interesting and entertaining that audiences will throng to see them. In time Ragna will learn about it, and want to see them for himself. He will summon you and your troupe for a command performance."

"And the Three Princesses will be part of the troupe," Cyrus said, seeing it.

"Exactly. Of course the Princesses will be in disguise. You will treat them exactly as ordinary girls. Which, really they are, apart from their power. No one must catch on to their identity as Sorceresses."

"I don't know how it can be concealed. The moment they do real magic—"

"They will weave an ambient spell to conceal their nature, and an aversion spell to make others incurious about them. But you will know, and help mask them, in the event one forgets and lets go with a spell. They are after all children, apt to be impulsive. You will be the responsible adult."

"That's ironic," Cyrus said. "And I don't mean to pun on my metal skeleton. I am only two years old myself."

"But crafted as a twenty-year-old adult. Your memories and responses are adult, even though you were never a child."

"I am adult," he agreed. "I will treat them as children. But I'll never forget that they are Sorceresses."

"That is sensible. If there is one person you never want to truly annoy, it is a Sorceress. A woman scorned is trouble, and a Sorceress scorned is downright dangerous."

"But neither can you afford to treat them with undue respect," Wira said. "Lest you give away their nature."

"I feel unqualified."

"The Challenges showed you had the necessary qualities," Sofia said. "You will handle it."

"I hope so. Still, the larger mission is daunting. I wish I had some guidelines."

"There is a guideline," Wira said. "Magician Humfrey told me. It is Two to the Fifth."

"Two to the Fifth? I am not making much sense of that. What does it mean?"

"We don't know," Sofia said. "Himself's pronouncements tend to be obscure. Sometime I wonder whether he knows their meaning himself. But they are invariably relevant."

"You will simply have to figure it out," Wira said.

"I am at a loss. Two perhaps I can understand. Could that mean that there will be two main characters in this play, I mean mission? Myself and another?"

"Maybe yourself and your woman," Sofia said. "The right woman can make a man."

"And the wrong one can break him," Wira said.

"So I had better be sure the right one selects me."

Both women nodded.

"But what about the Fifth?" he asked. "If we have two, must they go to find a fifth person? Who would that be?"

"We don't know," Sofia said. "But presumably you are the one equipped to figure it out."

"Maybe if I find the right woman, or she finds me, she'll be able to fathom it."

"There is that hope," Sofia agreed. "We have done what we can. Probably your best course will be to write a play, then go out to recruit players for it. In the course of that recruitment you can pass by Castle Roogna, where you will pick up the Three Princesses."

"But wouldn't that make their identity obvious? I should not go near Castle Roogna."

"Oh! You are correct. The Princesses will have to join you

elsewhere, somewhere along the way. They will surely find you."

"Just so long as they do so before Ragna Roc summons my troupe."

"They surely will," she agreed. "I have prepared a private room for you where you can work on the play. You can join us for meals, and there's a serviceable chamber pot under the bed. Will you be needing anything else?"

"Inspiration," he said grimly.

"That should seek you out when you are ready."

Wira guided him up the winding stairs, past the Good Magician's cramped study, and to an isolated turret. A single small window peeked out at the sunlight, which spilled in to touch the floor in one spot. This was his creative retreat.

"Lunch is in half an hour, in the dining room," Wira said. "Just come down to the ground floor and follow your nose. We'll all be there."

"All?"

"All except Magician Humfrey. I serve him in his study so he won't miss a line of his tome. The people currently doing their Services. You met them on your way in."

"Oh."

"And my husband Hugo. I wouldn't be here without him."

"Oh," he repeated dully. "Of course." Then, as she was about to depart: "What's it like, being married?"

"It's wonderful," she said dreamily. "There's always someone to hug." Then she was gone.

The chamber had a bed, and sure enough there was a ceramic pot under it. Also a basin and sponge, and a pitcher of water. He would be able to wash readily enough.

In a nook of the main room there was a small table and chair, with a quill pen, a bottle of ink, and a blank scroll. All he needed to write his first play.

He sat down at the table and lifted the pen. His mind went

utterly blank. So much for inspiration; it wasn't seeking him yet. He did want to write; he just didn't know how to begin.

He got up and went to the window. He peered out. There was the moat, and the countryside surrounding the castle. No inspiration there either.

He spied a door, and opened it. It was a closet, with a change of clothing. Including a nice clean pair of socks, of course.

He lay on the bed and closed his eyes, trying to imagine a suitable play. But all he could think of was how much nicer it would be to share the bed with a woman. Any woman. Maybe one like Tess, who was so clearly competent to educate him in the appropriate manner. When he had embraced her bare body in the pool—

He woke to find sunlight in his face. Time must have passed, allowing the sunbeam to move across the room. He jumped up. Was he too late for lunch?

He went down the winding stairs to the ground floor, where Wira intercepted him. "Just in time," she said. "This way." She led him to a new room.

There was a small group of people seated around a square table. Cyrus recognized them: Tuff Stuff, Acro Nymph, Dusti Devil, Sofia, and an unremarkable man who must have been Hugo, Wira's husband. "Hello," Cyrus said.

"Hello," they chorused in return.

The Sand Witch appeared with a platter of sandwiches. She was wearing her luscious young form. "Sorry, no more knuck-lers," she said. "They're reserved for Challenges." She leaned down to set them on the center of the table, showing rather more flesh than strictly necessary, and sat down herself.

He had thought of being in bed with someone like Tess. Now he realized that the Witch would also do. Of course she wasn't really interested; she had merely been playing a role in the Challenge.

The others reached for the sandwiches closest to them, so

Cyrus did too. His turned out to be hamhand on ryeder, his favorite kind. The others looked similarly satisfied with theirs. It seemed the witch knew her business. There were also cups of boot rear for a beverage.

"Did you finish your play?" Dusti inquired, sipping some boot and bouncing in place as it scored. That caused her décolletage to ripple intriguingly, surely by coincidence.

"I haven't even started it," he answered sheepishly. "No inspiration."

"Poor boy. Maybe I should join you up there. Give you a whirl. I'm sure I could inspire you."

"No you don't, tart," the Witch said. "I've got seniority." She turned to Cyrus. "I am more mature than I may appear at the moment, and thoroughly experienced." She inhaled. Full-figured women seemed unusually good at inhaling.

Cyrus's eyeballs had heated when she leaned forward. Now they heated again. He felt the steam rising from them. "You seem quite mature to me."

"Oh come off it," Acro snapped. "I can do that, and I'm only a fraction her age." She tore open her shirt, taking a breath.

Cyrus's eyes congealed in place.

"Now look what you've done," Dusti said. "I'll have the devil of a time getting his sight back." She dissolved into a whirlwind, hovered over the table, and blocked his view of the nymph.

His eyes thawed. But then in the whirling funnel he saw another bosom, formed of small clouds of dust, darkly inviting. The little devil! His eyes locked up again.

A stone plaque came before his face. It was a slab of volcanic rock, held there by Tuff. "Thank you," he said as his eyes recovered again.

"Spoilsport," Dusti muttered, reforming in her place.

"Somebody has to protect a poor helpless man from you teases," Tuff said.

"Some day one of us will find out just how durable your

stone is, Stuff," the Witch said darkly, taking a swig of her boot.

"Anytime, Sandy." Apparently he was calling her bluff.

The Witch aimed a Glance at him, but then caused it to veer harmlessly aside. "Perhaps."

"So have you figured out my talent yet, Cyrus?" Acro asked, changing the subject.

"Not yet. But I think it has to be related to your name. There must be some magic use for acronyms."

"But how can making words from words be magic?"

His mind started focusing. "Perhaps if such a derived word had magic properties. For example, if you encountered a magically closed door, and there was a sign saying 'Door's password needed. Closed until then.' You might excerpt O P E N and it would open."

"I wonder," she said. "It seems far-fetched. Those aren't even all first letters."

"It's not my specialty. Maybe you can do it right."

The others were silent, interested. Acro pondered. "Let's say I want to lift something magically, like this cup." She focused on her almost empty boot rear cup. "Under a **P**lump pillow. UP."

The cup sailed up, slopping out its remaining boot rear.

"It worked!" she exclaimed, thrilled.

"Try it with other letters," Tuff suggested, laying down a small tuff stone. "It would be a stronger talent if any letters would do."

"Under a pl**U**m**P** pillow." The stone flew up.

"Congratulations," the Witch said. "I suppose this means you won't be staying here any more."

"You just want to get rid of me!"

"Less competition," the Witch agreed, glancing sidelong at Cyrus. "Your plump pillows are too effective."

Acro considered. "I'll go when he goes. I want to be in a play."

"Don't we all," Dusti said.

"So one of you wants to go to his room tonight," Tuff said. "Why don't you compete for it more aptly? Say, the first one to get to his room without using the stairs gets him."

"I'm not agreeing to that," Cyrus protested, appalled.

"Who asked you?" Dusti asked. "This is our deal." The other two nodded.

Cyrus remembered about how some woman would select him. Maybe it was best just to let it happen. They were all interesting women. So he stifled any further comment.

"Very well," the Witch said. "I can fly my broom. Dusti can whirl through air. Now Acro can craft a word to fly or conjure her way there. Let's meet outside, and Tuff can give us a starting signal. Are we agreed?"

"What about the losers?" Dusti asked.

"They compete again for Tuff."

"Hey!" Tuff said.

"You devised the contest," the Witch informed him. "You're overdue for a comeuppance."

"One of us will melt your stone," Dusti said. "We were just waiting for the right pretext."

Tuff looked as uncertain as Cyrus felt, but he seemed to be stuck for it. The girls were showing their hand. Or whatever. Cyrus had had no idea that women could be like this, but he realized that it was just as well he was finding out. It put him on guard, for whatever that was worth.

He retired to his room and waited for what was to be. Which woman would win? Did he care? One part of him loved being the object of such attention, even if he knew it was just because they wanted to convince him to cast them in a play.

He looked out the window. There they were on the pavement just within the moat: three women and one man. Tuff raised one arm, then brought it abruptly down.

They were off. The Witch jumped on her broom and started flying, but it was slow; evidently the angle was too steep for it to handle. She had to start looping around an ascending spiral, slowly. The dust devil became a whirlwind, rising somewhat faster, but having trouble with nearby foliage that interfered with the circulation. And Acro stood in place, concentrating on her mental exercise. It would take her longer to start, but she might be much faster once she got it.

The broom and dust devil collided, probably by accident. The Witch dropped to the ground, cursing bleepishly, while the whirlwind went to pieces and had to reform. Both had lost time.

They got it together again. This time the broom flew to one side, and the whirlwind to the other. Acro still stood there, focusing.

Cyrus watched as the Witch gained elevation, achieving the height of his window. She was struggling with the effort of maneuvering her broom, her long hair flying back, her bosom heaving, her skirt fluttering up to flash her nicely formed legs. He found her quite intriguing, even if she was older than she looked, and half hoped she would be the winner. After all, he needed a woman with experience, so she would know exactly what to do.

Then he looked at the swirling dust devil, and thought about how evocative and shapely Dusti was in her solid form. She was interesting too, and spirited, and he would not at all mind if she won. She was young, but probably had more than half a notion what to do.

Meanwhile Acro remained on the ground, working on her words and letters. She intrigued him most of all, maybe because she had shown him the most flesh. She had freaked him out. If he had a choice, he would choose her. To bleep with experience.

The Witch oriented her broom and sailed toward him. But the dust devil was closing fast. They would arrive almost together.

Just as they did, Acro got her spell together and appeared

right between them, grabbing for the window ledge. The three collided in a tangle of limbs, tresses, and screams. They fell down, Acro grabbing the end of the broom for support, as the Witch spun in the whirlwind.

There was a splash as they all landed in the moat. "Your fault!" "Yours!" "Both of yours!" They were all as mad as wet poultry.

Cyrus sighed. It seemed that none of them had won. Now he had no choice but to return to his writing. Which wasn't happening.

4

WRITER'S BLOCK

F inally Cyrus went to Wira, who was helping Sofia put away armfuls of balled socks. "I'm supposed to be writing my first play, but my mind is utterly blank. I don't know what to do."

"I think I've heard of it," Wira said. "It's called Writer's Brick. Something like that."

"Block," Sofia said. "Writer's Block. It's a mundane phenomenon."

"But I'm not Mundane."

"True." She considered. "The specialists in plays are the Curse Fiends. You should go to them. They'll know what to do."

"But they'll curse me."

"I doubt it. They are seriously interested in all facets of play production. Go ask them for help. They'll be flattered, and will surely provide it."

"The right approach," he said, catching on.

Next morning he organized to depart. The three women

clustered close. "What about us?" the Witch demanded. "We want to be Actresses."

"Don't you still have your Service to the Good Magician to complete? There will be other querents needing dissuasion."

"I can go," Acro said. "I'm not bound, and I have my Answer, thanks to you, Cyrus. I will be happy to reward you for that, come nightfall."

"Unfair!" Dusti protested. "We deserve our chances too."

"The Good Magician will let you both go for this," Wira said.

That aroused the Witch's suspicion. "Why?"

Cyrus knew why, but couldn't say it. His real mission was to save Xanth from Ragna Roc, and the play was merely the means.

"I can tell you this much," Wira said. "It is important that the plays be as good as possible, with the best actors and actresses. But there may be danger. So you may go, as part of your Services, and completion of the troupe mission will also complete your Services. If you care to take the risk."

"What risk?"

"Possible extinction."

That made the three pause. But then they rallied. "I'm in anyway," the Witch said. "At least I'll get to be an actress first."

"Me too," Dusti agreed.

"Then you may go," Wira said. "But you may not mention the danger. It is a private matter that must not be exposed prematurely."

"No gossiping?" the Witch asked, disappointed.

"None."

"Bleep."

"Also," Cyrus said, "I will be recruiting other actors, according to the need of the plays. I can't promise you lead roles."

"Worse yet," Dusti said glumly. "Still, maybe we can persuade you. We can take turns sharing your tent. The three of us." She glanced at the others to get their agreement.

"No," Wira said firmly. "Such an arrangement would annoy the other actresses. Cyrus must not become intimate with any single actress, lest it prejudice the project as a whole."

"Awww," all three said together.

Cyrus was relieved. Had any of them been sincerely interested in him, he would have been interested in return. But he knew they were only trying to get preferential treatment. It was better to keep his distance from all of them.

So they set out as a party of four, carrying backpacks with spot supplies Wira and Sofia had provided.

Beyond the castle Don Donkey and Xina awaited them. "This is Don, my wood-burning robot ass," Cyrus said. "These are three actresses."

The donkey snorted. "They don't look like much."

"Neither do you, metal butt," the Witch snapped.

"Have you solved my problem?" Xina asked excitedly, her hair brightening.

"Yes. I am forming a repertoire company. You may join it and be an actress. Once I manage to write a suitable play."

Xina squealed with girlish delight, her hair shifting to blue. "Wonderful!" She kissed him.

"Hey!" Acro said.

"But I can't promise you a leading role," Cyrus said.

Xina looked as if she wanted to take back the kiss. "Oh." Her hair turned black.

"I told you he couldn't be trusted," Don said. "He's a cyborg."

"I have to warn you that there may be danger," Cyrus told Xina.

"There's always danger. I just want to be an actress."

"Join the throng," Acro said.

"We'd better move along," Cyrus said. "I want to reach the curse fiends tomorrow."

"The curse fiends!" Xina said, alarmed.

"He said there was danger," the Witch reminded her snidely.

Xina put on a show of resignation, her hair becoming dishwater blond. "What must be, must be."

"She *is* an actress," Dusti said.

"If you like that type," Acro said.

Cyrus marched on, and the four women fell in behind him. He could have ridden the donkey, but that would have seemed unfair to the women. They took turns, all liking the robot despite his taciturn nature.

The path curved to the north east. "We need to go south east," Cyrus said. "To Lake Ogre Chobee."

"Too bad," Don said. "We'll have to leave the enchanted path."

"But that will expose us to possible dangers," Acro protested.

"Duh, pseudonymph," Don said. "You knew it when you signed."

"Anyone who wishes to leave the troupe now may do so," Cyrus said.

"Oh, come off it," the Witch snapped. "We've got a dust devil on our side."

"And a robot," Dusti said.

They stepped off the enchanted path. Immediately a big cat appeared, the size of a panther, its head the shape of the letter A. It licked its angular chops.

The Witch strode forth. "I recognize you. You're an A-cat. So get your A out of here." She swung her broom, scoring on the cat's rear.

Surprised and dismayed, the cat bounded back into the forest.

"I probably shouldn't have done that," the Witch said.

"Why not?" Xina asked, evidently impressed.

"Because these cats hunt in prides, and each one is worse than the others. Worse, a person can abolish only one cat, then is vulnerable to the others. We'll have to take turns dealing with them."

Sure enough, another big cat bounded into view. This one's face resembled the letter B. It snarled at them.

"My turn," Dusti said. She whirled into dust devil form and moved toward the cat. "Get your B-hind out of here!" the cloud of dust cried, flinging grit at the cat's eyes.

This cat, too, was taken aback. It turned tail and fled.

"Well done," the Witch said. "But there'll be another."

In a moment there was. This one's face resembled the letter C, and it seemed to have sharp vision. It stalked them menacingly.

"My turn, I think," Acro said. "If I can work out a word fast enough."

"GO," Cyrus suggested.

"I've **GO**t it," she agreed. "GO!"

And the cat, seeing the magic of it, departed.

Only to be replaced by another, with a D-face that looked as if someone had scribbled on it. "This must be mine," Cyrus said.

"You look like a suitable morsel," the D-cat remarked as it contemplated him.

"I'm not. I'm a cyborg, with rubbery flesh and metal bones. Not that it matters. I'm a play director, and I will cast you into the awfullest role imaginable, the one that no other actor will accept." He lifted his arms as if about to cast a spell.

This cat was evidently not the smartest. It hesitated. Then as Cyrus began his invocation, it bounded away.

"So now who does get stuck with that role?" the Witch asked, smiling.

"The stupidest one," he answered.

But in half a moment there was another, an E-cat, with a face like the letter E. "Eeeee!" it screamed, charging them.

Xina jumped to intercept it, her hair billowing out in the most sickly green imaginable. The cat saw it and screamed again, in revulsion. She kept coming, and it finally turned tail and was gone, retching.

"What was that?" Cyrus asked.

"Ogress coif." Her hair was fading back to bearable.

The others laughed. That did explain it.

"It seems to me that talents aren't supposed to be repeated," Acro said. "I once met a girl who could change her hair color."

Cyrus sifted through his memory. "Talents don't generally repeat, except in the case of the Curse Fiends. But some can be very similar. Xina probably changes her hair in a different way than the other girl did."

Another cat appeared. This one's face was in the form of an ugly letter F.

"That's the worst," the Witch said. "It's from Mundania, where it terrorizes students. The F-cat won't allow anyone to pass unless he/she answers a silly question. No one with any sense can answer."

"Then it must be my turn," Don said, moving toward the cat. "I'm a silly ass." He oriented on the cat. "Avast, you funny feline formula."

The F-cat was more than ready. "If one dragon smokes from the east at three strides per moment, and another steams from the west at four bounds per trice, what will the temperature of the fire dragon be when they collide?"

"This is nonsense," Cyrus muttered. "A smoker and a steamer have nothing to do with a fire breather."

"That's the nature of the beast," the Witch said. "Normal folk can't even understand its questions."

"Four fifty-one Fahrenheit," Don said.

The dragon's jaw dropped. "You answered it!" it said, dismayed.

"Now get your tail out of here," Don said.

The F-cat did, and no more cats appeared. Apparently this party was too tough for them to prey on.

"How did you know the answer?" the Witch asked, impressed.

"It's one of the useless facts stored in my data bank," Don said.

"But suppose the cat had asked a different question?"

"All the F-cat questions are stored there. It's a real memory dump."

"We had better move on," Cyrus said. But privately he was impressed with all of them; each member of the party had come through when needed.

They found an enchanted path leading toward Lake Ogre-Chobee and followed it. By evening they were well on their way. They came to a camping site where there was fresh water, pie trees, and a cabin for five.

"But we are a party of six," the Witch said.

"I'll sleep outside," Don said. "Actually I don't really sleep; I merely power down my limited cranial circuits to let them cool. I'm about due to forage for more wood anyway."

"Five," Acro said. "We'll just fit."

Cyrus became alarmed. "I don't think I should join you."

"You'd *better* join us," the Witch said. "Otherwise one of us will sneak out to seduce you without the others knowing until it's too late."

"Now who would do a thing like that?" Xina asked innocently.

"Who wouldn't?" the Witch retorted.

Xina's hair went limp. She knew the Witch was right.

The women organized things effectively, and they had a nice supper of pot pies and tsoda pop. They let Cyrus wash up in the pond first, alone, then shut him in the cabin while the rest of them washed with much laughing and screaming.

At last they rejoined him. "We have decided that it's not fair to leave you completely alone," the Witch said. "So we'll take turns sharing your bed."

"Fair?" he asked, alarmed. "What's fair about that?"

"Fair to *us*," Dusti said. "Each one gets equal cuddling rights."

"Cuddling?"

"That's all that's allowed," Acro said. "Unfortunately. But we'll just have to make do."

"I'm not sure I—"

"Just lie down in the center bed and sleep," Xina said. "We've worked it all out."

Bemused, Cyrus lay down and closed his eyes. Immediately someone joined him on the bed. He tried to ignore her, but she slid a hand into his shirt and nuzzled his neck.

Her female nearness was intoxicating. He felt guiltily urgent to do what he shouldn't do and probably would flub anyway. "Who are you?" he whispered.

"Guess," she whispered back.

Because it was a whisper, he couldn't recognize the voice. "Will you answer a question?"

"No. I will merely whisper sweet nothings in your ear." She touched his ear with her lips. "Sweet nothings!"

The worst of it was that the nonsense words really turned him on. She was playing with him, and he was powerless to stop it.

He focused on business. So he couldn't fathom her identity by her answers. What else was there? "Then I'll have to feel you."

"Feel me," she agreed eagerly.

He put a hand to her head. She had hair, but he didn't know what any of their hair felt like, so that didn't help. He needed to see its color. He felt her face, but found that he could not tell one girl's face from another without seeing it. He felt for her clothing, but she wore none. All her identifiers were missing. "I give up," he said.

"The bleep you do! You haven't felt most of me."

"But that would be too—too familiar."

"Not when you have reason. Feel." She took his hand and set it on her chest. It was some chest.

He freaked out. He lay there with his whole body locked in paralysis, unable to move a muscle or anything else.

"Foul!" another woman cried. "You freak him out, you lose your turn. That's the rule."

"Bleep." She removed his hand and left the bed.

By the time Cyrus recovered control of his body, it was too late to ask who she had been. But her last "bleep" had been voiced, and that gave him the clue: Dusti. She was better endowed than he had thought, at least with her clothes off. If he had thought to feel her forehead he would have found her little horns and known her that way. She was truly a little devil.

Now there was another beside him. "Hello, Cyrus," she murmured, nibbling on his left ear.

"Xina," he said.

"You bet. Now let's see if I can prevent you from freaking out. Put on this glove."

"Glove?"

"Here." She fitted it to his hand, then found his other hand for the other glove. "Now touch my body."

"But—"

"Here." She carried one hand to her chest. He felt one or two marvelously soft mounds.

He reeled, but did not quite freak out. The gloves prevented direct contact, and that was enough. But it left him with deliciously naughty thoughts. "You—nice," he said.

"To be sure. Remember that when you cast the lead lady role."

"But that's supposed to be according to acting merit."

"Merit, smerit. It goes to the most evocative body. Do you have a problem with that?"

"Well, as I understand it—"

She guided his gloved hand across truly evocative surfaces. He was right at the very verge of freakdom, but not *quite*. "Are you sure?"

He was overwhelmed. "No problem," he agreed.

"Bleep!" someone else muttered.

"She used a prop," Dusti protested. "That's against the rule."

"So it is," the Witch agreed. "I had forgotten. We have to take the gloves off. Out of there, wench. You're disqualified."

"BLEEP!" Xina swore in wenchly fashion.

Now it was Acro's turn. She wore a sleek nightie that masked her body without the need for gloves. "And whose is the most evocative body?" she inquired dulcetly and she pressed it against him, placing his hands on her derriere.

Again, he was just barely (so to speak) shy of a freak. "Yours," he gasped.

She kissed his cheek. "That's good."

His face heated with the imprint of her lips. "Th-thank you."

Then she kissed his mouth. He started sliding into a freak. "Oops! Must stop that. You've got to be immune to kisses. **KI**ndly **S**tay **S**erene equals KISS. That should do it."

"It did," he agreed, no longer freaking. "Kiss me again."

"Foul!" Dusti exclaimed. "No magic!"

"Right," the Witch agreed. "That spell disqualifies you. Get your soft round butt out of there, nymph."

"Darn, I forgot," Acro said, doing it.

That left the Witch. "I knew those inexperienced girls would mess up," she confided. "The trick is to rev up a man just so far, and no farther."

"Doesn't he have a choice?"

She laughed. "I love your naïveté." She settled down against him, revving him up just so far. "Sleep well."

And, to his surprise, he did.

Cyrus scouted the way ahead, riding Don, to be sure of a route that all the actresses could handle without mischief. It was boring work, but necessary. "Too bad we can't be doing something interesting, like rescuing damsels in distress," he said.

"Or kicking some ass," Don agreed.

"I wouldn't do that to an animal!"

"I was not referring to an animal."

Oh. They moved on. He heard a scuffling and clamor, and hurried to investigate.

A comely young woman was being hounded by three brutish thugs. "No! Never!" she cried.

"Yes, and right now," a thug retorted, grabbing her by her long hair. "All three of us."

Cyrus realized that this was a maiden in need of rescue. Maybe even a Damsel in Distress. He hurried closer.

"I'll scream!" she threatened.

The thug pinned her against a tree trunk. "You're a real piece of resistance, know that?"

"That's pièce de résistance," Cyrus called, pronouncing it correctly. It was in his memory bank. "The main event. And not for you. Let her go."

"And suppose we don't?" the thug demanded belligerently.

"Then I will have to force the issue."

"Har har har!" The thug reached out to rip open the damsel's bodice.

Cyrus realized that these thugs were not going to be reasonable. He dismounted and strode forward. Don moved to block off the other two thugs.

"What the bleep?" the thug demanded as Cyrus caught his arm. "I'll pulverize you!"

Cyrus threw the arm into the brush. Since the thug remained attached, he followed it, landing on a stink horn. There was a foul-smelling noise and an awful-looking stench. The thug was soon enveloped in a noxious cloud, choking helplessly.

Meanwhile Don was kicking ass, his way. One hind hoof booted the bottom of the second thug, and the other hind hoof pasted the posterior of the third thug. Both flew through the air to land on their own stink horns.

In hardly more than a moment and a half all three stinking thugs were fleeing the scene.

"You saved me!" the Damsel exclaimed gratefully. "However can I reward you, handsome stranger?"

"Oh, there's no need. We were just passing by."

She glanced at him thoughtfully. Her ponytail flicked off a stray fly from her shoulder. "At least let's get to know each other. I am Algebra, good at math because I wear a bra made of algae." She glanced down at it, now exposed by the thug's bodice rip. It was somewhat green and furry, but supported very nice mounds. "I am a nymph with some equine ancestry." Her ponytail flicked off another fly.

"I am Cyrus Cyborg, a playwright, on my way to see the Curse Fiends."

"A playwright! Oh, I always wanted to be an actress!" Then she reconsidered. "But that doesn't compute. My real passion is mathematics. I must not be diverted from it. What is a cyborg?"

"I am half human, half machine."

"That's why you're so strong! And handsome too." She glanced at him again, taking a deep breath that stretched the living bra. "Are you sure I can't reward you with a kiss and perhaps more? I am really in your debt for rescuing me from those thuggees."

Cyrus was getting half a glimmer what she offered. But it

would surely delay him unduly. "No thank you. I have to be moving on."

"Then maybe you will accept this. It is exactly what you will need." She reached into the crevice between her full mounds and brought out a tiny vial. "Three drops of lethe elixir. It will make you forget something for three days."

"No thank you. I don't need to forget anything."

"Not now, maybe. But some time you will need this. It's a mathematical certainty. Please, it's the only way I can repay you for saving me."

When she put it that way, it was difficult to decline. "Thank you, Algebra," he said, accepting the vial and putting it in his shirt pocket.

"You are more than welcome, Cyrus." Then she laced her bodice back together and departed.

"You're a fool," Don remarked as they resumed their trek. "She was eager to make you deliriously happy for a calculated instant or two."

"I guess it's my nature," Cyrus agreed. "I don't really know how to handle women."

In due course they reached Lake Ogre-Chobee, where ogres and chobees roamed. As it happened, there was a middle-aged curse fiend standing by the shore. "Cyrus Cyborg, I presume?" he asked. "I am Curtis Curse Friend."

Cyrus was astonished. "You expected me?"

"Indubitably. We have an interest in those who set up competing play troupes."

That had not occurred to him. "I did not realize that it was competitive. I merely want to realize my destiny of writing and presenting plays."

"Precisely. And you are having a problem getting started."

"Yes. I am told I have Writer's Block, and that you would know how to deal with it."

Curtis laughed. "Indeed we do. But you have it garbled. In Mundania they have little or no magic, so their blocks get in their way and they have to dispose of them. But in Xanth they are magic, and every writer needs his own special one."

"I need a block?"

"Yes. Not just any block; the one block that is right for you. With it you will be able to write; without it you will be bereft of output, as you are now."

"Suppose I get the wrong block?"

"Then you will be no better off than the Mundanes. The wrong block will constantly thwart your efforts."

"How can I get the right block?"

"You will have to find it. You will know it when you see it, and it will know you."

"How do I find it?"

"That is what I am here for. I will produce your plays. That includes signing on your actors, arranging your travel schedule, organizing meals, and anything else the troupe requires. Getting you in fit condition to write and cast your plays is an aspect of it."

This was too much for Cyrus. "Why should you join my troupe? We are not curse fiends."

"Curse friends," Curtis corrected him gently. "We are hardly fiends. We are human beings with a common magic talent of cursing, and a common ability to produce fine plays."

"Curse friends," Cyrus agreed. "But still I don't quite understand—"

Don had been standing by. Now he spoke. "What's in it for you? We must beware of fiends bearing gifts."

"A talking ass!" Curtis exclaimed. "The first four-footed one I have encountered."

"He is Don Donkey, my robot steed," Cyrus said.

"I will answer forthrightly," Curtis said. "I have spent twenty years mastering my craft, rising through the ranks from spectator, through actor, to producer. Now I am ambitious to become Chief Producer, as there is an opening. To do that I must prove myself capable of managing the least likely material and producing a reputable play. If I can accomplish this with your motley untrained troupe, to the satisfaction of my peers, I will achieve the office."

Cyrus exchanged a look with Don. That was almost too candid. "You can help me find my block?"

"And organize your troupe. I mean to enable you to put on outstanding plays, thus demonstrating my genius for my peers."

Don opened his mouth. Cyrus quickly used his two hands to close it. "Thank you. We appreciate your sacrifice."

Curtis nodded. "Naturally. Now your physical block will be found anywhere, or you can craft it yourself."

"I don't understand."

Curtis rolled his eyes expressively. The orbs were evidently trying to avoid gazing on idiots. "Find a chunk of wood. Carve it into a block. Then I will explain how to establish the necessary rapport. Meanwhile I will set about organizing your troupe." Curtis walked toward the waiting women.

"So now you know where you stand," Don said.

"Knee high to a hopper," he agreed. "Well, let's get on it. The man seems to know what he's doing."

They checked around, and soon found a thick old gnarly wood root. Cyrus fetched a carving knife from Don's tool chest and carved. The wood was exceedingly solid and hard, but in due course he had a crude block. He used a rasp to work off the splinters, then sanded it and held it up. It was actually rather pretty, now that its grain was showing. "I have my block," he said. "I hope."

"Just don't let anybody knock it off."

Curtis appeared just as he finished. The man seemed to have an impeccable sense of timing. "Good enough. Now you need to make contact with the spirit of the block in the dream realm. There's a gourd down that path." He gestured. "Have your donkey supervise while you enter the scene. Keep your hands on the block so the gourd can orient. They will surely be expecting you."

Cyrus sifted through his memory bank. The gourd was an avenue to the dream realm. A person put his eye to the peephole and found himself there, but could not escape it until someone cut off his line of sight to the peephole. That was why Don was needed.

They followed the path, and soon found the access. It was a perfectly ordinary green gourd growing on a leafy vine. It was hard to believe that such a routine thing could perform in such manner. But there were many examples in his memory.

He lay down by the gourd, holding firmly on to the block. "Cut off my line of sight in one hour," he told Don. "Don't forget."

"As long as one of those lithesome nymphs doesn't come to ride me away."

"Don!"

The robot snorted. "It was asinine humor."

"That figures."

Cyrus put his eye to the peephole in the end of the gourd. Suddenly he was in another realm. It was some sort of city block, and before him was a blockhouse. This did seem to be the place. Curtis had advised him correctly. His memory bank did not have reference to any way to select a particular scene in the dream realm. The curse friends evidently had trade secrets.

The wood block was not in his hands. It seemed it had put him here, but could not enter itself. Well, that left his hands free, if that mattered.

He walked toward the door in the blockhouse. A voice challenged him: "Whatcha looking for, blockhead?" It was a demon guard who had just appeared. Across his burly chest was the word BUSTER. So he was the blockbuster.

"My personal Writer's Block."

Buster glanced at his empty hands, evidently seeing something there. "This is the place. Go on in." The demon faded out.

Inside was a veritable mountain of tumbled bocks. There were hundreds of them, of all sizes and colors. How was he to find his one personal one?

Considering the hopeless task, he realized that this was in its fashion like a Challenge at the Good Magician's Castle. He simply had to figure out how to handle it.

This was the dream realm. So maybe a dream would do it.

He closed his eyes and formed a picture in his mind: the somewhat nebulous image of the Perfect Block.

He felt a warmness in one direction. He walked that way, and the warmth increased. Then he tripped over a block and sprawled on the floor.

He opened his eyes. He was at the verge of another small mountain of blocks. There seemed to be a warmth coming from one section of it. So he didn't have to do it blind.

He delved into the pile, clearing the way. Blocks tumbled noisily down, but he kept going. The warmth was getting almost hot.

Finally he plunged his hand into the mass of blocks, feeling for the warmest one. He found it; it was almost too hot to touch. He hauled it out, scattering more blocks.

It was a statuette of a lovely young woman. Nude.

Now he became aware of the contours his fingers clasped. He dropped it, embarrassed.

"Ouch!" the little woman exclaimed angrily, rubbing her pert bottom. "Oaf!"

"You're alive!" he said, astonished.

"What did you expect, moron? A dead fish?"

"Uh, not exactly. I'm looking for my Writer's Block. The one that is meant for me alone."

Her eyes rolled in a manner reminiscent of the curse friend's. "I see I've got my work cut out for me."

"You mean—you're the one?"

"I am Melete," she said. "MEL-i-tee. The Muse of Meditation. It is my sorry chore to develop your inherent ability to write. It will help if you don't throw me on the floor."

"I didn't—"

She delivered a withering stare.

"I apologize," he said quickly. "It won't happen again."

She mellowed slightly. "I suppose you can't help being clumsy. You're a mortal man."

"Actually I'm only half a man. I'm a cyborg."

She sent another glance, this one apprising. "Well, that's new. A cyborg playwright. It does help to have a bit of novelty."

"You said you are a— I get a whole Muse to help me?"

"You get a tiny fragment of a Muse, as every writer does. Only when I have enabled all aspiring writers to be fully competent will I finally be freed of this miserable bondage. So you will do your best, or else."

"Or else what?" he asked, curious.

"Or else I will leave you forever, and you will never achieve your stupid dream. Now take me out to the real world. We'll talk further there."

"Yes ma'am," he agreed, picking her up carefully by the midsection. Whatever he had expected, it wasn't this.

He returned to the entrance, which turned out not to exist. "How do I get out?"

"You wait until your companion breaks your eye-line to the peephole," she said. "Duh."

"Oh. Of course."

And suddenly it happened.

5

MELETE

Cyrus found himself staring at the donkey's hoof, which
had broken the line of sight to the peephole. "Thank
you," he said.

"So did you get it?"

He looked at the block between his hands. It remained a
block. "I'm not sure. I made contact with a—"

He broke off, because the block had changed. Now it was a
statuette, or half of one. The upper half of the fragment of the
Muse, except for the arms, which were missing. "Melete!"

She made a moue. "You were expecting Clio?"

"But you're only half there."

"What are you talking about?" Don demanded.

"It's my Writer's Block, animated."

"Writer's bust," Melete corrected him, inhaling.

"Bust. Sorry."

"What did you bust?" Don asked. "Your block? It's un-
changed."

"Look closer," Cyrus said, holding up the bust. "Melete. My
muse."

"You named your block?"

"She named herself. Or identified herself. She's going to help me write my plays."

"That dull block of wood will help you write?"

"Not the wood. Melete. Look at her!"

Don looked closely at the wood, then at him. "Are you suddenly tetched in the head, cyborg? I told you, that's just wood. Looks good enough to eat."

"Don't you dare!" He turned to Melete. "Tell him."

She shook her head. "It's no use, Cyrus. He can't see or hear me. I am your muse, exclusively."

"Because he's a robot?"

"No one but you can appreciate me. To most others I'm just your original block of wood. Don't lose it."

Cyrus digested that. "I fashioned the block, you animate it—only for me?"

She threw her head back so that her hair flung out. Without arms that was her most dramatic gesture. "I believe he's got it!"

"I got it," he agreed. He turned to the donkey. "Let's just say I have a good imagination. It is as though this wood takes a form and talks to me. But now I should be able to write my plays."

"Let's hope so," Don said. "Otherwise this whole troupe is a bust."

"A bust," Melete agreed, laughing. That did more things to her own bust.

That reminded him. "Why don't you have arms? You did in the dream realm. In fact you had your whole body."

"Which remains there," she agreed. "I am your connection between reality and dreams. My better half must remain there until my job is done."

"But without arms—"

"I have arms. They just don't show at the moment. I have to choose."

"Choose?"

"Which portion of me to animate."

"I don't think I understand."

"Like this." She changed, in a weird kind of shifting upward. Her head disappeared from the top down, while her belly and hips came into view—and beside them, her arms. These continued traveling up and disappearing, as her legs appeared. At last there was only a nice pair of legs standing on the pedestal that was the lower half of the block.

And of course she couldn't talk in this position. They were very nice legs; had they had panties he might even have freaked out. But they were silent.

"I hope you can hear me, Melete," he said. "Please, bring your head back. Seeing only your lower half like this makes me uncomfortable."

The shifting reversed. Her feet disappeared into the block while her hips reappeared, followed by her belly and arms. For a moment or two or three she was a central torso, with bottom, belly, and breasts. Then the head came down, and she was back as a bust. "Now you know. You can have any part of me, but never the whole of me, except in your dreams."

"I see that," he said, impressed and somewhat disquieted. "Maybe it's just as well that no one else can see you."

"I am yours alone," she agreed.

"If you're quite through talking to your block," Don said sourly, "maybe it's time to get back to the troupe before that curse fiend absconds with it."

"Curse friend. They're not actually fiends."

"All in the viewpoint."

He mounted Don, and they headed off to rejoin the troupe. He held the bust carefully before him.

"Tuck me in your pocket," Melete said. "I must never leave you, because I am your creative spirit."

"But the block is too big for my pocket."

"Nonsense. Do it."

"If you insist." He lifted the block to his shirt pocket—and it fit. That had to be magic. Well, Melete was magic, so maybe it made sense.

"It does," she said from his pocket.

"You can read my thoughts?"

"I *am* your thoughts. I know everything that's in your mind."

"Everything?" he asked, alarmed.

"Everything I focus on. I can't help you meditate properly if I don't know your distractions. You have a problem with that?"

"Uh, no, I suppose. It's just that you're a—"

"I'm a what?"

"Nothing," he said hastily.

"I'm a woman?"

"Uh, yes. And women are—different."

"What's wrong with being female?"

"Nothing. It's only that—nothing."

"What don't you want me to pick up on?"

"Nothing."

"That means there's something. You'd better tell me, because if I have to ferret it out for myself by delving into your subconscious there's no telling what else I'll discover in those murky regions. Folk have all kinds of secret shames hidden in the nether realms. Make it easier on us both. Formulate your problem specifically."

He seemed to be stuck for it. "Men—women—they think about them. It can be embarrassing."

She delved on that. "Oh, those actresses. Why the naughty minxes! They're teasing you in bed."

"Yes," he confessed, feeling himself blushing.

"Well, we'll just have to put a stop to that. I'm the only one who can tease you now. We can't allow them to distract you from your creative writing."

"But I can't stop them. Women govern men."

"This is a special case," she said seriously. "Women govern men in secret. The moment it becomes open, it loses effect. They have been more than open; they have become blatant. That nullifies their advantage."

"It doesn't seem nullified to me. They—get me all excited, and I can't do anything about it."

"Precisely. You have to assert yourself."

"I wish I could!"

"You can. Here's how: call them together the moment we reach the troupe, and announce that you have found your Writer's Block and will now concentrate on writing the first play. Especially at night, because your dreams are essential. Say that any woman you find in your bed you will promptly nail to the mattress."

"I couldn't do that! I don't even have a hammer."

She laughed. "You do now. Trust me. Don't mistake subtlety for stupidity, or certainty for judgment. They'll get the message. Just make the statement, and they won't call your bluff."

"But—but suppose they do—call my bluff?"

"Oh, you're fun." She shook her head with some private amusement. "Then I will teach you how to nail a woman, as it were. One demonstration will make the point. But that should not be necessary. Henceforth women won't manage you, you will manage women."

"But you're a woman! Why should you betray your own kind?"

"Because I have a higher calling. I have to make a playwright of you. To accomplish that, first I have to make a man of you. It's a tall order, but I think I can accomplish it, by night if not by day."

"That's good," he said dubiously.

"I wish I knew what you think that block is saying," Don said. "Women, hammers, bluffs—I am not making sense of this."

"You're an ass," Melete snapped. But of course the donkey didn't hear her.

"It's a private dialogue," Cyrus said.

"If you do it in public, folk will think you are crazy."

"He's got a point," Melete said. "You had better not talk to me when in company."

"But then how can we have a dialogue?"

"Merely concentrate your thoughts as if you are talking. I will pick them up readily enough, and answer you."

I'll try, he thought.

"That's the way," she agreed. "You know, you should clean out your pocket sometime. You have cookie crumbs and a vial of lethe here."

A nymph gave me that. She said it's just what I'll need, sometime.

"Well, we'll see, sometime."

They rode along in silence for half a while. Then Cyrus thought of something else. "You said I should assert myself. Is that only with women?"

"No, it's with everyone. You will become a playwright of note, a man of importance. You must act like it."

"What about Curtis Curse Friend? He stepped right in, telling me what to do. In fact he directed me to you."

"I know him. I know all the curse friends. I have worked with their playwrights many times. Curtis is a good man, with a liability that doesn't affect the troupe. Just tell him that Melete is with you now. He will know exactly what that means."

"What exactly *does* it mean?"

"It means that if he opposes you, he will have to deal with me. I'm a minor Goddess to the curse friends. He will give you no trouble."

Cyrus's doubt remained. "But if he does give me trouble, what then?"

"Cyrus, there are three things never to antagonize, in ascending order: a woman, a Sorceress, and a Goddess. You can get away with the first, sometimes, if you're careful. The second is real trouble, and the third is disaster."

"Disaster?"

"Where would the curse friends be if they abruptly lost their creativity?"

"They wouldn't be able to make new plays."

"Or present the old ones effectively. They would lose their rationale for existence."

Which would be a terrible curse. "You can really do that?"

"Oh, yes. Simply by departing."

He believed it. "Suppose I, somehow, antagonize you?"

"Then you might as well go farm itch ants, because you'll never write another play."

"Oh, Melete, I couldn't stand that! How can I make sure never to annoy you?"

"It is easy. Never oppose my will."

"That's all?"

"That's enough."

"Your will is law," he agreed.

"That's an excellent start."

"Troupe ahead," Don said. "So shut up with your block."

He had forgotten to keep it silent. "Right."

The troupe had made a camp. Women were working industriously at various tasks, such as setting up tents and digging a trench to the side.

Curtis approached as Cyrus dismounted. "This will be our station while we recruit actors and rehearse them for the first play. When we are ready, we'll tour, making presentations to the villages on our itinerary. I have it all organized."

"Melete is with me."

The man took stock. "Organized by your leave, of course."

"Of course," Cyrus agreed. He had clearly risen from Nobody to Somebody. Melete did know what she was doing.

"Naturally I do," she agreed.

"Do you have any directives, Playwright?"

"Summon the women; I have an announcement to make."

Curtis clapped his hands, attracting their attention. "All actresses assemble here. The Playwright will address you now."

The women obeyed with alacrity. In a moment and a half the four of them stood before him.

"I have found my Writer's Block," Cyprus said. "Hereafter I will be concentrating on my writing. By day and night. I want no distractions. Any woman I discover in my bed I will promptly nail to the mattress. Any questions?"

"Bleep," the Witch muttered. "He's calling our bluff."

"What's that?" he asked sharply.

"We hear and obey, Playwright," she said immediately.

"Very good. Return to your chores."

They returned to their chores. So did Curtis.

"Dominance has been established," Melete said with satisfaction. "Now go to your tent and start writing."

"But I should help with the chores," he protested.

Don gave him a hard nudge with his nose.

"Right. Thanks," he said, to both Muse and donkey.

His tent was in the center of the camp, already set up with a bed, writing table, and chair. On the table was parchment, a quill, and a bottle bearing the label BLUE BOTTLE, INC filled with dark blue ink. Everything he needed.

"Apart from me," Melete agreed.

He sat down and lifted the quill. He dipped it in ink. And his mind went blank, exactly as before. "Nothing's changed!"

"Yes it has," Melete said. "You just need to organize your thoughts as well as Curtis has organized the site. Put down the quill and go lie on the bed."

"But that's not writing!"

"Are you opposing my will?"

"No!" He put down the quill and went to the bed. "Now what?"

"Close your eyes and meditate."

He lay on his back and closed his eyes. "How do I meditate? I've never done it before."

"Just think about life, the universe, and the play. What would move an audience?"

"Well, a romance, maybe."

"Boy meets girl, boy loses girl, boy regains girl?"

"Yes, I guess. But it doesn't turn me on."

"Because it's unoriginal formula. What would you rather write?"

"A really dramatic story of thwarted love that turns out well by surprise."

"That's not formula?"

He pondered. "I guess I want to write *my* formula."

"Very well. Now think of some completely different idea."

"Well, once I thought how nice it would be if I could see emotions. But that doesn't relate to this."

"Yes it does. Or it will as you craft it. How can you make it relate?"

"Maybe if he's looking for his perfect woman, by her emotion. He finds pretty women, but their feelings are not pretty, so he knows better than to mess with them. So he orients on the aura of feeling instead. And finds the best one. He can see this lovely cloud around her, and knows she's his ideal. But then he sees her body, and she's a monster."

"A monster?"

"She has the head of a frog. Something like that."

"So what does he do?"

"He's got a problem."

"What would *you* do?"

He laughed. "I'd probably take the pretty one with the bad feeling. I'm a typical male fool."

"Yes. Your protagonist should be typical. But then he must emerge as smart and decent, so that the average male viewer will identify with him, and be satisfied with his progress. The greater challenge will be the woman."

"The monster?"

"How can you make her someone the average woman would identify with and like?"

He pondered. "Maybe if she was beautiful, but was transformed by some evil magician or something. Or a really bad curse. So inside she's as beautiful as ever, but outside she's a horror."

"Exactly. Now go out and find your actress."

"A woman with a frog's head?"

"Or equivalent. A woman no man would want, yet who is utterly deserving and rather pretty. Make her the star of your play, 'The Curse.'"

"She's cursed, all right."

"But make him the one who is cursed."

"He has a frog's head?"

"No. He can see the auras."

"But that's a blessing, not a curse."

"And if it makes the woman of his dreams unsuitable, because he can see by her visible feeling that she is deceiving him and will destroy him if he marries her?"

"Oho! The blessing is really a curse."

"Until he converts it to a blessing by using it to locate his true ideal woman. Women will appreciate that, and men will also, if she has a good body."

"That's cynical."

"A writer must cynically craft a story that will evoke the maximum response in naïve viewers. Deserving romance for the woman, a sexy body for the men."

He nodded. "This is more practical than I expected."

"Cyrus, you are in the business of crafting dreams, not believing them. This is the down and dirty of sublime imagination. Now find your actress, and the play will write itself."

"I'll try." He got up. "Won't the troupe members think I'm goofing off, if I just walk out now?"

"You are the Playwright. A law unto yourself. They don't expect to comprehend your creative nature."

He left the tent. Don was there. "Have you written the play, you faker?"

"I'm working on it. At the moment we're going in search of an actress."

"As if we didn't have four too many already."

"A special one."

"So you say." The donkey was mechanically cynical.

He mounted and rode out of the camp. No one challenged him.

"Stay off the enchanted path," Melete said. "The woman we want won't be using it."

"Why not?"

"Because she'll be ashamed of her condition. She'll be lurking in some hidden cranny, avoiding exposure. We'll find her there. The most wonderful things are found in the least likely places."

"If you say so." He was feeling as cynical as the donkey. He guided Don onto a disreputable trail that led into the thick of a thinnet, and on to a half-hearted village of shacks. It was about as unpromising as a mud puddle.

There were large, stout weeds growing along the sides. These had bugs clustered on their stems, sucking the juice from them. They looked like giant aphids.

Then something flew in from the side. It was a huge bug. No, it was a Lady Bug. She landed beside the stems, stood straight, folded her gauzy wings, and covered them with glossy wing covers. Now she looked just like a girl in a red cloak.

"Hello," Cyrus said behind her.

She jumped, her wing covers spreading to unleash her wings. She hovered, looking wildly around, somewhat in dishabille as her gown flung out to expose her legs. "Oh," she said, spying him. "You startled me."

"I apologize. You have pretty—"

"Nuh uh," Melete warned.

"Wings," he finished. Actually her whole body was pretty, especially from the underside.

"Thank you." She settled back to the ground, and her gown closed about her front as her wing covers did around her back. "I am Lady Bug. I'm just tending my aphid garden."

"Aphids?"

"They make sweet syrup." She stroked the back of a bug and offered him her hand. "Taste it."

Cyrus sucked off her fingers. The syrup was marvelously sweet. "Delicious."

"We collect it and trade it for other goods," she explained. "To others, aphids are a pest, but to us they are valuable."

"Yes." Cyrus couldn't think of anything else to say, so he introduced Don. "This is Don, my robot donkey. We are looking for actresses."

Lady Bug straighted. "Actresses?"

"I am a playwright assembling a troupe. But I need a special actress for the lead role."

She touched up her hair. "Special in what way?"

"She has to be a monster."

"You mean like a winged monster? I am one."

"You're no monster!"

"Technically all winged creatures are winged monsters. It's a classification, not an insult."

"Like a woman with the head of a frog. Do you know of any?"

"Oh. No, I'm afraid I don't." She looked disappointed. "I

always wanted to be an actress. Do you have any other roles?"

"I may. I haven't written the play yet. But the lead has to be a monster."

"I'm afraid I can't help you," she said sadly.

"But check by the camp when you have time," Don said. "Once he has his play written."

"Oh! You talk!"

"And you fly," the donkey retorted. "You're just lucky your panties didn't show when you hovered over us."

"Don!" Cyrus snapped.

But she laughed. "That's not luck. I know exactly what I'm showing. If I wanted to show panties, I'd do this." She pulled aside a portion of her gown.

Cyrus freaked out. When he recovered, he was riding the donkey farther along the trail.

"I warned you about annoying women," Melete reminded him.

"But Don did it!"

"She knew that. So maybe she was just trying to impress you."

"She succeeded. I think."

They continued along the trail. The sky darkened. "It looks like rain," Don remarked.

"We can handle it," Cyrus said. "But can she?"

For a woman was approaching them. She was brownish in color, and had an interesting walk.

"She's not the one," Melete said.

"It may rain," Cyrus said to the woman as they met. "You should get under cover."

"No need. I am Umber Ella. I never get wet in a rainstorm." She walked on by.

Don groaned without other comment.

"We are meeting women, but not the one I'm looking for," Cyrus said.

"Keep looking," Melete said. "I am sensing her nearby."

The rain held off. They encountered another girl. She was painting red and white stripes on bushes, making them look like candy.

They paused to introduce themselves. "What are you doing?" Don asked.

"I am Candy Striper. I paint the bushes so that they become candies that heal people. It is my little way of making Xanth a nicer place."

She was right, but she was not the actress he needed.

Now they encountered a man. He turned out to be Weslee Weredragon, who could breathe any type of dragon breath: fire, smoke, or steam. That wasn't the actress either.

But Cyrus inquired anyway, explaining what he was looking for.

Weslee nodded. "It happens I know a girl who fits your description. She does not have the face of a frog, but she's just as bad."

"In what way?"

"Her arms terminate in giant crab pincers. No one wants to embrace her. That's too bad, because she really is a sweet person, and very nice looking apart from that one problem."

"She could be the one," Melete said.

"Can you lead me to her?" Cyrus asked, interested.

"Yes." The man paused. "Would you by chance have any likely role for a man with dragon breath?"

"Find me my ideal lead actress, and I'll write a bit part for you."

"Done." Weslee set off, and they followed.

"What's her name?" Don asked.

"They call her Crabapple. She pretends to like it."

"So as not to hurt their feelings?" Cyrus asked.

"Yes. As I said, she's a nice person. If only—" He shrugged.

"But can she act?" Don asked.

"I don't know. I see her only when she needs her weeds burned back."

"Do her pincers work?"

"Oh, yes. That's how she earns her keep: cutting vines into short length for ready storage. That's why the villagers treat her with respect. But there's not a man among them who would ever marry her. All she wants is to find true love and settle down to raise a family, but it will never happen."

"Notoriety can work wonders in such respects," Melete said. "Make her famous, and she'll find a man."

They reached Crabapple's house. Weslee knocked, then announced himself before the door opened. "Crabapple! It's Weslee Weredragon. I brought you visitors from elsewhere."

"Please take them away," a voice replied. "You know I don't like to be an exhibit."

"This is different. It's a Playwright. He wants to cast you in a play."

"As a monster? No!"

"Talk to her," Melete said.

"Crabapple!" Cyrus called. "I am Cyrus Cyborg. I am writing a play with a mon—a woman like you. I need her for a role."

"Don't tease me! It's not nice."

"Please! Let me in. Talk to me. I think you're the one. But it will help if you can act."

The door opened. There stood an elegant young woman in a voluminous cloak.

"Well, now," Melete said. "But is she just a pretty face?"

"You're beautiful," he said honestly. "May I see your body?" That didn't sound quite right, but he wasn't sure how to fix it.

She spread her arms, wrapped in the cloak. It drew away from her torso, showing it bare. It was stunning.

"Well now, doubled," Melete said appreciatively.

Cyrus jammed his eyes closed before he freaked out. "I didn't mean nude. I thought you were—well, clothed."

"It's hard to put on clothing over these."

He opened his eyes cautiously. She had covered up her body and revealed her arms. They were ordinary to the elbows, but then became giant greenish pincers. Indeed, it would be difficult to don any ordinary shirt or dress with those in the way. So she was being practical. He simply hadn't expected it. "Can you act?"

"I could if anyone let me."

"Put her in a scene," Melete said. "A romantic one."

"Pretend you're my girlfriend, angry with me but willing to be persuaded."

"Come in."

He left Don and Weslee outside and joined her inside the house. She closed the door behind him.

"And where have you been, you rascal?" she demanded. "I have been waiting these three weeks for news of you, but there was nothing."

"I was—busy," he said, already impressed by her delivery.

"Busy! *Busy!* Whatever could keep you so busy you couldn't at least send me word? Were you with some village hussy? Answer me!"

"Demur," Melete said. "Proffer her a mock gift."

"No, no," he said, hastily improvising. "I was—making this gift for you. I couldn't tell you, because that would ruin the surprise."

"Gift?" she asked suspiciously.

"Here." He held out an empty hand.

She took the invisible object. "Oh, it's lovely. Thank you so much! I'm so sorry I was suspicious. It's only because I love you."

"And I love you. I—"

She stepped into his arms, keeping her own arms clear, and kissed him firmly on the mouth.

His arms closed automatically about her marvelously slender yet shapely body. Then he realized that it was still bare. He freaked out.

"Bleep," Melete muttered helplessly.

He recovered, uncertain how much time had passed. Crabapple had sat him in a chair and covered up again. "I'm so sorry. I got carried away. For an instant it seemed almost real. I get that way when I'm reciting lines. It's as though I really am the part I'm playing in my fancy. I apologize for putting you through that."

"She will certainly do," Melete said.

"You'll do," he said. "You *can* act. It felt real to me too. Then when I realized that you were—I don't have much experience with women."

She smiled. "I don't have much experience with men. Only in my fancy."

"Tell her of the role," Melete said.

"Let me tell you about the play I'm writing. A young man can see feelings, so he knows how women feel about him. But the pretty ones have ugly personalities. They conceal these, so as to seem nice, but really they hold him in contempt. So he knows they are no good for him to marry. So he searches for a woman with perfect feelings, not even looking at her body. Until he finds her—and she looks like you. Because you will be the lead actress."

"The lead!"

"It's all about how he comes to terms with you. Because you are the best, if he could only get over your—you know."

"I know."

"Something will happen—I haven't figured it out yet—that makes him come to truly appreciate your—your—"

"Pincers."

"Yes. You use them in some way that saves him from danger, or something, and then he comes to like them as an aspect of you. So it will be a happy ending, after considerable doubt. Can you accept that story line?"

"Oh, yes."

"Oh, yes," Melete echoed. "She's perfect. Caution her and sign her up."

"You will need to emote, to make the audience truly feel your pain, and to come to love you, pincers and all. You have the face and features, and the acting ability. I simply need to write a play that will bring out those qualities. Will you join my troupe?"

"Who is the lead man?"

"Sharp question," Melete said. "She's hoping it's you. Better damp that out immediately."

"He hasn't been selected yet. But he'll be competent, I assure you."

Crabapple sighed. "But he won't be falling in love with me for real."

"Not for real," he agreed. "It will all be an act."

"I wish it could be real."

"Actually, you could do worse," Melete said.

Cyrus shook his head. "Crabapple, I can't promise it won't become real. Your body freaked me out, and I'm fully clothed. So it is possible he will—sometimes actors do fall for each other, and fulfill the roles they play. But—"

"But I have these pincers."

"That is the case. I need you for the play, and I believe you can do a good job. But whether men will want you for anything more than a passing dalliance, I can't say."

"But keep her in mind," Melete said. "You do need a woman."

Unless you *are the second of the* "two," *Melete,* he thought.

That set her back, for once. "Not a wife, but a muse. I suppose it is possible."

Meanwhile, Crabapple was nodding. "In short, you are telling me the truth."

"Well, yes."

"That's the way I want it. Yes, I will join your troupe. Is it far from here?"

"Not far. But you can ride Don. That's my robot donkey."

"Perhaps I will."

"We are on our way," Melete said.

$\overline{6}$

CURSE

Cyrus was back in his tent, writing madly. He had his lead actress, but as yet lacked the lead actor. He would have to assume that role himself, until he could cast some other man in the role.

"Maybe we should bring in some pages," Melete said.

"Pages?"

"Folk that find things. White and yellow pages, good at finding things or people. Set them to searching for a good male actor."

"That would help. But how do we find the pages?"

She laughed. "That's the problem. They aren't always where you need them."

"You've got a visitor," Don said. The donkey had become the guardian of his necessary privacy for writing the play. Cyrus trusted the animal's judgment, to an extent. "A girl."

"Tell her to check in with the Witch."

"She demands to see you personally."

Cyrus flung down his quill. It splattered blots of ink on his parchment. "How can I work, when I keep getting interrupted?"

He realized that he was displaying Artistic Temperament, but didn't care. He flung open the tent flap.

There was the girl. She wore a red dress, had red hair, and green eyes. She was about twelve years old. She wore a little golden crown. "Hi," she said, a bit shyly.

"Look, I don't have a part for a child," he said. "You'll have to do drudge work around the camp. Otherwise go away."

She entered the tent, brushing rather closely by him. "I know. But I had to talk with you first."

"Well, I don't have to talk with you! Now stop wasting my time."

She gazed at him with a cold expression. In fact in this moment her face reminded him of an eye sickle, a plate of ice with eyes. This was not the look of an ordinary child. That should have made him wary, but he was too impatient to be properly cautious.

A small drum appeared in her hands. She produced an oddly shaped little baton and beat gently on it. There was a single small boom.

Cyrus found himself frozen in place, unable to move half a muscle. What was happening?

"That's a Sorceress!" Melete exclaimed from the desk where the block had been parked.

"Right, Muse," the girl said. "I am Rhythm."

"The Princess!" Cyrus exclaimed, recovering or released from his stasis. "One of the three who were going to join us."

"Just one, for now," Princess Rhythm said. "All three of us together would be a live giveaway. For one thing, we always speak in turns, completing each other's thoughts. So I had to come alone to let you know. In private."

"You can hear me," Melete said, taken aback.

"Oh, sure. I'm a Sorceress, remember? But I won't tell. I know Cyrus needs you." She studied the tiny bare upper torso. "Don't you freak him out?"

"He's used to me," Melete said. "But I could freak him out if I tried. I won't, because I want him to write the play."

"It must be nice to be able to freak out a man."

"You should be able to do it, in six more years."

"Two more years. Cousins Dawn and Eve were able to freak out men when they were fourteen."

"They were naughty girls."

"So are we," Rhythm said defiantly. "This whole Adult Conspiracy business is a pain in the pants."

"You will need to blend in," Cyrus said, uneasy with the direction the dialogue was taking. Rhythm was a child, after all. "Different clothing, different hair. The crown has to go."

"I'm not really a child," the girl protested. "I'm on the very verge of teendom."

"Different attitude," Melete said. "You should work on the silver lining, the talent to discover advantages in any situation, even that of childhood."

"I'll consider it." The girl paused, considering. "Nope, I have a better idea. I've heard that if you walk in someone else's shoes, you can live that person's life and do the same magic."

"That's not true," Melete said.

"So if I borrowed a grown woman's shoes, maybe then I could kick a stork or two in the tailfeathers."

Ouch! This child had dangerously adult ideas.

"So what?" Rhythm demanded, looking him in the eyeball. "Maybe the wood bees exist only on Ptero and will never be in Xanth, but we can still dream, can't we?"

Cyrus remained uneasy. "You can read my thoughts?"

"Some," Rhythm said. "Except for the Adult Conspiracy stuff. It comes with being a general purpose Sorceress."

That was a relief. The fact was, she was a rather winsome girl, her status as a Sorceress Princess adding to her intrigue, and he didn't want her picking up any untoward thoughts.

Especially when the actresses teased him, as they continued to do on occasion.

"They tease you?" Rhythm asked. "How?"

"Never mind," Melete said. "Just get changed."

Rhythm sighed. She put her hands on her dress and tugged it upward. Her knees showed.

"Not here!" Cyrus and Melete said together.

"Why not?"

"Because a man isn't supposed to see a girl—not even a girl child—unclothed," Cyrus said. "Because—" He broke off, staring.

For Rhythm was now dressed in green jacket and shorts, the crown was gone, and her hair was dull brown. She had changed magically.

She was, indeed, a Sorceress.

"Are you going to write a part for me?" she asked, being the girl again.

"Immediately," he agreed, returning to his desk. "But I can't call you Rhythm in the play, or in life. I'll call you Rhyme."

"Okay," she agreed. "Rhyme or Reason."

"It will be a bit part, so as not to attract undue notice. No one must know your real identity."

"Actually I'll spread a disinterest spell, so no one will inquire. But it's true: no one must suspect."

"No one," he echoed.

"I'll go meet the Witch." Rhythm left the tent.

"You've got to watch those thoughts," Melete said. "Winsome girl indeed. She's a child."

"I know. She just took me by surprise." He focused on writing the part.

"But also a Sorceress," she continued. "And a Princess. Never forget that."

"How can I treat her as a garden-variety child when I'm not forgetting she's nothing of the kind?"

"You have to be an actor, playing a role. In this case the

role of yourself, addressing her role of unspecial child. You know better, and she knows better, but the rest of Xanth is the audience that doesn't know better. Play your roles well, and all should end well."

Cyrus realized something. "You know my real mission? You read it in my mind?"

"Yes. I would have suspected anyway. A beginning Playwright does not warrant the assistance of a Princess Sorceress. So I am helping you fulfill it."

"Thank you," he said somewhat drily.

"Now pick up your pen and kiss bust or kick butt," she said, her head sliding off the top as her bottom slid into view. Bust and butt.

Cyrus was wickedly tempted to jam the quill at the butt. But he remembered her prior caution: not to needlessly aggravate a Sorceress or a Goddess. He focused instead on his scroll.

"Good thing, too," Melete muttered as her head slid back into view.

"Suppose I *had* done one or the other? Kissed or kicked?"

"In your dreams, rascal."

"I can dream of you?"

"Naturally. I am largely made of dreams. Now quit dallying and start writing."

"I'm ready to write the whole thing," he said. "But I don't know where to start it."

"With the Curse," Melete said promptly.

"How does that happen?"

"Your lead man must aggravate a witch. That's another no-no in life, but a yes-yes in fiction. So she curses him."

"I don't have a lead man cast for the role yet."

"Put yourself in the role, in your mind. Every writer does."

"Oh." He bent to the task.

It went surprisingly well. Every time he paused to ponder, Melete goaded him with sharp remarks. He couldn't goof off while she was watching him. Which was perhaps much of the point of the Writer's Block: it prevented the writer from *not* writing.

When he went out of the tent later, he found things well organized. The others were doing their menial parts, playing their social roles, making it a viable temporary mini-community. Rhythm, who had introduced herself as Rhyme, had blended right in; no one noticed her particularly, or seemed to realize that she had just joined them this day.

"Talk to them," Melete advised. "They are desperate for news of the Play."

She was of course correct. So after the evening meal he bonged on a glass to attract their attention. "I have my Writer's Block," he announced. "And it is enabling me to write. I have fairly started the Play today."

They broke into applause.

"The lead man—we don't have an actor for him yet, so I will have to substitute in rehearsals for now—will aggravate a witch." He glanced at the Witch. "Your role, of course."

"Goody!" she exclaimed. "I can handle that part."

"She will curse him to see people's natures and emotions as colored clouds or auras surrounding them. He can't actually read their minds, but he will know immediately how they feel about things, including him."

"That's a curse?" Acro asked. "I'd love to have it."

"It's a curse," he said. "It will take him a while to realize it. That's part of the point of the play. He is looking for his ideal girlfriend, and this is where the curse begins to register. His first girlfriend—you, Xina—will be beautiful, but her private feelings are mercenary and unkind. She wants only to use him for convenience."

"I can play that role," Xina said, thrilled to have the part.

"Once he realizes that she is not ideal emotionally, he looks at the auras instead, hoping to find the perfect one. Feelings are more important than appearances. He needs to marry by a certain deadline; that may be part of the curse. The witch wants him to marry foolishly and be unhappy ever after. Finally he finds her, his ideal aura—but she has crab claws instead of hands."

"Oh!" Crabapple exclaimed, delighted. "I can play that role!"

Obviously she could; he had written it for her. "But that turns him off; it's too much of an adjustment. So he decides to shut out the aura and live with illusion, staying with the pretty girl even though he knows she's just using him." He smiled a trifle grimly. "Appearances are important to a man."

All the women nodded. They understood perfectly.

"The witch realizes that her curse is no longer working properly, so she decides to kill Xina just before the marriage, forcing him to make a last moment substitute. He won't have time to find a lovely woman both outside and inside, and will have to settle for an unsatisfactory one. So she sends her daughter—Rhyme—with a gift that will kill Xina. But Crabapple saves her, not only winning Xina's friendship but convincing him that Crabapple's his best match after all. Pincers have their place. That's the gist of it."

"But what of us?" Dusti asked, gesturing to herself and Acro.

"You'll have smaller parts, and I'll try to write you lead parts in subsequent plays. This is an ensemble; there will be several plays. Each actress will have her turn."

The girls exchanged a glance and a half, then smiled. They were satisfied. He was coming through.

That night he slept alone, and dreamed of Melete. She was full figured and nude, as she had been when he found her in the gourd.

"You did well, Cyrus," she said, expanding to full human size.

"Don't freak me out!" he said as his eyeballs began to lock up. "I'm trying to walk the causeway."

"Walk the what?"

"The causeway. Walking along it makes a person do things for a good cause. You are thoroughly distracting me from anything like that."

"Oh, all right." A gauzy gown formed around her body. "But you're going to have to get used to me in this version as well as in the bust version. You have a lot more writing to do."

"Yes. But it is going well, now, thanks to you."

"And it will continue well. I will see to that." She came up and kissed him.

His head threatened to float away. He struggled to recover equilibrium. "Are you trying to seduce me? I thought you were here to stop that."

"I am here to make sure you write your plays. Part of that is to make you more immune to the seductions of the actresses. They haven't given up on you; they are just being more subtle. Until we find you a suitable woman to marry, we have to be on guard."

"This is just like the play!"

"By no coincidence," she agreed. "You are animating your own aspirations and fears. All writers do. But we need to stop you from freaking out too readily. That's too much of a distraction."

"Lots of luck," he muttered.

She powdered her face and scowled. He realized that she had just used scowling powder, which was a caustic glare dried out and rendered into powder form for use as necessary, usually as a cleanser. It was possible to know such things in dreams. "Luck has little to do with it. All women have similar equipment; it merely varies in size and exposure. Once you are desensitized there should be no further problem." She squeezed him close.

"No problem!" he exclaimed. "I'm just about ready to—"

She did not withdraw. "Ready to what?"

"Ready to write a great love scene," he said, surprised.

"That's it. The closer you get to me, the more urgent your need to write becomes. That's my nature. Now wake up and write that scene."

He woke up. He discovered he was holding the bust, his fingers clasping the torso section. No wonder he had gotten ideas in his sleep.

"No wonder," Melete agreed, half fondly.

He got up, set her on the desk, lit a candle, and started writing. Soon he had a great near-seduction scene.

In a few days he had the first draft of the play. He wasn't quite satisfied with it.

"Don't be concerned," Melete said. "A true artist is never fully satisfied with his work. Go into rehearsals, and modify what doesn't work well."

"I can do that?"

"You can do what you choose. It's all part of the creative process."

"I'll need to copy the play, so the actors can read it and memorize their parts."

"No need. Rhythm will do that for you."

"She will? But she shouldn't show her magic."

"She won't."

He went out to find Rhythm, realizing that he didn't need to talk openly to her. He just focused the thought clearly: *I need copies of the play.* She saw him and nodded, but did nothing.

Yet when he returned to his tent, there were five copies of the play on his desk, with a sign: COURTESY OF A PASSING COPY CAT.

"There's your explanation," Melete said. "The Princess must not be credited."

He nodded. "She is turning out to be useful on occasion. I like her."

"Beware."

"She's a child!" he snapped. "Can't I like her for her use-fulness?"

"No. It's not safe to like a Princess or a Sorceress of any age for any reason. She must not get ideas."

"How could a child get ideas?"

"Ignorance of the content of the Adult Conspiracy does not mean there is no interest in it. Children are fascinated by the mystery, and sometimes seek to abridge it. They can get unrealistic notions, and she's a prime candidate, as she her-self says. Do not let her do you too many favors."

He shook his head. "You're paranoid. She's just a girl."

"A girl with phenomenal powers."

It seemed pointless to argue with her. He picked up the copies and went out to distribute them to the actresses, cour-tesy of the visiting copy cat.

He gave them two days to start memorizing their parts, while he pondered sets and costumes. "The first scene should be at the witch's residence," he decided. "Maybe a haunted house. Except that's too complicated to put together on a traveling stage."

"Make it her garden," Melete suggested. "Where she grows her witchly herbs and maybe brews the less savory concoc-tions."

"Yes! And he can be just passing by, not realizing it's a private garden. Maybe he steps on some of her plants, not realizing. Like butter fingers, which look like lady fingers, but make whoever touches them get clumsy. Witchy stuff she hates to have ruined. That sets up the dialogue, and gets him cursed. I'll have to make a spot revision of the script. Too bad I didn't think of this before we got the copies."

Rhythm appeared, fading in beside the desk. "It's been done."

"Done? I don't see how."

"The copies have been modified, per your description," she explained. "No one will notice."

"You've been snooping on my mind!"

"I like your mind."

"But—"

"Magic," Melete said. "Thank you, Princess."

"You're welcome, Muse." Rhythm turned to face Cyrus. He couldn't help noticing again how pretty she was, in her bright red dress with her red hair bound by a red ribbon. She was indeed on the very verge of becoming a woman.

"Nuh-uh," Melete murmured.

Rhythm frowned. "What's wrong with being pretty?"

"You're in your Princess outfit," Melete said.

"Only for Cyrus, alone. Everyone else sees the dull girl." She smiled at him. "Do you think I'm dull?"

He opened his mouth, and stifled whatever he might have said. How could he compliment her without encouraging one of those unrealistic notions? Yet she was almost beautiful.

So he changed the subject. "I am working on costumes and sets. Do you have any ideas?"

"Sure. Show that curse. You know, the colored auras."

"I don't think that's possible. The audience will just have to suspend its disbelief."

"It's possible."

"You don't understand. It would require serious magic to show them. We don't have it."

"Yes we do."

"No we don't! That kind of spell—"

He broke off, for there was a white haze forming around Rhythm.

"A different color for each actress," Rhythm said.

"You could do that?" he asked, awed.

"Oh, sure. It takes me a while to work up a new spell, but I can do it. I think it would really enhance the play."

"It would," he agreed. "But—"

"But what?" she asked, turning a look on him that he couldn't quite fathom. It wasn't the kind of look he expected from a child. Part innocence, part knowing, part something else. What was in her mind?

"But it would give away your identity," Melete said.

"Not if Cyrus went out and found the spell in the woods. The same way he found the copy cat."

"I suppose that's true," Cyrus agreed. "It would be very nice for the play. Thank you, Rhythm."

"Any time, Cyrus," she said, with a faint blush as she faded out.

"These are treacherous waters," Melete said darkly. "That girl has womanly ambition."

Cyrus didn't even try to understand that remark.

They still had not found a lead male actor by rehearsal time, so Cyrus played the part. For the moment it became his life.

He walked along the path, missing the detour sign that would have steered him right. Suddenly he was crunching herbs underfoot.

"You clumsy oaf!" the Witch screamed in full Old Crone mode. "You squished my bleeding heart orchid!"

"I'm sorry," Cyrus said. "I didn't see—"

"Didn't see? *Didn't see!* I'll make you see, numskull! I'll curse you with Feeling Sight! Now begone!"

Cyrus hastily departed. "What kind of curse was that?" he asked himself aloud. Thoughts in a play had to be spoken aloud. "I never heard of Feeling Sight. Well, I had better resume my quest for the Ideal Wife."

He encountered Acro, in a skimpy outfit. "Now here is a pretty woman," he said. "Maybe she's the one."

"One for what?" Acro asked, smiling.

"One to be my Ideal Wife."

"Oh, I am surely that," she said, smiling beatifically.

But now he saw something else. "What is that glowing cloud around you?" For indeed, she was surrounded by greenish light. He didn't have to imagine it; the color was there for a whole audience to see, though it was theoretically only visible to him. This was the special magic of the play.

"What glow?" she asked.

"The light around you. Don't you see it?"

"There's no light around me," she said, irritated. Now the green was shot with streaks of black. "Now are you going to marry me or aren't you? I don't have all day, you know."

"The Witch cursed me with Feeling Sight," he said to himself. "This must be it. I sense that the color of my Ideal Wife will be pure white. But this woman is green. She's not the one." Then, to her, "I will not marry you. Your glow is wrong."

"Why kind of bleep is this?" she demanded. But he had already moved on, leaving her to gesture her frustration theatrically behind him. He had just done a dramatic no-no, Scorning a Woman.

Next he encountered Dusti, in a fetching if slightly dusty dress. Her glow was pink. "No, she's not the one either," he said regretfully.

"Not the one for what?" she demanded.

"Not the one to marry." He walked on, leaving her, too, with black streaks across her glow.

"Nobody asked you!" she called after him, another Woman Scorned.

Then he came to Xina, in spectacularly skimpy shorts and halter. Her glow was blue.

"Now I appreciate the curse," he said. "Every woman is wrong. I can't marry this one either."

"Are you going to make decisions based on some stupid glow?" Xina demanded. "Instead of this?" She dropped her halter halfway.

Cyrus's eyes locked up, as would those of any male members of the audience. "Yes," he said regretfully, and managed to walk on, eyes scrunched up.

"You're a fool," she muttered angrily. "What man cares

about a glow, as long as a girl's got a body?" Not only had she been Scorned, she had wasted a perfectly good half-Flash.

"That witch certainly did curse me," Cyrus said as he walked, still speaking his thoughts carefully aloud, so the audience could hear. "Every nice-looking girl is wrong, and now that I can see that, I can't be satisfied with her. Am I doomed not to marry?"

He continued to walk, and had another thought. "Maybe I should look for the Perfect Glow, instead of for the Perfect Body. That might find me the Perfect Wife and save me from the rigors of perpetual bachelorhood."

Encouraged, he peered around, seeking the glow. And soon he found it, surrounding a shapely young woman in a cloak. "Hello," he said to her. "I am Cyrus. I am looking for the Perfect Wife, who I know by her pure white glow. You have that glow. Who are you?"

"Thank you," she said, smiling prettily. "I am Crabapple. But I don't think you want to marry me."

"Why not? You seem to have the qualities I require."

"Because of these." She drew back her cloak to reveal her forearms and hands. Except that they were not hands; they were giant greenish crab pincers. She clacked them in the air so that every member of the future audience could see them.

Cyrus was dramatically appalled. His gaze went back and forth between a Perfect Glow and her imperfect extremities. "I can't do this," he said.

"I understand," she said with regret. "I have encountered this reaction before. I wish you well in your continuing search."

Cyrus stumbled away. "What a curse," he exclaimed. "It puts me in the pincers of an awful dilemma." There should be a laugh from the audience at that line.

Then he reconsidered. "But maybe if I shut my eyes to the glow, I'll be able to return to my prior state, and be happy with a girl's exterior. What man really cares about what's inside, so long as what's outside is appealing?"

He turned around and walked back the way he had come. He came to Xina, who remained in place. "I have changed my mind," he said. "I want to marry you."

"What, despite my wrong glow?" she asked sharply.

"What glow? I don't see any glow."

She nodded. "In that case, okay, I will marry you. When is the wedding?"

"Tomorrow," he said.

"Good. That gives me time to prepare my wedding gown." She kissed him, an Unscorned Woman. "See you tomorrow."

"Right," he agreed, staggering in place to show how he had been half stunned by the kiss.

"I can't believe that such a good catch just fell into my hand," Xina said. "I will surely have lots of fun with him before I throw him away." She hurried off.

"I hope I'm doing the right thing," Cyrus said, his posture showing that he doubted it. He stepped behind a tree.

The Witch came onstage. "Curses! He's no longer responding to my curse. He's going to marry anyway, and avoid a lifetime of loneliness. That is the waste of a good curse. What can I do?" She pondered a moment. "I know. I'll kill the bride before the wedding. Then he'll be truly stuck. Hee hee hee!" She made a wonderfully witchly cackle.

The Witch beckoned someone offstage. Rhythm came to her. "Daughter Rhyme," the witch said. "Take this feather boa to Cyrus. Tell him you found it in the forest and thought it would make a perfect wedding gift for his bride."

"Yes, Mother Witch," the girl said dutifully. She took the feathery scarf and carried it across the stage to Cyrus, who reappeared from behind the tree, reactivating his scene. "Look at what I found, Cyrus," she said. "Wouldn't this make the perfect gift for your bride, right before the wedding?"

"Why yes it would," he agreed, taking the boa. "Thank you, child. Who are you?"

"I'm Rhyme," she said. "I'm someone's daughter." She departed.

Cyrus held up the boa. "This is beautiful. I'll give it to Xina tomorrow, just before the wedding."

The scene ended. The crux had been set up.

Then it was next day, in the play: the next scene. Curtis Curse Friend had to play the part of the King, so as to have the authority to marry them, until they found a suitable actor. What about a Best Man? That was Weslee Weredragon, who had decided to join the troupe. But Xina needed a Maid of Honor. That was covered in the play.

"I will do it," Crabapple said. "I want to see him satisfied."

Xina did not object, though obviously she thought Crabapple was a fool. Except for one thing: "Keep your claws covered. I don't want my wedding ruined."

"Of course."

"I have a gift for you," Cyrus said, proffering the feather boa.

"Oh, how nice," Xina said. She took it and wrapped it grandly around her neck and shoulders. It looked elegant.

Then something went wrong. The boa tightened around her neck, choking her. Cyrus and the King tried to pull it off, but its coils were too muscular. Xina was about to dramatically expire, waving her arms helplessly.

Crabapple threw off her cloak, uncovering her pincers. She clamped them on either side of Xina's neck and squeezed. The boa was cut into three pieces that dropped to the ground, wriggling helplessly, shedding its mortal coils. It had been destroyed.

"I'm sorry I ruined your wedding," Crabapple said.

"You saved my life!" Xina exclaimed. "You were a true friend after I treated you like a freak."

"Well, you couldn't marry him if you died first."

"And you love him yourself. Much better than I do. You should marry him."

"He doesn't want me."

But Cyrus was suffering a dramatic reassessment. "Those pincers are good protection. Now they look pretty."

"I'd rather be a live Maid of Honor than a dead bride," Xina said. "Marry her."

"Her aura is perfect," he agreed. "And so is her body." He looked at her bare form, which was now artfully posed for the appreciation of the audience. There was no audience yet, but the rehearsal pretended there was.

So Crabapple stood beside Cyrus, and the play-King pronounced them married.

"Oh," Acro said, mopping her eyes. "Weddings always make me cry."

"Me too," Dusti said. Her tears were dust.

"That's not in the script," Xina snapped. "It's not a real wedding."

"If they can cry at it, they should be there," Curtis said. "It lends verisimilitude."

All of the others paused to look at him. "Lends what?" Cyrus asked, sifting through his memory banks.

"It is from 'very similar,'" Curtis said. "It means that it has the appearance of truth. We always strive for that in our plays."

"That's what we want," Cyrus agreed. "I'll revise that portion."

"Now if we can return to the play proper," Curtis said. "It is time for you to kiss the bride and walk happily off into the sunset."

"Oh." Cyrus embraced Crabapple, struck again by how nice her torso was. He kissed her. That was nice too. Then they held hands, in a manner, and walked offstage. The play was done.

"That seems viable," Curtis said. "With some tweaking, and a full roster of actors."

Cyrus agreed. He knew it was far from perfect, but for his first effort, he was well satisfied. They would sharpen it up with later rehearsals.

"Thank you so much for this part," Crabapple murmured. "When you held me and kissed me, I almost thought you meant it."

He had almost thought so too.

$\overline{7}$

COMPLICATIONS

B ut we are forgetting that hint, Two to the Fifth," Melete
said. "You are only one. You need a partner. Then you
can tackle the rest of it."

"But I have no prospects for marriage," he protested. "Besides, I like being a Playwright."

"You can be a Playwright. Just find the right woman. Consider the actresses. They are all interested in you."

"I wish there really was a visible aura," he said. "So I could see who was right for me."

Rhythm appeared with the sound of the beat of her drum. "I can make it real."

"You can?"

"Sure. Melete's right; the way those stupid actresses flirt with you, you need to be married to fend them off."

"She has a point," Melete agreed.

"Go look at them now," Rhythm said. "They will have auras that only you can see."

"They will?"

"Like this." She used two chicken leg drumsticks to beat

her drum again. That was why they had looked odd, before; he hadn't picked up on their nature. A white light appeared around her.

Bemused, he tucked Melete into his pocket and went out to look at women. They did have auras—the same ones that showed in the play, but turned off after the rehearsal. "The little minx," Melete murmured. "She gave them their real auras."

And the only play-aura suitable for him was Crabapple. This made him pause. She was a nice person, without doubt, and he had gotten used to her pincers, and she was very nice to hold close. But this was not the play, and he was not at all sure he wanted to marry her.

"Too bad," Melete said. "You men are too locked into perfection of form. Let's check again."

So he walked about the lot again, considering auras. Now, with Melete's remarks, he saw how the other actresses were flirting with him. Rhythm was right about that. They weren't too direct, but they were definitely smiling at him, and subtly posing, showing off their figures. They all knew how to catch the eye of a man, without being obvious.

Acro was sitting in the kitchen area sorting potatoes for dinner, and somehow her skirt rode up on her thighs, showing off her nice legs. "That exposure isn't by accident," Melete said. He disliked admitting that those legs nevertheless turned him on. They reminded him of the rest of her body, when he had first seen her in the moat along with her myriad copies.

Dusti was scrubbing the dust off a tent, and as he passed she had a low place to work on, so that she bent well down and he could see into her halter. "She saved that spot for when you came by," Melete said. Regardless, those dusky globes turned him on too.

Xina, seemingly oblivious to his presence, was scrubbing clothing at the pond, nude at the edge of the water. That almost made him jump in to join her. "Water is marvelous for bodies," Melete said. "It conceals some and flashes some, attracting the eye. One has to admire her technique."

"I do," he said, tearing his eyeballs away with slight sucking sounds.

The Witch was harvesting assorted pies for the next meal, as the cast had gotten tired of sandwiches. She was fully clothed but in a voluptuous state. She darted him a glance that fairly heated his clothing and straightened out his hair. She knew what she was doing, and knew he knew it, but it remained effective. It made him want to find out what else she could straighten. The others were young and fresh, while the Witch was thoroughly experienced. She knew exactly what to do, and how to do it, and that was something that he in his inexperience appreciated.

"Any of them would marry you," Melete said. "They all regard you as a good catch. You are handsome, strong, talented, and diffident, so they could readily run your life. But all of their auras are wrong. You would have fun with them for a while, but then would discover objectionable differences and be less than satisfied. Only a pure white aura is right for you."

"The kind Crabapple has," he agreed morosely.

"And she's the only one who is not flirting with you."

That was interesting. So he went back to Crabapple. "Suppose I could see auras, as in the play, and yours was the right one for me. Would you marry me?"

"No, Cyrus," she said regretfully. "You're a nice man, and very attractive, but I would be bad for your public image. You'll never become a famous Playwright if I'm with you."

"What if I don't believe that?"

"Unfortunately, I do believe it. I must not cripple your chances," she said, and turned away.

"That was as nice a turndown as could be imagined," Melete said. "She was careful not to hurt your feelings. She does like you, but doesn't want to harm you by her association. She's being extremely unselfish."

"She's too bleeping nice for me."

"That is the case. That is surely why her aura is white. She would be right for almost any man."

He returned to his tent. He set Melete down on the writing table and considered his script. He had spot revisions to do, but his mind couldn't focus properly on it.

"But there are other women," Melete said. "Why don't you take a walk around the area beyond the camp, looking at auras?"

"I'll do that," he agreed, rising. He stepped outside the tent and strode beyond the troupe camp.

Only when he was well clear of it did he realize that he had forgotten to put Melete in his pocket. Well, she could surely survive an hour without him.

Rhythm appeared. "I was naughty," she said, walking beside him.

"You were? I did not notice."

"I made you forget to bring her."

"You made me forget? But why?"

"Because I wanted to talk with you alone."

"I am ready to talk with any member of the troupe, at any time," he said. "All you had to do was ask."

"She wouldn't have let me be alone with you."

He nodded. That was true, though he wasn't sure why. "What did you want to talk to me about?"

"Two things. I know you are looking for a woman to marry, and aren't satisfied with the actresses. I thought I could help."

"Help? How?"

"By enabling you to broaden your search. Maybe sticking to women your own crafted age is too limited. That's a very thin slice of womandom."

"It is," he agreed. "But what use would I have for any that are too old?"

"Or too young," she said.

"I wouldn't even consider those."

She paused, evidently seeking the right phrasing. "Yet suppose one who is too young now, would be just right for you once she matures? Would you want to pass her by?"

"I suppose not. But that's academic. I need to marry now."

"Yes. So you can't wait. It's too bad."

"It's the way it is," he said shortly. "The Adult Conspiracy makes it impossible."

"I wish I understood the Adult Conspiracy better," she said. "But of course I don't."

"By definition," he agreed.

"Yet my sister Melody already has a boyfriend, and she'll marry him when they come of age. On Planet Ptero they are already of age, and doing whatever they want. They even have a child. I'm jealous."

This dialogue was making him uncomfortable. "This isn't Ptero."

"Piper's coming."

"What?"

"The girl you met on the way to the Good Magician's Castle."

"How could you know that?"

"I can read your mind, remember?"

He was taken aback. "I forgot about that."

"You think I'm a winsome girl."

"Oh, bleep!" For of course it was true. He knew he had no right to see her as anything other than a child. A Sorceress, and a Princess, but still a child. It was embarrassing to have such a wrong thought, and worse to have her know it.

Yet, oddly she seemed satisfied rather than confused or alarmed. What was going on in her mind?

"I'll never tell," she murmured.

Bleep!

A girl appeared on the path ahead. "Hello, Piper," he called.

"Hi, Cyrus," she replied. "Who is your friend?"

"This is—" he paused, remembering that Rhythm was supposed to be anonymous.

"Rhyme. A girl in his play," Rhythm said. "He's a Playwright now."

"Oh, that's so wonderful," Piper said, clapping her hands. "I wish I could be an actress."

She and every other girl. "Maybe when you get older," Cyrus said.

"But I'm thirteen. Rhyme looks only twelve. She's in your play."

"And he is looking for a girl to marry," Rhythm said. She elbowed him. "Note her aura."

The little mischief! For Piper's aura was pure white.

Now Piper eyed him in a disturbingly appraising manner. Why did he suspect at times that girls were not always entirely innocent about the Adult Conspiracy? "I wonder," she murmured. "A girl could certainly do worse."

"You're too young!" he said desperately.

"But it happens we have a spell," Rhythm said. "It ages a person one decade, for an hour."

"That's interesting," Piper said. "I'd like to try it."

"Here it is." Rhythm handed her a little ball. "Bite it."

Piper bit it. It burst into vapor, for a moment obscuring her. Then the mist cleared.

A fully adult, twenty-three-year-old woman stood before him. "Suddenly I know all about the Adult Conspiracy," Piper said. "It is a necessary thing." She adjusted her dress, which fit her somewhat tightly now. In fact rather more bosom showed than was usual, as it strained at the girl-sized bodice lacing. "So you are looking for a wife?"

"Well, not exactly," he said.

"Yes he is," Rhythm said. "But she has to be just right for him."

"But is he just right for her?" Piper asked.

"What do you mean?" Cyrus asked, bemused by this abrupt shift.

"Now that I am mature, it occurs to me that my girlish dream of marrying a handsome man and living happily ever after is not well grounded in reality," Piper said seriously. "You're a nice man, but I think not my type for a long-term relationship. I am concerned about cyborg qualities I might come not to appreciate. Would our children have metal bones?"

Yet her aura was white: right for him. This was a new concept: she was right for him, but he might not be right for her. There needed to be a match both ways.

"This is sensible," Cyrus agreed.

"Still, since in permanent life I am still a teen, I believe I will indulge myself for a while. I will join your troupe, hoping for some small part on stage. By the time I am grown, that foolishness will have been expended, and I will be ready to settle down with a man who loves oak trees."

"Welcome to join," Cyrus said. He had no interest in devoting his life to tending oak trees. So it was turning out that her caution was justified. Perfect women, it seemed, had sensible concerns. "The troupe is farther along this path."

"Thank you." Piper walked on. By the time she reached the troupe, she would revert to her real age.

Cyrus turned to Rhythm. "That was certainly interesting. Your magic amazes me."

"I am a Sorceress," she reminded him. "Because I am general purpose, I can do just about any magic. But I have to craft it beforehand, as I did with the Decade spell. It's not an automatic talent like flying or growing ears on tree trunks. When I am with my sisters, we can do things much faster."

"But their presence here would give away your nature," he said, remembering.

"That, too," she agreed.

"There's something else?"

"I need to get out on my own. To discover my own identity. My own dreams. Not to be an almost perfect copy of my two sisters."

"That makes sense."

"I'm a sensible girl."

"Yes you are. You have been an enormous help to the troupe."

She blushed. "Thank you."

"You said there were two things you wanted to talk to me about. One was the Decade spell, so I could seek more widely for my perfect woman. That dialogue with Piper taught me something: that it's not just how good she would be for me, but how good I would be for her. That was very helpful of you. Now what was the other thing?"

"I will tell you in the right place," she said. "There's a special path. This way." She led the way to a side path he hadn't noticed before.

He followed her, feeling guilty for noticing again that she moved lithely, with nice legs. She would be a lovely woman when she matured. She was already well on the way there.

"Thank you."

Now he blushed. He had been caught again by her mind reading ability. That would be another one of the talents she had crafted in advance. "I shouldn't have been thinking that. I apologize."

"Why?"

"Because it's not right to look at girls as if they are women. The Adult Conspiracy—"

"Is a pain!" she exclaimed. "I wish it didn't exist."

"There is good reason for it."

"I don't believe it. It's just a plot to torment children, and some who aren't really children."

He did not try to argue the case. No child was capable of understanding that particular thing. So he changed the subject. "Where is this place you are taking me?"

"It's a nice little glade with a nice little pond. Very special."

"Special?"

Now she changed the subject back. "You shouldn't think of me as a child, Cyrus. I'm really not."

He could almost hear Melete muttering "Treacherous waters!" He needed to stop this line of discussion. "You are twelve years old, Rhythm."

"No. Only in my body."

He smiled indulgently. "That defines you."

She paused in the path, facing him with disturbing intensity. "Let me explain something, Cyrus. Not long ago I was seventeen. That's Old Enough."

He knew better than to ask old enough for what. She was too close and too pretty. "That temporary aging spell? I don't think that counts."

"This was different. Do you know much about Mundania?"

"Not much," he admitted. "Oh, there's data in my bank, but—"

"They have something called Daylight Saving Time."

He sorted through his memory. "Yes, I find it now. They get up an hour earlier in summer to take advantage of extra daylight, then revert in the fall. It strikes me as like cutting one end off a stick and gluing it to the other end to make it longer. But what can you expect? It's Mundania."

She laughed, almost falling into him. He had to put his hands on her elbows to steady her. Somehow his arms wound up partly around her as her large eyes lifted to meet his.

There was a faint pleasant scent. He remembered the rest of
Melete's remark: the girl had womanly ambition. He stepped
back, embarrassed.

"Thank you," she said. There was something in her manner that made him suspect that she hadn't really lost her balance.

"Welcome." He felt himself blushing, for no reason.

"Those extra hours need to be properly handled," she continued after a fetching moment. "They come to the village of
Century, where a giant century plant stores excess time. The
villagers catch the hours as they drift in and stack them
safely around the plant. Then in fall they send them back.
There would be real disruption if they got lost; Mundania
might get stuck permanently on the early time. Those folk
wouldn't like that."

"They wouldn't," he agreed. She was still standing too
close, and he couldn't retreat farther on the narrow path. Was
she trying to spin a story to keep him there? "Is there a point
to this discussion?"

"There is, Cyrus. There was an accident a few months ago,
and a number of skilled villagers were rendered impossibly
old, putting them out of service."

"Old? I don't see—"

"It's complicated, but the essence is that when a person
handles an hour, he or she ages that hour. Since there are
thousands of hours, this can have considerable effect. They
become significantly older in the summer, and then return to
their younger ages in fall. They are used to it, but it's not a
job anyone else can do. So when things went wrong—"

"You stepped in!" he said, finally catching on.

"The three of us stepped in," she agreed. "As general-
purpose Sorceresses we were able to adapt and fill in until
the village was able to obtain youth elixir to restore their
aged workers. That was a job that required twenty-five days,
but of course the hours couldn't wait without causing real

mischief. So Melody went first, to do the first third of the job. She's always first. She went there for six days, and handled the hours for them, and in that time she aged three years, then reverted when she returned to Castle Roogna."

"So she was still twelve," he said.

"In body. But she had been fifteen at the village. She said it was a unique experience. For one thing, her body bloomed, and she got odd notions, but didn't know how to implement them. It was frustrating."

"I think I can appreciate that."

"Then Harmony went. She's always second. She was there eight days, because there were more hours than Melody had realized, and aged four years before she reverted. She said she was a full-blown woman of sixteen, and loved it, but couldn't keep it when she left."

"That was surely fortunate."

She eyed him obliquely. "Perhaps. Then I went, and there were still more hours, and I was there ten days before catching up the hours, barely a day before they returned with the youth elixir so their regulars could return to work. So I was seventeen, in the full flush of lovely womanhood, before I reverted." She gazed at him. "My body returned to twelve, but my mind is seventeen. I actually lived those years, Cyrus, and the villagers told me I was pretty. I wanted you to know that."

Cyrus did not find this reassuring. What could he say? "I suppose it does explain your maturity of outlook."

"Yes. My girl body sometimes carries me away foolishly, but my mind is capable of much more, especially emotionally. I wish I could make you believe that."

"I believe it," he said insincerely. This whole business made him profoundly uncertain. Had she been seventeen physically, and approached him like this—no, he must not go there.

Now Rhythm turned and resumed walking, leading him along the path. "What is your ambition in life, Cyrus?"

He laughed. "That is what brought me to the Good Magician's Castle. My father, Roland Robot, wanted me to become a leader of robots. My mother, Hannah Barbarian, wanted me to capture and marry a lovely wild-haired uncivilized woman. I couldn't reconcile the two, so I went to the Good Magician—and garbled my Question. And he told me my true ambition: to write and direct plays."

"You could still be a leader and marry a lovely wild-haired rebellious woman."

"Maybe. I do think I need to marry, because of this Two to the Fifth hint. I think it means that I need to become two by marrying the right woman."

The path opened out into the glade with the pond. "Isn't it pretty?" she asked as they came to stand by the water.

"Yes." He was beginning to wonder what the point was. He was almost certain she had more in mind than just telling him about her timely experience.

"It's a love spring."

"A love spring!" he exclaimed, stepping back. "They're dangerous."

"That depends."

It seemed best to change the subject again. "Now what did you want to tell me?"

"About your conflicting ambitions: you could please both your parents."

"I'm not sure how. Writing plays isn't the same as being a leader, and I'm beginning to think that there is no other woman quite like my mother. The other actresses—"

"Who flirt shamelessly with you," she said, frowning.

"Yes. But they are civilized women. None of them would do anything really wild."

"You could marry a wild princess."

He laughed. "You know, that would fulfill my parents' ambitions for me! I would become a leader by definition, and her wildness would thrill my mother. But there's one flaw in that idea."

"What flaw?"

"What princess would ever want to marry a cyborg Playwright?"

She faced him squarely. "I would."

"Theoretically, when you grow up, if your mature judgment didn't make you see the foolishness of it."

"No. Now."

"You must be joking."

"Look at my aura. It's right for you."

So it was. "But—"

"I have come to know you, Cyrus. I have a crush on you," she confessed, blushing again. "In fact it's more than a crush. I love you, and always will. I am old enough at seventeen to understand my feeling. I can see some aspects of the future, and know this for sure. I'd do anything you wanted me to, even if I don't understand it, age no barrier." She made a little gesture, as of opening her shirt. "Please, Cyrus, take me. My body isn't quite there yet, but my spirit is." Her blush had become furious; she knew she was making a forbidden offer.

He was appalled. "But you're a child!"

Something faintly barbaric crossed her features. "Are you rejecting me, after I bared my secret heart to you?"

"Of course I am. I would never touch a child. The Adult Conspiracy forbids it."

"Even though you now know I'm really more like seventeen?"

"You would have to be seventeen in mind and body, or more, to have any right to—to do what you ask. You're not."

"So it's like that," she said grimly. "Well, then we'll do it the hard way." She reached into a pocket.

"Rhythm, you're making me nervous," he said, remembering again that she was a Sorceress. As he had been warned, any woman spurned was dangerous, and a Sorceress especially so, regardless of her age.

"You should be." She brought out a little sphere. She bit into it. It puffed into vapor, surrounding her.

Then the vapor cleared. Rhythm had activated another decade spell. Now she was twenty-two, lovely and wild-haired. "Oh, my," Cyrus breathed, awed by the transformation.

"I'm not a child any more," she said. "Am I?"

"N-No. But—"

"Now I have much the same body I had at seventeen. This dress is way too tight," she said. She ripped it open and dropped it on the ground. Her bra and panties were splitting at the seams, and she ripped them off too, letting her abruptly mature body spring to its full unfettered dimensions. It wasn't just her flaming red hair that was wild; it was her whole personality. She stood resplendently, defiantly nude.

Cyrus freaked out. He stood immobile, unable to rip his gaze from her remarkable body. It might exist only for an hour, but it overwhelmed him. This was the very image of his Perfect Woman. Doubly dangerous because he knew she was really a child, despite what she said. All he could do was gasp a single syllable. "No!"

"I love you, Cyrus," she said. "My mature perspective doesn't change that. But it seems you don't love me. Fortunately I can do something about that."

"No!" he repeated. What awful folly was she contemplating?

She stepped into him, threw her arms about him, and kissed him. If he hadn't already been freaked out, this would have done it. She was the most exciting contact he'd ever had, thrilling him in all manner of illicit ways. Then she drew back slightly. "Are you quite sure you don't love me, Cyrus?"

"No," he said weakly. But he wasn't sure how he meant it.

"That can be taken two ways. So we'll make it one way."

She clasped him tightly, half lifted him, and jumped into the pond, hauling him along with her. The love spring.

Oh, no! Now they were both sprawled in the water, thoroughly soaked, and it was indeed conducive. Suddenly he was ardently loving her. To bleep with the awful guilt! He held her and kissed her avidly.

"That's more like it," she said. "Fortunately I am unaffected by the spring, being already there." She kissed him back, passionately.

Then somehow his clothing was off, and they were in the throes of utter abandon. He couldn't get enough of her, nor she of him.

He wasn't sure how long the passion lasted, but finally they both dragged themselves out of the pond and lay panting on the bank. "Do you love me now, Cyrus?" she asked with two fifths of a smile.

"I love you now and forever, Rhythm," he said. "I don't think you even needed the love spring. You won me with that first adult kiss."

"That's nice." She rolled into him, and they clasped again. "I dreamed of doing this with you. Only I was too young to know the details. I might have suspected them at seventeen, but I lost that information when I reverted. I just wanted your complete devotion."

"You have it," he said, kissing her. "But there's a problem."

"I'll be twelve again, within the hour," she agreed.

"You know this love can't be."

"Unfortunately I do, now that I am conversant with the hidden details of the Adult Conspiracy. I was foolishly irresponsible. I won't remember those details when I revert, but I will still love you."

"And I will still love you," he said with sadly mixed emotions. "But this love is forbidden."

She nodded. "So we had better work it out now, while I

still have my knowledge. I will forget the details, but you won't. I will still be more than willing to indulge those details, if you guide me."

"No! I love you, but I can't do that."

"I understand. You are an honorable man, which is one of the qualities I like about you. But will you let me kiss you, after I revert? You can just stay still, doing nothing, so you're not at fault."

"I will be at fault if I let you," he said miserably. "Rhythm, I will want desperately to do everything with you, but I must not do anything. This is awful."

She nodded again. "I did not work everything out, as a child. I was not equipped to. But I think I will remember that I did work them out as an adult, so will know that I have to leave you alone. We must tell no one of this tryst."

"Yes! But Melete will know."

"She will have the sense to ignore it."

"Yes."

"Suppose I sneak into your bed at night, and——"

"No!"

"No," she echoed regretfully. "Bleep."

He had to laugh. "At least we understand each other's pain. You will revert, we'll recover and patch up our clothing, and there will be nothing more between us. No one will know."

"So that's settled," she agreed. "Anything else I want of you, I'll have to have now." She clasped him again, kissed him, and they had another desperate bout of passion.

"I think the hour is about over," Cyrus said with infinite regret.

"Yes. It is time to repair my outfit so that there is not an illicitly bare girl in your presence. Now that I am adult, I honor the Adult Conspiracy too." Then she looked past him. "What's what?"

He followed her gaze. "It looks like a stork. It must be passing here coincidentally."

"We did summon the stork," she reminded him. "Several times. Emphatically. I am now in a position to know."

That was a coy understatement. They had probably jolted several storks out of their flight paths. "But they take at least nine months to deliver. This can't be ours."

But the stork came in for a landing beside them. "Stymy Stork, at your service," he said. "I have a delivery for Princess Rhythm." He set down his bundle.

Both of them stared at stork and bundle, stupefied.

"I don't make many deliveries myself, these days," Stymy said. "But this one is special. Congratulations, Princess." He turned about, spread his wings, and took off.

"It's impossible," Cyrus said. "There has to be a mistake."

Rhythm reached for the bundle. She opened it. There was a precious baby girl in a basket. "Oh," Rhythm said, picking her up and holding her close. "She *is* mine. I know it. The stork works must have gotten confused and delivered her immediately."

Cyrus looked at the basket. It contained several bottles of milk, some diapers, and a sponge. The word "Kadence" was printed neatly on it. "She is Kadence," he said.

"Of course. I always knew my daughter would be Kadence. Rhythm—Kadence. I just didn't expect her so soon." She picked up a bottle and started feeding the baby. "This comes so naturally."

"But you're about to revert!"

"Then you will have to take care of her," she said. "She's your baby too."

"How will I ever explain a baby?"

She smiled ruefully. "Consider it a challenge."

Cyrus rescued his clothes from the love spring, and picked up the torn pieces of hers. "These won't be usable, for more than one reason. They're messed up, and mine are soaked with love elixir."

"I'll make a spell," Rhythm said. She focused, her drum

and drumsticks appeared, she beat a brief pattern, and in a moment both their outfits were repaired and dry. "You had better get dressed. I'll wait until I revert."

"You remaining bare until then will drive me crazy."

"Wonderful," she said. She glanced at the baby. "She's ready for a nap." She set Kadence back into her basket and gently covered her over. Then she turned to Cyrus.

No words were spoken, lest they disturb the baby. They both knew what they wanted, and they went at it almost savagely, knowing that it was probably their last chance for it. He hoped that didn't bring another immediate delivery from the stork.

"Something's odd," Cyrus said as he dressed.

"Yes indeed," Rhythm said, startled.

"It has been more than an hour, I'm sure, and you haven't reverted."

"Kadence is growing."

They looked at each other. They had been talking of different things. "She is," Cyrus said, peeking into the basket.

"And I haven't reverted," Rhythm said. "But by the position of the sun, it has been at least an hour."

"This is remarkably strange," he said. "Could it relate to the way the Stork delivered so fast?"

"I fear I messed up the spell. Or maybe our passion distorted it."

"Or maybe using it on yourself changed it," he suggested.

"That might be the case. But how would that account for the effects we're seeing?"

"Suppose it is somehow accelerating? So that it didn't stop at a decade." He hesitated. "Rhythm, you're still beautiful, but you look older."

She fetched a small mirror from somewhere. It couldn't have been a pocket, because she remained beautifully nude. "Oh, my! I *am* old! I look twenty-three or twenty-four!"

Or twenty-five or -six. "If time is moving faster, it would

mean that maybe the stork did take nine months to deliver the baby, and now she's a year or so older."

Kadence woke. "Mommy!" she cried.

They exchanged a startled look. Kadence was talking already.

Rhythm went to lift Kadence out of the basket, but the child was already crawling over the rim on her own. She went on hands and knees, then got tired of that, and lifted unsteadily to her feet. She was walking!

"Accelerated time," Rhythm said. "I *did* mess up that spell."

As they watched, the child became steadier on her feet, visibly growing. She was now a toddler, two or three years old. She was wearing a little dress. Had that been in the basket too?

"You're locked into adulthood," Cyrus said. "I love that, but it's dangerous. At this rate you'll soon grow too old for me."

"I'll never be that!" But she looked worried.

Meanwhile Kadence was walking up to Cyrus. "Daddy!" she said. "Pick me up."

He picked her up. She was now three to four years old, a healthy child. "Can you nullify the spell?" he asked. "So that at least nobody ages rapidly any more?"

"I don't know. I think I just have to cancel it."

"Do it soon," he said. "I'd rather have you underage than dying of old age in minutes."

"So would I," she agreed. "Let me concentrate." She beat lightly on the drum, her eyes closing.

"What's mommy doing?" Kadence asked him.

"She's trying to abolish a bad spell," he explained.

"That's nice," the child said. She kissed his ear. "I love you, daddy."

"I love you too, Kadence," he said, realizing it was true. His emotions were keeping pace with the accelerated passage of time.

"Put me down, please daddy. I want to go help mommy."

He lowered her to the ground. She was now five or six years old. "Hurry," he said urgently to Rhythm.

"Got it," she said. "I garbled a parameter, so instead of terminating normally, it went into accelerator mode. I won't make *that* mistake again. Now to repair it so it can expire." She produced a sphere, and bit into it just before Kadence reached her. Vapor puffed out, surrounding her.

In hardly more than a moment, it dissipated. There was Rhythm, twelve years old.

Kadence stopped, a small swirl of mist passing by her. "Mother?" she asked doubtfully.

Rhythm opened her mouth, but didn't speak. Cyrus knew why. What was she to say?

He went to the child. "There was fouled-up magic," he explained. "It was making her get old quickly. She stopped it, and now she is young again."

"I felt the magic," Kadence agreed. "It just touched me. It stopped me growing. Now I'm staying at six, aging normally."

"Kadence, dear," Rhythm said as she got quickly into her clothes. "You were supposed to be with me for that spell. It would have—"

The child was innocently wide-eyed. "Would have what, mother?"

"Would have abolished you," Cyrus said with awful realization. "As it is, it merely returned you to a normal existence in your present form. I think."

"I'll have to make another spell," Rhythm said. Her drum and drumsticks reappeared.

Kadence clouded over. She was suffering a dreadful realization of her own. "Mother! Don't abolish me! I love you."

Rhythm burst into tears. "I can't do it!" she said. The drum disappeared.

"*We* can't do it," Cyrus said. "The magic stops here." Then he hugged Rhythm and Kadence together. All three of them cried with mixed love and relief. Whatever the future was, they would face it together.

But what a complicated mess it was! An adult father, a twelve- (possibly seventeen-) year-old mother, and a six-year-old child. How could any of that be explained?

8

KADENCE

"Father, what's going on?" Kadence asked bravely. "Please tell me the truth."

Cyrus looked at Rhythm, who made a token nod. She was leaving it up to him, the adult.

Cyrus tackled it as well as he could. Absolute candor seemed to be required. "Your mother Princess Rhythm is a Sorceress," he explained to the little girl. "She fell in love with me, but she's only twelve years old. So she made a spell to make her older, and we did Adult Conspiracy things, but the spell was wrong and the stork delivered you."

"You didn't want me?" The child's eyes were brimming pools.

"We know we do, now, but we didn't expect you so soon. Normally both parents are of age, and even then the stork takes much of another year to deliver. This happened unusually fast. So we were surprised, that's all."

"Okay."

But the worst was coming. "Now your mother is twelve again, and we can't be seen together, because other folk would not understand. We love each other, and we love you, but they would think we did something wrong."

"Wrong, Father?"

This was not getting easier. "They would think that Rhythm was only twelve when we signaled the stork for you, and that would be wrong. She was twenty-two, but only for an hour or so. It is far too complicated to explain to them. So we can't admit that we did it."

"Then what about me?"

Exactly. "Neither can we acknowledge you as our six-year-old daughter; they would *really* not understand that. So we need you to pretend you're Rhyme's little sister, at least for now."

"Rhyme?"

"That's what she is called by others, who don't know she is actually a princess. There is reason for keeping it secret; she might be in danger if others knew."

"Oh."

Did she really understand? He had to hope so. "In time Rhythm will be old enough, and then I'll marry her, and we'll recognize you as our daughter. Can you handle that?"

"Roles," Kadence said, brightening. "These are roles."

"Exactly. We'll even give you a part in a play, another role."

Kadence clapped her hands together gleefully. "I'll do it, Father."

"Call me Cyrus, please. For the role."

"Oh, yes. This is fun."

"But apart from our roles," he concluded, "we do love you, and you really are our daughter."

"That's what counts," Kadence said, satisfied.

"There is something else," Rhythm said. "All of the members of my lineage have Magician-caliber magic talents. You surely do too. Do you know what your talent is?"

"No, Mother."

"Call me Rhyme."

"No, Rhyme." The child was a quick study, fortunately.

"That's all right. Sometimes it takes many years to discover one's talent. We know you have one, and at some point you will find out what it is. When you do, be very careful, because some people aren't easy about Sorceresses. Try to learn it and practice it by yourself. Never use it to harm anyone who isn't trying to harm you."

"I won't, Mother. I mean, Rhyme."

They walked back along the path, away from the love spring. Cyrus knew Rhythm had artfully trapped him, then run afoul of the complications of her own magic, but he didn't mind. He loved her, and her aura was right. He suspected that he had always been destined to love her; she had merely pushed the cadence, no pun. In time they would be a happy family.

When they came close to the camp, Rhythm took Kadence by the hand, while Cyrus took a separate route. Their new roles were about to be established.

Melete was waiting for him like an annoyed mother. "Where have you be—" She broke off, reading his mind. "Oh, my, Cyrus! This is a picklement."

"It would never have happened, if you had been along," he said. "Yet I'm glad it did. She *is* the one for me."

"Whom you can neither marry nor acknowledge," she said severely. "I wish you had been more careful."

Careful? He had been literally swept off his feet. "What's done is done. My main problem now is that I hate being away from them. Either of them. I love them both, in different ways."

"I appreciate that," she said tiredly. "Well, we'll make the best of it. You have revisions to make on the play."

"My private life has become more like a story than the play."

"Yes, of course."

He sat down at the desk to work on the play, but he just couldn't concentrate. All he could think of was Rhythm and Kadence. What was he to do?

Melete threw up her hands. "We'll have to sort this out somehow. All right, Princess; come here."

Rhythm appeared, with Kadence in tow. "We just can't function without him," she said apologetically to Melete.

"Neither can he without you," Melete said. "When you soak in a love spring, and it's buttressed by real love, it's impossible to live apart."

"Yet we can't even touch each other," Cyrus said dolefully.

"That's the bleep of it," Rhythm agreed. "I'm too young to do what I can't even imagine doing with him, and I know he won't do it. But I long to do it anyway. I know it's the complete expression of our love. Curse the Conspiracy!"

They looked at each other with sheer guilty longing. What had been could never be.

"This is why the Adult Conspiracy exists," Melete said severely. "So children won't get themselves into exactly the kind of trouble you did. Your parents will utterly freak out."

"Don't tell my parents!" Rhythm cried, horrified.

"I won't," Melete said. "*You* will. When necessary."

"I'm ashamed," Cyrus said, wishing he could embrace Rhythm. "I'm supposed to be the adult."

"I'm ashamed too," Rhythm agreed. She met his gaze, reading his mind. "And I wish the same."

"You both should be, after that stunt! You should have known better."

"We do know better," Cyrus said. "Now."

"Yet we would do it again, if we could," Rhythm said. "Any time."

They continued to gaze at each other. The forbidden longing became almost unbearable. Cyrus saw tears in Rhythm's eyes, and felt his own tears starting.

"You're both crazy," Kadence said severely.

Melete glanced at her, startled. "You have a solution?" It was evident that she could be seen and heard by others when she chose to be. "Despite knowing nothing about what they secretly long to do?"

"Sure. Mother just has to make another Decade spell, a good one that won't go wrong, and be with him for an hour, doing I have no idea what. But then they won't be so sad."

Cyrus exchanged a burning glance with Rhythm.

Melete sighed. "Kadence, put me in your pocket," she said. "We'll take a walk around outside and get to know each other better."

"Sure," the girl agreed cheerfully. She picked up the Muse, and went outside.

"Our daughter understands more than she should," Rhythm said as she brought out a sphere.

"She understands that we desperately love each other."

Rhythm bit the sphere. The vapor puffed. She became beautifully adult. "Oh, beloved!" she exclaimed, rushing into his arms.

It was an intensely satisfying session, guilt and all.

After their furious passion had been satisfied, they talked, loving each other's company regardless of the whereabouts of storks. "I loved you from the moment I first saw you," Rhythm confessed.

"I couldn't let myself love you. Because—"

She put a finger to his lips. "I understand. I felt you fighting against it. 'Winsome' was a euphemism." Her vocabulary matched her body, full fleshed.

"It was," he agreed. "But I must say, when you became adult, you were surprisingly apt. You had no experience; how could you have known so perfectly what to do? You had no hesitation at all."

"I shouldn't tell you," she said teasingly.

"Tell me, or I'll tickle your lovely ribs. Like this." He touched one rib with one finger.

"Eeek!" she screamed, laughing. "Don't you dare!"

He held the rest of his fingers threateningly. "I *will* dare. Tell!"

"I'll tell! I'll tell!" she cried, vanquished. "But first a bit of background."

The three Princesses had always been excruciatingly curious about the secrets of the Adult Conspiracy, but of course no one would tell them. Melody was the pretty, charming one; she tried to charm adults into telling, but they didn't. Harmony was the agreeable one; she tried to make them want to tell, but they didn't. Rhythm was the bold, wild one, the little savage; she was the one that came up with the naughty idea.

They made two dolls, a boy and a girl, as correct in details as they could. That meant that the girl was perfect, as girls were, while the boy was somewhat fuzzy in the midsection. Then they put the dolls together. They discovered that the dolls could do just about anything with each other. He could put his nose in her ear; she could put her finger in his mouth. But there was one thing he could absolutely not put in one part of her. So by elimination they knew that was it. How that could signal a stork remained a mystery.

Then they took turns invoking the Decade spell. But the one who became mature would not tell the others the rest of the secret, and could not remember it when she reverted. Still, what she avoided answering when closely questioned was indicative. By the time they had been through it three times—once for each of them—they had a little bit of a notion what it was all about. But they knew they would have to do it with a real man in order to fathom the last of it.

"And so I did," Rhythm concluded. "I didn't know exactly how, but I knew you did, and I followed your lead. After the first time, the mystery was gone, and I had no further problem." She smiled. "Except when I reverted, of course."

"Do you really forget those details?" he asked, guiltily curious.

"I am a wild, naughty, unseemly girl. My parents would be appalled if they even suspected. So of course I can't confess anything like that." She loosed a smoldering sidelong glance at him. "Does that dismay you?"

"Certainly. I am outraged. You are a perfect, deceptive barbarian, inside." He held her close. "Exactly the kind of girl I longed for. The kind my mother would approve of. I love your wildness."

"I always wanted to be loved for my wildness," she said, kissing him wildly as her hair flared out similarly. And of course the passion took them again. It was wonderful.

The hour ended and she reverted. She hastily dressed while he averted his gaze so as not to compromise the Adult Conspiracy. But they couldn't honor it perfectly; they kissed once more before separating.

"Same time tomorrow?" he inquired.

"If not before," she agreed. "You know, if I concentrated, I might almost remember some details."

"Don't do that!" he said, alarmed.

Then they laughed together. It had become a private joke. How could either of them ever forget the fulfillment of their love? Regardless of details, they had a solution of sorts to their dilemma.

Kadence and Melete returned. "There are fun people here, Rhyme," the girl said. "Even an ugly old witch with a pointy hat."

"To be sure, little sister," Rhythm said. "Now let's leave poor Cyrus to his work. I fear I have worn him out."

"He doesn't look very worn," Kadence said.

"I conceal my fatigue well," Cyrus said. He changed the subject. "I'm glad you enjoyed your exploration of the camp."

Rhythm glanced at the child sharply. "Your hair!" It had been cut halfway short.

"It was all straggly with loose ends," Kadence said. "As if I inherited some barbarian blood."

"You did," Cyrus and Rhythm said together.

"But Crabapple helped me tame it. She used her pincers to trim the ends so they are even, not straggly. Now it looks nice. She's great."

"She is a worthy person," Cyrus agreed. "We hope she will do well as an actress."

"We certainly do," Rhythm agreed. Cyrus knew she was aware of his own passing interest in the woman, which had abruptly and permanently ended. "Now we really must go."

Kadence set Melete back on the table, and mother and daughter disappeared. No one had seen Rhythm come here, because she hadn't walked in, but conjured herself in magically.

"Kadence is a nice girl," Melete said. "She wants so much to help Crabapple, but doesn't know how."

"I want to help her too, and not just because I need Rhythm to be reassured she's no threat. It would be nice if she truly succeeds as an actress. But I fear the part I crafted for her isn't enough."

"So we will make it enough," Melete said. "Put your rear in the chair."

Cyrus sat down at the table. This time, with Melete's help, he was able to focus on the play with only occasional distractions.

The troupe was growing. Dusty Dust Devil joined, reuniting with his sister Dusti. On occasion the two would go out and stir up a horrendous swirl of dust. But both worked hard at the play.

There was also Guise, a young man who happened by and was promptly co-opted by the actresses. His talent was to make clothing that made its wearer resemble whatever creature it emulated. The effect was illusory, but that was fine for the play. He was drafted to assume the lead male role, freeing Cyrus to direct. Xina was especially taken with him, and he with her, as they acted out the pseudo romance in the play. In the play, he went finally to Crabapple, but in life he stayed with Xina.

In addition, the Witch flew back to the Good Magician's Castle and recruited Tuff, the rock salesman, because they needed his talent to make the raised stage and chairs for the audience. Exactly how she persuaded him to join the troupe Cyrus did not inquire, but thereafter he shared a tent with her. Cyrus knew how extremely persuasive women could be, when they wanted to be.

The modifications and rehearsals continued. There seemed to be an endless array of minor details that had to be settled before they could make their first official presentation. Cyrus found it frankly somewhat dull. Also, the actresses no longer flirted with him. Somehow they knew that he had been taken, though he was sure they did not know by whom or in what manner. He was sure because both Melete and Rhythm assured him it was so, reading their minds. That was a relief, but it also was a slight disappointment. Had it not been for the private sessions with decade-aged Rhythm, he would have been unduly bored.

However, there was Kadence. She had joined the troupe as Rhyme's younger sister, and was doing her best to be helpful. The actors and actresses liked her. In the guise of encouraging her to learn acting, he was able to be with her without suspicion.

He came upon her sitting on the ground, staring intently down. "Are you all right?" he asked.

"Oh, sure, Cyrus," she replied. "I'm just watching ants. I didn't know they marched in regular columns."

"They don't, normally," he said. He joined her, looking

down. There were the ants in perfect formation, as if marching to a common drummer.

Drummer. This was Kadence, surely a variation of cadence. A cadence was a measured sound, a rhythmic progression. Folk marching to a drumbeat had cadence, as he understood it. Did the ants have cadence? If so, could it be related to her name?

"Kadence, try focusing on the ants not marching in step," he suggested. "See what happens."

"Okay, Cyrus." She was being very careful never to call him daddy or father, and he appreciated that. She focused on the formation.

Immediately the ants broke into a tangled mess of nothing coherent. All signs of their formation was gone.

"Ooo, ugh," she said, and concentrated again.

The ants re-formed their formation. They were back in step.

"Kadence, I believe we have discovered your magic talent," he said, pleased. "You can make things have a cadence. To hear a common beat, as it were, and move in formation. The ants are doing it because you are making them do it."

"Wow," she said, surprised. "Is that good?"

"It's not good or bad; it's magic. Every person has a magic talent of some sort, and this must be yours. The talent of organization. Coordinating others efficiently. Some talents are stronger than others."

"Is this strong?"

He had to be honest with her. "It does not seem like a really strong talent. But talents can be deceptive. Some that seem slight can actually be quite strong. Much depends on the way you develop it, and the use you make of it."

"I'm supposed to have a strong talent."

He shrugged. He did not see much potential here, but according to Rhythm, Kadence was destined to be a Sorceress.

"Maybe you can learn more about yours, and enable it to become strong. It will take practice."

"I'll practice."

"Be sure to tell your sister Rhyme about it. She may be able to help."

"I will."

Three actresses were approaching. Kadence gazed at them intently. They got in step.

Cyrus made a silent whistle. "Are you doing that?" he whispered.

"Shouldn't I?"

"Maybe be careful with people. They might not like it."

"Okay." The actresses fell out of step.

"With luck, they won't have noticed," Cyrus murmured. Indeed, the three walked on by, paying him no attention.

"Is it good, Cyrus?"

"It is stronger than doing it with ants, yes. We need to discover what else you can do."

"I'll work on it, Cyrus," she said, pleased.

It was time to put on the first play. Curtis made arrangements with Crabapple's village, and it was scheduled.

Then things started to go wrong. Guise had done well with the costumes, but had not had much time in the part, and tended to forget his lines at key moments. That would never do.

"We need a prompter," Curtis said.

"A what?" Cyrus asked blankly.

"A person who follows the play, and prompts the actors when they falter. I should have remembered before."

It seemed like a good idea. "Who can do it?"

"Anyone with a script. But some are better than others. We'd better have spot rehearsals for the position.

They did. Dusty tried it, but tended to blow the lines. That was worse than no prompter.

Acro was willing, but tended to excerpt letters from key words. That didn't work either.

"Try Kadence," Melete suggested.

"But she's a child." Cyrus winced internally as he said it, remembering what had happened the last time he accused a girl of being a child.

"She's a likely Sorceress with a talent for alignment."

So they tried Kadence, and she was perfect. She didn't even need a script, which helped, because she had not yet learned how to read. She had memorized all the parts just from hearing them rehearsed and corrected.

Tuff made a small chamber of stone and set it into the ground at the front of the stage. Kadence sat in it, facing the stage; the audience could not see her, as it was on the other side of the stone. "Now forget a line," Cyrus told Guise.

He faced Xina. "I want to—to—"

"Marry you," Kadence whispered promptly.

"Marry you," he said, remembering the line.

She would do. She had found her role in the play.

Another problem was food. The group had pretty well foraged out the local pie plants and other natural sources, and were tired of the Witch's sandwiches and brews. They needed a new, independent supply. There were increasing complaints, and actresses were getting female-doggish, which spoiled morale. But how could they tackle this problem, when they had the play to perfect? They couldn't afford a serious distraction.

Rhythm got on it, in her fashion. Melete was the one who gave her the notion. "Dear, we need you here, for reasons we can't say openly."

"So I shouldn't mention things like the man and daughter I love, because I'm too young to know the proper meaning of the word, or the way I keep my identity clouded from the others?"

"Exactly," the Muse agreed with just a bit more than half a smile. "Don't refer to them at all, beyond the privacy of this tent. So I think this is an occasion where your sisters might be able and willing to assist."

"Melody and Harmony!" she exclaimed. "I miss them."

"But we shall have to conceal certain things from them, lest word reach parental ears prematurely."

Rhythm quailed. "They'll know."

"Then we must persuade them to keep the secret, at least for the time being."

"Maybe that will work. They love secrets."

"Then summon them now."

Rhythm produced her drum and drumsticks. She made a brief patter.

Instantly two cutely crowned girls arrived. One wore a nice green dress, had green/blond hair, and blue eyes. The other had brown dress, hair, and eyes. Both had somewhat impish expressions, as if about to participate in something funny.

"You called, sister?" the first inquired.

"Or drummed us up?" the other added.

"Meet my triplet sisters, Melody and Harmony," Rhythm said.

"Hello, Princesses," Cyrus said formally.

The two gazed at him with disturbingly aware expressions. He realized that they could probably read minds, the way Rhythm could. He tried to banish any thoughts of the true situation.

The two turned as one to Rhythm. "Ooo, you've been naughty," Melody said, delighted.

"Extremely naughty," Harmony agreed, smirking.

"Bleep!" Rhythm swore. "I never even showed my panties."

"You went beyond panties," Melody said.

"Way beyond panties," Harmony agreed. "Or inside them, as the case may be."

Rhythm, clearly overmatched, played her trump. "This is my daughter, Kadence." Kadence appeared beside her.

This shut them up, momentarily stunned.

"Hi, Aunt Melody," Kadence said politely. "Hi, Aunt Harmony."

Melody found her voice. "But she's—"

"Six years old," Harmony said.

"It's complicated," Rhythm said.

They regrouped. "You will tell us everything," Melody said.

"Especially including the forbidden details," Harmony agreed.

"First you must agree to keep the secret," Rhythm said.

The two exchanged a knowing glance. "On one condition," Melody said.

"We get to kiss him, once," Harmony said.

"What?" Cyrus exclaimed.

Rhythm looked pained. "We do need their help, Cyrus."

He realized that he had to go along with their mischief. They were after all Sorceresses, dangerous to offend. "Once," he agreed weakly. "But that must be secret, because—"

Suddenly Princess Melody was embracing him. "Because this, too, is," she said, and kissed him firmly on the mouth. The impact of it was half stunning. He remembered that her mind was actually fifteen.

Then her blue eyes became brown, and it was Harmony holding him. "A violation of the Adult Conspiracy," she said, and kissed him equally firmly. That impact was the other half stunning; her mind was sixteen. He fell back on his bed, unable to orient. But already he understood that Rhythm was not so much of a maverick after all; her sisters were equivalently naughty and daring, after allowing for their mental ages. Sorceresses, all.

Kadence came to join him. "They're just teasing you, Father," she said, taking his hand. That helped.

"Now you've done it," Rhythm said grimly. "You're both in it too. We're all in violation."

"So none of us will tell," Melody said.

"Any of this," Harmony agreed. "Now out with it, sister. We are already good and jealous."

"First, we need to find a way to provide plenty of varied food for the troupe," Rhythm said firmly.

The other two sighed, together. "Very well, let's focus," Melody said.

"On that problem," Harmony agreed.

"Then I'll cover the rest," Rhythm concluded.

They put their heads together. Cyrus felt an intensity of magic expanding outward. It was breathtakingly strong. He remembered that any one Princess was a Sorceress, and any two squared it, and the three together cubed it. If he hadn't believed that before, he certainly did now.

Then it collapsed. "Jim will be here tomorrow," Melody announced.

"His talent is making food," Harmony added.

"Which will solve our problem," Rhythm concluded. Then she told her sisters what had happened, abbreviating only the details of stork summoning, which inhibited her at this age.

Cyrus, Kadence, and Melete merely listened, finding the dialogue interesting despite their familiarity with the subject. The Princesses had their own take on its aspects.

At last, satisfied, Melody and Harmony gave Cyrus a knowing look, and vanished. They had come, helped, and learned the full naughty secret, and would not tell. Rhythm seemed satisfied, and relieved.

She came to him after that, as Melete and Kadence elected to take their walk. Abruptly a decade older, she was especially amorous. He gladly indulged her. Yet Cyrus had the uneasy feeling that someone was watching. The two sisters, surely, snooping on what was forbidden. He doubted he could do anything about it, so he did his best to ignore it. Maybe it was just his imagination.

"Not even a Sorceress can balk a Sorceress," Rhythm said. "Let alone two Sorceresses."

"I'm sure I don't know what you're talking about," he said, kissing her.

"Of course you don't," she agreed, kissing him back. "But the Adult Conspiracy will fuzz the details."

He hoped so.

Next day, Jim arrived, coincidentally, he thought. He could make any kind of food magically, in any amount. But in a land where pies grow on trees and beer formed in the thick trunks of other trees, there had been very little demand for his talent. Now he stumbled into a camp where they welcomed him. It was instant mutual appreciation. Thereafter each member of the troupe had whatever food he or she liked, whenever and in any amount liked.

Acro seemed to take an interest in him. It seemed that Jim would not be sleeping alone long.

The day before the presentation, Cyrus, Curtis, Tuff, the Witch, and Kadence walked to the neighborhood and surveyed the site selected for the play. It was in the center of the village, with space for people to stand or sit all around it. "Make a raised stone stage here, of this size," the Curse Friend told Tuff. "A dressing room here."

"But Guise makes their clothing right on them," Kadence said. "They won't need to change."

Curtis smiled. "Trust me, child, they will need privacy. Actors are a temperamental lot; they get nervous before a presentation."

"Nervous?"

"Sick to their tummies," the Witch explained. "They may even toss their cookies."

"They'll be eating cookies?"

Melete intervened. She was in Cyrus's pocket. "This is Adult slang," she explained. "She means they'll vomit."

The child burst out laughing. "Oh, that's funny!"

"Not to the actors," the Witch said, smiling wickedly. She had not heard Melete, of course.

"Privacy," Curtis repeated. "Better have two potties, and a mop."

Kadence tried to stifle her giggles. The men smiled.

"And the prompter's booth here," Curtis continued after slightly more than a moment. "With a circular stage, some of the audience will see her, but that won't matter; they'll understand."

"Can I wave to them?" Kadence asked.

Curtis winced. "Please don't wave. This is a serious play."

She looked mirthfully disappointed.

Tuff conjured blocks of greenish volcanic stone magically and formed a raised stage together with a pinkish changing room complete with brown stone potties. It looked very nice.

"Of course the stone won't remain for more than three days," he said. "My talent is to borrow it from old volcanoes, not to keep it."

"That is fine," Curtis said. "The villagers wouldn't want our stage cluttering their territory indefinitely."

They returned to their camp for the night. Cyrus was excited; the big event was almost at hand.

Next afternoon, even before the play, several actors were daunted by the expectant audience of villagers. They suffered butterflies and butterspiders in their innards, and made copious use of the facilities. Crabapple was especially nervous, because she wasn't sure how the folk who had known her all her life would react to her role as an actress. But they all rallied bravely in time for the presentation.

Guise walked out, garbed as a handsome young man, which he happened to be; his costume merely made him more so. He approached the Witch's Garden.

The Witch rose up to face him, fairly radiating ire. Her costume made her more dramatically witchly than she had ever been in life, despite being authentic. "You—" she started. And stalled.

"Clumsy oaf," Kadence whispered from the prompter's box.

"Clumsy oaf!" the Witch screamed. "You just squished my Bleeding Heart Orchid!" The audience never knew that the brief pause had been a mental blanking of her line.

Guise opened his mouth. "I—I—"

"I'm sorry," Kadence whispered.

"I'm sorry," he agreed. "I didn't see—"

"Didn't see? *Didn't see?*" the Witch screeched, having no more trouble now that she was fairly started. She went on to curse him with Feeling Sight.

Cyrus, watching from the edge, saw the audience become expectantly confused. They did not know what Feeling Sight was, but were sure it would soon turn out to be awful.

In due course Guise encountered Acro, in her marvelously nicely skimpy outfit, surrounded by greenish light. It was a very nice effect, and the audience clearly liked gazing at her body. He got his lines out, but she stood frozen.

"One for what?" Kadence whispered.

That got her started, and she completed her lines. Meanwhile the audience, seeing her glow, was beginning to catch on.

Guise realized that he couldn't marry the wrong color glow, and went on to Dusti, whose glow was pink. She, too, was beautifully costumed, but lost her line and had to be prompted.

After her, Xina, glowing blue, the prettiest yet, also needed prompting. So did Crabapple, who could barely force herself to go out onto the stage. In fact, the only one who didn't need it was Tuff, the least experienced actor. But apart from that, it went well, and the audience never knew. It shuddered when the Witch formed her plot, and screamed when the feather boa struck, and cheered when Crabapple cut it away, and cried when she married Guise herself. She was of course the female lead, and her nervousness lent her a quality that enhanced her role and made her almost eerily beautiful.

The applause at the end was long and loud. They made Crabapple return to the stage several times. She was crying so hard that she couldn't see, and Guise had to guide her by the elbow, but they were joyful tears. She had returned to her village as a success.

As it turned out, the other actors were crying too. It was a great event.

"They have been bloodied," Curtis said with satisfaction. "They will perform better in the future."

There was an atmosphere of camaraderie as the troupe returned to the camp. They had performed together and made it work. And Kadence was the minor hero of the day, for her apt prompting.

Only later did Cyrus figure it out. "That applause wasn't natural," he said.

"Kadence did it," Melete agreed. "She wanted Crabapple to be appreciated."

"Kadence did it?"

"Her talent is aligning people and things to the beat, the cadence," Melete said. "During the play she aligned each faltering actor to the play script, so that there would be no more blanks. Then toward the end she focused on the audience, causing the people to applaud together, especially for Crabapple. They did not realize they were guided."

"My daughter really *is* a Sorceress," he said, awed. The notion was just a bit frightening. He had already seen what a Sorceress could do.

9

VIOLATION

Cyrus was struggling to write his second play, titled "The Dream," with Melete's assistance. He was discovering that even with the help of the Muse, the story did not necessarily flow.

"Writing is ten percent inspiration, ninety percent perspiration," she reminded him. "You need to perspire. If I do it all for you, you'll never become a great Playwright in your own right."

"I appreciate your consideration," he said, not appreciating it at all.

"It's for your own good," she said sulkily. The problem with her was that she understood him too well.

"Sure." He concentrated, getting little or nowhere. So he had a great title; what next? Should it feature a night mare who brought a good dream instead of a bad dream? He had the suspicion that had been done before. In fact he seemed to remember Night Mare Imbrium getting fired for it. That had been an injustice to her; she was simply a nice creature.

Thank you. Then with a flick of her tail she was gone.

Oops. He had been daydreaming.

The day was late, and Rhythm arrived before he knew it.

"She just can't get enough of you," Melete murmured. "This time set me on the table so I can watch."

"I never took you for a voyeur," Cyrus told her, smiling. Rhythm's visits always cheered him up.

"I'm not. I'm merely jealous. She can distract you from your writing without even trying."

"That's the joy of it," Rhythm said.

Melete was jealous of his passion for Rhythm? That might explain why she was making him work so hard. But it was true that he never thought about plays when with Rhythm.

The paper appeared in midair between them just as Rhythm was about to invoke the Decade spell. She grabbed it before it drifted to the floor. She read it:

"VIOLATION. You have been charged with Violation of the Adult Conspiracy. Report to the Stork Works in forty-eight hours for the hearing. Fail not, on pain of penalty."

She stared at him, aghast. "Cyrus! They're charging you with—"

"Well, I'm guilty," he said, horrified.

"No you aren't! I have always been twenty-two for you, except when I was even older."

He shook his head. "Your true age is twelve. I knew it. The Decade spell is like an Accommodation spell, making it possible for two folk to get together who have no business being together in that manner. I must pay the penalty, whatever it is."

She shook her head. "That might be the abolition of Kadence."

He sank back on the bed. "That would be unbearable."

"Melete, what can we do?" Rhythm asked the Muse.

"You will just have to persuade the stork authorities that you were of age when the stork was signaled, and when the baby was delivered," Melete said.

"Well, we *were*," Rhythm said.

"But their records may not show it, understandably."

Rhythm nodded. "Yes, that could be the case. Once we explain, they'll understand. I hope."

Cyrus hoped so too. "It says to report there within forty-eight hours. I don't even know where the Stork Works is."

"I can find it," Rhythm said. "But—"

"But you don't want to give away your nature by helping me get there magically," Cyrus said.

"The notice should have instructions," Melete said.

Rhythm looked. "Oh, yes. I didn't read that far before. It says there will be a pastel-colored line showing a safe way." She looked around. "Oh, I see it now! It leads right out of the tent."

"But I can't go right now," Cyrus protested. "The play—"

"Will keep," Melete said. "Better than you will, if you don't make that hearing."

"What would be the penalty?" he asked.

"It could be anything from banishment from Xanth to abolition of your child."

"No!" Rhythm cried. "We already know we can't allow that."

But the notion clung to Cyrus like burning tar. "Kadence! We can't let her be abolished."

"So you will make that hearing," Melete said firmly. "Tell Curtis you have an urgent appointment and will be back in four days. Rhythm will help cover for you."

"The bleep I will," Rhythm said. "I'm going with him. I'm not going to let them banish him."

"Then who will watch out for Kadence?" Melete asked evenly.

That faint bit of barbarian wildness played across Rhythm's face. "We had better take her too. She has a right to speak, if she faces extinction. But I'm not going to let that happen, even if I have to do something rash."

Cyrus realized that her dangerous Sorceress aspect was coming into play. He loved it. Even the Stork Works should be wary of crossing this girl. "I agree. But how can we explain the three of us departing together?"

"I will cast a small believing spell as you tell Curtis," Rhythm said grimly.

"That works," he agreed.

He went immediately to see the producer. Curtis offered no objection. "Just return with inspiration for the next play. We have a schedule to keep."

"We'll keep it," Cyrus agreed.

Next he talked to Don Donkey. "You have been faithfully and quietly guarding my tent all this time," he said. "Now I need you to do more."

"We're going somewhere," Don said.

"I am. You're not. I need you to stay here and keep an eye on things for me."

"Hee haw!" the donkey laughed. "As if I have any authority."

"I'm serious. I need to know that nothing goes wrong here while I'm away. So you can walk around the camp, keeping your eyes open, and I'll look through them every so often to see what you're seeing. You can also give me verbal reports."

"I'd rather travel."

"Maybe next time."

"Grumble."

"Hee haw," Cyrus laughed.

They found Kadence. "Come with us," Rhythm said. "It's important."

The child didn't argue. She respected her mother, more than ever since discovering the powers of Sorcery.

Soon they were following the pastel line out of the camp. Cyrus had some trouble seeing it at first, so Rhythm enhanced it with a spell so that both he and Kadence could see it clearly. That way there would never be any doubt about their route.

"But you know, Kadence," Rhythm said as they walked. "When we camp tonight—"

"Oh, I know. You can put a sleep spell on me so you can do naughty things with Father."

"Are you sure you have no idea what they are?" Rhythm asked suspiciously. She was increasingly like a regular mother when with her daughter.

"Of course I don't know," the girl said. "And of course Aunt Melody and Aunt Harmony haven't told me anything. I'm sure panties have nothing to do with it."

Cyrus had to bite his tongue. The girl was learning early what secrets to keep.

The pastel line led them to a campsite they hadn't known about before. It wasn't on the enchanted path network, which meant there could be danger, but Rhythm was sure she could handle it.

"There's even a nice bed," Kadence remarked. "Can I have it?"

Rhythm hesitated. "Let me borrow Cousin Eve's talent to check it. She can tell anything about anything that isn't alive, just by touching it." She poked a finger at the bed. And froze.

"Rhythm!" Cyrus exclaimed, alarmed.

"Mother!" Kadence said, also alarmed.

Rhythm just stood there, her finger touching the bed. She did not seem to be breathing.

Cyrus threw his arms about her and lifted her away from the bed. Then she came back to life. "Dear, I haven't changed yet," she murmured in his ear, then kissed it.

She meant her age. She thought he was embracing her. "You were stuck there frozen," he said, setting her down. "We feared for you."

"Now I remember. I touched that bed, and it was as if I died.

I couldn't even breathe." She faced the bed. "Now I know its nature: it's a Death Bed. Anyone who lies on it, dies."

"I was going to lie on it!" Kadence said, horrified.

"Don't touch it," Cyrus said, also horrified.

"Maybe this isn't the best place to camp," Kadence said, shuddering.

"I'll destroy it," Rhythm said, her drum and drumsticks appearing.

"Wait," Cyrus said. "This is not necessarily a bad thing. Maybe people who are tired of life come here. It would be an easy way to end it. All we have to do is leave it alone."

"You're so practical," Rhythm said, turning an adoring gaze on him.

"I wish you wouldn't do that when you're—twelve," he said uncomfortably.

"I got my crush on you at this age," she said. "That's what got us into this mess. But I don't want to waste any part of my adult hour on incidentals like talk or food."

She had a point. "Still, when Kadence is present—"

"As if I didn't know you love each other," Kadence said.

"Still, it's an awkward situation."

That sobered Kadence. "Are they going to abolish me?" she asked plaintively.

Rhythm hugged her. "Over my dead body."

"Don't lie on the Death Bed!" Kadence cried, half laughing.

That gave Cyrus an awful thought. "That Death Bed— could it be along this route not by accident?"

Rhythm met his gaze, appalled. "The storks—they wouldn't do that, would they?"

"Of course not," Cyrus said. But he was in doubt. The elimination of Kadence might be the first step in dealing with his Violation of the Adult Conspiracy.

"I'm going to tell my sisters," Rhythm said grimly. "They'll look out for us."

"Is that wise? They might do something rash."

She nodded. "They might indeed. All right, I'll leave them out of it, for now."

"Maybe that's best," Cyrus agreed. This was anything but an innocent trip.

There was a patch of pretty flowers shaped like mugs, each filled with nectar. Rhythm touched one cautiously with her little finger. "It's ale!" she said. "Fem ale."

"It's for you," Kadence said. "Female."

"No," Cyrus said firmly. "Ale—any ale—is an adult drink. You two stick to boot rear or tsoda pop."

"Awww," Rhythm and Kadence said together, smiling.

"I will stick with innocent drinks too," he said.

"That's nice of you," Rhythm said. But there was a mischievous twinge he didn't quite trust. She was too prone to naughtiness. He loved and feared that.

Cyrus remembered something. "I'd better check on Don."

"Your robot donkey?" Kadence asked. "He's nice. I wish he had come along."

"I asked him to stay, to keep an eye on the troupe. He is made with a robot radio that I can tune in on with the robot part of my brain." He closed his eyes, mentally dialed the number, and tuned in. "How are things, Don?"

"Routine," the donkey said, looking around to show nothing happening. "Dull."

"That's good." He tuned out.

"That's weird," Kadence said approvingly.

"Well, I am half robot."

"And half human," Rhythm said. "As I am about to prove again."

"Rhythm!" But he couldn't help liking the way she proved it.

They had pies and boot rear, then settled for the night away from the Bed. Rhythm did put a sleep spell on her daughter, then invoked the Decade spell she had not used before and embraced Cyrus.

"Technically Rhythm is of age now," Melete said, watching from the tree branch where he had set her. "If necessary, she can demonstrate that spell to the storks. The storks should realize that there is no Violation. Technically."

Cyrus hoped that was the case. But if the storks went by her regular age, he would be in severe trouble. Just how seriously were they taking his matter? That bed . . .

"Now I can have that ale," Rhythm said. She went to pick up the Fem ale mug, and he couldn't stop her. So he took a mug also. His turned out to be Reg ale, which seemed fit for a feast.

She tried a sip. "This is good," she remarked, and took a bigger sip. "I always suspected that Adults were hiding secret pleasures from children." She took a gulp.

"You should go easy on that stuff," he said.

"Really?" She swallowed more. "I'm feeling great."

"That's its effect. But too much can make you sick."

"I don't believe it." She drained the mug. She became visibly more voluptuously female.

Cyrus was nervous about this. She was adult, for the hour, but lacked much adult experience. He was feeling his own drink, and feared she was too. "I hope I'm not contributing to your delinquency."

"I'm not going to let them banish you, Cyrus—or Kadence," Rhythm said, her hair turning wild. "I *am* a Sorceress, and with my sisters' help I mean to set this whole thing straight." She got up to go for another drink.

He had to distract her before she got drunk. "Oh, I love you, I love you!" he said, kissing her. "Especially when you start being barbaric."

"Even though I used a love spring on you?" she asked teasingly.

"I told you: you won me with your first grown kiss. That love spring didn't make any more difference to me than it did to you."

"I know."

"You do? How?"

"Because it wasn't really a love spring. I just told you that so you wouldn't resist."

"You vixen! If I had known that—"

"You would have resisted despite loving me," she said. "Instead of abandoning yourself to the passion of it."

He nodded. "I would have tried to resist. I don't think you would have let me succeed."

"True. I would have done this." She did something naughty.

"Rhythm!" He had thought he was beyond shock. At her for doing it, and at himself for liking it.

"And this." Naughtier.

"I would not have succeeded," he agreed as he reacted. He was beginning to feel a bit barbaric himself. What a woman she was!

Then she lurched to her feet, staggered to the nearest brush, and spewed out the remains of her ale.

He got up and held her while she heaved. "I'm sorry."

"You warned me." After a messy moment she straightened up. "I'm okay now."

"That's good."

"Next time I'll drink slower."

"That will spare you the sickness."

"That will spare me from telling you more than I should."

So she hadn't intended to tell him about the fake love spring. "And doing more than you should."

"No, that's all right. I love you." She kissed him avidly. Her mouth was rather slippery, but he didn't mind.

"Are you sure you're up to—"

She hauled him to the ground with her. She was intoxicatingly female despite losing much of the drink. "Quite sure."

In due course their hour ended, Rhythm reverted, and they sank blissfully into normal sleep, side by side. If Melete found that improper, she didn't say. Maybe she had been freaked out by their naughtiness. Or just maybe she had enjoyed the show.

In the morning they organized and made ready to resume following the pastel trail. Cyrus assumed it would get them there on time. He checked on the troupe via Don, and was pleased that things there remained completely dull.

There was a swirl of smoke. "What is happening sound?"

Cyrus and Kadence stared. "Did that smoke talk?" Kadence asked.

"I think it did," Cyrus said.

"Metria, go away," Rhythm snapped.

"Happening how?" Cyrus asked, perplexed.

"Don't say that!" Rhythm said. "It will only get her started."

"Approved, solid, boom, bell, echo, noise, listen—"

"Hear?" he asked.

"Whatever," the smoke agreed, irritated.

"Here!" Kadence exclaimed. "What is happening here!"

"Exactly what I said," the smoke said, forming into a luscious human female body. "I recognize Princess Rhythm, but who the bleep are you?"

"I'm Kadence," the girl said. "I'm six years old."

"Ooof! You're a child. I take back the bleep."

"And this is the Demoness Metria," Rhythm said with resignation. "She's always a nuisance."

Cyrus sorted through his memory bank. There she was, a mischievous demoness with a speech impediment dating from the time she was stepped on by a Sphinx. "Hello, Metria," he said. "I am Cyrus Cyborg, and this is my—" He caught himself. "My young friend Kadence."

The demoness studied him, then Kadence, then Rhythm. "I'll be bleeped! There's a family favor. You must be related."

"Go away," Rhythm said. "It's none of your business."

"In fact she looks like a young Sorceress. I'd almost think—but you're too young for that."

"Obviously," Rhythm said.

"Not that obvious. You're a winsome girl who could almost pass for a woman and charm a man if she tried hard enough, if he didn't care about the Adult Conspiracy. Except that you couldn't have a six-year-old—" The demoness paused, noticing the bed. "What's that?"

"Don't touch it," Cyrus said quickly.

"Why so sensitive?" Metria asked, moving to the bed. "Did someone do something naughty on it?" She sat down on it.

And exploded into noxious vapor.

"Oops," Rhythm said, seeming not completely dismayed.

"What the bleep *is* this thing?" the vapor asked. "It feels like a goose melody!"

"A what?" Cyrus asked.

"Swan song!" Kadence said gleefully. It seemed she was also good at organizing words.

"It's a death bed," Cyrus explained. "I tried to tell you not to touch it."

"I never do what I'm told." The vapor coalesced into the sultry female form. "Good thing I'm not really alive."

"Good thing," Cyrus echoed. Now he understood why Rhythm had not wanted the demoness here. If she fathomed their situation, she would blab it all over Xanth. She needed to be diverted or distracted.

"So what are you three travelers up to?" Metria inquired.

Rhythm opened her mouth, but Cyrus spoke first. "I am a Playwright, and these two have parts."

"I'm the Prompter," Kadence said proudly.

"A Playwright," Metria said. "I always wanted to be an actress."

That was exactly the reaction he had hoped for. Let her get carried away by dreams of grandeur on the stage, and maybe she would forget about family resemblances. "I am currently recruiting for actors. But can you act?"

"Can I act!" she exclaimed. "I am always acting! Even *I* don't always know exactly who I am."

"Then maybe I'll write a part for you in the next play. But you will have to be able to memorize lines and deliver them clearly and effectively."

"I'll do it! See you there." She faded out.

"You may be smarter than you look," Rhythm murmured.

"I hope so."

They set out, following the line. Fortunately the demoness hadn't caught on to that, or the nature of their mission.

"However," Rhythm murmured again. "She isn't always as absent as she appears to be. So don't say anything about anything."

"Got it."

They came to a stand with an instrument on it. The instrument seemed to have a section attached to a cord that could be lifted. Cyrus reached for it.

"Don't touch it!" Rhythm said. "I recognize it: that's a tell-a phone."

"A telephone?"

"It gives you a horrible urge to tell it things, heedless of your surroundings. You would surely tell it too much. Someone might overhear."

Oh. "I won't touch it," he agreed.

They moved on, but soon encountered another thing. In fact it was a pile of things. One was a big letter E made of iron. Another was the letter N made of gold. Another looked like a container filled with salt. "Are these safe to touch?" he asked, having learned caution.

"I know!" Kadence said. "Those are piled up puns! Irony, GoldeN, and a salt. Assault. Better not touch it, because it will attack you! And there's B-salt, that will turn you to salt if you touch it. And a pool of C-salt. And D-salt that will unsalt things. You don't want to mess with that either, because you don't want to lose the salt in your body."

"How do you know all this?" Cyrus asked, amazed.

"Well, they align," Kadence said. "They're all lettered salts."

"And you understand alignment, being the Sorceress of that sort of thing," he said. "Kadence, you just saved me an ugly experience." He picked her up and kissed her.

"Ugh," she said, wrinkling her nose. "Why don't you leave that yucky stuff for Mother? She actually likes it."

He set her down, laughing. "I will."

"Beep." That was as close as she could come to bleep, being too young to swear. It seemed that her protest had been more a matter of form than preference.

But again he wondered: these were more potentially lethal things. Could it be coincidence that the pastel line was taking them past such dangers?

"Where's Melete?" Kadence asked.

Cyrus felt his pocket. It was empty. "Oh, no—I forgot to pick her up from the tree branch this morning!"

"That bleeping demoness distracted us," Rhythm said. She evidently did not have the same trouble with swearing that her daughter did.

"I must go back for her."

"We don't have time to do it without being observed. We're already running late."

She was right. "I'll just have to pick her up when we return," he decided. He wasn't comfortable about it, though. If he lost the Muse, how could he ever write his next play?

They followed the pastel line, which meandered so that soon Cyrus had no idea where they were going. It did lead them past enough pie trees to keep them fed, and to another campsite as evening approached. This one was by a nice-looking lake.

Cyrus did not quite trust this. "Anything could be in there," he said.

Indeed, shapes were appearing. One was bare breasted. "A mermaid!" Kadence exclaimed.

"Hello," the figure said. "I am Carla, your mermaid." Her tail formed into legs, and she strode from the water. She was no longer bare, but formally clothed. That was just as well, because the maid's bare body in the water had tried to compel his gaze, and he had felt Rhythm's annoyance. She didn't like him staring at *other* women's bodies, for some reason.

A merman followed, similarly adjusting. "I am Carlos, your merbutler."

"But we don't need—" Cyrus said.

Rhythm concentrated for half a moment. "They mean no harm," she said, evidently having invoked more magic.

"Of course we don't," Carla said. "We are here to make you comfortable during your stay by our lake."

Cyrus did what he should have thought to do before, and riffled through his memory bank. "You have an estate under water," he said. "Where guests can breathe."

"Indeed we do," Carlos agreed. "This way, please." He walked back into the lake.

Cyrus exchanged a look with Rhythm. This might be worthwhile, but he didn't fully trust it, because the pastel line had been leading them past seemingly coincidental dangers.

Rhythm nodded. She would be alert. She took his hand, and Kadence's hand.

"You're beautiful, when you try, Mother," Kadence remarked.

Now Cyrus realized what he hadn't noticed in his distraction: Rhythm had assumed her adult form. She must have invoked the Decade spell when the merfolk appeared. Why?

"So they won't separate us, dear," Rhythm replied to his thought, squeezing his hand suggestively.

Oh. How had he won the love of such a passionate princess? He surely did not deserve it.

"You didn't win it," she said. "It was given to you, and you spurned it."

He had been trying to honor the Adult Conspiracy. He

should have known he never had a chance when a jealous Sorceress fixed her eye on him.

"Right on," she agreed.

They were now below the surface of the lake, breathing naturally. The distraction of Rhythm had made him miss the actual immersion.

"I'm a wild one," she agreed. "I'm barbaric." She loved teasing him about his quest for a barbarian wench.

"Mother, I wish you would stop answering his thoughts," Kadence said. "It drives me crazy wondering what horrible Conspiracy things he's thinking at you."

"That's the beauty of the Conspiracy," Rhythm agreed. "It tortures children every which way."

"I was just basking in the love of your mother," Cyrus said to Kadence.

The merbutler led them to a fine house. "Carla will make your bed while I serve your dinner," Carlos said.

"What about me?" Kadence asked.

A third mer person appeared. "I am your mernanny," she said. "I will see to your needs this night."

Kadence was surprised. "What needs?"

"For relaxation and entertainment. Do you like I-scream? Cookies? Tsoda pop? Pewter games?"

Kadence smiled. "Those are my needs," she agreed.

The butler was as good as his word. He served a sumptuous dinner with ent wine at the start and intert wine at the end. The first twisted Cyrus's mind pleasantly, and the second made the two of them socialize closely. He could hardly wait to be alone with Rhythm in the bedroom.

Then he had a horrible thought. "The hour has passed!"

"No it hasn't, dear. I'm using illusion to emulate my adult self. I'll invoke the spell when we're alone."

He stared at her. "But my thoughts—I didn't limit them. There may have been all manner of forbidden things. Especially after the second drink."

"There were," she said smugly.

"And your appearance, that dress—you're showing the upper surfaces of full breasts."

"It's nice to have my effort of illusion appreciated."

"Do you realize you're getting me deeper and deeper into Violation?"

"Deeper and deeper," she agreed dreamily. "I've got rhythm, of course."

He blushed. "I didn't mean it that way!"

"I did."

"You minx! You should be ashamed."

"Yes. Awfully. You should spank me." She sent a mental image of a bare bottom.

He was appalled. That was no child's bottom. "Rhythm—"

"Let's skip dessert," she said, producing the Decade sphere. "This will do instead."

He could not argue. He had been hopelessly compromised, and was even more hopelessly in love.

They adjourned to the bedroom, which the mermaid had prepared very nicely. They kissed and fell together on the bed and generated the most intense ellipsis yet.

Then, as they lay panting after the effort, Rhythm paused sharply.

"What?" he asked, bemused that she could do that. Other people's pauses were usually dull, not sharp.

"Kadence. She's in danger." She scrambled off the bed, grabbing for her clothing, which resembled her illusion dress exactly.

"We shouldn't have trusted her away from us," Cyrus said, diving into his own clothing, which he had somehow managed to shed beside the bed. "That nanny—"

"Not her fault," Rhythm said. "This is something else."

They hurried out of the room and went to Kadence's room. They charged inside without knocking.

The child was reaching for an object. It looked like a small statue of a mermaid, with beautifully flowing hair, a full bare bosom, and a splendid tail. The nanny was watching, unconcerned.

Both paused as the two burst in.

"Don't touch it!" Rhythm cried.

"It's harmless," the nanny protested. "It's just a statue of my grandmother in her prime. She was a supreme object of desire."

"*I'll* touch it," Rhythm said grimly. She went up and poked one finger at the statue.

The statue exploded into vapor. A noxious cloud formed, then shaped into a horrendous demon. "I am the object of D's ire," he proclaimed. "Anyone who touches me suffers my ire. Woe to you, you nasty brat." His huge hands moved forward as if to catch and squeeze someone's puny neck.

Only it was Rhythm's neck they closed on, not the child's. "Woe to who?" she asked evenly as electricity played about the contact.

"What the bleep are you?" the demon demanded, surprised.

"I am the Sorceress Rhythm. And you are about to be one hurting demon. Did you think you could attack my daughter and not answer to me?" The electricity intensified.

The demon tried to let go, but the current held his hands locked in place. "Ooooww!" he howled in pain.

"Exactly." The current intensified further. Smoke began to rise from his burning hands.

"I didn't knooow!" he protested. "I was just following orders. Oooo, that smarts!"

"What orders?" Cyrus demanded.

"To eliminate the child."

So there *was* a plot! "Who gave them?"

"It was—was—" But then the demon exploded into awful nothingness.

"Bleep," Rhythm swore. "I overdid it."

The nanny was staring at them, horrified. "I had no idea!" she said. "The nasty demon must have taken the place of my statue. I'm so sorry. I never would have led any child into danger."

Rhythm glanced at her, and nodded, verifying that she was telling the truth. "You had no way of knowing. But I think I had better keep my daughter with me now, just in case."

"Yes, by all means," the nanny agreed, shaken.

"Can she come too?" Kadence asked plaintively. "She's nice."

Rhythm laughed. "Very well, but she must agree not to tell what she sees of our private lives."

"Oh, of course," the nanny agreed. "Nannies see everything, and tell nothing."

It was surely true. So they retired to their own room, bringing Kadence and the mernanny along. As it turned out, the nanny continued to keep the child entertained, so that Cyrus and Rhythm could get some rest and sleep. Rhythm reverted to girlform, lying beside him, and the nanny pretended not to notice.

But Cyrus lay for some time awake. They had confirmed that someone or something was out to get Kadence, so the other dangers were not coincidental. Kadence had almost lain down on the death bed, and there were also the plants growing ales. But who could it be, and why?

The question suggested an answer: Ragna Roc. Cyrus was supposed to use his troupe to get Rhythm close to the nasty bird, so she could nullify him. If anything happened to her or her daughter, she would be unable to complete her mission. She might be only twelve, but she loved Kadence, as he did, and would be devastated. Rhythm could take care of herself, as the scene with the demon had just made uncomfortably clear, but though Kadence was a Sorceress in her own right, she lacked the experience to defend herself against anything as malign as a demon.

But if Ragna Roc knew about them, how could they ever get into his presence to nullify him? And why were the threats so devious? Why didn't he just send a warrior to take them all out? The bird lacked any inhibitions about foul play, and would happily destroy them. So that must mean the big bird didn't know about them.

Then how to explain the threats?

"Dear," Rhythm murmured sleepily, "your thoughts are disturbing me. If you don't stop, I'll distract you from them."

He knew exactly how she would do that, even if it freaked out Kadence and the nanny. He had to stop worrying.

She took his hand. "That's better."

Holding hands wasn't really a Violation, he told himself. Adults held the hands of children all the time. Still, he felt guilty.

"That, too," she said. "Go to sleep." And she backed it up with a spot sleep spell. He was unconscious until morning.

The merbutler and mermaid were jointly appalled when they learned of the incident with the demon. It seemed that, true to her word, the nanny had not told them. "We never!" the butler said.

"Never!" the maid agreed.

"We know," Cyrus said. "Your hospitality has been impeccable. We have been beset by similar problems throughout our journey. We thank you for an otherwise excellent night."

Rhythm added her endorsement, and when they still fretted, added an acceptance spell. Then they walked up out of the lake and resumed their journey.

"I dislike showing magic," Rhythm said, "but I think we had better hurry before something else happens. We're behind schedule anyway."

"Hurry?"

"Take my hand." She caught his hand and Kadence's.

The scenery around them changed. They were now standing at the entrance to the Stork Works.

Oh. Cyrus nerved himself for the challenge to come.

10

DREAM

S tymy Stork was courteous but regretful as the three of
them sat in his office. "I am sorry to have to bring up
such a matter, realizing that the two of you were swept
away by circumstance. But whatever the circumstance, Violation of the Adult Conspiracy is a most serious matter. As
Head Stork, and deliverer of the bundle, I share some blame;
this should never have been allowed to happen."

"I know it," Cyrus said. "And I am mortified to have
done it. I am ready to accept whatever penalty is required,
except—"

"This is irrelevant," Stymy said.

"Except I want no harm to come to Princess Rhythm or
Kadence, who deserve no rebuke."

"There seems to be a misapprehension," the stork said.
"You are not being charged."

"Not—what?"

"You are the Victim, not the Perpetrator."

Cyrus stared at him blankly. "Victim?"

"According to our records, Princess Rhythm was age

twenty-two when the Violation occurred. You were two. She is guilty of Child Molestation."

Now Rhythm and Kadence stared at him, open mouthed. "Two?" Rhythm asked after a ragged two thirds of a pause.

"I'm six," Kadence said, a little swirl of confusion circling her head.

"I was assembled adult!" Cyrus protested.

"I realize that," Stymy said. "But our records are somewhat literal minded. I remember when there was a five-year confusion that caused me to decline to make a delivery, leading to serious complications. I don't want to make any such mistake again. That's why I elected to handle this matter personally."

Cyrus had the ugly impression that no matter how apologetic this talking stork was, he would do what he felt was proper. That could be deadly to Kadence. Meanwhile Rhythm's silence was ominous; if there did turn out to be any threat to her daughter's existence, there would be serious mischief. So he had to ease the crisis however he could.

"What is required to straighten this out?" Cyrus asked.

"Three things. First we must establish that you are adult, so that no abuse occurred. Second, we must establish the current age for Kadence, so that she herself does not later suffer the same complication that Surprise Golem did." Stymy covered his beak with a wing. "Oops! I should not have mentioned her name. That record is supposed to be sealed. Please forget it."

"Forgotten," Cyrus said immediately.

"Third, Rhythm must be lectured on acting in a manner becoming to her age, and she must promise to reform."

"The bleep I will!" Rhythm snapped. "I love him." Kadence giggled.

Cyrus hastily interceded. "She means she will be glad to cooperate in any way feasible." He moved on quickly, before Rhythm could object. "How do I establish my adult status?"

"Merely sign a statement to the effect that you were created adult by definition, in the manner of a robot, as your father was." A paper appeared on the desk.

Cyrus signed it. "Done. Now Rhythm is not guilty of any infraction."

"Technically," Stymy agreed with a wry curve of his beak. He turned to Kadence. "How did you become age six in only a month?"

"Mother garbled a spell, and time accelerated," Kadence said immediately. "That's how the first nine months passed so quickly, and the following six years, before she could turn it off."

Stymy nodded. "That explains how it was that we received what seemed like a backdated signal. I assumed it was a clerical error. Evidently it wasn't."

"It was a local time warp," Cyrus said. "It seemed like only an hour or two to us, but we all aged six years. Then when Rhythm nullified the spell, she and I reverted to our natural ages, but Kadence didn't."

"We had better enter her as delivered at age six," Stymy said. "These things happen."

"They do," Cyrus agreed, relieved.

The stork turned to Rhythm. He had seemed like a rather benign bird, anxious to get the paperwork straight. Now he seemed uncomfortably serious. Cyrus remembered that he was the head of the Stork Works, and had considerable power, especially over the composition of families.

Rhythm evidently realized it too. She was a Princess and a Sorceress, but she quailed visibly. She knew she was in serious trouble.

"The royal children have been getting increasingly naughty," Stymy said. "Your cousin Princess Eve—well, never mind. All of you have put a serious strain on the Adult Conspiracy. But you personally have achieved new levels of naughtiness. In fact, you are giving naughtiness a bad name."

There was a pause. "Rhythm," Cyrus murmured.

She turned to him with an expression of fixed innocence. "What?"

"Mother, say you're sorry," Kadence whispered.

"Oh." Rhythm turned to the stork. "I'm sorry." But she did not sound completely sincere.

"Your clothing is too tight," the stork continued severely. "So that you attract the male eye—and you're only twelve years old."

"I'm pushing thirteen," Rhythm snapped before Cyrus could shush her. "I've got flesh. I'm a nascent woman."

"You're a child," Stymy said firmly.

"I wear a bra and panties. See?" She pulled down on the top part of her dress and up on the skirt, exposing critical fringes.

Both Cyrus and Kadence freaked out, for different reasons. But the stork took it in stride. "And you have an attitude problem as big as Castle Roogna," he said. "Do you want me to inform your mother?"

Rhythm collapsed. "Please, no!"

"Then you will henceforth wear clothing appropriate to your status. No tight binding around chest or butt."

"Appropriate clothing," she agreed, defeated. Her dress became two sizes larger, so that it was no longer tight.

"You flirted shamelessly with Cyrus, who was trying to be true to the code," Stymy continued inexorably. "When that didn't work, you took naughtiness to a new level. No one has done that before. You should be excruciatingly ashamed."

"Well, he called me a child!" she retorted.

"Not any more," Cyrus said, hoping to pacify her before she damaged her case. At least she hadn't mentioned spanking.

"You used magic to invoke a technicality of age, and shamelessly seduced him," Stymy said. "Thus signaling us to deliver your baby."

"Yes," she agreed smugly. "They're both wonderful."

"You must now renounce them both, and promise never to do it again. Not until you have aged naturally to maturity in six years."

She exploded, outraged. "The bleep I will! I love him! And my daughter too! I won't renounce anything! I'm glad I did it!"

Cyrus exchanged a horrified glance with Kadence, seeing the case abruptly lost.

But the stork wasn't fazed. "Do you not realize that you have brought a child into this realm who can not share a normal family life with you or her father? This is bad for her upbringing and social adjustment. You have made a man love you who can not marry you. This is bad for his sanity."

Rhythm froze. "Oh, I'm sorry! I didn't think of that."

"A child wouldn't. That's why cautionary rules exist."

"I can get along," Kadence said bravely.

"So can I," Cyrus said, though it really bothered him.

"Neither of you should be required to sacrifice in this manner," Stymy said. "You need to have a normal family life. Her action caused you to forfeit it."

Rhythm burst into tears. "I never meant to do that! If I have to, to make it right, I'll give you up. Maybe you can marry someone else, Cyrus, and adopt Kadence. Then you'll have a family."

"No!" Cyrus and Kadence said together.

"But it's not right to make you suffer. I alone should suffer for my naughtiness."

Cyrus hugged her from one side, and Kadence from the other. "We'd rather suffer with you, than without you," Cyrus said.

Rhythm tried to speak again, but was choked off by tears.

"Fortunately you have one significant thing in your favor, Princess," the stork said, as they sat sharing their misery.

"I do?" Rhythm asked, soggily surprised.

"Love, as you said. It conquers all. Even on occasion the Adult Conspiracy. We are required to compromise."

"You are?" Cyrus asked, hardly daring to believe it.

"It was in the nature of a test question. True love brooks no opposition. Therefore we will accept the status quo, except that we will ignore any signals we may receive from Princess Rhythm, regardless of her temporary age, until she comes of age naturally."

"But what about the family?" Kadence asked.

"This is unfortunate," Stymy said. "We hope that the troupe represents a feasible substitute. It allows you to interact frequently, and the members are supportive of each other. The three of you know your relationship, so you can act as a family when alone together. As I said, it is a compromise."

But now Cyrus was suspicious. "Why should you compromise? It can't be just that there is love."

"There are two other factors," Stymy agreed. "All of you are needed for the completion of your private mission."

"You know about that?" Cyrus asked sharply.

"Only that it is of vital importance to the larger welfare of Xanth, so we must not interfere. The Good Magician put out the word."

Now Rhythm spoke. "What's the other thing?"

"It is somewhat personal," the stork agreed reluctantly. "Punishing you would also compromise me, for making the delivery. I should have checked the situation more carefully. I much prefer that no issue be made. It could cost me my position."

Oho! Cyrus had to bite his tongue to keep from chortling.

"We won't tell if you don't," Rhythm said, amused but serious.

"I believe we have an understanding," Stymy said, his beak making a wry curve.

"Silence all around," Cyrus said, immensely relieved.

"Let's get out of here," Kadence said. "Before anyone changes their mind."

"That does seem best," the stork agreed.

Outside the Stork Works, on their way back, Rhythm thought of something else. "That silence includes you," she reminded Kadence. "In case you should accidentally see anything at night you shouldn't. Because we aren't going to let you be by yourself. Not while something is out to get you."

"Aw, you'll both be covered by a blanket anyway," the girl said. "It never shows anything."

Cyrus and Rhythm exchanged half a guilty look. It was definitely time to move on.

"Now we need to retrace our route, so I can pick up Melete," Cyrus said.

"Gee—can we visit the merfolk again?" Kadence asked brightly.

"I will make a Find spell that will guide us directly to it," Rhythm said with half a shudder. "No need to visit the merfolk."

Cyrus didn't comment. They all knew that the threat to Kadence had not been the mers' fault, but it remained a bad memory.

The Find spell showed the direction, which wasn't exactly the way they had come. Actually they had not passed this way at all; Rhythm had transported them. It also tried to lead them through the worst of thickets, so they couldn't go straight.

They walked along any enchanted paths they found, but few folk traveled to and from the Stork Works by foot, and the paths did not always go the direction they needed. So as night approached they looked for a safe spot to camp.

"We are close to Melete," Rhythm said. "Which is odd."

"Odd? Why?"

"Because we are nowhere near where we left her."

He did not like that. "Do you think this is more of the mischief we have been encountering?"

"It may be," she said grimly.

"But you can protect us, Mother," Kadence said, sounding not quite certain.

"She can protect us," Cyrus said reassuringly.

There was a peal of thunder. A thunderstorm was brewing. "Fracto has seen us," Rhythm said. "He's going to wet on us if he can."

"There's a cave," Kadence said.

"My Writer's Block is in there, or beyond it in that direction," Cyrus said, surprised.

"I will check it." Rhythm went to the mouth of the cave. "Hello in there. Are there any monsters or dangerous creatures lurking?"

"I am the only occupant," a nymphly voice replied. "I'm a Lady."

"She's telling the truth," Rhythm said. "I don't have the energy to do a full check. It should be all right."

The first drops of water spattered around them, encouraging their entry. They walked into the cave, which was of goodly diameter. They turned a corner, where faint light leaked around.

And came up against the snout of a fire-breathing dragon. "Uh-oh," Rhythm murmured as her drum and drumsticks appeared.

"Do not be alarmed," the Dragon Lady said. "I am not going to scorch you. You sounded like nice people, so I invited you in. I never toast a visitor."

So it seemed. "I am Cyrus Cyborg, and this is Rhyme, and her little sister Kadence." He was not completely easy with the deception, but it was for a necessary cause.

"I am so glad to meet you."

"You talk like a nymph," Kadence said, surprised.

The Lady smiled, the expression rippling from one side of

her long toothy mouth to the other. "I had a nymph as a roommate for some time. She taught me how to talk human style, and I taught her how to chomp a fresh man. It seemed like a fair exchange. She finally got lonely for her own kind, leaving me lonely for company. But local folk don't quite trust me, for some reason."

"She is telling the truth," Rhythm repeated. "We can trust her not to scorch or eat us."

"Ah, that's your talent," the Lady said. "To ascertain truth."

"Part of it," Rhythm agreed cautiously.

"You must be hungry after traveling. I have assorted roasts, and some baked potatoes and bread." She looked apologetic. "Everything is hot; it's my nature. You will have to go outside for cool drinks."

"I'll fetch some," Kadence said eagerly. She dashed outside the cave.

"I also have warm pillows," the Lady said.

"We'll make do," Cyrus said. He pondered briefly, then decided to ask. "We are searching for a certain wooden block, and understand it is in the cave. Have you seen it?"

"This block?" the Lady asked, lifting it in a curl of her tail.

"Get me out of this!" Melete called. "She's a nice dragon, but I can't help her."

"That block," Cyrus agreed. "I am a playwright, and that is my Writer's Block. I can't write at all well without it. In fact I am stymied on a play now." The word reminded him of Stymy Stork. "May I have it back?"

"Certainly." The tail swung around, delivering the Block. "I found it on the branch of a tree, and it intrigued me, as I recognized its nature, so I brought it home. But it doesn't work for me, perhaps because I am not a writer."

"It will work only for me," Cyrus said. "Thank you for returning it. Is there any favor I can do you in exchange?"

"I hesitate to ask. I have a dream."

"A familiar dream," Melete said. "She's a young female."

"You want to be an actress!" Rhythm exclaimed.

"I blush to confess it. But other dragons aren't interested in that sort of thing, and most humans won't trust me close enough to ascertain my ability. I even tried to query the Curse Fiends, but they cursed me away."

It was an easy decision. "You returned my Block. I will write you into the next play."

"Oh, thank you! I am so grateful."

"However, you will have to come join my troupe," Cyrus said. "And not eat any of the actors."

"Cross my tail and hope to fry," the Lady said in an evident oath. "This is so exciting."

"I will get on it the moment we return safely."

"May I ask a personal question? I do not wish to be offensive."

"Ask," Cyrus said, suspecting what was coming.

"The girl resembles you, Rhyme. You introduced her as your sister, and perhaps she is. But the two of you are clearly in love, yet you look to be only about twelve, Rhyme. This close to the Stork Works—well, I suspect your story is somewhat more interesting than merely being tourists."

Cyrus saw Rhythm doing a quick mental calculation. He knew she wanted to invoke the Decade spell and be with him, but couldn't do that with an intelligent dragon watching. Unless the dragon agreed not to tell. "Will you keep a secret? A big one?"

"Cross my tail and hope to fry myself to a cinder," the Lady agreed solemnly.

"Cyrus and I are in love, yes. I was naughty, and we got a daughter. We had to explain to the storks. Now we can't love each other openly, but I can invoke a spell to make me older. Do you mind?"

"Mind? I am in love with love! Especially forbidden love.

I dream of finding it some day myself. But male dragons aren't much into nymph-talking females, except as a staple of their diets. Do anything you want; I won't tell."

Kadence returned, somewhat wet, with three mugs of drinks. "These were all I could find close by the cave."

"Oh, those are rums," the Lady said.

"Rum!" Rhythm said. "You can't drink that!"

"Neither can you," Cyrus told her.

"Oh, yeah?" She brought out the Decade spell and invoked it before he could protest. Her loose dress became tight in places before she remembered and changed its size.

"Now that's an impressive transformation," the Lady said. "But about that rum: I see one of them is a Deco. Kadence could sip that without being adversely affected."

"I'm thirsty," Kadence said.

"Oh, drink the Decorum, then," Rhythm said petulantly. She took one of the others from the girl's hands and sipped it. "This is fantastic."

"That's Fulc rum," the Lady said. "It generally serves as the turning point of evening festivities."

"That's for me." Rhythm took a big sip.

Cyrus took the third one. "That is Cereb," the lady said. "Be careful; it goes to your head."

"Cerebrum," he agreed, trying it. Indeed, he felt smarter already.

"Let's get turning," Rhythm said, almost slopping her rum as she tried to embrace him.

"You are being disgustingly obvious, Mother," Kadence complained.

The Lady smiled. "Come dear; we shall play a game of nineteen questions while they do what we have no notion about."

Cyrus was getting to like the dragon. He gulped down the rest of his mind-enhancing drink, and Rhythm finished hers, and they embraced. In the background they heard Kadence and the Lady playing the game of questions.

Once the intensity of the ellipsis wore off, Rhythm spoke. "Are you really going to write her into a play?"

"Of course. I think it would be nice to have a play with a genuine dragon in it."

"But what about the night mare you were thinking of?"

"This is better."

"Much better," Melete agreed.

Then they slept, carefully doing it before the Decade spell wore off so that they could lie together embraced without doing anything contrary to the Adult Conspiracy. Actually the Conspiracy was wearing rather thin, but they pretended not to notice.

And, lying embraced, with Melete back, Cyrus dreamed creatively and romantically.

John was lonely. So when he learned that he could participate in a vast communal programmed dream populated by other lonely folk, he was happy to do it. He took a Happy Dreams pill and lay down on his bed to sleep.

Soon he found himself in a pleasant dreamscape, a scene set on the surface of a giant floating cloud, where trees grew, rivers ran, and nothing bad ever happened. People were everywhere, playing games, eating meals, and dating. All of them were quite attractive, so that he hesitated to approach them, because he was distinctly ordinary.

A handsome, friendly looking man approached him. "You're new here," the man said.

"I just arrived," John agreed. "How did you know?"

"Because you're just a blob of vapor." The man held up a mirror.

John looked at himself. He was a blob of vapor. "Oops. I didn't realize. I thought I would just be myself."

"No. You can be anything *except* yourself. That's the rule."

"But how can I be anything other than myself?"

"You need an Avatar."

"A what?"

"An image, a personality, that others can see and hear and interact with. It can be anything you want. Most folk want to be handsome, beautiful, noble, wealthy, whatever. Choose, and it shall be so. Then you can interact with others on an equal basis."

"But in real life I'm not like that."

"No one here is. That's the point: here you must be what you want to be. Everyone is."

"That doesn't seem very realistic."

The man looked at him condescendingly. "Realism is hardly the point. This is a *dream*."

So it was. "Thank you," John said. "I'd just like to be moderately tolerably handsome. Nothing special."

"That's too close to your real nature. Try again."

"How do you know my real nature?"

"I'm in your dream, remember. Now try to take this more seriously."

"I *am* taking it seriously. I never wanted to be more than I am. I just want to be accepted for *what* I am. And I'm ordinary."

"Bad attitude," the man said, and drifted away.

So John formed a modest Avatar somewhat but not perfectly similar to himself and walked on, uncertain whether he really liked this dream. If he couldn't be himself in his own dream, what was the point?

A pretty young woman approached him. "May I talk to you?" she asked.

"Sure," he said, gratified that he wasn't being ignored. "I'm John."

"I'm Marsha. I noticed that you gave the dream monitor a hard time."

"I didn't mean to. I just wanted to be myself."

"Why?"

"Because if I'm no good as myself, I'm no good as a faked-up Avatar. Maybe that's a stupid reason."

"No, no, it's a great reason. I wish I had thought of it. Then I would have been different."

"But you look and sound fine."

"Yes, but it's fake. I'm nothing at all like this in real life. I capitulated to the requirement, and made myself—" She shrugged. "Like this."

So she was another ordinary person. "You're welcome to be whatever you want to be. I don't hold it against you."

"Oh, thank you!" she said, and impulsively kissed him.

He reeled and almost fell. She had to hold him tight to keep him standing. "Sorry," he gasped. "I—no girl ever kissed me like that before."

"I apologize. I just got carried away. I won't do it again."

"No, no, no, no! I liked it. I'm just surprised that you did it. I'm so ordinary."

"You liked it?" she asked. "May I do it again?"

"Uh, sure, if you really want to."

She wrapped her arms about him, pressed her nice body close to his, and kissed him passionately. He reeled again, but couldn't fall as long as she was holding him so firmly. "Oh, this is so much fun!" she said, and kissed him yet again.

"Yes!" he agreed, and kissed her back.

After that, one thing led to another, and they found themselves in a miniature dream castle that formed around them, providing them privacy from other Dreamers. Soon they were both naked and trying to see how many storks they could signal with a single effort.

"I'm glad this is a dream," John said. "Because if it were real, we could be in trouble with the Stork Works."

"That's one advantage of dreaming," Marsha agreed. "We're not really doing it, so we can do whatever we want, no matter how naughty."

They lay beside each other and talked, discovering many common interests and some wildly divergent ones. John liked mechanical puzzles; Marsha liked hunting. He was nervous about the night jungle; she loved it. But their differences seemed only to enhance their mutual attraction.

At last it was time for the dream to end; they had talked away the night. "May I see you again?" John asked her.

"I'd love that," Marsha said. "I'll be right here tomorrow night."

"Then it's a date," he agreed, and kissed her again. And found himself kissing his pillow as he woke up. It was dawn.

All day he was in a daze, thinking about his nocturnal experience. Marsha was such a woman! So maybe in life she didn't look exactly the way she did in the dream. Did it matter? She was a really nice person, and she actually liked him.

The following night he took the communal dream pill again, and soon he was back on the clouds. There was Marsha waiting for him. "Oh, I was so afraid you wouldn't come!" she exclaimed, kissing him.

"I was afraid *you* wouldn't."

"Oh, I had to! It's so utterly nice to be appreciated the way you appreciate me, even if it is all illusion."

"It's a dream, but maybe not illusion," he said. "I really do like you, Marsha."

"And I really do like you, John. But maybe you wouldn't like me if you saw me in real life. No man ever has."

"Maybe those other men were stupid."

"No, they were afraid."

He laughed. "Afraid of you? They never gave you a chance."

"True," she agreed sadly. "That's why I came to the dream, and a false Avatar. I must say it has worked beautifully."

"Beautifully," he agreed, kissing her.

"What do you have in mind today?" she inquired. "We have talked and we have clasped."

"There's something else?" he asked, surprised.

"Once we have done something, doesn't it get dull? I assumed you would want to do something else."

"It doesn't get dull," he said. "Not for me, anyway. But if you are tired of it—"

"Oh." The miniature castle formed around them. "I am inexperienced in this kind of interaction, and don't really know what's what. You are the first man I have done either much talking or storking with."

"You're great at both," he said, kissing her avidly.

"I'm so pleased," she said, kissing him back. "I don't want to be boring for you."

"Never that!" He proceeded to storkly interest, and she cooperated more than willingly. Soon they were both pleasantly exercised.

"But when you do get tired of it, do let me know," Marsha said. "I like being with you so much, I never want to wear you out."

He concluded that she was naïve in the manner of women about the extent of male interest. "I will." Then they talked, and he told her more about himself, surprised and pleased that she showed so much interest, and learned more about her. It seemed that she lived alone in the jungle and had little contact with others. She was insatiably hungry for friendly interaction. But she never quite said exactly where she lived, or why she seemed to have no family. There were other oddities, but they merely added to the pleasant little mysteries of her.

They spent the night together, and John felt no desire to go out in the dream world to meet others. Marsha was all he needed. When the night ended, they agreed to meet again the next night.

This continued for some time. Finally John realized that he had to have a serious talk with Marsha.

"Oh, no!" she wailed. "You're tired of me!"

"By no means," he said. "My problem is the opposite. I think I have fallen in love with you."

"But you don't know me, only my Avatar."

"I know your personality. You're a nice girl, and you're always wonderfully nice to me. Unless that's all an act—"

"No, no! No act. I feel the same about you too. But there's something I haven't told you."

"Whatever it is, I don't think it will stop me from loving you. I admit it will be difficult if you're secretly married, or eighty years old."

She laughed. "Neither one. I'm your age and single. But you see, when I told too much, no other man had any interest in me. So I didn't dare tell you."

"Even if you're ugly—"

"I'm not. But—"

"What is it?" he demanded. "Tell me, and let me judge."

She winced, then visibly nerved herself. "You do have a right to know, though it could destroy our relationship. First let me say that I am more than willing to continue as we have been doing, meeting here, talking, and clasping. I love being close to you. I love pleasing you. I love you. So if you can find it in your heart to forgive me—"

"What is it?" he repeated firmly.

"I'm a dragon."

He gazed at her. "A what?"

"A dragon. I'm not human. So I can never be with you physically, only here in the Dream, with my human Avatar. Now you know." She waited, flinching, anticipating his reaction.

"You're—a—dragon lady," he said, now seeing how the hints about her nature came together. Living alone in a cave in the jungle, liking to hunt, men afraid of her. Now it made sense. No wonder she had concealed her identity. "What kind?"

"Old-fashioned fire-breathing, about twenty feet long, with wings. I'm a winged monster."

"But then why—why associate with my kind, even in a dream? Why go to all this trouble to—to please me? Letting me kiss you, and all? Surely you'd rather toast and eat me."

"I don't eat humans. Too dangerous. They send dragon killers after rogue dragons, armed with devastating spells. I stick to crows and rats, mostly, and the occasional troll."

"I can see how that would get dull. But to let me—have my way with you, when in real life you could chomp me. I'm so puny compared to you."

"You're so smart compared to me. Haven't you noticed how I'm always agreeing with you? That's because I'm not awfully good at thinking for myself."

"I thought it was because we shared experiences."

"The only experience we share is here in the Dream."

"Bleep!" he swore. "This can never be. But I still—" He broke off, appalled by the realization, then plowed on. "I still love you."

"You don't have to say that," Marsha said. "Just don't hate me. I'll do anything you want." Her bare Avatar spread her arms appealingly.

"You really do love me? Despite my not being a dragon? I should think you'd prefer to make it with another dragon."

"Do you know how dragons do it? It's more like rape. Scorching, steamy, smoky scenes are literal. It can take weeks to recover. You are so tenderly gentle."

"But isn't it your nature to scorch and chomp? Feeble kissing must disgust you."

"It is supposed to be my nature," she agreed. "I always felt guilty for wanting something else. I couldn't get it with my own kind. So I joined the communal Dream and took a human Avatar. I know there are other animals doing the same. Then when I saw you appear, and knew you didn't know your way about yet, I—I hoped you wouldn't mind, once you really got to know me."

"I don't. I'm glad to know you. You're a better woman than any other I've known."

She blushed. "You don't have to say that."

"I said it because I mean it. You're ideal for me."

She kissed him repeatedly. "Thank you, thank you!"

"And you really do love me, at least in the Dream?"

"I do, John. You have treated me so well. I know you would have preferred a human woman."

"I'm not sure I would," he said slowly. "No woman ever treated me the way you do. They found me too plain and dull."

"You were never that to me!"

It seemed to be true. What reason would she have to deceive him? "May I kiss you, knowing what you are?"

"Oh, yes, John!"

He kissed her, and her lips were just as sweet as they had been. He wrapped his arms about her, and her body was just as nice. Soon they were back in stork territory. Did dragons signal storks, or eat them?

"What about an accommodation spell?" he asked as they rested.

She understood exactly what he meant. "It would make it possible to do this physically. But you would still be a man, and I'd still be a dragon. It would be unnatural. I much prefer just being with you in the Dream, in a form that pleases you."

"Could we get a transformation spell? So you could become a real woman, or I a dragon?"

"It wouldn't work, John," she said regretfully. "I know nothing about real human society, and you'd never make it as a dragon. I'd be chomping things and you'd soon get toasted. We are what we are, regardless of our forms."

He had to concede the point. "Then can we make a life together here in the Dream?"

"But we're both asleep!"

"Our bodies are, but our minds are awake. Marsha, let's get married—in the Dream. Let's have a family here."

"But what of our real lives?"

"They will proceed as before. It can be our secret, that our real lives are in the Dream."

They hashed it over, and finally she agreed. They went to the Dream authorities, and set it up, and in due course had a Dream marriage attended by other Dreamers, who understood. They signaled a Dream Stork, and—

Then he was back in his real life. The night had ended, and with it the Dream. He was Cyrus again, not John.

$\overline{11}$

PLAY

I just had the wildest dream," Cyrus exclaimed as he carefully let go of Rhythm so as not to seem to be clasping a child. "I think it will make a perfect play for the Lady."

"Oh, tell me!" the dragon exclaimed, delighted.

He described the dream in detail as they ate hot cross buns and hot nog for breakfast. They had gotten accustomed to the heat of the cave.

"So they decided to have a family in the Dream," he concluded. "He'll still be a man, and she'll still be a dragon, but in the dream they can live together and have dream children and all. It's a happy compromise."

"It's a derivative of your own situation," Melete said severely.

The Lady's ears perked. "Is someone else here?"

"Better let her in," Rhythm murmured to the Muse.

"Let me introduce myself," Melete said, extending her perceptibility. "I am the Writer's Block you returned to Cyrus. I enable him to write his plays."

"Oh," the Lady said. "I had no idea you could talk."

"I normally talk only to him. But you need to hear this too. It's not really a story about you; it's about his forbidden love. He can't let others know he loves a child, so he has sublimated it in the dream, which he now proposes to render into a play. Instead of a child, the lady is a dragon. It's an attempt to justify his illicit passion."

"But she has a spell to make her older," the Lady said. "So it's all right."

"But he knows she's really a child. That's what makes it not all right."

"Oh, come off it, Muse," Kadence said. "They're in love. Who cares how old anyone is?"

"The Adult Conspiracy cares."

"But technically there's no Violation," the Lady said. "Just as there's no man/dragon problem in the play. It's all in the Dream. Forbidden love is forbidden love, and it's great drama. I don't care if there's a parallel. I think it's a great play and I love it."

"So do I," Kadence said.

"Just make sure you get a cute actress to play my Avatar in the Dream, and a handsome actor to love her."

"But I thought you were going to act in it," Kadence said.

"I'll be there, curling around the stage. I'll speak my part, once the audience learns that I'm Marsha. That way I'll be a dragon playing the part of a girl. It's wonderful."

Melete sighed. "Have it your way. But I'll expect something more original for the third play. I have to protect my reputation, after all."

They made an arrangement with the Lady to meet her at the Troupe, and resumed their trek. Now that they did not need to search for Melete, they were free to take whatever paths were most convenient.

They came to a clearing wherein a number of people sat. A

man stepped forward to meet them. "Hello, I am a Talent Scout. Do you need a new talent?"

Cyrus was tempted to brush on by, but paused. "I'm not sure I have an old talent, other than merely existing. I'm a cyborg. Half human, half machine."

"Everybody has a talent," the man said. "I can readily check yours. Give me your hand."

Bemused, Cyrus extended his hand. The scout took it and concentrated. "There it is. You can change one thing in any person's memory. It has to be a small thing, though, because big things have too many extensions and affect other things."

"Just like that, you know?" Cyrus asked, not believing it.

"It's my talent to know," the Scout said. "You can readily verify it. Change someone's memory."

Cyrus shook his head. "I doubt I can, but in any event, I wouldn't."

"If you have no use for it, I will gladly arrange a trade. That's why I set up my Talent Agency." He gestured around the clearing. "How about the talent of controlling a wisp of fog? That can be fun, especially if you make it dance. Or if it happens to be a forget whorl."

"I don't think—"

"How about the talent of conjuring assorted cloths?" the scout asked, refusing to be put off. "Your little girl would like that, wouldn't she? Or to make any cloth as hard as steel. That would protect her."

"I don't need those," Kadence said.

"Or of doing something perfectly on the first try," the Scout said. "Though I have to tell you, thereafter it is apt to mess up. That's why the owner wants to trade it."

"I don't need that either," Kadence said.

She finally got the man's attention. "Why not? Let me check your talent. It is surely worth trading." He put his hand on her arm. "Oh, my! You're a Sorceress!"

Cyrus acted before he thought about it, changing the man's memory of what he had discovered to a lesser thing. "You make ants march in step," the Scout said, not realizing. "That's interesting, though not really useful. You will surely want to trade. How about the ability to invoke the talent of dead people?"

"We'll trade," one of two young men said from the bench. "I'm In Crease; I make others gain weight, size, or whatever. This is my twin brother De Crease; he makes them lose it."

"But those are good talents," Kadence protested. "Why would you want to trade them?"

"Because we can affect only others, not ourselves," De Crease said. "We remain ordinary. That frustrates us no end. But maybe we could have some fun with ants."

Kadence considered. "I think I'd stay dull too, so I guess I don't want to trade." She was of course being careful not to give away her real reason.

"How about my talent?" a man asked. "I'm Pete. My talent is unbreaking. I don't mean mending or healing; I mean that I make it so it was never broken."

"Say," Kadence said. "I could use that when I accidentally drop a precious vase."

"You could," Pete agreed.

"You'd do better just learning to be more careful," Cyrus told her.

Kadence sighed. "I guess so."

"Then how about us?" a boy asked. "I am Melvin. I can read the minds of women. My sister Megan can read the minds of men."

"But those are great talents," Kadence said. "Why trade?"

"Because all the men are interested in only one thing," Megan said. "I get so tired of it."

"One thing?" Kadence asked, intrigued. "What is that?"

"My sister is six years old," Rhythm said firmly.

Megan nodded faintly, revising her answer. "Panties."

"Panties?" Kadence asked. "They're dull!"

"Precisely," Megan agreed with an obscure smile.

"Actually that's not true," Melvin said. "We are also interested in—"

Megan stepped on his toe. "Blouses," she said.

"Uh, yes," he agreed, wincing. "While all women are interested in is—"

Now Rhythm interceded. She made the people lose interest in them. They walked on by, and they paid no attention.

"Beep," Kadence muttered.

Only when they were well clear did Melete speak. "The talent Scout meant well, and has a business many folk will patronize, but he was dangerous for us."

"Yes, because our talents give away our identities," Rhythm said. "That's why I kept my mouth mostly shut."

"But he did me a favor," Cyrus said. "He identified my talent, when I didn't even know I had one. I can change one thing in a person's memory. I used it on him."

"Good thing you did," Rhythm said. "I was about to blank out his memory of the whole day. Your way was better."

"Still, being able to play with wisps of fog might be nice," Kadence said.

Rhythm glared at her, but the girl burst out giggling. She had been joking. Maybe.

"But you know, that *was* a danger," Cyrus said. "Even though the Scout meant well. Just as the Dragon Lady meant well, but that could have been dangerous if she had been a normal dragon."

"Something is still putting threats in our way," Rhythm agreed. "But they aren't really effective threats. That's odd."

"As if someone wants us to get into mischief seemingly by accident," Cyrus said. "An attack by a ravening monster would make it too obvious."

"Too obvious," she agreed, nodding. "But whatever is

doing it is not obvious either. I can't get a fix on it; there seems to be nothing there. Maybe I should get my sisters' help."

But Cyrus was wary of that. Melody and Harmony were too much like Rhythm, and entirely too interested in his and Rhythm's romantic life. "I have another idea: this is almost like a curse. Curtis Curse Friend is part of a culture that works constantly with curses. We should hurry back and ask him."

"But I would have to use heavy magic," Rhythm said.

"It was just an idea," he said. "I'm glad to be with you anywhere."

She smiled. "Let's proceed carefully. If we don't encounter any more dangers, okay. But if we do, then I'll think again."

"It's fun being out here, as a family," Kadence said.

"Yes it is," Rhythm said, hugging her, then hugging Cyrus. "I can love both of you openly, without anyone challenging my age or identity."

And that was the great thing about this excursion, Cyrus realized. Just being together, openly loving each other, without having to hide it.

Exactly, Rhythm agreed mentally.

They came to a river that barred their way. "Make a boat?" Cyrus asked. "I don't think it would be safe to swing across."

"There might be loan sharks or allegations," Rhythm agreed. "Things with teeth."

"Look!" Kadence exclaimed. "Water moccasins!"

Cyrus looked, alarmed, but it was only a patch of shoe-sized flowers, including dainty lady slippers and yes, snake-like water moccasins.

Kadence picked a pair and put them on her feet. She stepped on the water. The moccasins enabled her to walk on the water.

"I think we have our way to cross without swimming," Cyrus said.

They all donned water moccasins and started across the river. But then a dragon came charging toward them. It was translucent and ripply.

Rhythm raised one hand. The dragon paid no heed.

"Heed the warning, for your own sake, dragon," Cyrus murmured. But the dragon didn't.

A beam of color flashed from Rhythm's hand. It struck the dragon. The dragon's snoot flashed into steam, and the rest of it splashed into the water.

"It was a water dragon!" Cyrus exclaimed. "Made of water."

"It could still have chomped us with icicle teeth," Rhythm said grimly. "That does it. There's too much danger here. I'm using magic to take us back to camp."

"Make it safely beyond camp," Melete said. "So they won't know."

Rhythm nodded. "Take my hand," she said.

Cyrus and Kadence took her hands. Then they were standing in the glade with the love spring, where Rhythm had first seduced him. "Oh, my," he said, remembering.

Rhythm caught his thought. "Muse, take Kadence for a walk on the water," she said. "It's safe. Don't look back."

They were all still wearing the water moccasins. Kadence took Melete from his pocket and walked out on the pond, not looking back. Rhythm led him by the hand to the spot.

"You mean—" he asked, violently hoping.

The spell was already there, and she was biting into it. The vapor puffed and she was grown and beautiful. "What else?"

When he was able to speak again, after an especially intense ellipsis, he felt some faint regret. "You know we really shouldn't be doing this. I know your real age."

"Do you have a choice?"

"No." It was true. She was a Sorceress, and increasingly he was coming to appreciate the depth and breadth of that. She could do things he had never thought of, and he was powerless to resist anything she really wanted. She was a child, but he was nevertheless her captive.

"It's true," she said. "You were mine from the moment I realized I wanted you. The stork was right to haul me up on charges, not you; I always controlled the situation."

"You always did," he agreed. "When I called you a child— that wasn't what made you mad, was it?"

"I knew you would say that, giving me a pretext to react. I had already brought you here, after all."

"You already had," he agreed. "Oh, Rhythm, I don't know how I'm ever going to wait until you are truly of age. I love you."

"You're not mad that I made you love me?"

"With that first adult kiss? No. I think I was already on the way to it. I was trying to fight it, but there was just something about you."

"With a spell on your mind."

He stared at her. "Rhythm! You didn't!"

She looked guilty. "I did. It's like the losing-interest magic I use on folk who might get too curious about my identity, only this is positive. Intensifying interest."

"That's why I thought you were a winsome girl, and felt guilty!"

"You tried so hard to be honorable. I love that."

"But you really *are* a child! I love you, but you are. You should not have done that."

"I can reverse it, if you wish."

He pondered that. A spell to make him no longer love her? "Objectively, I see that that would make sense. But subjectively I can't stand the thought. And what about Kadence?"

"No reversal," she agreed. "Suppose I have my sisters get

together and fashion a spell that would age me permanently? Then I would never be a child."

"But I love you as you are, even though it's forbidden. And what about the mission to save Xanth? Your age would give away your nature, and that would mess up the mission."

She sighed. "You're hard to satisfy. I love that too."

"We'll just have to muddle through, as we have been doing, guilt and all."

"Before the hour ends," she said, and kissed him. That made him realize that she had always controlled every part of their relationship. And he loved it.

At least she always invoked the Decade spell before clasping him. Or did she? She had an illusion spell too. He had a sudden horrible thought. "Rhythm—did you ever use illusion instead of aging?"

"No. Not for this."

That was a vast relief.

"But I tried. The Adult Conspiracy wouldn't let me."

"You tried?" he asked, horrified. "Tried to seduce me when you remained a child?"

"Yes."

"Why?"

"So I would remember the details. Cyrus, I love you, but as a child I can't remember most of what we do when I'm adult. Only that it involves holding and kissing, and I can do that anyway. And that Panties relate, though I have no idea how; they don't seem to exist in my memory." She smiled grimly. "As an adult I know why they're absent, but that gets lost when I revert. It drives me crazy not knowing. I can't stand losing any part of you, even part of a memory. If I did it as a child, I would remember. Then I would know."

"That's sweet. But don't try it again." He was overwhelmingly relieved to know that he had never touched her as a child.

"Of course you could simply tell me exactly what happened,

after I revert. Then I wouldn't have to scheme to try to find out."

"No."

She frowned. "You're riling me."

"Better that, than a true Violation. You're adult now; you understand."

"I do," she agreed grudgingly. "But I don't when I'm young."

And she remained a Sorceress when she was young. He had to beware of her.

"You do," she agreed, kissing him.

The hour ended, and she reverted. "You're not going to tell me," she said.

"I'm not," he agreed.

She frowned, and there was a rumble of thunder in the background. "If I didn't love you, I might do this to you."

An unseen force took hold of him and lifted him off the ground. It shook him.

"I'm glad you're not doing that to me," he gasped.

She had to laugh, breaking the mood, and he returned to the ground. Then she lunged forward and kissed him, hard. "But I do love you," she said.

She was, indeed, a child, with childish impulses. Fortunately he was adult. She needed that discipline.

"I do," she agreed.

Kadence returned with Melete. "Time to return to the troupe," the Muse said. "Time for you to stop playing and write your play."

"Time," Cyrus agreed.

They walked to the camp. No one inquired about their absence. This was more evidence of Rhythm's sometimes frightening range of powers as a Sorceress.

Cyrus sought out Curtis. "We were out walking," he said, "and there kept being dangers, especially to Kadence. I thought maybe it's a curse. You're a curse friend, so I thought this might be in your area. Can you help me?"

"Let me examine the child," Curtis said.

Kadence approached, and the man put a hand on her head. "It's definitely a curse," he said. "I feel its ambiance. Let me check my reference." He fetched a tome. "Yes, here it is. This is interesting."

"Curses are listed in a book?" Cyrus asked.

"It is our business," Curtis said a trifle stiffly.

"Of course. I just didn't realize that that sort of thing could be tabulated."

"It is a magic reference, automatically updated," the Curse Friend said. "Let me provide some necessary background. The Muse of History, Clio, was cursed to suffer some danger every day of her life. Fortunately she had the means to handle those threats. Later she got together with a Magician who reversed that curse, and it has lain fallow for several years. It seems that someone has appropriated it and applied it to Kadence. It is an opportunistic curse, adapting whatever is convenient, and not always aptly."

"Not aptly?" Cyrus asked.

"For example, if there is a dragon nearby, it will lead the subject to the dragon," Curtis explained. "But the dragon may not be hungry at the moment, so does not consume the victim. The curse isn't smart about such details."

"That's exactly how it is," Cyrus said. "We encountered a friendly dragon we recruited for the next play."

"The next play!"

"She'll be here in another day or so," Cyrus said. "She talks. I have worked out a play with her as the lead female."

"So you weren't wasting your time during your absence."

"I never know in what manner inspiration will come. Can you stop the curse?"

"Oh, yes, now that I have identified it. I will simply disconnect it from Kadence so it can't find her any more. But why should anyone want to curse such an innocent child?"

"That's what we would like to know," Cyrus said. "At least she's safe now."

"Safe," Kadence repeated, relieved.

But later, with Rhythm, he was sure he knew. "Ragna Roc. The bird knows about us."

"I don't think so," Rhythm said. "He would simply have rendered us all into illusion, instead of doing something relatively ineffective like this. Why alert us that he knows, anyway? Why use some leftover curse?"

She was right. "How about this: Ragna doesn't know about us, but does know that Xanth folk aren't keen on being taken over by him. So he got someone to watch out for dangers, and maybe that person found this curse, and oriented it to focus on the greatest danger to Ragna?"

"So nobody knows about us, except the curse, and it's not very smart." She nodded. "So we're safe, for now. Except—"

"Except why did it focus on Kadence? It should have oriented on you."

"On me," she agreed. "She's a Sorceress, but making ants or people walk in step isn't going to hurt him. Whereas if I get close to him, I'll zap him with a conjured pineapple."

"Which he would render illusionary. And you too."

"Um," she agreed. "Still, Kadence can't be the worst threat. Maybe the curse got the wrong person."

"Maybe," he said. "At least she's safe now."

"Yes." But she seemed uncertain.

"Now write that play," Melete said.

Cyrus got to work and wrote the play. It was rapid, because he already had it worked out.

Next day the Dragon Lady arrived. Cyrus had warned the troupe, so there was only muted alarm. He went out to greet her, and escorted her to the campsite. "This is the Dragon Lady," he said. "She will be the lead lady in the play."

"Hello," the dragon said shyly. "I'll stay away except during rehearsals. Hunting, you know."

The other members of the troupe were happy to leave it at that.

Cyrus had Tuff, the volcanic rock salesman, try out for the lead male. Tuff had done all right playing the King in the prior play, and was getting into acting. But who would do for the Avatar of the lead lady?

"Let me!" Piper said.

"No way," the Witch said protectively. "You're thirteen. This role requires kissing and simulated romance."

"But nobody will really summon the stork on stage before an audience," Piper protested.

"The implication will nevertheless be there," the Witch said. "No child can play this role."

A cloud of smoke appeared. "What child is playing with her bread?"

"Playing with her what?" Piper asked innocently.

"Wafer, toast, loaf, pastry, bun—"

"Roll?"

"Whatever," the cloud agreed, crossly.

"That's role, not roll," the Witch said.

"That's what I said," the cloud said, forming into a dark lovely demoness.

Oh, no. "We are casting roles for the play, Metria," Cyrus said. "You wouldn't be interested." And knew as he said it that he shouldn't have.

"Oh? Try me."

So he explained. "We need a nice-looking girl who will be mute. All her lines will be spoken by a talking dragon, who is the real Lady. The actress will represent the Avatar, an image the Dragon Lady crafts to participate in a big dream."

"Demons and Dragons!" Metria said. "I love that dream!"

"Rehearsals will be long and boring. She'll just have to pretend to talk."

"And kiss," Piper said, pouting. "They won't let me. Something about the stork."

"I can kiss," Metria said. "I have no fear of storks. In fact I can freak out any man with just my panties." Her smoky dress evaporated to reveal bright red panties with flickering blue stars.

"No!" Cyrus cried, too late. He had already freaked. His gaze was locked on the wicked sight.

Then a hand covered his eyes, breaking the contact. "Nobody freaks you out but me," Rhythm murmured. Then she fired a glance that caused the panties to catch on fire. The demoness puffed back into smoke with an outraged bleep.

"Thank you, child," he said, reminding her to conceal her nature.

Meanwhile women were doing the same for the men, all of whom had similarly freaked out.

"No panties, Metria," Cyrus said. "She's a nice girl."

"Nice girls also have panties," the demoness said, re-forming. "Even if they're hidden." But her dress was back, intact. "So do I have the role?"

What could he do? "You can try it. If you foul up, or do anything mischievous, I'll boot you out of the play."

"I'd like to see you try." She posed, with her backside ready for booting. "You'd get your foot stuck in it."

That was surely no bluff. "I mean I would deny you the part. You must play it straight."

"Whoo, mee?" the demoness asked, assuming an owl shape before fading out.

"We may regret this," Rhythm muttered.

"I already regret it. But maybe it's better to have her cooperating than interfering."

The actors were given a few days to memorize their lines, while the workers set up the dream set, consisting of foamy clouds fashioned from extremely diffuse tuff. It was surprising how varied volcanic rock could be; some of it was mostly solidified gas.

Then came rehearsal. The Dragon Lady curled around the stage, concealed by clouds. In the center was a little pavilion, substituting for the closed mini-castle, because a real castle wasn't feasible and anyway, the audience needed to see the actors. Overall, it was a full-sized but quite simple setting.

John, played by Tuff, stood beside the stage. "I'll never get a girlfriend," he proclaimed in the manner necessary to reach the full audience. "I'm just an ordinary dull man with no special talent." After a pause, he resumed. "So I'm going to try one of these dream pills, so I can sleep and enter a communal dream where maybe things will be better."

John made a production of swallowing a pill. Then he lay down beside the stage, disappearing from view. But in a moment he reappeared on the stage: he was in the dream.

In due course the girl approached him: Marsha. She was innocently pretty, projecting niceness. That was surely a real effort for the actress, Demoness Metria, but she managed it. She herself didn't talk, which spared the audience her fouled-up vocabulary; instead she gestured theatrically, and it was the Dragon Lady's voice that spoke. Because the hidden dragon's head was close to the actress, it seemed as if the actress was talking.

In due course John and Marsha entered the pavilion and started kissing, certain they were unobserved, in the manner of dramatic presentation. They were obviously an ideal couple. But as the play progressed, and they became closer acquaintances, Marsha's evasions about her physical identity became evident. Then the dragon raised her head, and the covering clouds fell away to reveal her full body surrounding the stage. The audience could see that she was the one talking, not the Avatar. John, however, on stage, remained dramatically unaware.

This was only the first rehearsal, watched by stagehands and other members of the troupe. But even they gave a small gasp as they realized that John was falling in love with a dragon. Cyrus was thrilled; it was working.

Then came the revelation that John understood, and his problem accepting it. But when he finally was reconciled, and kissed Marsha knowing that she was really a dragon, there was a small moan of appreciation from the limited audience. They understood that this was truly forbidden love, and sympathized with the lovers.

When the play was done, the actors took their bows, and the Dragon Lady bowed her head. The troupe audience applauded; they really liked the play.

"I believe this is viable after all," Melete admitted grudgingly. "It's derivative of your own situation, but the audience doesn't know that. It's a nice love story."

"Thank you," Cyrus said, relieved. She was always his most severe critic. That was of course her nature.

"However," she continued inexorably, "it is axiomatic that a good rehearsal can lead to a disaster at the presentation. Anything that can go wrong, will."

"To be sure," he said, not believing it.

They arranged to put on the play at Crabapple's village again, because it was the closest, and the villagers had liked the first play. That morning Cyrus, Rhythm, and Tuff went to set up the stage, as they had done before.

Tuff conjured expansive foam-stone cloudbanks, including enough small stuff to cover the dragon for the first portion of the play. Rhythm would render the Dragon Lady temporarily invisible so that she could take her place without raising a commotion. Cyrus had found another spot spell: that was the explanation for the troupe, and they were not inclined to question it, thanks to another spot disinterest spell.

"The Lady's head will be here," Cyrus said. "We need to move one block aside."

"No sooner said than—" Tuff said, heaving up the block. Then he tripped over a lesser block, lost his balance, and fell. Rhythm screamed as the boulder block dropped down on his leg. As stone went, it was light, but as flesh and bone went, it was all too heavy. There was a sickening crunch.

Tuff lay there, writhing in pain. Rhythm ran to help him. "I can—" she said.

"You must not, Princess!" Melete cried. "That would show your power."

Rhythm paused in midrun, nodding. "Help ease your pain," she said. "I've got a spell I keep for emergencies." She kneeled beside the man and put her hands on his leg.

"Oh, thank you, Rhyme, you dear child," Tuff said. "That makes it bearable."

"I think the Witch has a full healing spell," Rhythm said.

"No she doesn't," he said. "I know her pretty well."

So he did. So they couldn't use that ruse. He would have to remain injured until they figured out a legitimate cover for Rhythm's magic.

"I could heal it," Piper said. "But it would take weeks for an injury that bad. My healing power is more for cuts and scrapes."

The villagers had seen the accident, and were sympathetic. They carried him to a cottage where he could rest. This, too, had to be accepted.

Tuff was out of the play.

"But he has the lead part!" Cyrus said. "No one else knows his lines."

"No one except you," Melete said. "You wrote them."

"That's not the same. I could garble them."

"You will have a prompter."

Rhythm smiled. "My little sister is very good at that."

So she was. Cyrus sighed. He would have to do it. "When are you going to say you told me so?" he asked Melete.

"Any time now," she said, smiling. "Poor Tuff."

"We'll have him healed for the next presentation," Rhythm said. "Even if we have to find a hidden cache of healing elixir."

"Piper will find it," Melete said. And that was of course the suitable cover for Rhythm's power.

That evening they came to do the play. Rhythm made a spot invisibility spell to hide the Dragon Lady, and a supplementary disinterest spell so that the other troupe members did not think to question this. When the dragon was in place, and suitably covered by foam blocks, the spell faded. She needed to be seen, when the time came.

Because Cyrus was acting, Crabapple took over the announcing. "Tonight's play is 'The Dream,'" she said. "And no, I am not the dream girl." There was laughter.

The play was a success. Cyrus was the only one needing prompting, and Kadence was teasingly happy to do it. But there was one problem Cyrus was powerless to eliminate.

It was time for John's first hug and kiss with the Marsha Avatar. Demoness Metria wrapped her arms around him, pulled him very close to her heaving bosom, and planted a kiss on him that made two of the more sensitive ladies in the audience swoon. "Nothing like realism," she whispered mischievously.

Rhythm's face, offstage, was studiedly neutral. That was a bad sign. The more the demoness smooched him, under cover of the actions prescribed by the play, the angrier the Sorceress got. Cyrus knew he was in trouble, and he couldn't do anything about it.

When the identity of Marsha was revealed, there was a gasp from the audience. But they soon came to accept it: a talking dragon who longed for romance. When they finally decided to have a dream family that never left the dream, there was applause: it was the right, romantic conclusion. When it was done, and the actors took their bows, some children even came up to pet the nice dragon. The Lady loved it; she was a dramatic success.

But Cyrus dreaded his next session alone with Rhythm. She might be a child, but she had strong passions and strong magic, as he knew so well. He was in a picklement.

12

RECRUITING

S he really worked you over," Rhythm said.

"It wasn't my choice." He doubted that would satisfy her, however. "I'm sorry."

"I'm not."

He was startled. "Not?"

"I got to see some techniques I can remember. Maybe I knew them when I'm adult, but I didn't as a child. She was trying to seduce you, right there on stage."

"That would have been awkward." It was an understatement. What the demoness had been doing in the name of acting pushed the limits of the Conspiracy. "It won't happen again. I'll get another actress."

"No, let her be. She's less mischief there than she would be if you provoked her by booting her. Woman Scorned, and all that, you know."

"I know," he agreed weakly. "But—"

"But we'll get Tuff healed, and then she'll be doing it to him, and it'll be the Witch's nose disjointed. That'll be fun."

"So—you're not mad?"

"Furious," she said. "But not with you."

He didn't trust this. "So it's all right, between us?"

"It's all right." But there was an expression on her face that would have been better on some other face. "But I may punish you a little."

"Maybe I deserve it."

"Oh?" Her glance was sharp. "Why?"

"Because she succeeded in arousing me. Some."

"Let's explore this." The spell appeared, and she bit it open. In half a moment she was lusciously adult.

Then she changed. The Demoness appeared in her place.

"Get out of here, Metria!" he said. "You've been more than enough trouble already."

She smiled. "I'm not Metria."

"That's what she would say."

"Metria would emulate me, to fool you into doing it with her. She wouldn't appear as herself."

"That's right," he agreed, surprised. "But why would you want to appear as her?"

"To punish you, as I said." She stepped into him, pressing close, exactly as Metria had. "Did she do this to you, up close?"

"Yes," he said.

"Did you like it?"

What could he say. "Yes. I hated liking it, but I did respond."

"And this?" She kissed him savagely.

"That, too," he agreed.

"And this?"

"Not that," he gasped. "Rhythm, please—"

But she refused to stop until she had seduced him in the form of Metria. Only when it was done did she revert to her own appearance. "So there," she said.

"But it means Metria could have done it," he protested.

"I don't think so. You knew it was me."

"Yes, but—"

"You would have kicked her out, if it wasn't on stage, and you knew it wasn't me."

"Yes, but—"

"So I'm satisfied. I'm sorry I punished you."

He shook his head. "You ought to be spanked." But he knew as he said it that he shouldn't have. She had a thing about spanking.

Sure enough, she turned over, exposing her plush bare bottom. "Spank me."

"Rhythm, stop it!"

"You brought it up. Now you have to do it."

The worst of it was that it was so illicitly tempting. "I shouldn't."

"Would you rather have me spank you?"

"No!" And that, in the odd logic of the situation, committed him. He wound up spanking her, not hard, and that led into another bout of storking. But he still felt horribly guilty.

Then he had a spot revelation. "You put that thought of spanking in my mind! That's why it kept occurring to me, when it never did before I met you."

"I'm a naughty girl," she agreed, unchastened. "I do deserve spanking."

"But the way you set it up, it's not punishment, it's something else."

"It sure is," she agreed languidly.

He saw that there was no point in arguing the case further. She was delightfully incorrigible.

She laughed, reading it in his mind, and he had to join her. He hoped she had worked out her ire. He had never been more conscious of both her female appeal and the fact she was a Sorceress. He knew she loved him, as he loved her, but she was dangerous when riled. It was a bad enough situation as it was, without jealous emotion interfering.

Curtis dictated that they needed at least three plays in their roster before they could tour. So Cyrus had to write one more. He knew it would be a struggle, even with Melete's help.

"Meanwhile it is time to arrange the itinerary," the Curse Friend continued. "You will be busy with the play and casting, so someone else will have to do it. Whom can we spare?"

"I won't know until I know the parts for the third play," Cyrus said.

"Which has not yet been written. How about sending Piper?"

"She's a child!" Cyrus protested.

"Hardly the only one. She can ride your mechanical donkey, who should be able to protect her, and take along her dust devil friend."

"But she really wants a role in a play."

The man shot him a glance that made him feel like an idiot. "Tell her two things: first, that this is a vitally important mission that only she can accomplish, and second, that when she returns she will have a suitable part."

"This is manipulative!"

"It is my business to get things organized and accomplished."

So it was that Cyrus sent thirteen-year-old Piper Nymph out with Don Donkey and Dusty Dust Devil to locate and enlist a number of villages to be sites for their tour. The girl was thrilled to be entrusted with such an important mission, and promised to do her very best. "Understand," he told her. "Don Donkey is a robot. He does not eat food, he burns wood."

"Oh, I know," Piper said. "We get along fine. He's given me rides."

"He also has a robotic device that enables me to see and hear what he sees and hears, when I tune in, and he can give me reports on what is happening around him. So if you get in trouble, he'll let me know immediately, and we'll arrange to help you."

"How can you help, when we're far apart?"

"I have a spell," Cyrus said. Actually he had Sorceress Rhythm, but couldn't say that.

"Okay."

"Here is a copy of the map that Don has in his data bank," Cyrus said. "If you lose it, don't worry; he can print out another. It shows all the villages within range, and all the enchanted paths you can use to travel safely, and all the safe camps for the nights. It also marks the worst dangers to avoid, like tangle trees."

Piper laughed. "You forget, I'm half tree. No tangler would try to eat me."

He had forgotten, which was embarrassing, because it was part of the reason he thought she would be able to travel safely through the forest. "And dragons."

That fazed her. "I'll avoid them." She took the map. Then she hesitated, blushing faintly.

"There's a problem?"

"Rumor has it that sometimes you kiss people. For luck, maybe."

Oh? Maybe the original actresses had been gossiping. Did all the girls in the troupe have ideas? "But you're—" Oops, he had first gotten in trouble by calling a girl a child. "Not supposed to know that," he finished.

"I don't," she agreed. "Maybe that's just as well."

"Just as well?"

"Because if I did know, I might do this." She stepped up and kissed him firmly on the mouth.

The kiss had impact, partly because of the surprise, partly because she was a pretty girl, and partly because he feared

Rhythm's jealous wrath, but he took it in stride. "Good thing you didn't do that," he agreed.

She smiled. "And I'll never say a word about Rhyme disappearing from her tent at night and nobody knows where she is or dares conjecture."

"Thank you," he said weakly. Now it was clear why the other actresses were leaving him alone. But did they think he was corrupting a child? "But you know she has that Decade spell, that can age a person ten years, for an hour."

"I know. I tried it, remember. Otherwise I might be jealous."

"I'm glad you understand."

Piper mounted Don, and rode away, with Dusty swirling along before, after, and to the sides, idly stirring up leaves. Cyrus watched them depart, and when they were out of sight, he tuned in on Don to watch some more. He saw the foliage beside the path passing toward the rear, and increasing detail when Don turned his head to peer at something.

"I shouldn't have teased him," Piper said to the donkey. "But I thought he should know the rumor."

"He'll survive it," Don said.

"There's something about Rhyme. It's as if she's an older woman pretending to be a child. We can't figure out why."

"I wouldn't know," the donkey said. Actually he did know, but Cyrus had sworn him to secrecy.

"So if she's not really a child, she can be with him all she wants. We just wish we knew why she doesn't act her real age. What is she hiding?"

"I wouldn't know," Don repeated. "I'm just an animal."

She reached forward to ruffle one of his ears. "A wonderful animal."

Don's circuits heated with pleasure. That surprised Cyrus. He hadn't realized that the robot had real feelings. Some of his components were more sophisticated than they seemed when collected as junk.

Cyrus tuned out, satisfied that the two were getting along well. He went about his business of writing the next play. It was a struggle, as always.

"You always make me work for it," he complained to Melete.

"The idea that writing is easy is an illusion," she replied. "Easy writing is apt to be junk. You have to bleed on the page, suffering for your art."

"Now she tells me," he muttered.

In due course Rhythm showed up. "Rumor has it that you disappear from your tent every night, and they wonder where you are," he told her. "They have a suspicion that it's with me, and that you are a grown woman masquerading as a child."

"Close enough," she agreed. "What else?"

"Piper kissed me."

"And you didn't slap her face?"

"I wouldn't do that!"

She evoked the Decade spell and bit into it. Then she assumed the form of Piper.

"Enough with your jealousy!" he snapped. "She's a child."

"And you won't touch a child," she said, reverting to her mature self.

"The only one I want to touch is you. I wish you'd stop being bleepchy."

Then they both paused as the bad word burned a trail through the air and scorched the material of the tent.

"That would have freaked me out, if I hadn't aged," she said. "It daunts me, even so."

"Well, I'm sorry. You're like a rose with thorns."

She surprised him by breaking down into tears. "I really am. I'm so sorry."

He stared, uncertain what to do. "Comfort her," Melete whispered.

He tried. He put his arms around her. "I love you as you are, Rhythm, thorns and all."

"This instant conversion—it makes me physically and mentally adult, but I lack experience," she said, the tears still flowing. "I can do the seductive part, but emotionally I remain somewhat childish. Temperamental. You don't deserve this."

"I don't think I deserve *you*," he countered. "You're a Princess and a Sorceress, while I'm only a cyborg."

"You're a Playwright," she said. "A good one. You've got fantastic imagination."

"Which I carry in my pocket," he said wryly. "Without my personal Muse, I am nothing."

"You are everything to me," she said. "Oh, Cyrus, I really do love you. I just don't quite know how to handle the unreasonable jealousy. I know better, but still it lurks."

"Maybe that simply takes time and experience."

"I hope so. I thought that all it took to be adult was stork summoning. It isn't, is it?"

"It isn't," he agreed.

"Hold me," she said.

He lay down on the bed with her and held her. Soon she was asleep. There had been no stork summoning, yet somehow he was more satisfied than if there had been.

The night was still young, and he was not sleepy himself. He loved holding Rhythm like this, but his mind wandered. How were Piper and Don doing?

He tuned in on them. There was a magic lantern illuminating the camp shelter, and Piper was sitting talking with a strange man while Don snoozed beside her. Of course Don never truly slept, he just powered down for a while. But not everyone knew that.

"What's going on?" Cyrus asked the donkey soundlessly. "She shouldn't be sharing a night with a man."

"He's harmless," Don replied, also soundlessly. "His name is John, as in your play, and his talent is creating a local Region of Madness."

"Harmless? That's dangerous!"

"No, because it is small, and temporary, and benign. Watch; there's another siege starting now."

Cyrus watched through the donkey's eyes. A cylindrical metal can flew into view with insect wings. "Hello," the can said. "I am your host for this canned show: Can Bee. I can do just about anything you can imagine."

"You can?" Piper asked, impressed.

"I am a can, yes," it agreed. "And here is my girlfriend, Can D." Another can appeared, filled with sweets. "And my clever brother, Can E." This can shone brightly. "And my cousin Can L." This one was long and thin, containing water with small ships sailing on it. "My military uncle, Can N." This can had thick sides. There was a bang, as it fired a Can N Ball that flew into the wall and exploded, making a hole. "And my incontinent child, Can OP." This little can had a cloth covering, and was filled with urine. "He likes nuts." The little can tilted, and poured out a stream of urine in which floated several corrugated nuts. "Real P Cans," Can Bee said proudly. "You are welcome to eat them."

"Thanks, but I have already eaten," Piper said, evidently trying to mask an expression of disgust.

One more can appeared. "Sorry I'm late," it said. "Had to carry water for the gang."

"And my other son, Can Teen," Can Bee concluded. "Now can we get out of here? Let's get canned." All the cans faded from view.

"Harmless madness," Cyrus agreed.

"Unfortunately it takes a few days for my effect to wear off," John said apologetically. "It is involuntary; I leave a trail of mild madness behind me. If you are going where I have been, you will encounter it."

"I am traveling that way," Piper said regretfully.

"Well, it's your sanity." John pulled a blanket over his

head and slept. Evidently once his local madness had manifested, it lay fallow for a few hours.

Piper shook her head. "Trees were never like this."

"Neither were machines," Don said.

Cyrus tuned them out. Piper and the donkey seemed to be all right.

Rhythm woke with a start. "Oh, I have reverted!"

She had, for more than an hour had passed. "Nothing happened," Cyrus reassured her.

"That's good. Or is it?"

"It's good," he said. "You were upset."

"That I remember. I was a bad girl, all nasty and jealous."

"You were a good girl, all contrite and gentle."

She gazed at him, knowing better. "You're so sweet."

He didn't argue.

Next day Piper and Don came to the state of Miss. Every resident was female, single, and fouled up. They had, it seemed, run afoul of Miss Adventure, who caused them to have the bad luck to get diverted into this territory. When they asked directions to get back on track, their informant turned out to be Miss Direct, who gave them the wrong information. The one they tried to explain their situation to turned out to be Miss Believe, who refused to accept anything they said. Then a new woman forgot anything they told her before she could help; she turned out to be Miss Remember. Miss Anthrope refused to talk to them at all. Miss Place couldn't find anything.

Finally Piper and Don both shut their eyes and forged on blindly, paying no attention to any of the women. That was the key; soon they blundered out of that region and were back on track.

Piper relaxed by pausing to drink a hot cup of dark liquid.

And burst into a fit of coughing. She had accidentally taken coughee.

As her vision cleared, she found herself in another section of madness. This one had a sign: PARODY PUNS. She quailed, but the only way out was straight through. Thus they passed by a bird with fancy tailfeathers: a P-Cock. Another creature insisted on peering at them from behind a bush: a P-Ping. Another was a nut in the shape of a P: a P-Nut.

"We've got to get out of here," she said, irritated.

"You're getting P-vish," Don said.

She kicked him in the flank.

Cyrus shook his head. He had not meant to send the poor girl into such a mess. But she was managing adequately.

Or was she? "Mischief coming up," Don warned him.

"How do you know?"

"I have excellent distance vision. There's a bad sign."

"A bad sign? Since when do you believe in signs?"

"Stay tuned."

So Cyrus did.

Finally they came to a village. "I'm hugely relieved," Piper said. "The gruesome puns have worn me out." Dusty had stayed largely clear, but he seemed tired too.

Only Don remained as ever. "Sticks and stones will break my bones, but puns only disgust me." He reconsidered. "Actually, I'll eat the sticks, and my bones are iron. So that part's not true."

Piper laughed. "It must be nice, being a robot," she remarked as they approached the village sign. "No emotions. You can't get upset."

"I'm learning emotions," Don said. "By studying you. I file each one in my data bank for future reference. For example, disgust is an emotion."

"Oh! I fear I'm a bad model. Too girlish."

"No, you have obvious emotions. That helps."

They paused at the sign. UNWELCOME.

"They can't mean that!" Piper said with spot despair.

Dusty compacted to his devil form and peered at the sign. "There's small print," he announced. "It says IF YOU ARE UN-INVITED AND UNEXPECTED, YOU ARE ALSO **UNWELCOME**."

"But it's too late to find another village!" Piper wailed emotionally.

"So we will stay here tonight," Don said. "There must be a hostel."

"We already know they're hostile."

"I meant a place to stay."

They walked into the village. From almost every window unfriendly glances speared out. The sign by the village hotel said HOSTILE, confirming Piper's understanding. That wasn't the same.

Don's keen eyes spotted a woman sitting on her porch. She looked nice. "Try her," Don suggested, stopping outside that house.

Piper dismounted and approached the woman. "Hello. I'm Piper. We need a place to stay tonight."

The woman smiled. "I am Shaunna. You are welcome to stay here. But you may not want to."

"Why not?"

"Because I am not popular in this town."

"The town of Unwelcome?"

"Yes. I tend to welcome people. That's contrary to the spirit of the village."

"We'll stay here," Piper said.

"As you wish." Shaunna got up and opened her door.

"What about Don Donkey?"

"I have a grass garden in my backyard."

"Any dry wood?" Don asked.

"You talk!" Shaunna said, startled.

"I'm a robot donkey. I have a robot talk box."

"A robot! So then you don't eat grass."

"I burn wood."

"I do have some dry sticks. You are welcome to them."

"I prefer to stay with Piper."

"You can come inside with her. And you also, of course, mister—"

"Dusty."

"Yes, I'm not surprised. It's a dusty landscape out there."

"Dusty Dust Devil," he clarified, briefly swirling into his other shape.

"Oh!" she said, laughing. "That's clever."

But the neighbors were scowling. "She should be burned out," one said grimly.

"Yeah?" Dusty demanded, starting to swirl again.

"Don't be concerned," Shaunna said quickly. "They won't do anything."

"They won't?" Don asked. "They look pretty determined mean to me."

"My talent is the Seldom Scene," she explained. "When I invoke it, as I do every night, they can't locate my house." She made a gesture. Nothing happened.

But the nasty neighbor seemed to lose his way. He looked all around except at the house. Then he departed, disgruntled.

"I don't understand," Piper said. "We are plainly visible."

"No. We can see out, but they can't see in. The scene is gone, for them. Even though they know the house is still here, they just can't find it. It keeps me safe when I sleep."

Shaunna served Piper and Dusty a nice meal, and brought in her dry sticks for Don. "I like this woman," Don remarked privately to Cyrus.

"You're really nice," Dusty said.

Shaunna laid her hand on his. "It's nice to be appreciated."

Cyrus, looking through the donkey's eyes, saw how thrilled the dust devil was with that touch.

"I have an idea," Piper said. "I am scouting for a play troupe.

We need villages to watch our plays. I don't think this one will be interested."

"It won't be," Shaunna agreed.

"But your talent—it could really help. You see, the stage and scenery needs to be set up, and the actors have to get their costumes on, without people looking. You could hide them, until playtime."

"It would really help," Dusty said eagerly.

"I suppose I could," Shaunna agreed.

"So why don't you come with us? I'll return to the troupe once I get enough villages lined up. Then you could travel with us. I know the others will like you."

"But you can't do that on your own," Shaunna protested. "Your director might not like it."

Piper smiled. "Let's find out. Don?"

"Bring her," Cyrus said immediately. "We can certainly use her talent."

"It's okay," Don said.

"But how could you know?" Shaunna asked.

"I am in contact," Don said.

"He is," Piper agreed. "You can come, if you want to."

"Oh, I want to! I don't like living here, but I had nowhere else to go."

"Then it's decided," Piper said.

In the morning they resumed their trek, and Shaunna came along. As they left the village, Don looked back. There was a column of smoke. The villagers were burning Shaunna's house, now that it wasn't protected by the spell.

"Bleep!" Cyrus swore, observing. "I wish I could burn the rest of them down."

Rhythm put a hand on his arm. "Don't be childishly vindictive. That's my prerogative."

He had to smile. "But it will be good to have Shaunna with us."

"You have a play to write," Melete reminded him.

So he did. Rhythm disappeared, and he sat down at his desk. The play was titled "The Riddle," and it concerned Good Magician Humfrey and his five and a half wives. He had most of his cast; all he lacked was a suitable story.

Well, there would have to be a problem only the Good Magician personally could handle. But for some reason he would not be able to handle it. Why? What could the Magician of Information not know? That was verging on a paradox.

Cyrus laid down his quill and got up. "I need to ponder," he said.

"All writers do," Melete agreed.

Vaguely annoyed by her lack of inspiration, he left her on the table and left the tent. Maybe a walk around the area would help.

A cloud of smoke formed before him. "We need to blurt," it said.

"To what, Metria?" he asked tiredly.

"Babble, blab, blather, ballyhoo, buzz—"

"Talk?"

"Whatever," she agreed crossly. "You didn't even let me get out of the Bs. There's a slew and a half more words to go, like chat, dither—"

"What's your concern, demoness?"

"That part is boring."

"You don't like kissing Tuff?"

"Oh, that was fun for one rehearsal. Making the Witch mad was fun for another. But now it's dull. I want to be on my way, stirring up mischief elsewhere."

"Metria, we need you for the next play. To play Humfrey's demon wife."

"Dara Demoness," she agreed. "I've known her for centuries. I can't rile her; she knows all my tricks."

Cyrus sighed. "If you are determined to leave us in the lurch, I can't prevent you. But I hope your half soul gives you half a guilty conscience."

"It will," she said. "Buy."

"That's 'bye,'" he said. But she had already dissipated.

Cyrus stopped himself from smiling, lest she still be watching. He could find another actress for the role of Avatar in "The Dream," and another for the role of Dara in "The Riddle." Meanwhile he was rid of Metria, who was really more trouble than she was worth. But it was essential that she not know that, lest she change her mind about leaving.

He still lacked a story, so tuned in on Don Donkey as he walked.

Piper was riding, with Shaunna riding behind her. Don was strong enough to carry any number of maidens who could fit on his back. It was a fine day, and the two were chatting idly as Dusty swirled ahead in his whirlwind form.

Then the dust devil returned and formed his devil shape. "There's something funny ahead, on a bypath."

"Funny hee-hee or funny odd?" Piper asked.

"Funny odd. It's a demoness crying."

"Now that *is* odd," Shaunna agreed.

"It's worse than odd," Don said. "It's weird. Demons have no souls, therefore no conscience. They don't get sad, they get mad."

"So we'd better investigate," Piper said.

The others didn't argue. They walked on, Dusty leading them to the bypath, which was plainly labeled BYPATH.

The demoness was there, still sobbing. They came up and stopped. The women dismounted.

"Pardon me," Piper said.

The demoness jumped, puffing into foul-smelling smoke. "Oh! You startled me," the smoke puffed. "I thought I was alone. I come here every day to cry for a few hours."

"You were alone," Piper said. "We came to ask why you are so sad. Maybe it's none of our business."

The smoke formed back into a woman. "You're a tree-nymph! What are you doing away from your tree?"

"I'm only half dryad," Piper explained. "I'm not bound to a tree, though maybe some day I'll adopt one. I am Piper Nymph. My mother married a mortal man."

"You're a half-breed!"

Piper bridled. "You have a problem with that?"

"No, not at all. I'm a half-breed myself. I am D Kay, a zombie demoness."

"Your parents—that must have been some romance!"

"More like a disaster in a love spring." Kay looked at Piper. "Do you have a problem deciding which heritage to honor? Human or dryad?"

"Yes, actually. So I'm out traveling, trying to make up my mind."

"That's my problem. My demon father doesn't want anything to do with me, and my zombie mother—well, her mind isn't very good, because of too much rot, and she sometimes forgets I exist."

"So you don't know who to associate with," Piper said. "I understand perfectly."

"Yes. So I try to fly with the demons, but they leave me behind. So I try to settle down in the local zombie village, but they don't much like demons. So I don't know where to go."

"Bring her here," Cyrus told Don. "We need a demoness actress."

"Ask her to join the troupe," Don murmured in turn to Piper. "They need her."

"I'm with a troupe," Piper said. "We put on plays. In fact I'm promised a small part in the next one. They need a demoness. Why don't you join?"

"I'm a *zombie* demoness," Kay reminded her. "I can't do all the things demons do, and I tend to stink. I don't think your troupe would want me, though I'd love to be an actress."

"We want her," Cyrus told Don. Don nodded his head to Piper.

"We can handle the smell," Piper said. "As long as you can remember your lines, and have the discipline to keep rehearsing."

Kay broke down in tears again.

"I didn't mean to make you sad," Piper said, alarmed.

"These are tears of happiness," Kay said. "You have given me reason to live. That's not something either demons or zombies find very often."

"Then come with us," Piper said.

"Gladly," Kay sobbed, smiling. Several of her teeth were bad, but she looked relatively nice.

Someone touched Cyrus's shoulder. It was Rhythm. "Is she joining?"

"You used magic!" he exclaimed. "To get a replacement for Metria."

"Well, I wanted someone who wouldn't try to seduce you in a play," she confessed.

"No zombie demoness will seduce me in a play," he promised. He looked around. "Are we alone? Is it safe to kiss you?"

"It is never safe to kiss me," she retorted, kissing him.

She was absolutely correct, unfortunately. Eventually there was bound to be a serious reckoning. But he loved her, regardless.

13

ITINERARY

Piper, Dusty, Don, Shaunna, and D Kay went on to the zombie village. "I never realized zombies had villages," Piper confided to the others.

"It's on the map," Don reminded her. "Zombies can do whatever they want."

Piper checked. "So it is. I guess I wasn't paying proper attention."

They went to the center of the village. All around them zombies were doing zombie things: smearing rot on vegetables, mold on walls, slime on old bread, and scum on water. Soaking new clothing in acid mud to make it deteriorate until a respectable zombie could wear it. Coating newly harvested shoes from a shoe tree with stale sweat to break them in.

"Actually, zombies are not bad folk," Kay said wistfully. "They're always willing to lend a hand, they never give anyone any lip, but they do go to pieces on you."

Just so. "Hello," Piper called. "I represent a troupe that puts on plays. Would you like to have us stop and do a play here?"

An old zombie man shambled up. "Any zombie actorrz?" he asked, spitting out a decayed tooth.

"Yes. One."

"Okaay." He returned to his business of scraping muck onto his porch.

"One presentation site signed up," Don said.

For some reason they did not dawdle at Zombie Village. They walked on out and headed for the next village on the map. This was a normal human one, they hoped.

It was. But there was a hitch. "Is this a curse fiend play troupe?" the Village Elder asked.

"Not exactly," Piper confessed. "It's a new amateur group, produced by a curse friend, yet to prove itself."

"Curse what?"

"Curse friend. They're not really fiends."

He nodded. "So you really do have contact with them."

"Yes." Piper wasn't sure whether this was good or bad, for this village.

"We'll try it, not expecting much."

Don marked another presentation site.

The next was a robot village, Rolando. Cyrus was surprised as he looked through Don's eyes: all the robots were humanoid, about the size of his father Roland, and looking similar. How far did the resemblance go?

This time Don did the talking. "You folk look like a robot I know," he said. "His name is Roland."

"We know of Roland," they said in chorus. "Our programs derived from his. We are all barbarians, and we all love anyone named Hannah."

Cyrus shook his head. That program should have been modified. He would have to talk to his father when he returned.

Don plowed gamely on. "Do you like romance?"

"We are all very romantic," they agreed.

"Some of our plays have romances."

"We'll watch them!" they chorused.

Don chalked up another site.

There followed several more human villages, all of which were interested. Then they came to a village of gnomes. Would they have any interest in human plays?

The map said this was GNOBODY, home of the Gnobody Gnomes. They were in Don's data bank, listed as largely unknown for some reason. They were a grumpy sort, seldom associating with humans, so this was a poor prospect. But they had to ask anyway.

"May I talk to your leader?" Piper inquired.

"We have no leader," a lowly gnome replied. He was only about half her height.

"Then may I talk to you? I am Piper Nymph."

The little man shrugged. "If you insist. I am Gnonentity Gnome. What do you want?"

"I represent a touring troupe. We are putting on plays, and would like to have places to present them. Would you be interested?"

"Why would anyone ever want to put on a play *here*? We are strictly a gnothing village of gno significance whatever."

"We just would like to have appreciative audiences."

"The only thing we appreciate is gnotoriety, because we have gnone."

That gave Piper an idea. "Don, ask Cyrus: does he have an actor to play the male lead in his next play? The one about Magician Humfrey?"

"A gnome!" Cyrus exclaimed. "He would be perfect!" Because Magician Humfrey was sort of like a gnome, being small and grumpy.

"Go for it," Don told her.

"Gnonentity, how would your villagers like it if one of you played a lead role in a play?"

Now the other gnomes gathered around them. "But that

would be significant," Gnonentity said. "Gno one would ever grant us that."

"We would," Piper said. "We need an actor to play the Good Magician Humfrey."

The gnomes looked at each other, awed. "Who among us?" Gnonentity asked.

"You, if you want. Come with us, and when we loop back to our troupe, you will be given the part and have to learn the lines. We'll put on a play here, in due course, so all of you can see it's true."

They were amazed, and hardly believing, but decided to find out. And so Gnonentity Gnome joined the group.

"That girl is good," Cyrus said. "Not only is she lining up villages, she's recruiting actors we need."

"Just don't get hung up on her," Rhythm said.

"Rhythm—"

"I was joking. Some. You're right: she's a good girl."

Cyrus accepted that. But privately he was bothered. Rhythm was getting jealous without reason.

"I know it," she said. "I'm trying to do better. Honest I am."

Bleep that mind reading!

"Bleep," she echoed.

Piper completed her circuit of villages, signing up halfway between a fair number and a goodly number for play sites. Her party rejoined the troupe in good order.

But there was one thing that concerned her. "Cyrus, I avoided a section, though it was on the map," she said. "Did I do the right thing?"

This surprised him. Maybe he hadn't been watching closely enough. "What did you avoid?"

"The section where the Villages became Cities."

"They did that?"

"Yes. Here." She pointed to a region on the map.

"Necess Village?"

"On the map," she said. "But the sign says Necess City. The same for the Villages of Adver, Pompos, Elasti and Verbo. They all claim to be cities now, though they still look like villages. That made me nervous for some reason, and I avoided them."

"That is curious," he agreed. "You did right to be cautious. I'll investigate."

"That's good," she said, evidently relieved. "Now you must meet the people I collected for parts. Don said you said it was all right."

"By all means," he agreed. "You did an excellent job, Piper."

She blushed. Girls were good at that. "Thank you."

They went outside where the others waited. "Hello," Cyrus said. "I am Cyrus Cyborg, the Playwright."

"Gnonentity Gnome," the gnome said gruffly.

"Yes. You will play the part of the Good Magician. You seem to be perfect for that role."

The little man did what seemed to be a rare thing for his kind: he smiled. Perhaps he had feared that the part would not actually be granted.

"D Kay," the zombie demoness said.

"And you will be Dara Demoness, the Good Magician's first wife."

She, too, relaxed, reassured.

"And I am Shaunna," the third new person said.

"We'll rehearse with the Seldom Scene," Cyrus said. "It promises to be really useful to protect our privacy in different villages. Thank you for joining us."

"You are more than welcome."

Cyrus turned to Piper. "And you will play MareAnn, Humfrey's half-wife, the one who likes horses."

Piper fainted.

Fortunately Cyrus's cyborg reflexes enabled him to catch

her before she fell. Had she thought he would not keep his promise?

"She's a good girl," Gnonentity said grudgingly.

"She deserves a good role," Kay agreed.

After a moment and a bit Piper revived. "Thank you," she said faintly.

He set her back on her feet. "Go and get a good night's rest. Tomorrow we start rehearsals."

Dazed, she departed.

Curtis appeared. "I will see to the accommodations for the new actors," he said.

When Cyrus was alone in his tent, he murmured one word. "Rhythm."

She appeared. "Already?" She brought out the Decade spell.

"Not yet. There's something else. Piper discovered that several villages have become cities, at least by their signs. That made her nervous, and she avoided them. I think she was right to be cautious. Can you check this?"

"Be right back," she agreed. She vanished.

Cyrus focused on the play. He had finally gotten it written, with Melete's help and prodding, and had distributed copies to the actors. The three newest ones would have some catching up to do, but the others would help them, and fluffs didn't matter so much in early rehearsals. He had done his best, and Melete approved of it, but he remained nervous about its reception. It was always thus, when a play was fresh.

"It's your artistic temperament," Melete said. "Perfectly normal."

Rhythm returned. "This is bad," she said grimly.

"Name changes are bad?"

"Those villages are now in territory controlled by Ragna Roc. He changed their names, maybe so he could keep track of his land conquests."

"Ragna Roc," he repeated. "Has he caught on to us?"

"I don't think so. He's just marking his boundaries. I didn't look closely; I wanted to be sure nobody saw me. But it shows what we're up against."

"How did he take over the villages? Were there battles? I wasn't aware of anything like that."

"No signs of violence," she said. "Maybe the villagers just decided they liked him better."

Cyrus snorted. "Do you believe that?"

"No."

"It certainly shows the importance of our mission."

"Yes."

"It makes it more immediate. Had Piper not been alert, we could have scheduled a presentation there. We might have fallen right into the power of the enemy."

"We might," she agreed. "Yet the people did not seem downtrodden. There's something odd about this. I should check more closely."

"Don't go back there!"

"Cyrus, I have to," she said seriously. "I promise I'll be careful."

He sighed. "You're growing up. Acting with maturity. I think I preferred you carefree."

"I think that's the nicest thing you've said to me." She kissed him on the ear and vanished.

Which was the problem with loving a Sorceress.

He focused on last-moment adjustments to the play. Somehow there always seemed to be more tinkering to do.

Rhythm returned an hour later. "The people aren't downtrodden," she reported. "They're being treated all right. But they are nervous. It seems that Ragna Roc's minions identified all villagers who might oppose him, and he deleted them."

"Deleted?"

"Rendered them into illusion. Ghosts, really. There are whole houses of illusion. I mean, the house and everyone in it. You can see them, but you can't touch them; they aren't really there. They are plainly horrified."

"The ghosts?"

"The ghosts. They know they are illusion, and they can't stand it, but they can't do anything about it. I think Ragna leaves them there as object lessons to the other villagers. If they don't behave, that will be their fate. So of course they behave. They are loyal to the big bird."

"This is awful!"

"Yes it is. I'm horrified myself. Oh, Cyrus, we have to stop this!"

"That's our mission," he agreed.

Then she invoked the Decade spell, and let herself cry. He held her and comforted her as well as he could. Their relationship seemed to be entering a new stage, where other emotions were becoming important, not just love or passion. That was probably good.

Next day was the first rehearsal. "We will practice with the Seldom Scene," he said. "This will give us privacy, because no one will see us until it abates. We don't need it here, but will find it useful when we tour, so we want to be sure we have it straight. You won't notice any difference, but this whole scene will be undetectable to outsiders."

The Witch nodded. "That will help, because we won't always be able to set up with complete privacy."

"Now with three new members of the cast, we'll have to allow reading from the scripts. But I will expect all of you to know your parts in a few days. The prompter will help you throughout. Now take your places." They did, and the scene faded out as Shaunna invoked her magic. "Announcer, I am your audience, this time. Proceed."

Crabapple stepped up to face him, her back to the unseen stage. Her arms were covered; they were not needed for this. She looked like an ordinary, attractive woman, with a talent for speaking clearly.

"It is our pleasure to present the play 'The Riddle,'" she said in her Announcing voice. "The opening scene is in the Good Magician's Castle, where Hell is breaking loose, figuratively." She smiled and stepped out of the way.

Now the scene appeared, as Shaunna turned off her talent. The gnomelike Magician Humfrey hobbled onstage, wearing one sock. "Where's the other sock?" he demanded grumpily. "I can't bury myself in my famous Book of Answers with a sock missing!"

A woman hurried up, carrying a long sock. She was Dusti, with a Mundanian hat concealing her little horns. "Here it is, husband dear." She handed it to him.

"About time, Sofia Socksorter," he grumped, struggling to put it on. He had big feet, which made the process awkward.

"You'll never get it on that way," another woman said. This was Xina, her modest garb masking her attributes. It had been a struggle to get the prettier actresses to understand that there were times when beauty was not the point. "Sit down and put your foot up."

"Stop ordering me around, Maiden Taiwan," he grumped as she kneeled to slide the sock over his foot.

"Dinner is served," a third woman said. She was Acro Nymph, gorgeously costumed and quite pretty.

"Already?" Humfrey grumped. Then he did half a double take. "Rose of Roogna—what are you doing here?"

"Don't you remember, dear? I'm your wife."

"I've got five and a half wives. You take monthly turns. Sofia and Taiwan are already here." He did the other half of the take. "Both? Who is the Designated Wife of the Month?"

"I am," the Witch said. She was heavily veiled, but shapely below.

He peered over his spectacles at her. "You are, Gorgon? Then what are these others doing here? There's supposed to be only one wife at a time."

"That's the problem," D Kay said. "Something has gone desperately wrong."

"*What* has gone wrong, Dara Demoness?" he demanded even more grumpily.

"Everything," Kay said grimly. She was very good at looking grim. Her costume and makeup concealed the fact that she was a zombie, but an impression leaked through.

Piper read from her script. "All of Xanth is up in a heaval."

"That's a different story, MareAnn. I can't be bothered with Xanth when my five and a half wives don't know their places. Who is responsible for this?"

"We don't know," the Gorgon said. "That's part of the problem."

Humfrey sighed grumpily. "Then I will just have to research it and find out." He tramped offstage.

Xina, as the Maiden Taiwan, shook her head. "He's not going to find it in his Book of Answers. It's a recent phenomenon."

"So what are we going to do?" the Witch (Gorgon) asked. "We'll never get along with all of us here at once. He's going to get five and a half times as grumpy as usual."

"We shall just have to solve the problem ourselves," Rose (Acro Nymph) said.

"And exactly how do we do that?" Sofia (Dusti) demanded. "We're not great at solving magical riddles. We're *wives*."

"We can get outside and survey the situation," Rose said. "Maybe we'll be able to make some sense of it."

A glance circled around the group. Kay (Dara) looked up from her script and nodded. "At least it will get us out of the castle for a while."

"We'd better tell Humfrey," MareAnn (Piper) said.

"Why?" the Gorgon demanded. "He'll only grump at us."

Now understanding laughter circulated. "We're better off on our own," Dara agreed.

The scene ended. "That's good," Cyrus said. "Next time we'll work on more feeling. You are all rivals for the Good Magician's attention, after all; you will tend to be waspish to each other. That's one reason you have to take monthly turns with him."

"We'll make it crackle," the Witch said with relish. "I love a mean-spirited role."

"MareAnn's not mean-spirited," Piper protested. "She's a nice person."

"That's why she's only half a wife," the Witch said. "Full wives are faceted."

"I like this part," Gnonentity said. "Great minds are grumpy."

"We could ruin that mood," Dusti said mischievously.

"I'd like to see you try."

Dusti glanced around. "He just invited me, didn't he?"

"He did," the Witch agreed. "Go ahead and ungrump him."

"It was a figure of speech." Gnonentity said, getting nervous.

Dusti dissolved into a whirl of dust. It swirled around the gnome. In a moment the woman re-formed, her arms wrapped around him. She kissed him on the nose. "Are you still grumpy?"

"Of course," he said.

She kissed him on the cheek. "How about now?"

"Yes. I—"

She kissed him on the mouth. Little hearts swirled around his head. "Now?" she inquired with half a hint of malice.

He tried to rally. "You shouldn't be making such a scene."

"But I'm your *wife,* Magician. Your most useful, sock-sorting one. It's part of the play." She kissed him again. More hearts swirled.

Finally he kissed her back. "You win, minx."

"Second scene is outside," Cyrus said before the other

mischievous women could get into the act. They had a new challenge, and soon enough one or more of them would be tempting the gnome in bed. "While still on stage, of course. Take a break while we get the props changed."

The rehearsal continued, as the women discovered the weird changes occurring in the Xanth of the play. Centaurs were having offspring that were either human or equine, not both. Harpies had straight bird and straight human children. Chimeras had triplets: lion, goat, snake. On the other hand, humans were having crossbreed children, such as one with the body of a human and the head of a fish: a maidmer. Chaos was developing.

Soon assorted magical creatures were coming to the Good Magician for Answers about this chaos. He could no longer ignore the crisis. He had to go out and find the origin of the problem. The five and a half wives insisted on going with him.

After seeing many weird things, they concluded that the problem was with the Demon Xanth, the source of all the magic of Xanth. That magic was just from the leakage from his body, a trace amount of his power. Decades before, when the Demon had departed on business of his own, most of the magic had dissipated, leading to the awful Time of No Magic. Later the Demon, on a Demon bet, had assumed the form of Nimby, a donkey-headed dragon, and taken up with a mortal girl, Chlorine. But that was another mere personification, only a tiny fragment of the larger Demon. Now the magic remained, but was imperfect.

"The Demon is distracted by something," the Good Magician pronounced. "I must go and undistract him."

"And what do we do while you're gone?" the Gorgon demanded. "Pull each other's hair out?"

Humfrey glanced at her. Her hair consisted of little writhing snakes framing her veil. "That might not be a bad idea."

For a moment her hand went to her veil, as if to lift it away and stone him with her gaze. Then she thought of a better way to get back at him. "We shouldn't stay home quarreling. We should go with you, to help you."

"Hear hear!" Rose agreed. "We hate being cooped up in the castle with no one to smooch except the moat monster." There was a murmur of agreement among the Wives; it seemed that the reference was not entirely fanciful.

"Absolutely not!" Humfrey said grumpily, but perhaps not quite as grumpily as in the first scene. For some reason he seemed to have lost his edge. Perhaps not all of the smooching had been imposed on the moat monster.

"If you go alone, who will tend your socks?" Sofia demanded. He had after all married her when his socks got out of hand, as it were.

That made him pause, visibly. Obviously he was incompetent to tend them himself.

"And who will keep you properly dressed?" Rose asked. She was the one who normally handled that, being very costume conscious.

"And who will protect you from stray monsters?" the Gorgon asked, touching her veil again. Normally she stoned any creature who threatened him.

"And who will find you a horse to ride?" MareAnn asked. Her talent had been to summon equines, until she lost her innocence in Hell, but she still got along well with them.

"And who will pop ahead to spy out the route for you?" Dara asked. As a demoness she was good at that.

"And who will make your bed?" the Maiden Taiwan asked. She was excellent at maid services.

Humfrey realized that he needed them after all. "Then come along if you insist," he said grumpily.

They all clustered around him, bestowing kisses wherever they could reach, mainly the top of his head.

"Enough, you disreputable wenches," he protested. He seemed to have almost run out of grumpiness at the moment.

That completed a scene. "Very good," Cyrus said. "Take a break while we get Don costumed for the next scene. Humfrey will ride, the Wives will walk, of course."

"Of course," the Wives chorused, amused.

The rehearsals worked out well, and in due course they were ready to take the troupe on tour. The new actors fit right in, and Gnonentity Gnome had turned out to be ideal for the role. One might possibly have suspected that the grumpy gnome almost liked being the constant center of attention by six appealing women, even if only onstage.

They skipped Shaunna's unfriendly village and went on to Zombie, where Kay had not quite fit in. They used the Seldom Scene to set up, then presented it.

It started well. Then Kay, as Dara Demoness, was so nervous she forgot her opening line.

"That's the problem," Kadence said, as prompter.

"It's a problem all right," Kay muttered under her breath. "I forgot my line." Then she did a double take. "Oh—that *is* my line." She faced Magician Humfrey. "That's the problem."

"*What* has gone wrong, Dara Demoness?" Humfrey demanded grumpily.

She opened her mouth—and forgot again.

"Everything," Kadence said.

"Everything," she echoed gratefully.

Then it was Piper's turn, as MareAnn, and Kay was able to relax. Not only had the audience not realized that she forgot her lines, they had not caught on to her identity. Her costume and makeup were so thorough, thanks to Guise's magic and the Witch's expertise with paints, that she did not look at all like herself.

Of course zombies were not noted for the quality of their observation, so maybe it wouldn't have mattered. They did seem to like the play, and applauded with much sloughing off of flesh.

Only "The Riddle" was presented here, because Cyrus

had wanted to see how Kay and the other new actors did before a noncritical audience. They stayed three nights, and presented it three times, and the zombies liked it better each time as they picked up more of its nuances. That also enabled the actors to gain experience and competence.

Next on the itinerary was the robot village. Here they presented all three plays, "The Curse," "The Dream," and "The Riddle." The robots had trouble seeing the magic auras, but related well to Crabapple's pincers, which resembled mechanical extremities. They liked the romantic theme, as wild romance was part of their programming. They had trouble understanding the second play, because robots didn't dream. But the intellectual conclusion of the third play thrilled them, as they were good at cold logic. They also appreciated the fact that the Good Magician rode a robot donkey; for this audience Cyrus had elected not to conceal Don's nature.

Then they went to Gnobody Village. All three plays were well received, because the gnomes liked the fact that a woman with pincers for hands, a sure nonentity, finally won acceptance and love. They also liked the way a dragon found true love with a man; if a dragon could do it, maybe so could a gnome.

But the major event was the third play. They were rapt the moment Gnonentity came onstage as Good Magician Humfrey. They knew him, of course, and now they could plainly see the importance of his role. When Humfrey solved the Demon Xanth's problem they applauded wildly. Indeed, he had become famous!

A gnomide approached him after the show. Gnomides tended to be quite petite and pretty, and this one was typical. "I did not properly appreciate you, Gnonentity, before," she said dulcetly. "But now that you are famous—"

"I regret my interest is elsewhere, Gneiss," he said.

The others were amazed. He was turning down what promised to be a very nice liaison?

"Oh?" she said, surprised. "May I inquire who?"

He fidgeted. "I'm not sure I should say. It's a private matter."

"I think I have the right to know who has preempted me," Gneiss said. It was evident that she was not accustomed to being turned down.

"I can't say," he repeated.

Then Lady Bug flew to him. She landed and folded her wings. "It is time to become open," she said. "I am the one." She kissed Gnonentity on the cheek.

Several jaws dropped among the cast. No one had known of this. Lady Bug had joined the troupe, hoping to be an actress. She had not yet acquired a role, but was a general-purpose substitute, ready to fill in where needed. Petite and beautiful, she was utterly unlike the gnome. Yet it seemed that opposites had attracted.

"Thank you," Gneiss said stonily, and retreated.

When the troupe was alone, the actresses clustered around them. "Why didn't you tell us?" the Witch demanded.

"We weren't sure it would work out," Lady Bug said. "But after seeing how well the Dragon Lady did in her play, it seemed more likely." This time she kissed Gnonentity on the mouth, and winged hearts radiated out from them. There was no doubt of their mutual devotion.

"Well, we softened him up for her," Dusti said, a bit grumpily.

Cyrus wondered how they would react to the truth about him and Rhythm.

They went on from village to village on the itinerary, and were generally well received. The actors became sharper with each repetition, and the plays were quite effective.

But the most critical presentation was the last: at the residence of the Curse Friends. This made even Curtis nervous. "My whole future career as a Producer rests on our performance there," he said.

Cyrus knew it was true. The Curse Friends knew more about putting on plays than anyone else in Xanth. Curtis himself had been invaluable, keeping the troupe organized. Without his supervision they would have messed it up badly. But what was very good for amateurs might be weak for the professionals.

Soon enough they found themselves in the Curse Friends' fabulous palace under the water of Lake Ogre-Chobee. They set up in a huge theater. Could there possibly be an audience to fill this place?

"Oh, yes," Rhythm assured him privately. "I have seen some of their plays, when I was a Princess. They take them very seriously."

"How do we compare?"

"We're not in their league," she said. "But they know that Curtis is working with amateurs, and will make allowances. We'll just have to do our best, and hope for the best."

"Actually, it is beside the point," he said. "It is a different audience we are trying for."

"Which has shown no interest so far," she said. "That worries me."

"The whole mission worries me," he said.

She looked around. "Do we dare do anything here? The Curse Friends are extremely observant."

"We don't," he agreed. "You must not do any Sorceress magic here."

"Yes." He knew she was as regretful as he was.

Cyrus warned the troupe: "This is apt to be a larger but extremely critical audience. Do not expect much applause. Just do your best."

"Is this the end?" the Witch asked. "No more performances after this?"

Cyrus smiled reassuringly. "This is the conclusion of the initial tour. If we receive the Curse Friends' stamp of approval, that should enhance our reputation, and more villages will ask for us. We will continue as long as it seems worthwhile." He couldn't say that what they were trying for was a far more dangerous audience.

"That's a relief," Crabapple said. "This troupe has become my home. I don't ever want to give it up."

There was a general murmur of agreement.

"You're a good group," Cyrus said, touched. "I like being with you too. But circumstances could complicate."

They adjourned for what they hoped would be a good night's rest. In the morning they would put on all three plays, one after the other, for the same critical audience.

Cyrus slept alone, except for Melete. "Will I ever lose you?" he asked.

"Not as long as you want me."

That was reassuring. "And what about Rhythm?"

"Cyrus, you know that affair can have no good conclusion."

He sighed. He did know, but refused to admit it.

Morning seemed to come instantly. Abruptly they were in it. The actors, perhaps enhanced by nervousness, did beautifully. They were the best three performances they had done, with very little Prompting required. But applause was restrained; they were not much impressing this knowledgeable audience. Cyrus was glad he had warned the troupe. Privately he was disappointed, however.

As the curtain closed on the last play, an official came forward. "This will do," he said to Curtis.

Curtis fell back into a chair, little stars and planets whirling around his head. He had passed!

The official turned to Cyrus. "The material is adequate, but has potential. We would like to adapt it for our own purposes, making our own productions with our own actors. Is this satisfactory?"

They wanted to steal his plays? Cyrus opened his mouth.

"Accept," Curtis whispered. "It is a sign of honor. We seldom adapt from outside sources."

Cyrus stifled his initial reaction, trusting Curtis's judgment. "This is satisfactory," he said. "As long as we can continue with our own tour."

"Of course." The official walked away.

"Curtis is right," Rhythm murmured. "They go outside their own base maybe once in a generation. We have scored."

Now Cyrus checked his mental data bank, and found that it was true. The troupe had done very well.

But was it well enough for the real challenge?

14

ANDROMEDA

Next morning as they were preparing to depart, Curtis approached Cyrus. "This concludes my association with your troupe," he said. "It has been a pleasure."

"You're leaving us?" Cyrus said. "Somehow I hadn't realized."

"This was my qualifying examination," Curtis reminded him. "I passed, and now can achieve my life's ambition of producing my own plays."

"But we need you! You have been invaluable, with your organizational expertise. It would be difficult to continue without you."

"I am sure you can manage. You will train in another producer. Time and experience will bring expertise."

Cyrus sorted through his memory bank. "But you spent twenty years mastering your craft. We can't afford that much time."

"Why not? A thing worth doing is worth doing well."

Cyrus did a quick calculation. Could he afford to tell the truth about the mission? This man had proved to be competent, patient, and reliable. He could surely be trusted. "Because this is more than an amateur troupe. There is a vital mission."

The curse friend lifted an elegant eyebrow. "Oh?"

"I must ask you to keep a confidence."

"Granted."

"Do you know of Ragna Roc?"

Curtis shook his head. "Oh, my. If you plan to associate with that ill bird, we must part company immediately."

"My mission is to destroy him."

"You have my complete attention."

"I need to put on plays that will interest the bird enough to summon my troupe for a presentation. In that way we can get close enough to do what we have to."

"That bird is Magician caliber, and strengthening. You will have to have similar power, to have any chance at all."

"We do."

"Who?"

"Princess Rhythm."

"She's a child."

"I heard that," Rhythm said, appearing.

"Rhyme! You are she?"

"I am the one he needs to smuggle in. Then my sisters will join me to tackle the Roc."

"That is why you have been associating with Cyrus?"

"Yes."

"Rumor had it that—never mind."

"When I associate, as you put it, I am like this." She invoked the Decade spell and stood in her full adult splendor.

"Oh, my," Curtis repeated. "I envy you, Cyrus."

"This is why we need you," Cyrus said. "We must be the best that we can be, to attract the attention of the Roc without arousing his suspicion."

"I appreciate that," the man said, wavering. "Yet—"

"You said you envied Cyrus," Rhythm said. "But you have

evinced no interest in the actresses. Dusti, Acro—they would have been glad to tease you unmercifully, had you ever glanced their way."

"They are not my interest."

"So you do have an interest," Cyrus said, pouncing.

"Yes. But she never gave any indication."

"Crabapple!" Rhythm said, reading his mind. "I'll fetch her."

"Don't!" Curtis said. But she was already gone.

"She is a very nice and beautiful person," Cyrus said. "But any semblance of condescension or pity would alienate her. She is completely realistic about her condition."

"She is," Curtis agreed. "I appreciate realism."

Rhythm reappeared with Crabapple, who looked amazed. "I had no idea!"

"I have been incognito," Rhythm said. "But this is important. Please listen." She turned to Curtis. "Make your case."

The curse friend looked extremely uncomfortable, but made the best of it. "I do not wish to embarrass or offend you, Crabapple. I find myself attracted to you. These folk wish to persuade me to remain with the troupe instead of departing it at this point. If you should have any potential interest—" He shrugged.

"Why should you have any such interest in me?" Crabapple asked evenly.

"Apart from your beauty and character?"

She almost smiled. "Apart from those."

"I think you would not laugh when I removed my boots."

"I don't think I understand."

Curtis sat down and pulled off a boot. Beneath it was a club foot. It was a solid club, capable of doing some damage if swung at anyone. But as a foot it was ludicrous. Obviously he needed the boots to preserve his balance and mobility, not to mention his pride.

"Oh, Curtis, I didn't know!" Crabapple said.

"It has been my secret." He removed the other boot to expose a matching club.

It was almost possible to see the wheels turning in her head. "You understand about—limbs, Curtis."

"Oh, yes!"

"I never liked being patronized. But your affinity is legitimate."

He looked at her. "Is there then a prospect for your interest?"

"There is a prospect," she agreed. "Not a guarantee."

"That will suffice." Curtis turned to Cyrus. "I will remain with the troupe for the duration."

"I would appreciate a pretext to associate with you," Crabapple said. "Without generating unkind rumors."

"We're going to need to train in a new producer," Cyrus said.

"That intrigues me," she said. "If—"

"I should be glad to share my expertise," Curtis said.

Cyrus exchanged a glance with Rhythm. It seemed they had a deal.

Once they were clear of the Curse Friend's residence, Cyrus called the troupe together for a briefing. "We have completed our tour successfully," he said. "Now I have in mind a more challenging tour. Any of you who do not wish to participate will be free to leave."

"We know the plays," the Witch said. "What's so challenging?"

"I want to tour territory controlled by Ragna Roc."

"But he might delete us!"

"For what reason? We're entertainers."

Several of the troupe members had been at the Good Magician's Castle. They understood that Cyrus had some sort of special mission. They were nervous, but did not protest.

"It is a potential audience," Curtis said. "The curse friends are barred from touring there."

"The Roc's people may be hungry for entertainment," the Witch said.

"Who knows," Curtis said. "The big bird might even take notice, and summon us for a demand performance." Now that he knew the nature of their mission, he was helping.

The other troupe members let it be, though obviously not particularly keen on the notion. No one decided to leave.

The troupe traveled. Crabapple developed an interest in producing, and Curtis graciously started showing her how. The Witch observed that, and nodded; she smelled an interesting new relationship developing.

The closest Roc-controlled village was Adver City. They reached it in two days. They camped at the edge of Roc territory, and Cyrus prepared to go in alone to make arrangements, if the residents were amenable. The other members of the troupe watched, not comfortable about it.

"You're going alone?" Rhythm asked. "Suppose you get deleted?"

"That's why I prefer to go alone," he said. "If I don't return, the visit is canceled."

"Why don't you go with him, Rhyme?" Curtis asked. "Then you can return to let us know if he gets in trouble."

"Well, I will."

Again, the other troupe members let it be. They knew there was a relationship, even if they didn't know its full nature.

They walked to the village. "I've got a bad feeling about this," Rhythm said. "I'm slightly precognitive, when I try to be."

"Trouble?"

"Not exactly. I just know I won't like it."

That made Cyrus nervous. "I can call this off."

"No, it's necessary. I feel that too."

That did not make him feel easier.

The village looked normal. There were normal-seeming people going about normal business. But there was a certain hush about it. For one thing, the villagers did not seem friendly. It was as if they were antagonistic to strangers.

They came to the center house, normally the residence of the village elder. "Hello!" Cyrus called. "May we talk?"

The door opened. A woman emerged. Both Cyrus and Rhythm took stock, impressed. She was tall and graceful, with huge emerald green eyes, blond hair braided to her knees, and a small brown crown. She wore a closely fitted dress that flowed out at the bottom, in two layers: earthy brown under, lighter grass green outer. She had light green wings, veined with brown.

"Hello, visitors," she said. "I am Andromeda, Queen of the Dragonflies, and appointed elder for Adver City. Who may you be?"

"Cyrus Cyborg, Playwright. This is Rhyme, a member of my troupe. We have been touring the area, and wondered whether your village—uh, city—would have any interest in viewing our plays."

"We are interested. We have little current commerce with outside villages, and life gets dull." She frowned. "The folk here are accustomed to adversity, having worked very hard all their lives, and do not trust strangers, as you may have noticed. That is why I, an outsider, have been appointed by Ragna Roc to handle their public relations. But they should enjoy your plays, particularly if they contain interpersonal stresses."

"They do," Cyrus said.

"I will tell them to attend."

"Then, with your permission, we will come and present three plays, on succeeding evenings."

"Are you married?"

The question caught him completely off guard. "No!"

"Then you will stay with me for the duration of your stay here. We will arrange other accommodations for the members of your troupe. Will that be satisfactory?"

Cyrus was flustered. "I prefer to remain with my troupe."

She gave him a disconcertingly direct look. "I understood you to say that you wish to present your plays here."

"Yes, but I see no need to—"

Then he caught on. "I am not married, but I do have a relationship. I would not feel free to spend nights with another woman."

"Oh? And with whom do you have this relationship?"

"I do not feel free to say."

Andromeda smiled. "So you are not a stranger to adversity yourself, it seems."

"That is true," he agreed uneasily.

"But you *are* free to accept my hospitality. I'm sure your significant other will understand."

Cyrus looked helplessly at Rhythm, who was completely impassive: a bad sign. "I am not at all sure she will."

"Lovely. Well, perhaps I will meet her tomorrow. Tonight you are mine."

Cyrus made a difficult decision. "I think we shall have to bypass Adver City. It is too contentious a site."

"The troupe wouldn't like that," Rhythm said. "I'll go explain." She hurried off.

"Thank you, Rhyme," he said after her retreating form. She had decided to go along with the dragonfly lady's demand? He really mistrusted this.

"Bonita!" Andromeda called.

A surly-looking village girl appeared. "Yes, Elder?"

"Tell the welcoming committee to make space for a visiting troupe. There will be—" She paused, glancing at Cyrus.

"Twenty," he said.

"Twenty in that party."

"Yes, Elder." The girl departed, clearly not pleased with this assignment.

"Now please come inside," Andromeda said briskly.

Cyrus entered, helplessly. The inside of the house was painted to resemble a forest glade, with tree trunks for walls and flowers around the edges. In fact there were flowers and assorted mushrooms throughout. They looked completely real.

He bent to touch one, to verify its illusory nature—and discovered it *was* real. They were all real.

"It is my talent," Andromeda said. "They grow where I walk."

Indeed, there was a trail of small flowers and mushrooms following her. "I am impressed." He sat on a tree stump chair, so as not to step on any of the clustered blossoms.

"Would you like anything to eat or drink? I have Hop Scotch that has a bounce, Upsc Ale, a higher quality beverage, or one imported from the land of the imps, Imp Ale, that goes right through you." She looked in her pantree. "There's also gin, but all that's left is Vir, and I can no longer drink that." She glanced sidelong at him. "But perhaps you can?"

"No!" he exclaimed. "I don't want any of those."

"Please, I am trying to be a good hostess in a difficult situation. You should try to be a good guest." She looked again. "Ah, I do have some tonics. Mono is very consistent, never changing. In contrast, there's Tec, that really causes a rumble. There's also the friendly effect of Pla Tonic."

"That one will do," he said desperately.

Amused, she poured him a glass, and took one herself. She brought him his, then sat opposite him, crossing her legs. They were splendid legs, all the way up to the very brink of, but not quite showing under her skirt, panties.

"You must consider me to be very forward," she said.

He could not deny it, but didn't want to affront her. "Perhaps."

"Let me show you something."

"There's no need," he said quickly as she lifted a leg.

But all she did was get up and walk to a wall. It was covered by a curtain. She drew the curtain aside, revealing a wall-sized glass window to her backyard. The yard was filled with trees, flowers, and dancing dragonflies.

"Beloved," she murmured.

A singularly bright dragonfly flew close to the window—and through it. It formed into a handsome man wearing the garb of a king.

"This is Perseus, my husband," she said.

"Your husband!"

"So you see, I too have a significant other. But there are constraints."

The man stepped toward Cyrus, extending a hand. He wanted to be friendly? Cyrus stood and took the hand.

Their hands passed through each other.

"He is illusion," Andromeda said. "As are all my people. I alone remain of all the dragonflies." She turned to Perseus. "Thank you, dear." She lifted her face to kiss him, and it almost looked real, but their lips overlapped a bit. Then the King of the Dragonflies returned to his natural form, and flew back through the window.

Cyrus went to tap his finger against the glass, verifying that it was solid. And thus that Perseus was not.

He turned back to Andromeda—and caught her wiping tears from her face. "I apologize," she said. "It's just—not easy. I love him so." She drew the curtain back across.

"Now I am really confused," Cyrus said.

"Understandably. Believe me when I say that I would have no interest in you if Perseus were solid. Just as you have no interest in me. But if you do not wish to share my fate, this is a painful game you must play."

"Ragna Roc!" he said. "He deleted your people."

"He did. We rejected his request that we winged monsters

join him in taking over the Land of Xanth. He did not take it well, as you can see. And if they are ever to be restored, it will be only by dint of my effort. I must recruit for him something equivalent in value. Then, perhaps, he will deign to give me back my beloved, and perhaps also my people. Now you understand the essence of my situation."

"I do," Cyrus agreed, touched. "But I am just a Playwright with a Troupe. We put on plays. We're not anything special apart from that." He was getting used to that lie, though it still made him uneasy.

"But you see, you are special," she insisted. "First, we are desperate for entertainment, especially since the curse fiends blacklisted us. Second, I suspect the Roc gets bored at times, and might well appreciate some plays. If I can bring them to him—" She shrugged. "It just possibly might be enough."

"How is it that you are here in a human village, uh, city? Instead of with the dragonflies?"

"Not by my choice. The roc assigned me here, because among other things I have experience governing. I don't like it, and the villagers don't like it, but we all understand that if we don't play along, all of us will be deleted. So we do what we have to do." She mopped up another tear. "And I must say, the Roc is not a harsh master. All he requires is our fealty, and that we do anything he asks. It is power he is after, not misery for his subjects."

"I don't see how you can persuade me or my troupe to welcome being deleted, as you put it."

"You won't be deleted if you swear fealty. You may not be deleted if you don't; it depends on whether the Roc wants your service. At the moment his attention is elsewhere, and we are idle. But I can't stand to wait any longer than I have to, to get my King and people back."

Now Cyrus really appreciated her position. But it didn't make him want to cooperate. "I think I just want to get out of here and hide from the Roc."

"You can't hide," she assured him. "I serve him reluctantly, but I do serve him. I will send word to him who you are, what you do, and where you go. Please don't make me do that."

He was sure she was serious, as he would be if Rhythm got deleted and he had to do something to save her. Could he escape the Dragonfly Queen by canceling her memory of him? Probably not, because she now had a half slew of related memories, while his talent was strictly one spot memory. So what could he do?

He realized that he might not have to do anything, because Rhythm had taken advantage of the opportunity to get away and report to the troupe, and she was not about to leave him in the arms of a glamorous queen. All he had to do was wait, and hope for the best.

Andromeda feted him nicely enough, then took him out to see where the troupe was camped. They had made a nice spot in a vacant lot near the center of the village, and the tents were pitched there.

Bonita hurried up. "Elder, they wouldn't accept hospitality in our houses. They said they insisted on staying together, and that their tents were good enough."

"That is true," Cyrus said quickly. He could well understand why the troupe members didn't want to get separated from each other in strange homes. "We are accustomed to doing for ourselves, and averse to being governed by others." The inhabitants of this city should really understand that. "All we need is space."

"As you wish," Andromeda said.

Curtis spied them and came forward, accompanied by Crabapple in an arm-concealing toga. "This is Curtis Curse Friend, our Producer," Cyrus said.

"Pleased to meet you, Elder," Curtis said with studied insincerity.

"And his companion, Crabapple."

"Charmed, I'm sure," Crabapple said, nicely emulating Curtis's tone.

Then the Witch, Dusti, Acro, and Xina came out. "I'm so glad you're safe, dear," the Witch said, kissing him on the cheek.

"I can hardly wait to get you back in my bed," Dusti said, kissing his other cheek.

"It's hard for me to sleep without you by my side," Acro said, kissing his forehead.

"There just isn't any other man like you," Xina said, kissing his mouth.

Cyrus was nonplussed, perhaps even nonminused. Why were they coming on to him so obviously? Then he saw Rhythm standing in the background. She had somehow put them up to it, so that Andromeda would not know his real interest. They were cooperating with enthusiasm. It wasn't anything personal at this stage; they just liked teasing men.

Then Rhythm's thought came to him. *I told them to make a pretense of interest in you. They asked "pretense"?*

Just so. Because if Andromeda discovered his actual beloved, she might report her to the Roc to become a hostage.

Exactly.

Andromeda was unfazed. "Will you be able to present your first play tomorrow?"

"Yes," Cyrus said. "This is our business."

"Then it seems that things are in order. We can now return to my abode."

And Cyrus had to accompany her. Her situation might be desperate, but she had effective control over him for the time being.

As evening came, back at the house, Andromeda made her next move. "I think that none of those women are yours. They are all actresses."

"They are," he agreed cautiously.

"Yet you do love somebody, as do I. Understanding that

our liaison is temporary, why not appreciate it? I have been uncomfortably lonely since losing Perseus."

He did not like this. "What are you suggesting?"

"That we night together. I will pretend you are Perseus, though you are not the shadow of a man he is, and you may pretend I am your anonymous girlfriend, who I think is not the shadow of me. We may thus have some pleasure of each other."

He started to protest the derogation of his beloved, but caught himself. Andromeda was trying to make him inadvertently identify her. "That is surely the case," he agreed.

She glanced at him, a quarter smile hovering near her mouth. "You are not stupid, at least. I like that." She led him to the bed.

"I really am not ready to—" he began.

She lay voluptuously nude against him, her wings folded flat against her back and evidently crush-proof. "Are you sure?"

"Yes," he said uncertainly.

She kissed him. There seemed to be an explosion of mixed hearts and flying storks. "Really?"

"Really," he agreed, but it was an obvious lie. This woman was as bad a tease as any actress.

"Let's be practical," she said. "We each want something of the other. I want to persuade you to swear fealty to the Roc. You want something of me, or you would not have come here, knowing the danger posed by the Roc. I will accommodate you in any way I can, that does not betray my mission. What do you really want?"

And he did want something: to ascertain the limits of the power of Ragna Roc. But he couldn't ask that, lest he give away his mission. So he temporized: "I fear the Roc, and wish I knew how to stop him. I don't want all of Xanth to fall under his sway."

She shook her head. "Nobody does, Cyrus. But it isn't as if

we have a choice. The best we can do is cooperate and gain preferential treatment for ourselves."

"Then I guess there's nothing I can ask of you."

"That's too bad. Well, let's get down to business." She kissed him again, potently.

Cyrus tried to struggle, emotionally, but short of scrambling out of the bed and out of her house, he knew there was no way to escape her. She was too experienced and too determined.

"I'm not going to swear fealty," he gasped.

"Not even if I do this?" She did something that not even the grown Rhythm had done, and it turned him on unbearably.

"No," he said faintly.

"Or this?" She did something else. It was so naughty he could hardly imagine it. Any more of this, and he was lost.

"I—" he said, unable to field a reasonable protest.

Then something changed. It was dark, so he could not see her face, but there was a difference in her manner. "What is going on here, Cyrus?" she asked.

He recognized the voice. "Rhythm!"

"Bleep! Quick, make her forget that name!"

He did, striking into Andromeda's memory with his talent. She would not forget the episode, but she would at least lose the name. "How did you—?"

"It's a talent," she said. "Taking over a body. For a while."

"You know I was trying to resist her," he said. "But she's got such a body, and she was using it so well."

Her hands felt his hot body. "So I gather. Well, let's get on with it."

"But you—aren't eligible."

"But this body is." She kissed him, and it was Rhythm's kiss.

He could resist no more. An internal dam broke, and he clasped her to him and kissed her passionately. "Oh, anonymous, I love you!"

"And I love you," she said, kissing him back.

After they had severely battered the ellipsis, she eased off. "I must leave you. But it was nice."

"It was awesome!"

She was gone. He felt the change.

"What just happened?" Andromeda asked.

How could he explain it? "You don't know?"

"Someone just took over my body and made wild love to you. It must have been your lover."

She had nailed it. "Yes." How angry would she be?

"So that's her talent: occupying the bodies of other women. Does she do that often?"

Did Rhythm's changes to age twenty-two count? "I can't exactly say."

"Does she ever do this in her own form?"

"No."

"That's interesting. She must be very ugly."

She was still probing. "Maybe," he agreed.

"Well, she certainly wore me out. Good night." She dropped off to sleep.

Just like that! But of course she was a dragonfly; they rested often and briefly. Relieved, he relaxed and slept also.

In the morning, she remembered. "That is some girlfriend you have. No wonder you're not free to identify her. But you did speak her name."

"Did I?"

"But I can't remember it, oddly. I am normally excellent with names."

"That's too bad," he said, relieved on at least two counts: she couldn't remember the name, and she seemed not to be angry.

"You may be more of a challenge than I anticipated," she said, getting up nude and stretching her arms and wings. She was a beautiful specimen. Fortunately she seemed not to be amorous in the morning.

She let him rejoin the troupe to organize for the evening play. "But you will be with me again tonight," she warned him. "Maybe this time I'll identify your mysterious girl-friend."

He certainly hoped not. He stayed studiously away from Rhythm, knowing how dangerous it could be if Andromeda ever identified her. Rhythm, understanding perfectly, coop-erated.

The first play, "The Curse," was a success. The villagers really were starved for entertainment, and loved it. They ap-plauded heartily. Their original unfriendliness faded.

"That actress," Andromeda said that night. "Could she use other bodies to come to you because of the awkwardness of her pincers?"

"Maybe."

She sighed. "So it's not her."

Then Rhythm took over. "No, not her," she agreed with Andromeda's mouth. "She's too nice."

"Obviously you're not," Andromeda replied in her own voice.

"You're talking to each other?" Cyrus asked, amazed.

"She sees I'm not angry, merely intrigued," Andromeda said. "So she lets me have some freedom. This way, not only do I get your passion, but technically I'm not being unfaith-ful to my husband. That's a fair deal."

"I'm not sure there should be any deal. This is weird."

"Really?" they said together, and tackled him.

After the horrendous ellipsis, Rhythm departed. "I think I like her, whoever she is," Andromeda said. "Is she a member of your troupe?"

"I'm not telling."

"So she is." The Dragonfly Queen was entirely too apt at reading his responses.

After she fell asleep, Cyrus had an awful thought. How old was Rhythm physically for these sessions? Was she invoking the Decade spell? Or was she really participating as a child? Somehow he hadn't thought it through before.

He decided not to ask. After all, as she had said, Andromeda's body was adult. It was like the Decade spell in that respect.

The second play, "The Dream," was also well received. And it gave Andromeda another idea. "Could she be the dragon!" she exclaimed. "That really makes sense."

Cyrus said nothing, hoping she would take it as confirmation.

"Almost too much sense," she concluded. "Why would you reveal it in a play, if you wanted the liaison secret?"

Oh, well.

The villagers liked the third play also. "Tomorrow we must let you go," Andromeda said regretfully that night. "I can see you are not a prospective convert."

"You're giving up?" Cyrus asked, surprised.

"Your girlfriend will not give you up, or allow you to join the Roc," she said. "I can feel it in her nature when she possesses me. All I can do is whisper one last private plea." She put her mouth to his ear.

"That's not necessary," he said.

"Get out of here, you and your troupe, quickly," she whispered urgently. "Lest you suffer our fate. You are decent folk. Please don't betray my confidence." Then she kissed his ear.

"Uh—" he said.

She drew back, smiling sunnily. "Isn't that persuasive? I am bound to do my best to enlist you in our cause."

She was a nice person herself. She had whispered the truth, and the Roc would surely delete her if he knew. "You are extremely persuasive," he agreed, kissing her. "If it were solely up to me, I would do what you say."

She sighed. "Well, I tried." She looked around. "Where is your woman?"

"She hasn't come to you?"

"No. I remain myself."

They were in bed together, both bare. "You could have faked it," he said. "I might not have realized."

"I wouldn't do that."

"Oh, Andromeda, I think you're a fine woman, and I will help you any way I can. But this—"

"I understand. You can't help me."

"I don't think I could resist you, if—"

"There's a peculiar ethic. Let's sleep."

"Of course," he agreed faintly.

They slept.

"Cyrus."

He woke, recognizing the voice. "Anonymous!"

"Sorry I was late. I got involved in something. Did I miss anything?"

"When she realized you weren't coming, she let me be."

"Suddenly I like this woman."

"I do too. We have to help her somehow. But I can't swear allegiance to the Roc."

"We'll think of something."

"We'll think of something," he echoed. But he feared there was nothing.

15

ORIENTA

In the morning the troupe pulled up stakes and moved out of Adver City. On the surface it had been a successful presentation, and they knew the performances had been appreciated by the villagers. But they also knew that the village was under the sway of a malign creature the people could not escape. That damped down any joy they might have felt.

Andromeda came to bid them parting. "We do appreciate your visit," she said. "It was a rare pleasure, and we loved your plays. Especially the strife between the good Magician and his bothersome wives."

"Thank you," Cyrus said. Then, lowering his voice: "Somehow, someday—"

Andromeda shook her head. "There is nothing." Then she transformed into a lovely dragonfly and flew away.

Cyrus felt horribly guilty. But she was probably right. Not only was there nothing he or anyone else could do, it was dangerous even to mention it.

Curtis joined Cyrus as they walked. "I had expected a

malign atmosphere. Instead I found decent folk under the shadow of repression."

"That is the case," Cyrus agreed. "What is next on our itinerary?"

"Necess City, governed by a woman named Orienta."

Cyrus quailed. "Why do I suspect I will be nighting at her house?"

"The Roc has set things up to try to welcome and convert visitors. It seems persuasion is easier than outright conquest. Attractive women are a likely means."

"Andromeda was attractive more than physically," Cyrus said. "She's no enemy."

"I wouldn't know. But I suspect it will be no easier in Necess."

"That is my fear."

Curtis moved on, and Cyrus saw Crabapple join him. Evidently that relationship was working out.

Then Rhythm's mind joined his. *I can't get over how she let you be when I wasn't there.*

"I think Andromeda first saw me as a prospect for conversion, possibly saving her people," he murmured subvocally. "But as she got to know me, her conscience came into play and she had to warn me of the danger. So she sacrificed her hope."

She still could have taken you in bed.

"Not when she started to appreciate me as a person. Sex was one of the tools she was willing to use on a stranger, not a potential friend."

We've got to help her, somehow.

"If we destroy the Roc, will his spells dissipate?"

Not according to our information. Most spells survive their makers.

Which left them helpless in that respect. Cyrus felt miserable.

Me too.

He thought of something else. "You might have read her mind to learn the Roc's weakness."

I tried. She doesn't know it.

"Maybe the next one—Orienta of Necess City—will. If she takes me in, and you come to her, maybe then you can read her mind."

I can try. It will help if you pose the question to her. She may not answer you, but I would still be able to read it in her mind.

Cyrus wondered again whether Rhythm had invoked the Decade spell before coming to Andromeda, but still hesitated to ask.

I did. I tried to come without it, but the Adult Conspiracy bounced me from her body.

"You tried to cheat!"

I love you regardless of my age, she thought defensively. *I want to possess you, or whatever it is, as I am now. And remember.*

He did not argue the case, but was glad she had not succeeded in cheating. He loved her, but she was after all a child, and he supported the enforcement of the Adult Conspiracy.

I read that!

Oops.

Necess was a village very like the last. This time Cyrus went in with Piper, so as not to seem to favor one messenger over another. She rode Don Donkey, with whom she got along well, and her friend Dusty tagged along as he usually did, whirling up stray leaves.

As before, the people largely ignored them. They were doing the regular village things, harvesting pies and milkweed pods, repairing their houses, and the children were playing children's games. But none of them seemed to have much enthusiasm; they were merely doing what was necessary. It was as if they were under a looming cloud, and Cyrus had a fair notion of its nature.

They came to the Elder's house in the center. The door opened as they arrived, and a petite winged girl came out. She looked barely older than Piper.

"Hello," Cyrus said. "I am Cyrus Cyborg, and this is Piper, and Don, my robot Donkey. And Dusty Dust Devil," he added as Dusty coalesced to solid form. "We represent a touring troupe. We were wondering whether—"

"Yes, the news is around," the girl said. "You played at Adver. I am Orienta, appointed Elder of Necess."

Cyrus's data bank whirred. "Daughter of Gloha Goblin-Harpy and Graeboe Giant?"

"Why yes! How did you know?"

"I am part machine. I have a memory bank that contains the public record."

"Ah, you are another crossbreed!"

"Yes. My father is a robot, my mother a barbarian human. There are many crossbreeds in Xanth."

"I am one too," Piper said. "My father is Hiatus Human, and my mother is Desiree Dryad."

Orienta smiled. "Welcome to our village. I mean, city. But I have to tell you—"

"That this place is under the sway of Ragna Roc," he said. "We learned that at Adver."

"Yes. That frightens some folk." She opened the door. "Do come in. Your donkey too, if he's housebroken; I love equines."

Cyrus exchanged half a glance with Piper. "Don doesn't leave poop, just ashes." He did not say more about the donkey, preferring that his full nature not be known, and Don understood. They followed Orienta inside.

The house had an opening in the ceiling, but no stairs. Orienta, being winged, didn't need stairs. But above that

Cyrus could also see a hole in the roof. She evidently liked the freedom of the sky.

"Let's get to know each other before we talk business," Orienta said. "I am fourteen, and my talent is to conjure things from the East."

"East of where?" Piper asked.

"East of wherever I happen to be. They tend to be artistic and ornate. I don't do it much because I can't be sure whether I am stealing them from someone who needs them."

"I am thirteen, and my talent is healing," Piper said. "I have a small part in a play: one of the Good Magician's wives."

"So you're an actress!" Orienta exclaimed. "Oh, I envy you!" She turned to Dusty. "Are you an actor too?"

"No, just a friend," he said. "We've known each other ever since she was one and I was two. I bashed my arm coming out of a spin, and she grabbed it and healed it. Or at least made it hurt less so it could heal in peace, in time. She didn't mind my being a devil."

"So you're my age," Orienta said. "I don't mind either. I think your horns are cute."

The two looked at each other. Then both of them blushed.

"I fashioned Don from spare robot parts," Cyrus said, to fill in what might have become an awkward silence. "So he's a bit clunky, but he understands human talk."

"May I pet him?"

"Certainly."

Orienta went to pet Don on the shoulder. "Oh! You're warm! And you smell wonderfully smoky."

"He burns wood," Cyrus explained. "He has to eat another stick or log every so often."

Orienta returned to her chair. She sighed. "I don't think I can postpone it any longer. We have to get down to business. That is always the case, in Necess City."

"We would like to put on our plays for your villagers," Cyrus said.

"That, too," Orienta agreed.

"What other business did you have in mind?" Cyrus asked, already knowing it.

"To convert you to enlisting with Ragna Roc. It's why I'm here. To talk any visitors into it, if I can. Especially ones with useful skills, such as putting on plays. I really have to try."

"Why?" Piper asked.

"Because my parents are here in Necess City. They found it to be a nice village with nice people who didn't mind them being crossbreeds. Well, Father isn't, technically; he's really a changebreed."

"A what?"

"He was an invisible giant. Then he fell in love with Mother, who is a goblin-harpy crossbreed, and agreed to be transformed to a male goblin-harpy so he could be with her. Some folk don't like crossbreeds or changebreeds, but here it was okay, so they settled. It was nice, until—"

She paused, but no one else spoke.

"Until Ragna Roc came," she resumed after a moment. "He changed everything."

"But things look much the same," Cyrus said. "The villagers are going about their normal lives, as far as we can tell."

"They have to look that way, or they will be punished," Orienta said. "Ragna prefers to take over by persuasion, but if that doesn't work, he does it by force. Sometimes there doesn't seem to be much difference."

"But there should be all the difference in the world of Xanth," Cyrus said.

"That depends." She looked uncomfortable.

"How did he persuade you?" Piper asked.

"He sent his Minions in to give us the word. We all had to swear fealty to him, and serve his interests henceforth, or be deleted."

"Please," Piper said. "Tell us the whole story."

Orienta started describing it, and Cyrus found he was able

to imagine it as if he had been there. Two men marched into the village. They were nondescript, but carried themselves with authority. "Gather round folk," one called. "We are Damien and Demetrius. We have a message from Ragna Roc, the Emperor of Birds."

The people gathered, curious. Orienta's family was among them. "What's going on?" Graeboe demanded.

"You—all of you—will hereby swear fealty to the Roc, and serve him loyally the rest of your lives, doing whatever he or his appointed Minions require of you," Damien said. "Or else."

This presumption annoyed more than one villager. "Or else what?" Graeboe asked.

"Or else you will be deleted."

"I don't understand."

"You will cease to exist on this mortal plane. You will become an illusion."

Graeboe shook his head. "This is laughable."

"The Roc's first directive is for this village to be renamed Necess City, and to provide good housing for us, and appealing women." Damien glanced around. "You," he said, beckoning to a pretty farmer's daughter named Lita. "Come to me."

Lita looked around uncertainly. She was too young to know what any man would want with her.

"Now," the man snapped.

Lita heeded the voice of command and went to him.

"And for Demetrius—" He glanced around again, then fixed on Orienta. "You."

Orienta wasn't sure what this meant, but it seemed that her father did. "My daughter is fourteen."

"Who cares? She's pretty. This is the new order."

"No," Graeboe said firmly.

"You are refusing a direct command?" Damien asked, surprised.

"You have no authority to issue any commands," Graeboe said. "And certainly none to bother innocent girls."

"Then we shall have to do it the hard way," Damien said with a certain ugly relish. "Ragna will make a demonstration." He lifted one hand to the sky.

In half a moment there was a dark blot in the distant sky. It expanded rapidly. It was a bird—a big bird. In fact it was a roc. The monstrous creature glided down to land behind the two men.

"This family is balky," Damien said, pointing to Graeboe, Gloha, and Orienta.

The giant bird's huge glittering eyes fixed on the three of them. Then something changed. Orienta felt oddly light. "What happened?" she asked her parents. But no sound came out.

Her mother's mouth moved, but again there was no sound. Something was definitely wrong.

Orienta ran to her mother, needing her warm comforting embrace. But instead of contact there was nothing. She ran right through Gloha.

She turned, astonished. How could this have happened? It was as though her mother didn't exist—yet there she was.

Then the truth sank in. They had been deleted. They had no material substance. They were ghosts.

"Oh, Mother! Father!" Orienta wailed. "This is awful!" But all that issued from her mouth was silence.

The three of them turned to look at the other villagers. Another man was stepping forward to address the intruders. He was Nathaniel, a kindly neighbor. "Now see here," he said boldly. "Those men were taking underage girls for nefarious purposes. We had to resist."

Suddenly the two minions quailed. The Roc's gaze fixed on them. There was Lita standing beside Damien, looking frightened.

In an act of inspiration, Orienta stepped forward and raised her hand. She was the other underage girl.

The roc glanced first at Damien, then at Demetrius. Both men's faces broke out in horror. Then the Roc glanced at the deleted family, his eyes glittering.

Suddenly Orienta felt weight. She was solid again! So were her parents. They had been restored.

"If I understand you correctly," Nathaniel said, "you have restored the family on the assumption that they will now swear fealty to you."

The big bird nodded.

"And deleted the two Minions for exceeding their authority."

Another nod.

"All you want is fealty, not violation of the natural order. The Adult Conspiracy holds."

The huge bird shrugged.

Nathaniel glanced back at the other villagers. "The demonstration is persuasive. We hereby agree to serve you. Who will you appoint to govern us in your name?"

The Roc considered, then slowly lifted one wing to point at Orienta.

"Me?" she asked, unnerved. "But I can't possibly—"

"She agrees," Nathaniel said, with a sharp glance at her. "Orienta will be the village elder, and do your will."

Ragna Roc nodded once more. Then he spread his enormous wings and took off. Soon he was a mere dot in the distant sky.

"And so it has been since," Orienta said. "The Roc returned us to life, and we are grateful. I am doing his will as I understand it. I am trying to convert visitors peacefully, so that Necess City will be left alone. We are all doing what we have to."

"What happens if you don't convert us?" Piper asked.

"I don't know. Maybe nothing, if the Roc doesn't care about you. But if he does—"

"Deletion," Cyrus said.

"Yes."

"We can't swear fealty," Cyrus said. "Our troupe must remain free to travel and present its plays wherever it chooses."

"Maybe it will be all right," Orienta said, a tear squeezing from the corner of one eye.

Cyrus wanted to get away from there, but did not want to be obvious about it. "You are too young to entertain guests my age."

"But not for our age," Piper said. "Why don't Dusty and Don and me stay with you while the troupe is in town? I know Dusty would like that."

Dusty blushed.

"That would be nice," Orienta said.

Piper knew that Don could hear and understand everything, and relay it to Cyrus. So if they learned another important clue, he would know.

Cyrus stood. "Then I will return to the troupe," he said. "I will be in touch."

"You will need to designate a place for the troupe to camp," Piper told Orienta. "About twenty people, including a dragon."

"A dragon!"

"She won't eat anyone, I promise."

"She's another actress," Dusty explained.

Cyrus departed. Things were working out reasonably well.

We learned more about the Roc, Rhythm thought. *Surprisingly fair minded.*

"But nevertheless a tyrant," Cyrus murmured as he walked.

Sure, we have to stop him. But now we know him better.

"He doesn't brook any violation of his rules," Cyrus said.

"The way he deleted his own Minions—that's instructive and scary."

It sure is. Also the way he can delete and undelete. That bird's a potent Sorcerer.

Cyrus reached the troupe and assembled it for an update. He described what he had learned about the conversion of the village. "So we must be exceedingly careful what we say and how we act," he concluded. "We don't want the give the Roc any reason to come here and delete us."

"We understand," Curtis said.

"We do," Crabapple said, taking his hand. That was interesting, because of course her hand was a pincer; the man would have snatched his hand away if he didn't trust her.

In due course the troupe entered the village and camped at the designated spot. The people set about pitching their tents and making their evening meal. Several villagers came to watch. They were clearly impressed by the way Jim made food for each person. But especially by the Dragon Lady, who settled down for a snooze without eating anyone.

That night Cyrus tuned in on Don. Piper was teasing Dusty about how he liked Orienta, and Orienta was pleasantly embarrassed. "He may want to remain here, when the troupe moves on," Don said.

"Well, maybe he can," Cyrus agreed. "He's not a member of the cast, and even if he were, we'd let him go if he wanted."

"But he's Piper's friend," Rhythm said.

"But not her boyfriend."

She nodded. "It will be their decision. Orienta's a nice girl."

"That's the weird thing about these captive villages," he said. "They have nice people. We couldn't just destroy them to get rid of the roc."

"We couldn't," she agreed. Then she invoked the Decade spell, and their dialogue ended.

The first play was a big success. The villagers, uncomfortable about becoming isolated, related well to both the curse and Crabapple's dilemma.

After the play, Orienta brought her parents up to meet Cyrus. Gloha Goblin-Harpy was a petite winged woman of thirty-four, and Graeboe was a winged man, with no trace of his former identity as a giant. It certainly seemed that they had been happy here until the Roc came.

The second play was also well received, perhaps because the villagers related to the plight of the Dragon Lady, able to love a man only in the dream. The villagers' dream was freedom.

Piper, Dusty, and Don continued to visit with Orienta, between presentations. The four seemed to be getting along splendidly well. "Orienta has company her own age," Rhythm said wisely. "She must really have missed that."

As the audience assembled in the big tent where "The Riddle" was to be presented, there was a distant rumble of thunder. "Bleep," the Witch muttered. "That's Fracto. I know his voice. He's found out that folk are having fun."

"And it's not just parades he wets on," Demoness Kay said. She was getting her considerable makeup applied, to mask her zombie component.

"Maybe we can finish it before he gets here," Xina said hopefully.

The others just looked at her. But what else was there to do, except to hope for the best?

The third play seemed to relate less well, but the villagers plainly were enjoying it. Cyrus watched faces as the Good Magician and his five and a half wives traveled and finally found the Demon Xanth, who was in the form of a donkey-headed dragon. The costume crew had done a great job making the Dragon Lady up with a donkey head.

"Nimby!" the Good Magician said. But the dragon ignored him.

"Demon Xanth," Humfrey said.

The Demon still paid him no attention.

"Let me try," Dara Demoness said. She put on a hula-hula dance that made the male eyeballs in the audience sweat. But still the Demon did not react.

"Poophead!" the Gorgon shouted. That brought the usual laughter from the audience. Naturally that would never happen in real life. But this was a halfway humorous play.

Now at last the donkey head glanced at them. "Um?"

"All Xanth is going haywire," Humfrey said. "We conclude that the magic has diminished to half strength because you are seriously distracted. What is your problem?"

"I *am* distracted," the Demon said. "By a riddle. I can't figure it out."

"Ha!" Dara Demoness said. "Humfrey's good at riddles."

"Not necessarily," Humfrey grumped.

"He's the Magician of Information," the Maiden Taiwan agreed.

"That has its limits," Humfrey said, obviously ill at ease.

"He knows everything," MareAnn said.

"Untrue. I don't know how to handle five and a half bossy wives."

"You're sweet," Rose said, kissing his eyebrow, which was as low as she could reach in her elaborate costume dress.

"Nobody knows how to handle one wife, let alone six," the Demon said.

"Five and a half," MareAnn said. "I'm the half."

"You look whole to me."

"Half a *wife*. It was a small ceremony. I'm a whole woman." She lifted her skirt enough to show the barest glimmer of the hint of a panty. That was the most the actress, Piper, could afford to flash onstage. The audience, unaware of her age, loved it.

The donkey head managed to look slightly confused. "I still haven't figured out Chlorine."

The Demon's wife Chlorine came onstage. "I heard that!" she snapped. She was portrayed by the Lady Bug, whose folded wing covers made a perfect robe. She was beautiful, as her role was supposed to be. "What are you doing with all these women?"

"They are my wives," the Good Magician said. "The magical glitch in Xanth caused them all to appear at once. It is driving me to distraction."

"You poor man," Chlorine said, sympathetically. "Let me fetch you a glass of water to calm you down."

"No thanks!" he said quickly. That brought a laugh: everyone knew that Chlorine's talent was poisoning water. "I'm merely here to see what I can do to fix the magical disruption."

The Demon focused an eyeball on the Good Magician. "Then perhaps you can help me."

"He will certainly try," Sofia Socksorter said. "He can sort out just about anything except socks." That brought another laugh.

"What is your riddle?" Humfrey asked. If there was an incongruity about the Magician of Information having to ask a question, it passed unnoticed.

"My son Nimbus brought it to me. It perplexed him, and now it perplexes me."

"Is it about whose hair a barber cuts?" the Gorgon asked. "You know, he cuts everyone's hair who doesn't cut his own hair, so does he cut his own hair?"

"Woman, get your snaky locks away from here before I cut off their heads!" Humfrey snapped.

"Well, it could be that riddle," the Gorgon said as her snakelets hissed.

"It's nonsense," Humfrey said. "It belongs to a class of riddles that are paradoxical because they are self-referential. None of them are worth bothering with." He returned to the

Demon. "You can see why I am desperate to get things returned to the natural order."

"That is no riddle," Nimby agreed with half a smile. The actor, the Dragon Lady, had practiced assiduously to craft that degree of a smile on the donkey face.

"So what is your riddle?" Humfrey asked again, with a circular glare to silence all his wives and also Chlorine.

"The babysitter is tutoring our son Nimbus, and posed it as a riddle for him to stretch his mind with. He did not want to admit he couldn't solve it, so he brought it to me. Now I don't want to admit I can't solve it, and it is distracting me most annoyingly."

"I'll say," Dara agreed. "The only thing a man is supposed to be properly distracted by is a panty." She hoisted her skirt to flash the male half of the audience. She had extremely well-filled panties, and would have been a seductive terror and a danger to herself and all men in the vicinity, had she not been portrayed by a zombie. As it was, half the men in the audience freaked anyway, not knowing she was a zombie demoness, until she dropped her skirt. They really liked this play. The women were for some reason mildly annoyed, but did like the notion of the wives running the Good Magician's life.

"Ignore Wife Number One," Humfrey said tiredly. "She's got a demon hotbox." That of course brought another laugh, for the naughty reference.

"Ignored," Nimby said, shaking the glaze off an eyeball. "The riddle is this: why don't two chips of reverse wood nullify each other? Nimbus tried putting them together, and they didn't. Yet reverse wood reverses anything."

"I have three answers for you," Humfrey said, dramatically relieved that it was a simple question that would not require research in the Book of Answers. "You may select what pleases you."

There was a deafening crack of thunder, followed by instantly heavy rain. Fracto had arrived.

They tried to continue, but the wind and thunder drowned out their lines, and the water collected in the pockets of the tent, weighing it down. The malign cloud wanted nothing less than to bring down the tent on their heads. They had to evacuate in a hurry, the play unfinished.

Fortunately they were able to extend their tour and finish it the following night. Then it was time to move on.

Cyrus talked with Orienta. "You aren't going to urge us to swear fealty to the Roc?"

The girl was appalled. "Why would you ever want to do that?"

"Andromeda, at Adver City, tried to persuade us."

"That's hard to believe. She hates the Roc."

"She wants to protect her village." He did not mention how the woman had whispered other words, which confirmed the girl's statement.

Orienta nodded. "That's true. She does what she has to, as do we. But that didn't work, so I know there's no point. But I will say this: those who join voluntarily are treated well, and a number have high places in the Roc's forming Empire. You could do well for yourselves if you joined him."

"But you aren't urging us?"

"I hope you don't. But I was obliged to tell you."

"Thank you for your candor," he said. "But we will be moving on."

"Please don't tell that I didn't try to convert you. The Roc would be furious."

"I will pretend that you tried very hard," Cyrus said. "But that I was immovable."

"Thank you. In public of course I have to make the case. But we're alone now."

"Ah." That explained her seeming change in attitude. She

resembled Andromeda in this respect, doing what she had to, but not liking it.

"Can Dusty stay?"

"That's his choice."

"Thank you." Impulsively she kissed him on the cheek.

"You are welcome," he said, moved.

16

LAYEA

The third city was Pompos. After the first two, Cyrus
knew better than to expect anything similar. They
could encounter something entirely different.

That turned out to be the case. At first the village looked
normal, though its buildings were fancier than those of the
others, as if the occupants were higher class. The people
were also better dressed, as they went about their assorted
businesses. As before, they ignored the visitors.

But that wasn't the remarkable thing. There was something distinctly different about this normal scene. Cyrus was
appalled when he caught on.

"These folk are all deleted!" he said.

Curtis stared. "You're right!" He passed his hand through
the wall of a house. "It's all illusion."

"So it is," Crabapple agreed, touching the trunk of a tree,
and passing her shrouded hand right through it. "Even the
trees!"

"Something must have truly annoyed the bird," Cyrus
said, awed.

They proceeded to the village center. "Hello," Cyrus called. "Is anybody home?"

The door opened and an ordinary looking girl emerged. She held up a sign printed on a papered tablet: I AM LAYEA. MY TALENT IS TO MAKE ANY MAN DO MY BIDDING, TO A DEGREE. WELCOME TO POMPOS CITY.

Cyrus took stock. "You are illusion?" he asked.

She nodded.

"And you can see and hear me?"

She nodded again.

"I am Cyrus Cyborg, and this is Curtis Curse Friend. We represent a traveling troupe that puts on plays for village audiences. We were going to ask to make our presentations here, but if no one here is real any more, there may be no point."

Layea hastily printed on the next sheet on her tablet. NO, WE ARE INTERESTED.

"But if—" He broke off, as she was already printing.

WE ARE ILLUSION TO YOU, BUT REAL TO OURSELVES. WE DESPERATELY CRAVE DIVERSION FROM OUR CRUEL FATE.

Oh. "Of course. I misunderstood. We shall be happy to present our plays here. Just designate a suitable spot for us to camp, and we will put them on one each evening."

Layea smiled. THANK YOU SO MUCH! YOU MAY CAMP RIGHT HERE.

"On the street? But that will obstruct your passage."

YOU CAN'T OBSTRUCT US. WE WILL WALK THROUGH YOU.

Oh, again. "Thank you. We will do that." He turned to Curtis. "Why don't you see to that, and I will try to learn more about the local situation."

Curtis understood perfectly. He nodded and walked away.

Cyrus faced Layea. "I would like to know how it came to this, if you care to tell it." Because there was surely a lot to be learned about the nature and power of the Roc here.

I WILL BE HAPPY TO TELL YOU, BUT YOU MAY FIND IT UN-BEARABLY DULL.

"We have seen evidence of the Roc's powers and actions in other villages," Cyrus said. "But they were not like this. Something extraordinary must have happened here."

She nodded. COME IN. She held the door open for him, though of course it had no substance; he could simply have walked through it.

Her house was typically organized inside, with nice curtains, a table, chairs, and a comfortable couch. I REGRET YOU CAN'T USE THE FURNITURE, she printed. YOU WILL HAVE TO MAKE YOURSELF COMFORTABLE ON THE FLOOR. THAT IS ALL THAT REMAINS REAL.

"I understand." He felt a chair, verifying that it had no substance, and eased himself to the floor. Layea sat on the couch; for her it was solid. He remembered how Orienta had said she passed right through other illusion people, after being deleted herself; maybe stationary objects were different.

From his low vantage, he couldn't help seeing her legs. They were ordinary, like the rest of her, but the view under her skirt made them intriguing. He looked away, embarrassed.

But then he had to look back, because he had to read her printing. This was awkward.

OH—I'M SORRY, she printed. I WASN'T THINKING. She rearranged her legs so that less flesh showed. It seemed she was not trying to vamp him in the manner Andromeda had; she just had not fully adjusted to the perspective of a visitor on the floor instead of on a chair, understandably.

"Is there any way to manipulate your illusion?" he asked. "So instead of slow print, you could show me what happened?"

She scribbled: KATRIANA.

"She is someone who can do this?"

YES. SHE CAN REPLAY REAL SCENES VIA ILLUSION.

"That's what we need," he agreed.

ONE MOMENT, PLEASE. She walked out of the house. He remained, getting comfortable on the floor. His metal bones made it easier.

Soon Layea returned with another woman. Katriana was older, and completely undistinguished. Except when she invoked her talent. She lifted her hands, and something appeared between them. It was a picture. She spread her hands, and the picture expanded between them. It showed the village of Pompos.

Layea held up a sign beside the picture. WHERE SHOULD WE START?

"At the beginning," Cyrus said. "I want to understand the whole story."

THAT WOULD BE OUR FIRST PROBLEM, AND OUR FRIEND ETTE.

"Ette?"

SHE'S A ROC. VERY PRETTY.

Roc Ette, surely a shapely bird. "Thank you."

Katriana expanded the picture farther, until it was like a picture window into the scene. It showed a rock mine. Villagers were busily working with picks, hammers, and sieves, extracting small stones from the ground. On the hill above the mine was a huge nest occupied by a giant but quite lovely bird: Ette, prettiest of roc hens, with lovely plumage.

IT IS ETTE'S MINE, WHICH WE HAVE A DEAL TO WORK, Layea's sign beside the picture said. WE TRADE HER THINGS SHE WANTS, LIKE THE LATEST ROCK MUSIC.

The scene showed a villager carrying a rock shaped like a musical note up to the roc's nest: rock music. Cyrus's memory bank confirmed that rocs did like rock music, rock gardens, and rock candy.

The scene showed a close-up of the pebbles the villagers were extracting from the mine. They ranged from nondescript to ugly.

"What kind of stone do you mine?" Cyrus asked.

UGLY GEMS.

"I can see that. But who would want those?"

The picture showed a very pretty young village woman, the kind any village man would want to take home. She put an ugly stone on a cord and hung the cord around her neck, so that the stone dangled before her evocative bosom.

Suddenly the woman was unpretty, and her bosom was repulsive.

"Oh!" Cyrus exclaimed. "Not only is the gem ugly, it makes its wearer ugly! But still, who would want it?"

The young woman took off her stone, and became pretty again. Immediately a dirty young man approached her. He said something that was inaudible to Cyrus, but the girl flushed angrily and walked away. The man pursued her, uttering more embarrassing things. It seemed that he wanted to do things with her that the girl preferred to avoid.

Finally she put the stone back on. The man took one more look at her, shook his head in wonder, and departed.

"Oh," Cyrus said. "It made her unattractive, so she was no longer bothered by aggressive men."

YES. YOUNG WOMEN FIND OUR UGLY GEMS VERY USEFUL ON OCCASION. SOME WEAR THEM ALL THE TIME, EXCEPT AT HOME WITH THEIR HUSBANDS.

"Got it," Cyrus said. "Pompos must have had a prosperous business."

YES. IT ENABLED US TO BECOME UNBEARABLY POMPOUS. WE COULD AFFORD THE VERY FANCIEST THINGS, AND WE FELT SUPERIOR TO EVERYONE ELSE AND LET THEM KNOW IT. THEREIN LAY OUR DOOM.

"Oh? Ragna wanted your mine?"

NO. THE GOBLINS DID. THEY THOUGHT THAT OTHER CREATURES WOULD LIKE THEM BETTER IF THE GOBLINS COULD AFFORD FANCY POSSESSIONS. SO THEY DECIDED TO TAKE THE MINE FROM US.

Now the scene showed a horde of goblins pouring out of a mountain. They organized themselves into a crude army and marched on Pompos.

The villagers saw them coming, and were plainly appalled. This was not a warrior village, and they had no way to stop the invasion. What could they do?

Layea walked up the hill to talk with Roc Ette, who would also be affected by this. Could she help them?

The roc nodded. There was further dialogue, then Layea and several village men climbed into a large basket outside of the village. Ette flew down and caught its handle in her talons. She lifted it and carried them away. Evidently Katriana did not go on this journey, because the scene did not follow it.

Meanwhile the goblin horde was rapidly swarming toward the village. Would the special party return in time to stop it? The villagers were horrified, knowing that nothing but death, rapine, and slavery awaited them if the goblins took over. Their prettiest girls were fleeing, because their fate would be awful.

"But the ugly stones," Cyrus protested. "Wouldn't they save the girls?"

NOT FROM GOBLINS. GOBLINS OFTEN DON'T FIND THEIR OWN WOMEN UGLY ENOUGH.

Oh, again.

ANYWAY, THE LADY GOBLINS WANTED THE STONES TOO, BECAUSE MALE GOBLINS ARE VERY AGGRESSIVE. AND THE STONES COULD BE TRADED FOR ALL MANNER OF FINE THINGS. THEN THEY COULD BE AS SNOOTY AS THE HUMAN FOLK HAD BEEN.

It was making ugly sense.

In due course the roc returned with the basket, and barely in time, for the goblins were upon the fringe of the village. There was no chance to land, so Ette flew over the swarm. The folk in the basket poured buckets of water out onto the heads of the goblins, thoroughly wetting them.

The effect was immediate. The goblins were enraged, and turned on each other, madly attacking. They hated everything, including their companions, and laid about them with their weapons.

"Like mundane rabies!" Cyrus exclaimed.

HATE ELIXIR, Layea agreed. OPPOSITE TO LOVE ELIXIR.

Which made the goblins mad, literally. The result was sheer carnage. Before long there was nothing left but a pile of brutally slain goblins.

There was an awful mess to clean up, but the villagers went to work in good spirits. They had to wear protective clothing to avoid being touched by any lingering hate elixir, and the growing stench was appalling. They persevered, and Ette carried baskets of pure water to rinse off the contaminated landscape, and in a few days they had the area clean again. Things returned to normal.

Roc Ette had enabled them to save their village and their mine. They owed her a huge favor.

"I should think so," Cyrus agreed.

Time passed. Then a stranger appeared. He talked with Layea.

A MINION OF RAGNA ROC.

Layea listened courteously. Then she did something odd. She invited the Minion in, fed him a nice dinner, put on a dress that greatly enhanced her appearance, and took him to her bed. Her bare body was quite enticing, and the man was clearly enticed. So was Cyrus, who realized that she looked ordinary only when she wasn't trying. That was an inherent talent many women seemed to have.

"You really don't need to show me this," Cyrus said, embarrassed.

IT IS NECESSARY.

In bed, naked, she balked, gently holding him off. There was something she wanted in exchange. What was it?

I PROFFERED A DEAL. I WOULD DO ANYTHING HE WANTED, ALL NIGHT, IF HE DID SOMETHING I WANTED NEXT MORNING.

"Of course he wanted something," Cyrus said. "He's a man, and you're naked. Men want mainly one thing." He winced internally as he said it, remembering how he had learned what it was. "But what did you want of him?"

THAT HE DRINK FROM A NEARBY SPRING.

"That seems like an unequal exchange."

IT IS A SPECIAL SPRING.

The man shrugged and agreed. They made the deal. Then he took hold of her and stirred up some stork feathers. The Adult Conspiracy came into play, fudging out the details, but there was no question what was going on.

Cyrus found it voyeuristically interesting despite the lack of detail, and was ashamed of himself. Why did she regard it as necessary that he witness this private spectacle?

In the morning the Minion, evidently satisfied with the night, nevertheless returned to business: his gestures showed that he wanted Layea to swear allegiance to Ragna Roc, on behalf of the village. Layea still demurred, evidently protesting that she couldn't possibly make such an important decision in such a hurry; there would have to be a village meeting, discussion, and so on. When he became impatient, she kissed him and drew him back to the bed. He was nettled, but yielded; she had done well for him in the night, and had evidently not yet exhausted his passion.

When a full day had passed, and it was the same time it had been when the Minion arrived, her attitude shifted. She begged him to accompany her to a special place not far outside the village. It was a small spring, with a warning sign beside it: BEWARE—LETHE.

The Minion read the sign, and gesticulated. He wasn't touching that! But Layea insisted, pointing to the spring, reminding him that he had agreed to do it. He had, indeed, and finally, reluctantly, he lay down beside it, put his mouth down, and drank.

Then he got up, evidently dazed. Layea was gone and he was alone. He wandered away, remembering nothing. The village had been saved.

"But how—?" Cyrus asked, bewildered. "He saw the sign. He *knew* it would wipe out his memory."

MY TALENT. I CAN MAKE ANY MAN DO MY WILL TWENTY-THREE MINUTES OUT OF TWENTY-FOUR HOURS. SO I KEPT HIM WITH ME THAT TIME, THEN ASKED HIM TO DRINK. I MUST ASK, NOT COMMAND, AND IT HAS TO BE WITHIN HIS CONSCIENCE. BUT HE *HAD* AGREED, AND IT WAS NOT CONTRARY TO HIS CONSCIENCE, SO MY TALENT WAS ABLE TO MAKE HIM DO IT. A DEAL IS A DEAL.

Cyrus worked it out. She had to know a man twenty-four hours before her talent became effective on him. So she had done what she had to, keeping him with her, doing whatever it took, until she could invoke her talent. Then she wiped him out.

"This is ugly," he said.

Layea nodded. I HAD TO TELL YOU, EVEN IF IT MAKES YOU HATE ME.

"I don't hate you! I'm just—appalled."

WHAT ELSE COULD I DO?

He pondered. He had seen the other two villages. The Minions of the Roc were merciless. She had a weapon, and she used it. "Nothing," he said.

She looked relieved. She had not wanted to alienate him, but she had had a cruel choice to make. Submission to Ragna, or a desperate use of her power. She had done what she had done, to save her village.

"Yet my opinion isn't worth much," Cyrus said. "You could have simply told me you distracted the Minion, without showing me exactly how. That would have saved you some embarrassment."

I FEEL GUILT, AND NEED A LIVING OPINION. THE VILLAGERS OF COURSE SUPPORT ME, BUT YOU ARE MORE OBJECTIVE. I WANT TO KNOW THAT I DID THE RIGHT THING, EVEN IF I HAD TO DO A WRONG THING TO ACHIEVE IT.

So it was a confession. He wished he could do the same about his own guilt with Rhythm.

A bulb flashed over his head. "I have a similar confession, requiring similar objective judgment," he said. "Will you listen?"

Layea gazed at him, half in surprise, half in gratitude. YES.

"I was seduced by a Sorceress, a stunning creature twenty-two years old. I love her still. But her real age is twelve. She used magic to age herself a decade, and I knew it, but did it anyway. How great is my guilt?"

YOU ARE A MAN.

"Yes. But that doesn't excuse it."

MEN DON'T NEED EXCUSES. THEY DO WHAT THEY DO REGARDLESS. YOU COULDN'T HELP YOURSELF.

"Still."

THE GUILT IS THAT OF THE SORCERESS, WHO KNEW WHAT SHE WAS DOING.

"I don't blame her! I love her."

YOU ARE A MAN, she repeated. THE MINION WAS A MAN. ALL A WOMAN HAS TO DO IS SHOW HER PANTIES OR HER BRA OR EVEN SOMETIMES JUST HER BARE FLESH AND SHE CAN DO ANYTHING WITH HIM SHE WANTS. SHE USED YOU AS I USED THE MINION. YOU ARE GUILTY ONLY OF BEING WHAT YOU ARE.

"Somehow I'm not relieved."

AT LEAST YOU LOVE HER. THE MINION DIDN'T LOVE ME; HE USED ME. YOUR GUILT IS MINIMAL.

He hadn't thought of it that way. A burden was easing from his conscience. "Thank you, Layea."

WELCOME. Then they resumed the illusion presentation.

A month later a second Minion arrived. THEY HAD FOUND THE FIRST, WHO HAD FORGOTTEN HIS MISSION. HE DEMANDED TO KNOW WHO HAD DONE IT.

"But they couldn't know it was you," Cyrus said. "Because of the forgetting."

THEY KNEW WHERE HE HAD BEEN SENT.

The second Minion was a canny brute. He wanted Layea to swear fealty, but he also wanted whatever the first had gotten.

SO I TOLD HIM. IN FACT KATRIANA SHOWED HIM.

"Showed him! The way she's showing me?"

YES.

"But then she must have been there, to see it herself!"

NO. I TOLD HER, AND SHE RE-CREATED THE SEQUENCE.

Cyrus shook his head. This was desperation indeed. There were women who would literally die rather than expose themselves to the potential humiliation of having their illicit seductions publicized.

The picture showed a picture within the picture, as the Second Minion watched what the first had done with Layea. The sight evidently excited him greatly.

WE MADE A DEAL. HE COULD DO THE SAME AT NIGHT. IN THE MORNING I WOULD FILL TWO CUPS WITH WATER. ONE WOULD BE NORMAL; THE OTHER, LETHE. HE WOULD CHOOSE, AND WE BOTH WOULD DRINK.

"He agreed to that?" Cyrus asked incredulously.

THE ILLUSION SHOW MUST HAVE TURNED HIM ON.

As it had turned Cyrus on. It was, as she had said, the condition of being male.

So the Second Minion had at her all night, and in the morning she fixed two clear drinks. She held them up before him, inviting him to choose.

He picked one, then gestured: he wanted her to drink first. She put hers to her mouth and sipped. She smiled, not losing her memory.

Ha. He took her drink from her, and gave her his.

"Hey!" Cyrus said. "Isn't that cheating? You should have drunk simultaneously."

I CHEATED TOO.

"How? You gave him his choice."

WATCH.

Layea was clearly reluctant to drink from the second cup, but he insisted. She evidently reminded him that he must drink too, and her talent was making him conform, so they drank together. One sip each.

Layea looked slightly confused, affected by a little bit of memory loss. The Minion smiled, then glugged down the rest of his drink, while Layea sipped more delicately.

Then he stood dazed. He had forgotten everything. She turned him about and sent him walking out of the house and village. He was done.

"But he switched drinks!" Cyrus protested. "You had the lethe!"

I FAKED CONFUSION.

"But if that wasn't the one—you drank from both."

I FILLED EACH HALF FULL OF LETHE, AND HALF FULL OF SAFE WATER. THE LETHE IS THICKER, AND SETTLED TO THE BOTTOM.

"And you never drank down to the bottom, as he did! You tricked him."

I DID. WAS I WRONG?

Cyrus considered. The Minion had been so determined to cheat that he had fooled himself. He had thought he had the safe one, and glugged it. "Less wrong than he was."

THANK YOU. I DO FEEL SOME GUILT.

"Ragna Roc must have been pretty mad when he lost a second Minion."

HE DIDN'T NOTICE.

"Didn't notice! Then why did he destroy your village?"

Layea smiled. The illusion picture moved again.

This time it showed Roc Ette gracefully flying. When she nested on the ground her plumage was drab brown, but when her wings spread they displayed rainbow colors. She was beautiful when she tried, typically female in that respect.

One day as she foraged she encountered a male roc. He admired her wings and squawked to her in bird talk. He wanted her to come with him, to be his companion and perhaps more. She was interested, and followed him to his lair, which was beside a huge castle being constructed from rock candy.

Then she saw three other roc hens nesting, and realized that she had not been invited to be his sole companion, but a member of a harem. Revolted, she wheeled about in midair and departed.

The three other hens vaulted from their nests and pursued her. They boxed her in, flying before, above, and below her. "Halt, hen!" the one above squawked. "Do you not know who asked you? Don't be coy." There was no actual sounds in the picture, but Layea printed the words so that the full scene was re-created.

"Whoever he is, he has some nerve," Ette retorted. "You may be satisfied to share, but I am not. We do not practice plural marriage in Xanth."

"That's the old order. He is Ragna Roc, establishing the new order. You would do well to seek his favor, as we do."

"Why should I want the favor of a philandering cock bird?"

"Because otherwise he will delete you."

"What me?"

"Delete you. He will render you into illusion. That's his talent. He is a Magician Roc, and he will govern, or see the end of Xanth in a mighty battle. He is a god."

"He's deluded! There are no gods."

"There *were* no gods," the hen squawked. "Now there is Ragna. Join him now, while the position remains open."

"Hardly," Ette said with contempt. Then she folded her wings and plummeted past the lower hen. She got a new direction and flew away before the three could reorient. She dodged behind a mountain, turned at right angles, and shot off again, flying barely over the ground, losing them.

But after that her life was not her own. When she foraged, there were spy rocs that reported her position, and the three hens came after her. It was evident that Ragna intended to capture her for his harem, regardless of her preference. What was she to do? She had to forage, lest she starve, but then she could be spotted in the sky. Rocs are big birds; they can not readily disappear in flight.

It got worse. Ette made evasive maneuvers whenever she spied another roc, be it hen or cock, but even so they were narrowing down her home range. Soon they would locate her nest, and then she would be doomed.

Then the villagers repaid their debt to her. They constructed a tent over the deepest section of the mine, coloring it to resemble that section so that it would be invisible from above. It was big enough for Ette to roost under. They also masked her nest, so there was no indication that a roc had ever roosted there.

But how was she to eat? They handled that too. They brought her a constant stream of assorted foods to eat, ranging from trapped welsh rabbits to giant pot pies harvested from the village orchard. It wasn't pleasant having to stay hunched down all day, but she was essentially invisible, and safe.

Days passed, and the search died down. Ette emerged, desperate to resume hunting for herself.

And the rocs spied her. They had been waiting in ambush, knowing she was somewhere in this sector. Now they had narrowed it down further.

She tried to escape, but they had her surrounded. She fled to the very edge of Xanth, but could go no farther, because without the magic ambiance she could not fly at all. She had to land and await her fate.

Ragna came. "Swear allegiance to me," he squawked.

"Never!" she squawked back.

He didn't argue. He merely looked at her—and she felt something strange in her wings. She tried to lurch into the air, to fly—and discovered that her wingfeathers had become illusion. Ragna had clipped her wings, in his fashion. She could no longer fly.

They strung a harness around her, made a captive centaur flick her to be light, and the three roc hens used the harness to carry her up and on to Ragna's castle. She could not fly away, and was doomed to belong to his harem until she could slowly grow new flight feathers. If he didn't delete them too.

"What a fate," Cyrus said sadly.

Then the Minions backtracked, and located the concealed roost in the mine. They understood what the villagers had done.

Ragna came and stared at the village. One by one the houses were deleted, along with whatever was inside them, including people. Those who tried to flee were deleted in midmotion. The Roc did not stop until the entire village and all its inhabitants were illusion. Then they set a sign saying POMPOS CITY and departed, leaving it as an object lesson for anyone else who might think to oppose the Roc.

NOW YOU KNOW, Layea concluded.

"I'm sorry," Cyrus said, feeling inadequate.

NOT YOUR FAULT.

"Thank you for showing me what happened here."

WHY DID YOU WANT TO KNOW?

Cyrus pondered, and decided to take a risk, because he really wanted to give Layea and her village some hope. "I have a secret."

Both women smiled. WE WILL KEEP IT.

"My mission is to destroy Ragna Roc. I am gathering information."

Both women looked highly gratified. WE WISH YOU SUCCESS. IS THERE ANY WAY WE CAN HELP?

"Do you know the limits of his power?"

They shook their heads. IT SEEMS TO HAVE NO LIMIT. HE IS SURELY THE MOST POWERFUL SORCERER IN XANTH.

"Thank you," he said regretfully.

Cyrus did not return directly to the troupe. Disturbed by what he had learned and the magnitude of the mission, he walked out of the illusion city until he came to a region where the trees and objects were real.

Something attracted him to a particular tree. There was a sadness here, a loneliness. In fact it felt like a maiden weeping. Grief was something he had a fresh appreciation for. But he saw nothing. Yet it was here, beside the tree. Was it another virtual ghost?

No, human man, the lady's thought came faintly. *It is I, Anona.*

He looked around again. "Anona, I don't see you."

Look down.

He looked down. All he saw was an ant.

Yet. Anona Ant. I am sadly lost from my Pique ant hill, and fear I will never find my way home.

"An ant! How can I hear you?"

Lift me up near your head.

He reached down and put out one finger for the ant to climb on. She did. Then he brought the finger to his face. Anona was a surprisingly pretty ant. "You can read minds?"

It's a complicated story. The essence is that Che Centaur fed me some royal jelly, two years ago, and it made me more female than is good for me, and had a side effect of making me slightly telepathic.

He spoke aloud, because that focused his thoughts specifically so she could read them. "That explains that. But how did you get lost?"

I was foraging alone—my untoward femaleness makes me unwelcome among other workers—and found a nice grain of wax on a snoozing bird. But when I pried it loose, the bird woke and took flight, and carried me away. I finally got off when the bird landed, but I was far far away from home. I have been crying ever since. Can you help me?

"I don't know. I am not conversant with ant geography."

I believe we are guided, sometimes in ways we don't understand. There must have been reason for me to get lost, and for you to find me. Let me nest in your pocket, and perhaps you will find a way to return me to my hill.

Cyrus was about to demur, but the grief of Anona ant threatened to burst out again. So he tried reason. "I am on a very dangerous mission. It would not be safe for you stay with me for any length of time."

Does it relate to Ragna Roc?

"How did you know that?"

Because you are here at the edge of the village he recently destroyed. It is also uppermost in your mind.

"Yes. Then you know the danger."

Help me, and I will help you, if I can. I doubt an ant can do much, but there must have been some higher purpose in our meeting.

Cyrus sighed. He put the ant in his front shirt pocket.

Ah, you have some cookie crumbs here I can eat.

"I guess I do," he agreed. "Sometimes I store them there." He turned around and walked back to the troupe. He never thought of Anona again, and she didn't remind him, though she was close enough to reach him telepathically. Maybe it was her notion of manifest destiny.

They put on the plays, staying three days. The illusion villagers loved them all. They might have no substance, but their human passions remained.

THANK YOU FOR TAKING THE TROUBLE, Layea printed. YOU ARE THE FIRST REAL FOLK TO TREAT US LIKE PEOPLE.

"You're welcome," Cyrus said, a lump in his throat. The village had helped a friend, and paid a horrible price.

"Maybe we'll visit again, when we have more plays," Kadence said.

Cyrus had caught the troupe up with the general history of the village, and they all sympathized. There were nods of agreement. They would return—if they had the chance.

17

LULLABY

"We have two cities to choose from," Curtis said. "The left fork of the trail leads to Elasti; the right fork to Verbo. Do we have a preference?"

"Elasti City and Verbo City," Cyrus repeated thoughtfully. "I am growing tired of the big bird's penchant for puns."

"Actually, Elasti has been named that all along," Curtis said. "Perhaps it served as the inspiration for the Roc's renaming of the others."

"Let's go there, then," Cyrus said.

Elasti City turned out to be a wonder of rubber and elastic, with buildings that swayed in the wind and snapped back into shape as it passed. The people, too, seemed resilient, being friendly and not illusory. They were not bent out of shape by the appearance of outsiders.

"This is beautiful," Rhythm said, looking around.

"Mind-stretching," Kadence said, giggling.

But Cyrus knew that there was danger here, as in all the areas taken over by Ragna Roc. What special challenge would they encounter?

The central building was especially interesting, looking partly like a limber palace and partly like a lady's garment that flexed gracefully with every suggestion of a breeze. "I could almost wear that, when I mature," Rhythm remarked.

"In what venue?" For she was both princess and girl.

"Both, of course." She was probably correct.

"Hello!" Cyrus called.

The laced door opened and a woman appeared. She was elegantly garbed in a dress that stretched in all the right places, and she wore a petite elastic crown. "Yes?" she inquired, her voice wonderfully resilient.

"I am Cyrus Cyborg, and these are Rhyme and her sister Kadence," Cyrus said. He never liked lying, but there was no alternative in this case. "We represent a traveling troupe. We would like to present three plays here, if you are interested."

The woman nodded. "I am Princess Lullaby of Elasti City, and we have been expecting you. Do come in."

"Expecting us?" Cyrus asked, nonplussed.

"Did you suppose your travels were secret? We have considerable candor to share. Enter."

"Thank you, Princess," Cyrus said, hardly nonminused by her words. What did she mean by candor?

Lullaby seated them on ornate bouncy stools, and sat in a thronelike chair herself. It gave springily under her weight. Everything here was resilient to some degree.

"You will want to know about our association with Ragna Roc," Lullaby said. "That is simply told. We have always had a fine business in the export of elastic clothing and materials; it helps stretch our budget so that our people don't get bent out of shape by hard work."

"So we have seen," Cyrus agreed cautiously.

There was a boom!, the sound of a nearby explosion, making them jump. "Don't be concerned," Lullaby said soothingly. "That's only Rocky, helping with construction. His talent is to make stones or other small things explode. It's very handy when we have to clear a cluttered lot."

"You are still doing construction?"

"Oh, yes. We like building new things. We posted a sign saying BLOCK LONG ERECTION."

Cyrus bit his tongue. Rhythm looked slightly suspicious, and Kadence noticed nothing. Had Lullaby said it on purpose? What was she up to?

"It's good to keep working," Cyrus said noncommittally.

"Then Ragna came and offered us more. Working with him, we are in a position to extend our range and expand our influence. Naturally this interested us, and we gladly joined his realm."

"Realm?"

"He is a god, Cyrus. He doesn't have a kingdom but a realm."

This was too much for Cyrus. "He's a rank impostor!"

"You will surely change your opinion, once you know more of him. We did."

"He's a power-hungry birdbrain!"

She nodded benignly. "I see you will need some persuasion. I think it is merely a matter of discovering your price."

"I have no price! I am loyal to the present order."

"Really?" Lullaby opened her gown to show the curvy upper lines of a jeweled bra.

"That won't work," he said, disgusted.

"So it seems. The actresses of your troupe all got into bed with you and tried to seduce you, without success. That might indicate sterling reserve."

"Might," Cyrus agreed, shaken by her knowledge of that particular situation.

"Or it might suggest disinterest in their bodies," Lullaby continued resiliently. "Because then you took up with a child."

He stared at her. So did Rhythm and Kadence.

"A twelve-year-old girl. You seem to be having a regular affair with her. Now you are getting interested in her six-year-old sister."

"I—" Cyrus said, but further words clogged in his throat.

Rhythm put her hand on his. "She's baiting you," she murmured.

Kadence put her hand on his other hand. "Don't let her get to you."

"But this is outrageous!"

Both hands squeezed his warningly, and he shut his mouth.

"Cyrus," Lullaby continued inexorably. "You are a pedophile."

The hands continued their warning squeezing. The girls evidently knew something he didn't. He kept silent.

"Consensual, it seems," Lullaby said. "Interesting."

Then he realized: the woman knew only part of the story. She had made an assumption that might have been reasonable, based on her incomplete information, and was playing him for her own purpose. It was better to leave her in ignorance.

That gave him command of the situation. "My relationship with these two girls is consensual," he agreed. "What are you leading up to?"

"Swear fealty to Ragna Roc, assist him in ushering in the new order, and not only will you be among the privileged, you will be free to maintain any relationships you want, with any amenable children, not merely these two."

She was trying to blackmail him into enlisting! Now maybe he could play her, for vital information. "I doubt it. Ragna deleted two Minions for trying to take over two underage girls."

"He did delete them, but not for that reason. Ragna does not care about interpersonal relations, apart from those directly with him: loyal, unquestioning obedience to his will, expressed or implied. He deleted them because they exceeded their authority. They could have had those girls, had they cleared it with Ragna in advance. Instead, they presumed. Ragna has little tolerance for presumption."

"They didn't ask," Cyrus said, appreciating the distinction.

"They lost track of their place," Lullaby agreed. "A smart and loyal Minion never does that."

"You are such a minion," Cyrus said.

"Indeed, and you are free to leave it uncapitalized as long as you are not one yourself. Are you now amenable to joining the new order?"

"No."

"You are honest and direct. That's good. Ragna needs officials of that description."

"No. I am not honest and direct. I am concealing the nature of my devious relationship with these girls."

"As you have to, in the present order. Let's move on. We have been aware of your mission and movements throughout. We did not expect the other city elders to recruit you. If I do not succeed, I will forward you to one who will."

"What do you think my mission is?"

"To destroy Ragna Roc."

"How can you know that?"

"Because your mission started with the Good Magician. He is laboring to find a way to stop Ragna's advance without danger to himself. So he made this your Service to him. That's the way he works. Thereafter we have tracked you via the spy we have in your midst."

Cyrus had thought he was recovering ground, but this dropped it from under him again. "A spy?"

Lullaby laughed. "So you see, nothing has been secret. The Roc has seen you coming throughout. At first he sent a curse after you, but that seems to have gotten lost."

"There was a curse," Cyrus agreed. "But our producer is a

Curse Friend, and he defused it. It wasn't very effective anyway. I understand it was a used one."

"That was common cents."

He was startled again. "What?"

She brought out several small copper coins. "Hold these. They facilitate reasoning." She handed them to him.

He looked at them. They were completely ordinary mundane pennies, dull and worn. Common cents.

"It made cents to use a used spell," Cyrus said. "Not only was it cheaper, it couldn't be traced to its source. If it worked, good enough; if not, little was lost."

"You see, common cents helped you work it out."

"It wasn't directed at me, but at the greatest danger to Ragna," Cyrus continued. "Evidently I'm not it."

"Evidently," she agreed, taking back the pennies. Now it was clear why she was so logical; she had the cents. "I have little belief in the efficacy of mindless curses. I expect to do a better job."

"Regardless, I am not signing up with Ragna," Cyrus said.

"You can't escape him. You are not an Escape Pea."

"A what?"

She brought out a small pod. "These. Consider them." She handed the pod to him.

It popped open as he took it, and the peas rolled out. He tried to grab them, but they cleverly avoided his hand and spilled onto the floor. Rhythm and Kadence tried to catch them, but they danced around and got away.

"Escape Peas," Cyrus said. "You are right; I'm not clever at escapes the way they are."

"It's their talent. Every person has his talent. I like Dale's."

"Who?"

"Dale. He's one of our citizens. His talent is to knock the socks off people. You can tell when he's annoyed, because everyone in the neighborhood is barefooted, or at least sock-less."

"She's teasing us," Rhythm said tightly.

"She should try it on the Good Magician," Kadence tittered. "He has more socks than anyone."

"I think it is time for us to go," Cyrus said.

"By no means," Lullaby said. "You must stay the night, all of you. In the morning I will give you a tour of the city, beginning with our hydraponics pool."

This was a word not in his data bank. "What kind of pool?"

"Hydraponics. We grow hydras from nothing but water," Lullaby explained. "Some have seven heads, others nine heads. They are really quite impressive."

That did it. Cyrus stood to go. "We are not interested."

Lullaby shrugged. "Sleep on it, and we'll discuss it further in the morning."

"I have no intention of—" He broke off, for she was doing something odd. She was making a sound, like a sustained note, or a croon. In fact, she was singing.

Then he became aware of the slackening grips on his two hands. He looked, and discovered that both Rhythm and Kadence had fallen asleep beside him.

"I am named for my talent," Lullaby explained. "I sing people to sleep. Now carry them to the bed, so they can rest comfortably. This way." She stood and walked to a doorway.

There seemed to be little else to do except what she asked. He couldn't carry both girls at once, and couldn't leave them alone in this house. He had to stay with them. He stood, bent to pick up Rhythm, and carried her in the direction Lullaby was going. This turned out to be a fancy bedroom with a huge soft bed. He laid the girl down on it, hoping she would be all right. She slept throughout; the enchantment was strong. Then he went back and picked up Kadence, and laid her beside Rhythm.

"That's good," Lullaby said. "They have a knight light." So it seemed; it was in the shape of a glowing mounted knight.

"What are you trying to do?" Cyrus demanded.

She smiled. "You are such a handsome man. You must have a fans club."

Cyrus drew yet another blank. "A what?"

"To beat off obsessed fans."

Oh. "No."

"Now you may if you wish join me in my bed, or sleep here."

"I am not joining you."

"Just verifying." She resumed her singing.

"I won't—"

When he woke, it was morning. He was lying beside the two girls, who were now stirring.

"What happened?" Rhythm asked.

"Her talent is to sing folk to sleep. She put us down for the night."

"That's all?"

"All I know of. I slept too. She was demonstrating her power."

"Let's get out of here."

"If she lets us."

"Make her forget," she murmured.

Good idea. They walked out the doorway, and into the main part of the palace.

Lullaby intercepted them. "Ah, you are up. It is time for breakfast." She gestured to a set table. "I have blue bread and gray V. But watch the Mugs; they will steal from you if you aren't careful. You don't want to get Mugged."

"No thanks," Cyrus said, refusing to ask about the food. "We're returning to the troupe."

"Not yet." She started to sing.

Cyrus made her forget her intent. By the time she remembered, the three of them were back on the street and walking rapidly away from the castle.

"Well done," Rhythm murmured. "I didn't want to show my power."

"Don't even speak of it," he murmured back. "Their spy might be near."

You're right, she thought. *Who is that spy? She doesn't know. She gets her information from a little bird.*

A little bird! He had to smile. But he knew she meant it literally, and it did make sense: Ragna was after all a bird. A big bird, but a bird. He would have bird allies.

"Who could be the spy?" Kadence echoed, evidently receiving the thought too. "Nobody in the troupe would betray us."

"That's my impression," Cyrus said.

"Mine too," Rhythm said.

They continued to mull it over, mostly silently, as they walked. They were sure that none of the regular troupe members would do it. But what about the peripheral ones? And there they zeroed in on a possibility. *Dusty!* Rhythm thought.

Dusty had associated with Piper, and with his big sister Dusti. They would have shared troupe gossip with him. And that was Lullaby's information: troupe gossip. Most troupe members did not know or even suspect Rhythm's identity. Or that she used the Decade spell to age herself for an hour at a time. Or that Kadence was their daughter. So the real secrets had been maintained. That was good.

Dusti and Piper would not have realized that Dusty was a spy; they were innocent. But why would Dusty join the Roc?

Orienta! Rhythm thought. *The Roc must have promised him a nice girlfriend—and delivered.*

And there it was. They had solved that riddle.

What were they to do about it? Nothing, Cyrus concluded.

Just continue their secrecy about the things that mattered. Ragna had little reason to fear Cyrus or the troupe, but excellent reason to fear Princess Rhythm.

Meanwhile the Roc wants to win you over, Rhythm thought. *Are you tempted?*

The Roc thought Cyrus was a pedophile! No, he wasn't tempted.

I was only teasing. But she was angry too, and so was Kadence. They would have to live with that suspicion, not refuting it, until this mission was done, one way or another.

But don't turn him down flatly, Rhythm advised. *Let him think you are considering it. Maybe you'll learn more.*

Good point.

The troupe had moved into the village and set up in the vacant lot provided. It seemed that a villager had come to tell them that the Elder approved the presentations, and Cyrus and the girls were being entertained at the palace.

"I was concerned," Curtis said when they rejoined the troupe. "It's not like you not to inform me."

"She put us to sleep with her magic lullaby," Rhythm said. "We had no chance."

"She called me a pedophile," Cyrus muttered.

Curtis knew much of the truth. He tried with reasonable success to stifle his laughter.

"She said he could have us both, openly, if he joined the new order," Kadence said. Theoretically she was too young to know what a pedophile was, but this was a special situation.

"And that there's a secret spy in our midst," Rhythm said.

"A what?" Curtis asked, startled.

"Who provides information about the troupe."

"There is none," Curtis said with certainty. "I know these folk. None of them would do that."

Cyrus took him aside and whispered their conclusion. The Curse Friend nodded and departed, shaking his head.

That evening they put on the first play. It was well received.

After the play, Lullaby approached Cyrus. "You may have until your stay here ends, to reconsider the offer," she said.

"And if I still decline?"

"Ragna will decide. Probably he will let you go. He can't trust involuntary Minions. But it's a good offer."

"I'll think about it."

"Very good." She moved on.

That night Rhythm joined him, but was hesitant. "Considering what Lullaby thinks, I don't know whether to—you know."

Whether to invoke the Decade spell. Surely there were ways for Lullaby to know what happened here, and if she learned that Cyrus was not a pedophile she would realize that she had no real hold over him.

"Let's just be innocently together," he said.

Will you settle for that? she asked mentally.

"Of course. I love you regardless."

But you're a man.

"I am," he agreed.

Men care only about one thing. Even children know that.

"Not everything children know is true."

You keep surprising me, she thought, snuggling close.

"We'd better talk aloud or sleep, lest some realize" *that you can read my mind,* he finished as a thought for her to read.

"So what is on your mind, Cyrus?" she asked.

"Two things. One is trying to figure out the weaknesses of Ragna Roc."

"We haven't found any."

"The other is what the prophetic riddle means: Two to the Fifth."

"We are the Two."

"And maybe the Roc is the Fifth. And we're going to him.

But that's just asking to be deleted when we don't join him. That's no good."

I can't say this aloud: that I am a Sorceress who will enchant him. "No good," she agreed aloud.

Suppose he is immune to your Sorcery? "So there must be something else, because the Good Magician doesn't speak nonsense."

I'll bring in my sisters. Actually that's the plan: to get the three of us together. Nothing can stand against our cubed power. "What else could there be?"

Ragna knows of the three of you. He must have something in mind. "I have no idea."

Deletion. If he catches us. "Surely something bad."

"Horrible."

"Awful," she agreed, snuggling closer.

They slept, innocently. It was wonderful.

In the morning they went to see Lullaby. The plan was for Cyrus to ask leading questions, and for Rhythm to read the answers in the woman's mind, perhaps gaining some clues.

"Why hello, Cyrus and Rhyme," Lullaby said as they stood by her door. "Do come in."

Inside, comfortably settled, Cyrus got blunt. "You tell me that Ragna Roc wants my fealty. I have difficulty understanding why he should want me."

"You are a cyborg—the first we know of in Xanth. You thus can relate to both the human and the robot species. That could be useful."

"How could he be sure my fealty was good? That I wasn't lying, to get close to him and somehow hurt him?"

"You are a cyborg," she repeated. "You have machine components. An iron skeleton, a data bank, a crossbreed outlook."

"I do."

"Machines can't lie. They have to be true to their programming."

"But I can lie. I'm half human."

"But only for good reason. Such as to protect yourself from condemnation for violating the Adult Conspiracy. If you make an oath, you will honor it."

She had him there. "Still, I might somehow annoy Ragna, and then he would delete me. Why should I risk that?"

"Apart from free access to your child love? A fine residence? Power over others, in the name of the Roc?"

"Apart from those," he agreed.

"Because your risk of deletion is much less if you are with Ragna, than if you are against him."

"Is it really? I am wary."

"I can give an example. There was a man here in this city who annoyed Ragna by trying to steal food reserved for a favored Minion. Ragna deleted him. But the man had a useful talent, so after a few days Ragna undeleted him. Then the man annoyed him again, being unreformed. This time Ragna banished him. So he was spared, and now he lives elsewhere, we care not where. Ragna is cautious and not vindictive. Maybe some day he will need that man's talent again."

"How does Ragna delete something?"

"He merely peers at it and exerts his power."

Cyrus's mind made a connection. "He has to see something to delete it."

"Why yes, I suppose he does," Lullaby agreed. "Does it matter?"

Cyrus reconsidered. "Maybe not. When he deleted Pompos City, he did it building by building, and that included everything inside the buildings. So there were things he didn't directly see, but they were still in range."

"Maybe the deletion proceeds from the outside in," she agreed, evidently intrigued.

"Could he delete himself?"

"Maybe with a mirror?"

"Probably the mirror would be deleted," Rhythm said, smiling.

"But if he could delete himself—could he then undelete himself?" Cyrus asked.

Lullaby shrugged. "I wouldn't know. It is academic, because he has no reason to delete himself."

"I suppose not," Cyrus agreed. "Unless he got captured and imprisoned."

"He would delete the prison and walk out," Lullaby said.

That gave Cyrus another idea. "Is there anything he *can't* delete?"

"I doubt it. As you noted in Pompos, he deleted everything."

"So he did," Cyrus agreed. "Well, thank you. We'll put on the second play tonight. I hope you enjoy it."

"I'm sure I will."

They departed, returning to the troupe. Cyrus wondered whether Rhythm had gotten any useful information from the woman's mind.

I did. She didn't like the sharpness of your questions. She truly serves the Roc, and hates any indication of weakness in him. His having to be within sight of something to delete it or undelete it is a limitation. But there's more.

Are you teasing me?

No. You really scored with the question about what the Roc can't delete. There is *something. But she doesn't know what it is.*

That was really interesting. The bird had to see it, and something still couldn't be deleted.

We need to find out what that is, he thought.

Yes we do.

There it lapsed. But they had made significant progress.

The folk of Elasti City really enjoyed the second play, with its stretching the nature of reality and romance. They applauded heartily. They certainly didn't seem to be oppressed; they liked being under Ragna Roc's wing.

The third day Cyrus walked around the beautiful city, openly admiring the architecture. But his mind was on the twin mysteries: what could Ragna Roc not delete, and what did Two to the Fifth mean? Were they related?

Two had to be himself and Rhythm. The Fifth must be the Roc. But why the Fifth, and not the Fourth or the Third? What about the intervening numbers? It just wasn't making any sense.

Lullaby approached him. "I will expect your answer after the conclusion of your third play."

"I may not be able to give it."

"You will give it. If you are not for Ragna, we shall have to assume you are against him."

"That seems fair." Because Cyrus already knew he would never sign up with the big bird.

The audience was right with the play. The actors were impassioned, knowing that a crisis point was approaching. Were the folk of Elasti City going to let them depart next day in peace? What would happen if they didn't?

Lullaby is planning something, Rhythm thought. *I don't know what, but she had definitely made some sort of decision.*

That did not ease Cyrus's concern. But all he could do was see it through.

The play proceeded to the point at which Nimby, the Demon Xanth, posed the riddle for the Good Magician Humfrey: why didn't two chips of reverse wood nullify each other?

"I have three answers for you," Humfrey said. "You may select what pleases you."

"I will," the donkey-headed dragon said.

"First, it is indeed a member of that nonsensical class I mentioned before, so should not be taken seriously."

"Nevertheless, I am taking it seriously."

Just so. "Second, the two chips are part of the larger re-verse wood tree that fragmented eons ago, so don't affect each other any more than two hands on a person cancel each other; they are part of the same whole, and act together, even if somewhat separated physically."

"But if they do affect each other, what then?"

"Then, third, they would each reverse the other, causing it to enhance rather than reverse, and it would enhance the re-versal ability. So instead of losing reversal, they would re-verse other things twice as strongly. So there is no conflict and no paradox."

The donkey head angled thoughtfully. "It seems so simple when you clarify it."

"That's my business," Humfrey said, looking gnomishly smug.

"That resolves my dilemma. Thank you." The Demon Xanth faded out. That was a spot effect of the Seldom Scene, impressive onstage.

The Good Magician looked around. Suddenly five wives also faded, leaving only MareAnn, the half wife. "Let's go home, dear," she said, leaning down toward him. "We haven't had a moment alone together since the Demon got distracted. We have a lot of thwarted love to make up."

"Don't try to kiss me!" Humfrey grumped.

But she tackled him, dropped him to the floor, and planted a huge slobbery kiss on his face as the scene faded. The audi-ence roared, loving the gnome's obvious embarrassment.

After the curtain calls, Lullaby approached Cyrus. "Have you come to a decision?"

This was the crunch. What did she have in mind? He would simply have to bring it on.

"Yes. I don't want to swear fealty to Ragna Roc."

She nodded. "I suspected as much. You have been stead-fast in that respect. Ragna respects that. Therefore he wants to meet you."

"I prefer to remain with my troupe." He had to have Rhythm along, and not for personal reasons; she was the key to the defeat of the Roc.

"Of course. Therefore Ragna is extending an invitation for your troupe to bring your plays for performance at Castle Rock Candy, his official residence."

"An invitation!" Cyrus did not have to pretend astonishment. Just like that, they were to reach the big bird?

"A word of caution. Such invitations, however politely phrased, are not subject to refusal. Your only option is to accept with gratitude."

"But none of us have agreed to swear fealty!" he protested. "We are not his allies."

She nodded again. "Two things about that. First, Ragna does receive visitors who are not his disciples. It is a matter of governance. As an entertainment troupe, you may perform for him and go your way thereafter. Second, if he truly desires your fealty, you and the members of your troupe will be subject to persuasion by Ragna's Minions. So you may not remain separate."

"I don't like the sound of that. I don't want my actors pressured. Certainly I don't want Rhyme and Kadence held hostage against my enlistment."

She shook her head. "No, no, no! That would be duress, and would not lead to ultimate loyalty. There will be nothing of that sort. The only problem for you might be if some of the members of your troupe were persuaded, and you were not. That might lead to dissension in your ranks."

Why was she playing this so cautiously? "So maybe it would be better not to go."

Suddenly she is afraid, Rhythm's thought came.

"Cyrus, please. If you decline, not only will you bring the Roc's ire upon yourself and your troupe, you will bring it on me for not persuading you. I assure you that the invitation is good, and that you will be subject to no coercion or unpleasantness, only reasonable persuasion. He can be a most congenial host, when he tries, and he has a great deal to offer. Only if you try to attack Ragna or his subjects will there be repercussions. I beg you, accept."

She's sincere.

Cyrus was oddly moved. He had merely been playing a role, that of a wary troupe master, so that there would be no suspicion of his real mission. So he did what his role required. "I apologize for alarming you. On behalf of my troupe, I accept."

"Oh, thank you!" She flung her arms about him and kissed him.

That, too, was interesting. She thought him a pedophile, with no interest in grown women. But in fact, were he not already taken, he would have found her interesting indeed. She *was* interesting.

She recovered her composure. "The Roc's entourage will arrive tomorrow morning. Pack your things early." She departed.

She'd have taken you to her bed, had you been interested.

If you took over her body, I would be interested.

But it would reveal you as a normal man.

And that was the rub.

18

RAGNA

They packed before dawn, knowing that this was the big event. Jim made food for them all, so that there would be no delay for breakfast. They were tensely ready.

"Wait outside the city," Lullaby said.

They marched out to the plain beside Elasti. There was a giant basket sitting there. It was the size of a house.

"Get in," Lullaby said.

They got in.

Then the birds came: a squadron of monstrous roc hens, a winged brown mass that darkened the sky. They came in for a landing all around the basket: six of them. The ground shuddered as each put down her landing gear: enormous metallic talons. Sparks sprayed out as those claws slid across the hard surface of the landing field, braking the giant bodies.

"Farewell," Lullaby said, stepping back. "I sincerely wish you well." She got well clear of the rocs, who waited impassively while she passed under the beak of one to get beyond their hexagon. The monstrous bird could have snapped her up and swallowed her in half a flick of an instant, but did not. That was another impressive example of the discipline of Ragna Roc's Minions of whatever species.

Then the great birds caught lines in their talons, spread their wings, and taxied in formation for the takeoff. The lines stretched taut, connected to the basket. The rocs leaped into the air together, their wings blasting powerful downdrafts. They forged upward, and the basket hung between them, buffeted by peripheral turbulence. The troupe members hung on to the handholds all around the edge. This was a trip like no other. Their entire troupe, together with its folded tents and other paraphernalia, was being lofted as if it were just an incidental package.

The rocs achieved traveling elevation, then stroked forward at cruising velocity. The wind of passage was so strong that vapor trails formed, obscuring the surrounding scenery. There was no way to tell exactly where they were going. This was not accidental, Cyrus realized; most folk had no idea where Ragna Roc lived. The Good Magician knew, but kept the secret, so as not to invite the malign attention of the Roc.

Soon they arrived. Rocs flew so fast that all of Xanth was within minutes. They glided down toward Rock Candy Castle.

There was a concerted gasp of awe from the actresses. "It's absolutely beautiful," Xina said.

"Good enough to eat," the Witch agreed. "I'd love to have some of their leftover rubble to build a little candy house in the forest to attract children." It was humor; the Witch actually liked children, and both Rhythm and Kadence liked her.

Tuff made as if to press her into the ground with his fist. "Volcanic rock is good enough."

"I can duplicate rock candy," Jim said.

"On that scale?"

Jim sighed. "No. That's a whole mountain."

And it was. The castle perched on a mountain of multicolored rock candy with outcroppings of translucent projections. The base of the castle was chocolate brown, giving way to lime green, and on up through other colors to the highest glassy tower. And what a tower it was! It had no spire, but was shaped into the form of a monstrous bowl.

"It's a nest!" Acro Nymph exclaimed.

"For Ragna Roc," Dusti agreed.

The nearer they came, the larger the castle became. Stones that had seemed the size of dominoes turned out to be the size of cinder blocks, then of brightly faceted boulders. Tiny peepholes became sparkling windows. A mousehole of a door expanded into an elephant avenue. Rock Candy Castle was not only beautiful, it was enormous.

The hen formation glided down onto a raised landing field that turned out to be quite large enough. The basket bumped to a halt. Then the rocs released the lines, spread their wings, and took off again. Their job was done.

"I have to admit to being impressed," Cyrus murmured.

Rhythm squeezed his hand. He glanced at her, and noticed she had two ribbons in her hair, one green, the other brown. He did not remember them; she must have done a quick primping just before the journey.

They scrambled out of the basket, uncertain what was next. Would they be pitching their tents here? But the shining pavement was too hard for them to drive stakes into.

A group of people appeared. "Hello, honored visitors," a man said. "I am Alex, and my talent is making stone invisible. We used it for windows in the lower stories. It is my pleasure to welcome you to Castle Rock Candy, and to make your stay here as pleasant as possible."

"I am Cyrus Cyborg," Cyrus said, not completely at ease. "This is my troupe. We are here to present plays for the entourage of Ragna Roc."

"Of course. But you are also much-appreciated guests.

Because you may be understandably perplexed by the multitude of people and wonders here, we will provide each member of your troupe with a personal guide and assistant who will cater to your every need and inclination."

"Oh, we don't need anything like that," Cyrus said. "All we need is a place to camp and pitch our tents, and a stage to put on our plays."

The trace of a frown hovered in the vicinity of Alex's mouth. "This is standard procedure for visitors, by order of the Roc. We hope you don't find it burdensome."

So it wasn't an option. Ragna would be keeping a close eye on every one of them. "In that case, thank you," Cyrus said. "But we shall want to camp together. We become uneasy when separated." Because who knew what mischief could befall them, without the others knowing?

"Perhaps a compromise. We will provide you with a cluster of cottages your troupe may use as it wishes."

"That would be nice," Cyrus agreed warily.

"Let me introduce your guides." Alex snapped his fingers, and two almost identical young men stepped forward. "This is Obvious, who is quick to see the nature of any situation, and this is his twin brother Obvious-Lee, who cancels out that ability. They would like to assist sisters."

Rhythm smiled. "I am Rhyme, and this is my little sister Kadence. We hope you know where the best rock candy for eating is." She was being deliberately childish, Cyrus knew, so as to conceal any hint of her real nature.

"We do," Obvious said. He shot a glance at Lee. "And don't cancel that!"

Kadence clapped her hands together. "Oh, goody! Let's go." She was playing her little sister role, which wasn't difficult for her because she'd been doing it all along.

"Now be careful, dears," the Witch said, playing her motherly role. "You may eat only three pieces, so you won't get sick to your tummies."

"But she didn't say how big those pieces can be," Rhythm stage whispered to Kadence. The two went off with the brothers, just like naughty children.

"Maybe you had better keep an eye on the children," Cyrus said to the Witch. "Just in case. Their mother would be most annoyed if they got tummy aches."

A woman stepped forward. "I am Kim. My talent is that I can't be harmed by mundane means, only magical means. I will guide you and help you keep an eye on the children. I have children of my own."

"Thank you," the Witch said. Like Cyrus, she was not really easy with all this assistance, but all they could do was make the best of it. "But Kim, if you can't be harmed by magical means, you have nothing to fear from the Roc. So why are you here?"

"By mundane means," Kim corrected her. "Regardless, I did not join Ragna from fear, but from promise: I will have a much better life serving the god than I ever would in garden-variety Xanth. I shall be glad to talk to you about it, because you, too, can have improvement."

The Witch shot Cyrus a helpless glance. It seemed that each assistant was going to be working on a troupe member for conversion.

The little party went off to find candy. Alex continued to assign guides to the members of the troupe. For Cyrus there was a man named Gole. Gole did not meet his gaze.

"Is there a reason?" Cyrus asked, slightly puzzled and slightly more annoyed.

"My talent is to gaze into a person's eyes and make an illusory copy that is exactly opposite in nature and talent," Gole said. "It lasts for only an hour, but anything it does with its talent is real and endures. So I will not meet your gaze unless there is reason, because you would probably not like what resulted."

"I wouldn't," Cyrus agreed, shuddering. A talent like that could be dangerous.

"But should anyone else try to bother you, then I would look into his or her face, and that person probably would be distracted for an hour." Gole allowed half a smile to escape. "But no one here will try to bother an honored guest."

And what if Cyrus did something the Roc didn't like? Gole was surely an effective guard, but also a threat. Maybe that was the point: letting Cyrus know that he and his troupe had better behave.

The last human member of the troupe to get an assistant was Curtis. This was Ray, who had the ability of rearranging his body in unusual ways. For example, he put one of his hands on the end of a leg. Then he put his head on the end of his arm where his hand had been. "Do you think I could be an actor?" he asked, smiling from that vantage.

"Possibly," Curtis said, taken aback.

Then came the Dragon Lady. Her assistant was a woman carrying a large dragonhead mask. "I am Masque," she said. "I make very special masks from living creatures. They imbue the wearer with one quality of the creature. This one is a dragon mask I will use myself." She put it on, and blasted out a jet of fire.

"I'm impressed," Lady said. "What other masks do you have?"

"A number," Masque said, removing the mask. "I have one for ogre strength, ugliness, or stupidity. Another for nymphly beauty. Would you like to see my collection?"

"Yes I would. I wonder whether it would be possible to obtain a few masks from you, if I have anything to trade for them. Such as one to make me seem more human."

"Certainly. You can have any you like, if you swear fealty to Ragna Roc."

Oops. Cyrus winced.

"I will think about it," the Lady said noncommittally. Bless her.

Even Don Donkey got a companion, a silly ass named

Burrito who constantly cracked lame jokes about digesting beans or cutting cheese, but was ever alert. It seemed the Big Bird didn't trust even a robot animal to be alone.

They went as a group to the cottage cluster. This was on an open rock candy plateau at one side of the larger castle, and there were several pie trees growing in big tubs beside the cottages. Overall, it was a very nice site.

"Here is yours," Gole said, bringing Cyrus to a cottage. It was beautiful, with pale blue translucent rock candy walls, a berry-straw thatched roof, and lovely flowers growing around it. "You may occupy it alone, or have company of your choice."

"Company?"

"Rhyme."

Of course they knew about that; Lullaby would have informed them. "Thank you."

"We have in mind giving you a day and night to acclimatize, then showing your three plays on consecutive nights following," Gole said.

"That's considerate." It also gave the Minions longer to try to persuade the troupe members to defect.

"But first, if you are ready, comes the interview with the Roc."

"Interview?"

"Ragna wishes to converse with you and Rhyme. Something about a prophecy."

"Prophecy?" How much did they know?

"Two to the Fifth. I don't pretend to understand what it means, but I am merely a lowly Minion. Ragna will surely have a greater perspective."

They knew too much. "We will meet the Roc when Rhyme returns from her rock candy shopping."

"She is already waiting outside the cottage."

He was being channeled, but seemed to have no choice. "Thank you."

Cyrus used the basin and pitcher provided to wash up, and the rock candy glass mirror to verify his appearance. He was nervous about this meeting, uncertain what would happen. Ragna might simply delete him, thus preemptively canceling his mission.

Rhythm was indeed waiting outside, with Obvious, who had guided her to exactly where she needed to be. Obviously.

"Did you hear?" Rhythm asked with girlish excitement. "We are getting to meet Ragna Roc!"

"Yes," Cyrus agreed shortly. He was under no obligation to pretend naïveté about this dangerous encounter.

The guides conducted the two of them through several large arched chambers, up an enormous circular stairway, and to the lofty nest that was the Roc's residence. They came out onto a raised rim that surrounded the nest.

And there was Ragna Roc. He was a giant dull brown bird, undistinguished as rocs went, but still dauntingly impressive. Beside him, on the ledge, stood a kind-faced woman.

The bird squawked.

"Leave us," the woman said to the two guides. They walked quickly away.

The bird squawked again.

The woman turned to the two visitors. "Ragna Roc greets you, Cyrus Cyborg, and Princess Rhythm," she said. "I am Em Pathy, translating for the god. My talent is to alter emotions." She smiled briefly. "Do not be concerned; I am under strict orders to leave yours alone. Ragna desires an honest dialogue."

So Rhythm's disguise had been penetrated.

"Thank you, Em," Cyrus said. "It seems we are not fooling anyone."

Ragna squawked.

"He understands human talk," Em said. "And you are correct: he recognizes the Princess, and her two sisters."

"Sisters?" Cyrus asked blankly.

Squawk.

"The two ribbons," Em translated. "Please resume your natural forms now, Princesses."

Rhythm drew the green and brown ribbons from her hair and dangled them before her. They fluttered, shimmered, and fuzzed into vapor in the manner of a demon. The vapor coalesced into Princess Melody in a green dress, and Princess Harmony in brown.

"You didn't tell me!" Cyrus exclaimed, astonished.

"Secrets are best kept secret," Melody said.

"So that they don't leak out," Harmony agreed.

"And this one was important," Rhythm said.

So they were back in their threesome mode. Cyrus was not completely pleased with the deception.

Ragna squawked, amused.

"Your purpose was to bring one Princess here," Em said. "She then conjured the others. So that the three of them could face Ragna together."

"So it seems," Cyrus agreed wryly. "But how did Ragna know, if *I* didn't know?"

Squawk. "We have telepaths. It was in Princess Rhythm's mind."

And there had been opportunity for telepaths to get close to Rhythm, as she toured the premises.

"Ragna saw us coming," Cyrus said. "But why would he welcome his worst enemies to his home? That's dangerous."

Squawk. "It is fated," Em said. "The climactic battle between the god and the mortals must come, to decide which shall govern hereafter. Ragna welcomes that decision, though it destroy much of what currently exists."

"Welcomes it?" Cyrus was having trouble assimilating this.

Squawk. Cyrus was beginning to hear the translations as part of the squawk. Maybe he was learning roc language.

"The suspense is uncomfortable," Em said. "He would rather have it done with. It is better to have the battle at a time and location convenient to him, than to wait until the enemy precipitates it at a time convenient to the enemy."

"I suppose so," Cyrus said. "But it seems the Princesses have been as eager to get to it as he is."

"Yes, we are," Melody said.

"We are uncomfortable with indecision too," Harmony agreed.

"The issue must be settled," Rhythm concluded.

The enormous beak twitched in the suggestion of a smile. Squawk. "And the three of you have never found any magic to match your merged power. You want to test it against a worthy opponent."

"Of course not," Melody said insincerely.

"We never considered that," Harmony agreed dubiously.

"We're not like that," Rhythm concluded skeptically.

Squawk. "Such a pleasure to deal with children. I am now too old to have such certainty about anything. Do you believe them, Cyrus?"

"No." And somehow the bird had found a way to put the two of them on the same side. The two of them? "Oh, no!"

The three Princesses looked at him suspiciously. "What?" Melody demanded angrily.

"You don't think we're up to it?" Harmony asked grimly.

"I thought you loved me," Rhythm said tearfully.

Squawk! None of them needed the translator's smirk to recognize the laughter.

"None of the above," Cyrus said hastily. Now they had him embellishing with adverbs too. "It's that we may have misinterpreted the prediction."

"Two to the Fifth," Em said, not needing the squawk.

"We don't understand," Melody said, definitely not amused.

"The Good Magician's words are meant to be confused," Harmony agreed, certainly without mirth.

"So what the bleep are you talking about?" Rhythm concluded, positively annoyed.

Her two sisters, Cyrus, Em, and the Roc all looked at her, startled. She was, after all, a child, and a female one at that. She should never had heard the word, let alone understood it or been able to utter it.

"So to speak," Rhythm amended, embarrassed.

"Methinks somebody has had too much adult experience," Melody said.

"And remembered too much of it," Harmony agreed.

Rhythm opened her mouth. A wisp of steam emerged.

"What I mean," Cyrus said before she could speak, "is that we assumed that the Two were Rhythm and me. The question was who was the Fifth, which we thought was probably Ragna Roc. But suddenly I'm agreeing with Ragna against the three of you. As if he and I are the Two in this party of Five, and the three of you fill out the Five. That daunts me."

The three Princesses looked dismayed.

"Oh, no," Melody said, horrified.

"It can not be," Harmony agreed, appalled.

"You were always true to me," Rhythm concluded, distressed.

Squawk. "If Cyrus joins Ragna, Rhythm will not oppose the Roc," Em translated. "He will win by default."

"I'm not joining Ragna!" Cyrus exclaimed. "I just am not sure about that prophecy."

Squawk. "We had better fathom it," Em said. "I think we are agreed that it signals the victor in this war."

"War?" Cyrus asked.

"The war between the god and the mortals. Whose final climactic battle will settle the issue for all time. The battle between Ragna and the combined magic might of the three most potent Sorceresses Xanth has to offer."

Oh. *That* war. "And it seems that the first to fathom the

real meaning of the prophecy will win that battle," Cyrus said.

Squawk. "Again we are agreed. But as we know, it can be avoided if you will join me. There need be no ugliness at all."

"Why are you talking with us, instead of blasting away at the Princesses?"

Squawk. "That is not the way such things are done. There is a protocol. Also, I would much rather have the Princesses serving me, than deleted. Their merged power is surely second only to my own. And we have not yet enjoyed your plays."

Cyrus shook his head, bemused. "You would delay the final battle so as to watch a play?"

Squawk. "Indubitably. It won't be possible to watch them after the battle. Either I will be gone, or all of you will be gone."

That put it in chill perspective. "How do any of us know someone won't cheat? A sneak attack, or something?"

Squawk. "Surprise is impossible. We have been feeling each other out throughout."

Cyrus looked at the Princesses. They slowly nodded, together. Now he felt the tingling atmosphere of powerful magic. They were already in the battle, or at least the preliminaries of it. It hardly seemed to matter that it was a bird against children; it was sheer brutal magic force.

"Then suppose we schedule this final confrontation for the day after the last play," Cyrus said. "That is, the fourth day hence?" And realized as he spoke that this made it a five day event. The battle on the Fifth?

Squawk. "And ponder the prophecy in the interim," Ragna agreed.

The three Princesses nodded again, in concert. They seemed slightly distracted, and he realized it was because of the stress of opposing magic.

"Agreed," Cyrus said.

Squawk. "And if the prophecy turns out to favor me, the offer remains open, for you and the Princesses. Meanwhile, you have the freedom of Castle Rock Candy. Enjoy yourselves."

"Thank you."

Ragna closed his eyes, dismissing them. Em Pathy smiled. "That went well. Ragna likes you." She walked along the ledge to the exit.

Their guides appeared. It was time to return to the camp.

Now the girls relaxed. "That was interesting," Melody said.

"He's very strong," Harmony agreed.

"Maybe too strong," Rhythm concluded.

"How can you say that?" Cyrus demanded. All of them were ignoring their guides, as there was nothing secret remaining.

They turned a triply serious gaze on him. At this moment, none of them seemed childish. "We have to assess the matter accurately," Melody said.

"Because to do otherwise would be to invite disaster," Harmony agreed.

"And his power is equivalent to ours," Rhythm concluded.

Cyrus was taken aback. "To your cubed power?"

They nodded in concert again.

"And if he can defeat the three of you, there is no other magic in Xanth that could oppose him?"

"Only one," Melody said.

"The Demon Xanth," Harmony agreed.

"And he won't interfere," Rhythm concluded.

"And the prophecy Two to the Fifth is the key to victory," Cyrus said.

"You had better figure it out soon," Melody said.

"Within three days," Harmony agreed.

"Before the final battle," Rhythm concluded. "Now, if we

are through being triplets, why don't the two of you go tour the castle?"

"Nuh-uh," Melody said.

"He'll never figure out anything if you have at him," Harmony agreed. "Those decade-aged panties are deadly."

"Bleep," Rhythm concluded. This time the other two laughed, together. They definitely knew more about panties than girls their age were supposed to. The Adult Conspiracy was surely struggling to keep some sort of restraint on them.

Thus it was that Cyrus returned to his cottage, alone. Rhythm would not be visiting him tonight. "Bleep," he echoed.

"She's right," Melete said. "You have to focus on the prophecy. That's the key."

"But there are so many ways it can be interpreted! I'm at a loss." Actually they were talking silently, so as not to alert listening spies about either his thoughts or Melete's existence as more than an inert block.

"Cyrus, you are the creative one in this troupe. You write the plays. You have to work this out. No one else can do it. Not even the Roc, it seems." She was nagging him, as was her wont. He had long since ceased resenting it, as her constant prodding was largely responsible for his success as a playwright. He might be creative, but she was the one who kept him at it. Without that writer's block he would never have made it.

"The Princesses say that his power matches theirs. How can an obscure prophecy have any effect?"

"That is for you to discover," she said firmly. "The fate of Xanth may depend on it."

He tried to focus. "I suppose if the sides were evenly matched, any slight tilt could decide it."

"Keep working it out," she agreed.

"Two to the Fifth. If Two's not Rhythm and me, who is it?"

"Does it matter? You're both here regardless. It's the Fifth that's the real mystery."

So it seemed. "It has to be the fifth of some series."

"Why?"

That stopped him. "Why not?"

"It could be anything."

Cyrus groaned. "Like a fifth of whiskey? The Mundane Fifth amendment about not incriminating yourself?" He paused. "That's tempting. Could it get me out of trouble associating with a child? What about the Fifth Commandment, to honor your father and your mother? Only I'm a father now, and Rhythm is a mother. How can that relate to defeating the Roc?"

"Don't dismiss anything," Melete warned. "It may relate in a way we haven't yet thought of."

"Then there's math: two to the fifth power. That's thirty-two. That has nothing to do with anything."

"Oh, I'm sure the Muse of History could think of something."

"What about the fifth dimension?"

"What is that?"

"I'm not sure. My data bank says a dimension is any measurable extent or quality, and specifies four: length, breadth, depth, and duration."

"Space and time," Melete agreed. "You need one more."

"Well, there's mass. You can measure it in the form of weight or inertia. A rock and a puffball may be the same size, but the rock has a lot more mass, so has more impact. Without at least some mass, a thing would not exist, any more than if it were missing one of the other dimensions. It might look the same, but it wouldn't be real."

"What would it be?"

"Illusion."

Then he paused, a revelation spreading through him. "Illusion! That's what Ragna Roc makes of real people. He deletes their mass!"

"He uses the fifth dimension," Melete agreed.

"We have figured out the Fifth! The fifth dimension! It is the Roc's power!"

"I believe we have," Melete agreed. "So maybe you and Rhythm have to find a way to nullify that power."

"But the Princesses can't just block it; they say Ragna is as strong as they are."

"In a straight contest of magical power," Melete agreed. "That is surely where the prophecy comes in: to point out a way to nullify the Roc's power."

"But if Rhythm and I are the Two, and even all three Princesses can't nullify the Fifth, what is left?"

"*You* are left. The Princesses can oppose the Roc without any clear decision. You must be the missing factor."

"And what can I do? All I've done so far is mess up Rhythm's life by providing her with a daughter. And Kadence is a fluke, not supposed to exist at her age for another sixteen or seventeen years."

"She's like another illusion," Melete agreed.

"Yes. She should exist only in our imagination, but instead she's solid. As though she has been undeleted. A gift of the fifth dimension."

Then Cyrus and Melete exchanged a glance of sheer wonder. "Could she be the key?" Melete asked.

"But her talent doesn't relate. She makes folk march in step. That won't stop the Roc."

Melete nodded. "There must be something else."

May I say something?

It was Anona, the Pique Ant. Cyrus had put her in his pocket and completely forgotten her.

"Of course, Anona," Melete said.

"You two know each other?" Cyrus asked.

"We communed when you brought her home," Melete said. "We're both telepathic. It helps. She's a nice person."

Cyrus felt guilty for forgetting her. "What do you wish to say?"

I have picked up on your discussions, and pondered the matter of Ragna's weakness. It seems to me that maybe he can't delete something twice. He's never done it, as far as you have heard.

Cyrus considered. "That's right. That Minion he deleted, then undeleted, he didn't delete again, but banished him instead. I thought he just didn't want to hurt someone unnecessarily."

"Yet he had no compunctions deleting an entire innocent village," Melete said.

So maybe he didn't do it out of compassion, which he seems to lack, but because he couldn't, Anona thought. *If so, that's a weakness, isn't it?*

"A huge one," Cyrus agreed. "If we could just figure out a way to use it against him."

Well, I thought that maybe if you build a big cage out of undeleted material and put him in it, he couldn't escape. That would defeat him, wouldn't it?

"Build a cage of undeleted material," Cyrus echoed. "Confining him. Maybe a big egg shell so he couldn't see out of it. That just might do it. But how could that be done? He's not going to just sit around while we collect all that loose material and assemble it. He'll delete anyone who tries."

I thought maybe we ants could do that. He wouldn't even notice us, and we're very good at collecting and assembling. Except we're somewhat disorganized, so it would take a long time.

"We don't have a long time."

"But we do have Kadence," Melete reminded him.

"Whose talent is organization!" he agreed. "She could direct a mound of ants to do it in hours instead of months."

"And Ragna would never suspect, because he wouldn't see the ants and Kadence is just a child who shouldn't exist," Melete said.

"I think we've got it," Cyrus agreed. "Our secret weapon is a person from the fifth dimension. Except that all we have is one ant."

The Princesses could summon the rest of my hill, conjuring all the ants here. If they wanted to.

"I'll ask them!"

"No," Melete said. "*I'll* ask Rhythm, so there's nothing spoken aloud. You go about your business of putting on the plays."

"Talk to Kadence too," he said. "But assuming we get the cage made, how can we get Ragna in it?"

"That will be your challenge," Melete said.

He had been afraid of that.

There is something else, Anona thought.

Cyrus had learned respect for the ant's thoughts. "What is it?"

Won't they read your mind, and know your plan?

Cyrus shared a devastated glance with Melete. Of course the Roc's tame telepaths would do that! "What can I do?"

What about the lethe elixir?

"The what?"

When you put me in your pocket, there was a vial there. I recognized it as containing three drops of lethe. We Pique Ants have had some experience with that sort of thing, and are largely immune. That's why you forgot about me; it has an ambiance. That dose would be enough to make you forget this matter for at least three days. Four at the most; it hasn't been tested on cyborgs.

"The lethe Algebra Nymph gave me!" he exclaimed, remembering. That ambiance, as she put it, must have made him forget the vial as well as the ant. "She said I would need it at some point."

"This is that point," Melete agreed. "Take it. We can't let you carry that plan in your head these next three days. Not with those anonymous telepaths lurking. We have to clear it out immediately."

"But then how can I plan to lead the roc to the shell?"

"You will have to think fast then. Take the lethe."

Cyrus sighed. It did seem necessary. Still, he hesitated. "Suppose it wears off too soon—or too late? They could read my mind before the battle, or I wouldn't be able to invoke the plan. Either way is dangerous."

"Stop temporizing," Melete said severely. "Anona and I will know what's going on, and we'll direct Kadence without explaining, so she can't give away the plan either. We'll divert you or prod you as necessary."

He reluctantly fished the vial out of his pocket. It was so small he couldn't uncap it. "How do I open it?"

"Just chew it up," Melete said. "It's not glass."

He put the vial in his mouth. "Let me forget about the plan to stop Ragna Roc," he said. "And that I even have a plan." Then he chewed down hard.

"Now it's our turn," Melete said. Cyrus wondered what she meant by that, because he couldn't remember anything relevant.

19

Battle

The troupe members enjoyed being feted, each attended by an attentive guide, and they loved the luxury and beauty of Castle Rock Candy. They didn't like the constant solicitations to enlist with the Roc, but were cautious in their demurrals lest it end their royal treatment.

Cyrus stayed away from the Princesses and focused on the presentation of the three plays. They were well received, especially the second one, "The Dream," because of the prominence of the Dragon Lady. It seemed they related very well to the association with a nonhuman creature.

"We have let it be known," the Witch said to him, "that you are the troupe leader and we will stay with you. So if you join the Roc, so will we."

"I'll never do that!"

She cautioned him with a finger. "Be not so emphatic. We want to give them serious hope, at least until the showdown. It keeps them helpful."

"Less emphasis," he agreed. "But you know, if we lose the showdown—"

"Then we will join rather than be deleted. It is the sensible course. But we hope not to lose. We trust that you have some secret strategy for a surprising victory."

"I appreciate your trust," he said wryly. How could he tell her that he had never figured out any plan? The members of the troupe were trusting him, and he wished he were more deserving of their trust.

The last play concluded. The battle would be the following day.

Em Pathy approached Cyrus. She was attractively dressed, and quite pretty. "As you know, I speak for Ragna," she murmured.

"Yes."

"He would really like you to enlist, and not merely to avoid what is bound to be a bruising battle. He respects you, and would like to have your creative imagination supporting his realm."

"If he defeats the Princesses, who can say what I will do? I love Princess Rhythm."

"If he defeats the Princesses, there will be a separate negotiation. But the chances are that Princess Rhythm will be gone, and you will be intent on vengeance. It might be dangerous to bring you in then. He prefers to bring you in voluntarily, before the battle."

"I can't do that," Cyrus said uncomfortably. "I am loyal to the old order."

"It is that loyalty he appreciates, in part. For your sake, he will try to spare Princess Rhythm. But this may not be possible. Should the worst happen, he wants you to know that he will try to make it up to you."

"Oh?"

"By providing you with another compatible woman. He now knows you are not a pedophile."

So their telepaths had been reading his mind, and knew

the real nature of that romance. Cyrus repressed an angry retort. "I don't want any other woman."

"For example, me," she said. "I can be extremely understanding." She inhaled, smiling.

Suddenly she was more than attractive; she was compelling. He found himself overflowing with desire for her. He wanted to take her in his arms, kiss her, and go oh so much farther, reveling in the sheer awareness of her closeness.

Then he caught on. "You're altering my emotion!"

The effect faded. "Merely a demonstration. If you should lose the Princess, I could ease your pain and make you happy. Do not close off that option carelessly."

He realized that what she said was true. She could change his feelings. In order to avoid that, he answered very cautiously. "I will keep that in mind. But I do not want to stop loving the Princess."

"You are loyal. I value that. I am loyal to Ragna. But if by some foul chance he loses the battle, you may recruit me if you choose." She gave him a last tender tinge of desire, then walked away.

"That woman is dangerous," he said later to Melete. "And not just because of whom she serves."

"True. Do not make an enemy of her. She could be extremely useful if we win."

"Oh, I see. But if he wins—"

"Rhythm may be gone."

He had to see that they beat the Roc! But how? It was almost as if he had lost interest in formulating a plan of action. What was wrong with him?

"I'm sure you'll think of something," Melete said.

"But I *haven't*! I have no idea what to do!" With her, at least, he could be honest.

"Maybe the Princesses will defeat the Roc tomorrow," she said. "Then it won't matter any more."

"I wish I could be sure of that. But I'm afraid I have led them into a deadly trap. If they die it will be my fault."

"Cyrus," she said seriously. "This battle was fated. They would have had to meet Ragna sometime. It is better to do it now, before he takes over any more of Xanth. Win or lose, it's not your fault."

"But it *feels* like my fault."

"I would comfort you if I could."

"Rhythm could comfort me. Where is she?"

"She and her sisters are preparing to battle Ragna tomorrow morning. They can't afford to have you distracting them at this time. It could be the death of them."

"I know it," he said miserably. "I'll leave Rhythm alone."

"Now sleep," Melete said. "You will need your wits about you tomorrow."

"To watch a battle I can't affect? To betray the trust of my troupe?"

"Trust me, Cyrus. You are doing your part."

He gazed at her. He did trust her. But he couldn't believe her.

Yet, somehow, he managed to sleep soundly. Maybe someone had put a sleep spell on him.

In the morning the three Princesses were waiting by his door with their guides and the rest of the troupe. Rhythm stepped forward. "In case I don't make it," she murmured, "remember that I love you, regardless of my age." Then she kissed him in front of everyone.

"Oh, Rhythm!" he said as he held her. "I'll always love you!"

"Stay with Kadence, please. Make a family for her." She wiped away a tear. At this stage, she was only technically a child.

"I will!" he said, half blinded by tears himself.

She returned to her sisters. They began the march to the Roc's nest.

Kadence came up. He took her hand. They followed the Princesses. The rest of the troupe was behind.

They came to the Nest. There was Ragna Roc, huge and imposing. Beside him stood Em Pathy.

"The battle will commence when I lower my hand," Em said without preamble. She raised her right arm.

Melody, Harmony, and Rhythm stood together at the rim of the nest, facing Ragna Roc. They nodded together, ready.

There was no other preliminary. Em dropped her arm.

Nothing happened. The troupe members looked at each other, perplexed. When was it going to start?

Then Cyrus saw that Ragna Roc was absolutely still. Not a single feather moved. And the three Princesses were frozen in place like statues. Bird and girls were staring intently at each other, doing nothing else.

Nothing? They were doing everything! Ragna was trying to delete them, and they were fighting back and perhaps using his own power against him, maybe reflecting it or converting it to something else. The battle was invisible, but it was being waged.

Now Cyrus felt a tingling in his hair and on his skin. All the hairs of his body were trying to lift themselves up, as if electrically charged. There was enormous magic suffusing the area, touching them all peripherally.

"Daddy!" Kadence cried, scared.

He looked at her. Her hair was drawing itself up from her scalp, spreading out, radiating from her head like a spiked helmet.

"It's the magic," he whispered. "It's not directed at you. It's because of the battle. It's so intense it infuses everything and spreads out, like a hot potato cooling. They are trying to destroy each other."

"Oh," she said, not seeming very much reassured. "I thought I was terrified." She reconsidered. "I *am* terrified!"

Cyrus looked around. The hair was spreading out on all the troupe members, and on the Minions too. "We all are, dear. But all we can do is wait, and hope."

Something changed in her expression. "No. Anona says we have more to do."

"Anona Ant?" He had quite forgotten her since first putting her in his pocket. How did she relate?

"She's in my hair," Kadence said. "Hanging on desperately. She's directing me."

"Directing you?" Cyrus was at a loss to comprehend this.

"Come with me, Father."

"But the battle isn't finished."

"Go with her," Melete said from his pocket. He didn't remember putting her there, but he must have done so.

Kadence took him by the hand and led him from the Nest. No one else moved; they were all standing distracted, hair spiking, hardly breathing. The magic was so thick it seemed difficult to pass through it. Oh, yes, the battle was happening!

As they passed through the halls and chambers of the castle, Cyrus noticed something else. The rock candy stones were melting. Not a lot, but their sharp edges were rounding off, and their flat planes were warping slightly. The intense magic was evidently generating heat that softened the material. If that continued, this castle would became a physically dangerous place, because there was an awful lot of candy rock in it.

He remembered how daunting it was to be in the vicinity when the three Princesses focused together on a spot project. They were children, but their merged and cubed magic was as strong as any in Xanth. Yet Ragna Roc was attacking them with confidence, and so far, making it stick. It was awesome and, yes, scary.

There were Minions here and there, but none of them paid attention to the two visitors in their midst. They were standing in place, hair outstretched, taken by the awful power of the surrounding magic.

They came to the roof where the roc hens had landed. The basket remained, and beside it was a huge egg with a hinged top. It was big enough to hold several rocs. Ants were swarming over it, applying the finishing touches.

"What is this?" Cyrus asked.

"It is your project, Father. Don't you remember?"

"No. I know nothing of this."

"Because you took those three drops of lethe elixir to make you forget. They should be wearing off any time now. This is an egg made from undeleted material—stuff the Roc deleted, then undeleted, so can't delete again. Anona Ant is directing me, and I'm coordinating all the other ants in her Hill, which the Princesses conjured here three days ago and then took sniffs of some lethe elixir they also conjured from where Roc Ette used to live, to make them forget. Ragna will not be able to get out of this egg, once it closes about him. But there's one problem."

Cyrus did not need to remember anything to understand that. "Getting him into it."

"Yes. That's your job. If he beats the Princesses, we can still win, if you get him in there. But there's another problem. That lid is too heavy for the ants to move quickly. He'd escape long before they could close it."

Cyrus looked at the huge lid. "Too big for me too."

"Think of a way, Cyrus," Melete urged him.

It was beginning to come back. "I worked this out," he said. "Then took lethe so the telepaths couldn't find out from my mind. But I didn't think of that detail."

"Think of it now," Melete said.

Cyrus focused his creativity. A dim bulb flashed. "Roc Ette!"

"Who?" Kadence asked.

"The roc hen he captured after deleting the entire village that had helped her escape him. She's part of his harem."

"What's a harem, Father?"

He opened his mouth, but was abruptly balked by the Adult Conspiracy. "A special group of women. The point is, she doesn't want to be there. She surely hates Ragna."

"She could close the egg!" Kadence exclaimed. She was a bright child.

"Yes. If I can find her in time."

"I know where there's a flock of roc hens," Kadence said. "I saw them when we toured the castle."

"That has to be them. Take me there."

She led him to another section of the castle. The trip was harrowing, because rock candy blocks were starting to fall into the halls, and here and there they could hear roofs collapsing. The castle was being destroyed, yet no one was touching it. How long could this go on?

They reached the hens. These, too, were mesmerized by the transcendent magic atmosphere. They perched hunched, their feathers extended in the manner of the hair on the humans. But which one was Ette?

"Call her," Melete advised. "The others won't care."

"Roc Ette!" he called.

One huge head turned toward him. This was a very pretty roc. Now he saw that her wingfeathers were not extended. He remembered why: they had been deleted. They were illusion. She could not fly. It was a horrible punishment for a bird, any bird.

"Roc Ette," he said. "I am Cyrus Cyborg. I saw how the entire village of your human friends was deleted. I am fighting Ragna, but I need your help. Together maybe we can put him away."

She nodded. She understood him. She hopped down from her perch.

"This way," he said. "To the roof." He explained as he and Kadence ran around the growing rubble and melt, and Ette followed.

Fortunately the landing area was more solidly constructed than the more decorative portions of the castle. Maybe it was underpinned by regular rock instead of candy. It remained firm enough to support the roc hen's weight.

"So if you can hide behind the basket, then jump out and push the lid closed when he's in it, he will be trapped," Cyrus concluded. "Will you do that?"

Ette nodded. There was something very like a grim smile on her beak.

The trap was set. Now all he had to do was get Ragna here, and into the egg. If he could just figure out a way.

"I must go," Cyrus said. "I congratulate you, Anona, Kadence, and the Pique Ants. You have done an excellent job."

Kadence remained by the shell, organizing the ants as they shored up any possible weak spots. They would have the shell ready for occupancy on time.

The collapse of the castle was accelerating as he returned to the Nest. He had to climb over forming piles of half-melted rubble. Yet still the contest of magic continued. It seemed that the opposing forces were so nearly equal that there was no way out except to continue.

How was he to get the big bird past all this and into the shell? Cyrus still had no idea.

He came to the Nest. Ragna still faced the three Princesses. None of them had moved. But now the rest of the castle was collapsing around them. The people were fleeing, both Minions and troupe members. It wasn't any change of loyalties so much as fear that they would be crushed in falling blocks of rock candy, or stuck in melting goo.

Now at last there began to be some change. Ragna's feathers were drooping, and the Princesses were wavering. Then Melody sank to her knees.

"No!" Cyrus cried in anguish.

"Yes," Em Pathy said, returning to the scene. "Did you really think mere Sorceresses could defeat a god?"

"I did," he said, seeing Harmony also sink.

"I'm surprised they lasted as long as this. I thought he would delete them in the first few minutes."

"Go poop your panties, pooch."

"In a few more minutes you will belong to me, Cyrus. Then you will welcome my panties."

The awful thing was that he knew she meant it. She had taken a fancy to him, and would rule his emotion once the way had been cleared.

They watched as Rhythm sank to her knees. The ambiance of magic was overwhelming the three; they could not hold out much longer.

And when they lost, what of his love? A bulb flashed over his head, and such was the intensity of magic that it overheated and exploded with a pop. He could make a difference!

Cyrus jumped into the Nest and slid down its curving side to the roc's giant feet. "You big pile of piffle!" he yelled, kicking a talon. "All you can do is attack little girls!"

"Cyrus!" Em called, horrified. "Get out of there! You can't attack a god!"

He ignored her. "You must be really proud of yourself, birdbrain! Beating up on children!" He stomped the talon.

Now he got Ragna's attention. The roc glared down at him. But to do that, he had to remove his deadly gaze from the Princesses. He could not focus his magic without looking.

"Why don't you try to delete someone your own size, feather-face?" Cyrus demanded. "Don't have the nerve, Raggy?"

Ragna stirred. He tried to orient his head so that both eyes could focus on the annoyance. That gave Cyrus a notion.

"You can't delete what you can't focus on!" he yelled. "And I'm too close for you to focus, cross-eyes!"

Now there was a stir of anger. A foot twitched up. But Cyrus was already scrambling over the other foot and around to the far side of the Nest.

"Get your tail in gear!" he yelled, kicking at a tail feather. He didn't do the huge thing any damage, but his effort was surely quite annoying. "You can't catch me, birdlime!"

He definitely had Ragna's attention. The Roc half spread his wings and spun about, trying to orient his beak for an attack. But Cyrus was on his way up the side and out of the Nest.

"You're crazy!" Em called. "You're throwing your foolish life away, when you could have so much fun with me!"

"I'm having fun with Ragna Rook!" he called over his shoulder as he ran from the Nest.

Now the chase was on in earnest. Cyrus fled through the rubble of the castle, dodging from side to side in an attempt to prevent the roc from focusing on him. Ragna pursued, enraged.

"Ragna!" Em called. "Don't let him distract you from the battle! The girls aren't dead yet!"

"Sure, go back to the girls, you horrendous hunk of deleted droppings!" Cyrus encouraged him. "They're more your speed."

"Let him go, Ragna!" Em called. "He's not worth your effort."

The Roc ignored her sensible advice. He was trying to focus on Cyrus.

Cyrus realized as he ran that his hair was no longer standing on end. The potent aura of magic had faded; the battle with the Princesses was no longer in progress. He had succeeded in distracting the bird, as he had intended.

Cyrus dodged around a pile of half-melted rock candy, staying out of the direct line of sight. There was a crash as the pile collapsed in on itself; Cyrus realized that the Roc had deleted the bottom of it, where he had just dodged, and so the top had lost support and dropped down. He was glad he was a cyborg, with half-machine strength; otherwise he would not have gotten clear in time.

He came up on a statue of a bare nymph. Actually that was redundant; all nymphs were bare until some became real women and donned clothing. She probably represented a morsel of food rather than a stork object. He ran around her—and her fair head plunged to the floor, leaving her deleted body standing in place.

Cyrus knew he had better get where he was going soon, because otherwise he would become illusion on the way. He ran behind more rubble, then dodged back the opposite direction as it collapsed.

The way was awkward, but he was angling for the roof and the shell. He kept yelling insults and lurching in different directions, hoping that the Roc would follow without ever getting the right range. He knew he would be terrified if he ever paused to think about it.

Somehow he succeeded. There was the basket and the shell. He ran straight for them, feeling the breath of the Roc right behind him.

"A place to hide!" he cried. "He won't find me there!" He ran up a convenient pile of rubble and leaped for the huge shell. He caught the rim, and heaved himself inside. He slid down the curving inner shell. Would this ruse work?

There was an angry squawk outside. The Roc must have tried to delete the shell, and been unable. That, with luck, infuriated him. His annoying prey was escaping.

Suddenly the top darkened. Then the huge body landed inside. Cyrus barely managed to scramble out of the way of the descending mass. "Curses! He found me!" he yelled.

Ragna oriented on the sound. His eyes found Cyrus, and started to focus.

The lid slammed shut. Suddenly it was dark inside.

"Squawk?" Ragna asked, surprised.

"Listen, rock-head, the trap has sprung," Cyrus said loudly. "This shell is made of undeleted material, and built to withstand any physical force you can apply. You are a prisoner."

There was a shaft of light from a large peephole. Cyrus went to stand in its wan illumination. "Go ahead," he said. "Delete me. Then you'll be entirely alone. You know they'll never let you out. They'll poke food into the hole so you won't starve, and remove your refuse, because the folk of Xanth aren't brutes, but they'll never free you."

There was silence. The Roc was listening.

"This was my doing," Cyrus continued. "I devised this trap, and had the ants make it, and I led you to it. It is not entirely unkind; there is a hypno-gourd here that you will be able to peek into and range the entire dream realm at your leisure. You won't be bored. But you will need a companion, if only to interrupt your eye contact occasionally so you will not starve to death. So now you have a choice: destroy me and be forever alone, or listen to the deal I proffer."

He paused, but there was no response, so he continued. "I will arrange an exchange, if you wish: me for a roc hen to keep you company and assist with the gourd. Or any other creature you choose, who wants to be with you. Maybe Em Pathy, your translator."

Now there was a negative squawk. "I thought not. She's loyal to you, but not your kind. You want the hen. Here is how we will arrange it: you will delete me, I'll walk through this shell and arrange for the hen to come here, you will peer at her through the peep hole, and if you are satisfied you will undelete me and delete her so she can come in here where you can undelete her. Then she will be yours forever. Is that satisfactory?"

There was half a squawk.

"Ah yes. How can you trust me to do as I promise? The

answer is, you will have to. There are reasons why you
wanted to recruit me to your team, and trustworthiness is
one of them. I never pretended to you or your Minions that I
planned to join you; I always served the other side. I was true
to my commitment. I will be true to this one. But since I can't
necessarily trust *you*, I will insist on your undeleting me before the hen joins you. I will obtain her commitment to join
you after I am undeleted, and to refuse to join you if I remain
deleted. That is the deal I proffer. If you don't like it, make
me a counteroffer. We can surely get Em Pathy to come to
the peephole to translate."

There was a pause. Then Cyrus felt a change. His substance was gone. He had been deleted!

"Thank you," he said. But no sound came out, because he
had no solid vocal cords.

He turned and walked through the shell wall. Em Pathy
was there; she had followed them. She had evidently had experience with this sort of thing before. She pointed to a fragment of slate lying beside the big basket.

Cyrus went to it and picked it up. It was deleted; it felt
solid to him and came up in his hands. There was a stylus
attached. He took that and wrote:

WE MADE A DEAL. BRING A ROC HEN TO SHARE HIS EXILE.

She shook her head. "They all hate him," she said. "They
have already flown the coop. None will come."

Oops. What was he to do now?

Then Roc Ette appeared. She read his sign. She nodded.

This astonished him. BUT HE TOOK YOU BY FORCE. YOU
HATE HIM WORST OF ALL.

She nodded again.

I DON'T UNDERSTAND.

"I do," Em said. "She wants to make him absolutely miserable for the rest of his life. This is how."

This astounded him. I PROMISED HIM A FAIR DEAL. THIS IS
NOT THAT.

But Ette went to stand in the view of the peephole. She was ready to go.

Cyrus hurried to print another message. RAGNA. THIS IS NOT WHAT I PROMISED. SHE HATES YOU.

He felt the change. The plaque was no longer solid in his grasp. He had been undeleted.

Ette glanced at him, satisfied. Then she walked to the shell. She walked through its wall and disappeared inside.

"He accepted the exchange," Cyrus said. "But he had to know what was on her mind."

"He did. But any hen is better than no hen, and she was the prettiest in his harem. He doesn't mind that she hates him." Her mouth quirked. "He's male."

The bewilderment was wearing off, like his lost memory. "What about you, then? Your master is gone."

"I remain loyal. I will supervise the supply of food, to be sure he is not mistreated. Go to your Princess. If she is dead, I will still be here. I will make you forget."

A bulb flashed over his head, and this one didn't explode. "Like Ette! You want to make the rest of my life miserable."

"Oh, yes," she agreed. "And you will agree. If your child bride is gone."

Cyrus rather feared he would. But there were other details to attend to. "Where is Kadence?"

"I am here," Kadence called. "With Anona and the ants. There's a crisis."

"A what?"

"All this was too much for the Queen Pique Ant. She has decided to retire. That leaves the Hill without a queen. They don't know what to do."

Cyrus smiled. "Fortunately, I do. Anona, take another bite of royal jelly. That will make you fully female, and you will be the new queen. You have earned it."

Even from this distance he felt Anona's thought. *Oh!*

"But we must revive the Princesses," Cyrus said. "So they

can send all the ants back to their Hill." That was hardly the only reason. Had he diverted Ragna in time?

"Yes," Kadence agreed.

The two of them, and Anona riding in Kadence's hair, made their way back to the Nest. A woman was there, bending over the still forms of the Princesses. "Who are you?" Cyrus demanded.

"I am Princess Ivy, their mother," the woman replied. "I felt my beloved children in danger, and had to come. And who are you?"

Cyrus was shaken, and unable to respond immediately.

"He is my father, Cyrus Cyborg," Kadence said. "And Princess Rhythm is my mother."

Ivy was shocked. "Your *what*?"

Kadence smiled disarmingly. "Hello, Grandma Ivy. We just saved Xanth from Ragna Roc."

Something crossed Ivy's face, but it was not exactly joy. "I'll deal with this in a moment." She put her hands on Melody.

In a stretched moment Melody's eyelids fluttered. She woke. "Mother!" she said tearily. "You came!"

"Of course I came, dear," Ivy said. "Who else could Enhance you back to wellness? Now let me tend to your sister."

Melody sat up and saw the others. "Mother's Sorceress talent is Enhancement," she said. "She can make any good quality better. She just Enhanced my deleted will to live."

"You girls need better supervision," Ivy fussed as she put her hands on Harmony. "You know you had no business getting into a mess like this."

"Yes, Mother," Melody answered with just a hint of a ghost of a smile. Then she looked at Kadence. "Did it work?"

"Yes, Aunt Melody. Father led Ragna into the shell, and Roc Ette slammed the lid on, and now she's in there with him."

"Ouch!" Melody said. "Poor Ragna."

They laughed.

Harmony was slower to revive. "This is awful," Ivy said. "I can barely manage her."

"Oh, you used up most of your power on me," Melody said. "I'm sorry."

"The three of you tackling a creature like that, without your father or I knowing," Ivy fussed. "Whatever possessed you?"

"We're naughty girls," Melody confessed. "But we're older than we look."

Finally Harmony revived. "Mother! You're here!"

"Yes I am," Ivy said. She looked worn. "But I fear I lack the power to save Rhythm. You're all simply too depleted." Tears were running down her face.

"But if you don't Enhance her, she'll sink into illusion and be lost forever," Melody wailed.

"I know. But the three of you were struck by terrible magic. You never should have tackled Ragna Roc alone. We shall have to learn to survive without Rhythm." She was clearly grief-stricken but exhausted.

"No!" Melody cried.

"There must be something," Harmony agreed.

There was no conclusion from Rhythm. She lay there, almost as still as death.

Cyrus was devastated. "Rhythm!" he cried, gazing at the still form. "You can't go! I love you!" He flung himself down and kissed her passionately on the mouth.

At first she was passive. Then she began to respond. Finally she kissed him back, ardently.

As their kiss broke, he lifted her and held her against him. "Oh, Rhythm! I couldn't let you go."

She smiled weakly. "Let's get married, Cyrus."

Then they became aware of the others. Rhythm turned and saw her sisters and mother. "Hi," she said faintly.

"You're a child!" Ivy said severely.

"Mother," Melody said. "He revived her."

"Mother," Harmony agreed. "He saved her life."

"Mother," Rhythm concluded. "I'm seventeen, really. I love him."

"And I'm their daughter," Kadence repeated proudly. "And we just saved Xanth."

Ivy put her hands to her face. "I think I'm going to have a headache."

Another man appeared. "Gnonentity Gnome," Cyrus said. "What are you doing in costume? The play is over."

"Father, that's not Gnonentity," Kadence said.

Then he realized who it really was. "Good Magician Humfrey!"

"Who else?" Humfrey asked grumpily. He turned to Ivy. "Cyrus was doing a Service for me. Rhythm was helping him. It was the only way to save Xanth from Ragna Roc. The mission had to be secret, because Ragna would have deleted all parties had he caught on. What happened between them was necessary."

"Necessary!" Ivy exclaimed. "She's a child!"

"Necessary to summon Kadence from the future," Humfrey said. "She was essential to the effort. Without her it could not have been accomplished. Two to the Fifth: they were the Two, Kadence the fifth. Which is to say she was an idea they filled out by summoning her and borrowing mass to give her solidity. She can not remain here."

"But my child can't have a child! The Adult Conspiracy forbids it!"

"I made an aging spell," Rhythm said. "I was twenty-two when we did it."

"Be that as it may," Humfrey said. "And much as Xanth may owe the two of you, Cyrus and Rhythm, the old order has been salvaged. Cyrus must be banished to Counter Xanth for six years, to abate suspicion, and Kadence must return to her own time."

"No!" Rhythm cried. She gathered Kadence to her, and the three of them stood together.

"When in due course she will rejoin you, when you are of age and married, and can make a proper family," Humfrey continued inexorably. "Her job here is done."

They all saw the inexorable logic of it. They knew they couldn't fight it.

Humfrey brought out a vial. "Drink this," he told Kadence.

The child took it. "Mother, Father, I love you," she said. She drank the fluid in the vial.

Then, softly and silently, she faded away. Rhythm cried quietly into Cyrus's shoulder, and his own eyes were flowing.

"Now you," Humfrey said, proffering another vial.

I know Counter Xanth, Rhythm thought rebelliously. *Everything there is reversed, only you can select how it happens. I'll visit you and I won't be a child.*

Cyrus nodded appreciatively. Exile didn't bother him, but he would not be able to stand being separated from her. Humfrey was sending him to where their love could be legitimate, seemingly coincidentally. The Good Magician was on their side. He drank the vial.

He found himself in an unfamiliar land. It was filled with zones where odd reversals happened, but he was able to step back and unreverse himself. That was fortunate, because one section reversed him to an old man instead of a young one; another to an ugly man; and another into a woman. He didn't want to be old or ugly or a woman. It made a difference how he crossed the lines; he had to do it right, or the reversal didn't unreverse.

When he found a section that rendered him into a two-year-old child, he pondered as he backed out. Two was his technical age. What would it do to a twelve-year-old child?

He found a way to get behind that section without being childified, and made a camp there. Then he waited.

Soon Rhythm appeared, evidently having conjured herself there. "You found it!" she exclaimed, pleased. Then she strode forward, and when she reached him she was a full adult.

She hugged him and kissed him and squirmed rapidly out of her clothes. "All you want is one thing, right?" she asked without giving him a chance to demur. "Over and over." She took him through it, over and over.

But meanwhile she talked, catching him up on events back in Xanth. "We took the ants back to their Hill, and Anona is Queen. She really likes it, but she doesn't have a Consort. She sort of likes you—"

"What?"

"But I told her you were taken," she said teasingly. "They're finding new homes for all the former Minions of Ragna Roc. He thought the final battle would destroy everything, but all it destroyed was his Rock Candy Castle. They're working on recovering the deleted folk of Pompos City, starting with Layea. And they're working on the dragonflies, for Andromeda. You liked her, didn't you?"

"Rhythm—"

· She giggled. She had been teasing him again. The child Rhythm had never been much of a tease; this adult version was. In fact she was adult in a different way, not merely an aged child. Her personality had filled out, enhancing aspects that were only hinted at in the child. The discovery of this more mature yet still playful woman promised to be rewarding.

"And Em Pathy," she continued. "She's sort of sweet on you. Maybe we should send her here."

"Maybe you should," he agreed, trying to play her game.

She ignored it. "The troupe isn't disbanding. Just about all the members want to stay with it. Piper and Don are already scouting for new locations for presentations. Curtis and Crab-apple are running it, and they will develop new plays and put them on."

"New plays?"

"If you write them, I'll deliver them. You should have time to write. Melete's still with you, isn't she?"

"Yes, of course," Melete agreed. "Where would he be, without me?"

"Nowhere," Cyrus said sincerely.

"And in six years, when I'm eighteen," Rhythm continued, "you'll return to Xanth and marry me. Then we'll see about getting Kadence back, and she won't suddenly jump to age six, either. Do you think she'll remember?"

"We'll tell her."

"Yes we will. We couldn't have saved Xanth without her." She paused, then thought of something else. "Do you know the best part of all this?"

"Loving you," he answered promptly.

"That, too. I mean, both my sisters are jealous."

He laughed. "Are you sure you're adult?"

"At the moment. But when I'm a child, that's really fun. And there's another thing."

"What would that be?" he asked warily.

"I remember."

Oops. "You mean—what we do? But you're a child! You're not supposed to—"

He stopped, because she was bursting out with laughter. She was teasing him again.

Taken as a whole, this promised to be a bearable exile.

AUTHOR'S NOTE

On Mayhem 3, 2006 (I use the Ogre Months), I made my first notes on this novel, *Two to the Fifth,* the thirty-second in the Xanth series. I pondered the relevance of the title to a fantasy novel, and realized that the Fifth could be the fifth dimension, which I have always regarded as mass. I checked the reader suggestion list and saw Kadence, Princess Rhythm's daughter, with a useful talent. So I had a start on the novel. But there was a problem: Kadence did not yet exist, and her mother Rhythm was at this stage only twelve years old. That required some pondering. How could she be brought into existence in time for this story? The answer batters the nefarious Adult Conspiracy almost beyond recognition and gives naughtiness a bad name, as remarked in the novel.

Next day my computer crashed. That generated a distraction of several months, because naturally I had not backed up certain key files. It's always the files you never think to back up that turn out to be the most important when they are lost. I use Linux, an open-source operating system that can be properly understood only by elusive Mundanian magicians called geeks. I had lost the geek who set up my system, so was in trouble. There are a number of Linux distributions, all of which are fundamentally similar but different in detail. All of them claim to be easy for anyone to install. None of them are. We struggled with several, some of which installed imperfectly, demanding nonexistent passwords, graying out essential dialogue boxes, and pulling other annoying stunts. Others refused to touch my system at all. We would put in the disk and tell it to install, and the disk would reset the system, start over, and reset the system again, indefinitely. We're not geeks, and obviously Linux was not about to let us have it geeklessly. We did get Xandros, but it started trashing my files. I tried SUSE, but didn't like its environment. They all had trouble addressing backup discs and the Internet. Thus went the dull month of Jejune.

We had to buy a new system and juggle things around, before finding a hardware combination that would allow one distribution, Linspire, to install and work well enough. It wasn't perfect, and I couldn't get it to go online at all, but at least it was close enough to use. (Linspire lives online, but I live in the backwoods and have only dial-up, which it mostly ignores. So I had only a fraction of what it offers others.) So in the months of Jewel-lye, Awghost, and SapTimber I used Linspire to write this novel. After this I'll try Kubuntu to see if I like it better. The point is, I worked out the bypaths of the novel while struggling with the bypaths of Linux.

At this writing I am seventy-two years old, with a bad back (a collapsed disk—could that be why my computer had trouble addressing discs?) and my wife is struggling with her health. Age is a bleep. Those who want to track my ongoing activities can click my website, www.hipiers.com. Every so often a fan asks if he can take over the writing of Xanth novels after I croak, and I politely decline. As Mark Twain said, reports of my death are exaggerated. Also at this writing there are three movies based on my books being worked on; by the time of publication more may be known about that.

Once again I used more than a hundred reader suggestions, but more kept piling in. Some readers sent pages of puns, too many to use in one novel. I considered having special regions made up of all these puns, but feared that would slow the story. So I used a few, and saved the rest for future novels. I try to use puns by everyone else before using several by one person, as a matter of fairness. Some notions were simply too good to use in the late stages of this novel; I'm saving them for better treatment in the next. I hate to use a good idea as a peripheral mention, when it could be so much more. Some relate to characters that don't appear here, so again they have to wait. But in a general way, I used up the available ideas through July 2006. It's likely to be two years before they see publication, but at least they are in the pipeline.

About character names: some I invent, often with alliteration, like Cyrus Cyborg or Don Donkey. Some are suggested by readers. And some I borrow from readers, generally without their knowledge. Some readers write me asking that they be put into Xanth; the answer is generally no. But when I need a spot name for someone with a particular talent, then I may use the suggester's name. It is pretty much chance, so don't deluge me with talents, hoping to get your name used as a character; you're likely to be disappointed.

Here are the credits, in general order of use, but when a person has more than one, I list them together.

Novel Title: *Two to the Fifth,* for the thirty-second Xanth novel, Assorted Cans, Em Pathy—Tim Bruening. Golden Retriever, grape and strawberry jellyfish, shedding mortal coils, Rhythm's chicken-leg drumsticks, Deathbed—Robert. Piper as a significant character—Piper Misna. Dust Devil that is really a devil—Chase Kelly. Selective Friction—Trevor Brogan. Tess Tosterone, S Trojan—David Witchell. Like-ens and Dislike-ens—Amethyst Stever. Robot, Synthe, and Roman tics—Scott Wheeler. T-Tree with hot cups of tea—Mary Rashford. Xina—Ken Kirschenman. Flying Turtle Dove, Bed Rock, Sea Urchin—Alex Paris. Knuckle Sandwich—Niku Larang. Tuff, the volcanic rock salesman—Carlos Plascencia. Strip Tide, Feather Boa Constrictor, Gray V, Mugs that steal—Kelsie O'Dea. Serendipity Serpent,

White and Yellow Pages—Judi Trainor. Gene Pool—David Seltzer. A Void Dance—Norman McLeod. Beaten Path— Cassi. Ants: Defend, Correspond, Persist, Convers, Inf, Antiperspir, Adjudic, Expector, Miscre, Disinfect, Mendic, Contest, Merch, Eleph, Inform, Flagr, Claim, Consult— Donna Macomber-Cassidy. Adverbi, Bronchi Ale—Jennifer Katz. Ragna Roc—Steven Zimmerman. Magnet Monster vs. Com Pewter—Evelynn Moore. Navel Oranges—Shannon Arney. Talent of making mirrors appear—Johnny Maio. Excerpting letters from words to make magic, boy and girl who read minds of women and men—Megan Higgins. Lady Bug—Christina Pirnie. Umber Ella, Copies of Roland's program make other robots barbarian, and loving Hannah— Mark O. Burson. Candy Striper—David J. Browlee. Weslee Weredragon—Weslee Scott. Eye Sickle—Tom Marrin. Walk in someone else's shoes, use their magic—Tom Koerber. Talent of the Silver Lining—Christa. Wood Bees—Ethan Suntag. Causeway, for a good cause—Daniel Forbes. Scowling Powder—Susan Lepper. Butter Fingers—Dale Ashburn. Algae Bra—Hercilla A. Dillard. Daylight Saving Hours— Rachel Vater. Kadence—Maura Guerrero. Guise, making special clothing; Layea, who makes any male do her bidding, 23 minutes of 24 hours; Gole, able to make reversed copies of people; talent of rearranging one's body; Masque that imbues one ability of creature it's made from—Joseph Raymer. Talent of organization: coordinating others efficiently— Mary Eriksen. Talent of making food—Jim Egerton. Magic Drinks: Ales, Gins, Rums, etc.—Avi Ornstein. Telephone— Andrew Palmer. Iron E, Gold N—Andrea Duquette. Lettered salts, Talent of changing one thing in a person's memory, Talent of making small rocks explode—Joseph Laurendeau. Mermaids, merbutlers, mernannies—Carlos Plascencia. Object of D's Ire—Frederick Love and Aunt Dee Dee. Talent Scout—Jen Bartlett. Talent of controlling a wisp of fog—Tommy Yarbrough. Talent of conjuring assorted cloths, or of turning cloth as hard as steel—Blackadder. Talent of being perfect on the first try, not thereafter—Donna Duffy. Ability to invoke the talents of dead people, talent of making stone invisible—Alex Aylor. Twins In Crease and De Crease—Jessica Becker. Talent of unbreaking—Pete. Water moccasins—Norm McLead. Water dragon made of water—Dale DellaTorre. Talent of creating a local Region of Madness—John Frey. Disastrous Misses—Blaine Conner. Coughee—R. J. Craigs. Talent of the Seldom Scene—Shaunna Gyorki. D Kay, zombie demoness—Norm McLeod. Zombies lend a hand, never give lip, go to pieces—Kiti Williams. Cities of Necess, Adver, Pompos, Elasti, and Verbo—Melanie Nunnelee. Hell Breaking Loose, basis for the play "The Riddle"—Daniel Colpi. Andromeda, queen of dragonflies—Ashley Williford. Orienta, who conjures Eastern things—Carrie Foster. Names: Damien, Demetrius, Lita, Nathaniel, Katriana—Sharina Van Dorn. Lullaby, who sings folk to sleep—Jessica Becker. Block Long Erection—George Steele. Common Cents—Jill King. Escape Peas—David Witchell. Talent of knocking the socks off people—Dale Ashburn. Hydraponics—growing hydras from water—Lizzy Wilford. Knight Light—Niko Laranang. Fans Club—Norm McLeod. Obvious and Obvious Lee—Patricia Blalock. Talent of can't be hurt by mundane means—K. Adams.

So what is the future of Xanth? Well, I'm working on completing the letters of the alphabet for the titles. The next one is probably Xanth number thirty-three, *Jumper Cable,* featuring a descendant of Jumper Spider, who appeared in Xanth number three, *Castle Roogna*. He is marvelously adept with spun silk cables, and Com Pewter needs one for a key connection. But we'll see.

Turn the page for a preview of

JUMPER
CABLE

Piers Anthony

Available now from
Tom Doherty Associates

TOR®

A TOR HARDCOVER
ISBN 978-0-7653-2351-4

I

PROPHECY

J umper was going about his business as usual, hunting succulent bugs to eat. He had happened upon a puddle of ointment, and knew there would be flies in it. He was just about to nab a fat fly, taking care not to get stuck in the slimy stuff himself—whereupon a hook swung down from the sky and caught him by the scruff of his chitin. It hauled him up, up, and away, dizzyingly.

Then it dropped him into another scene. This was strange beyond his experience. The ointment was gone, and with it the delectable fly. The plants were thick-stemmed and woody, reaching into the sky, sheathed in clusters of green leaves. Some were small green blades hugging the ground. There was a bird, but no threat to him because it was so small as to be no bigger than a mite. Weird!

Jumper suffered a tweak of memory. His great-to-the-nth grandfather, the original Jumper, had had experience with such a realm. Where was it?

There was a scream. Jumper reacted before he thought, getting there in a single bound. Jumping was of course his nature; he could cover many times his body length per jump, and make a perfect landing. He was, after all, a free-ranging spider.

It was a—his distant tenth-hand memory tweaked—a man, grabbing a girl. Girls needed protecting. So he extended a foreleg, caught the man by the scruff, heaved him up, and threw him away. The man landed in a prickle bush, yelped, looked at Jumper, yelped again, and fled.

"Xx, xxxxx xxx!" the girl cried, getting to her two thick feet.

Jumper clicked his mandibles in confusion. He did not speak girl talk. He was trying to figure out what a girl was doing in this scene. Girls were properly of the giant realm.

She gazed at him, then went to the side and fetched something squirmy. She brought it to him. She held it up with one of her forelegs.

Jumper reached out a foreleg and took it. It seemed to be a writhing nest of greenish leaves. What was he supposed to do with it?

The girl made a gesture as of putting something in her mouth part. Oh—this was edible? He lifted it to his own mouth, to taste it. But the thing immediately squirmed into his mouth and filled it with twisting strands.

"Oh, thank yew!" the girl exclaimed, exactly as before.

"You're welcome," Jumper said.

Then he paused, astonished. Not only had he understood her, he had replied in her own language. How could that be?

"It's the tongues," the girl said. "I gave yew the gift of tongues. So we could talk."

"Tongues?" he asked, perplexed. There was something funny about the way she talked, without any clicking of mandibles; could this explain it?

"It's a kind of plant," she clarified. "It enables a person to relate to any language. Yew saved me from getting abused by that village lout, and I wanted to thank yew. So I had to enable yew to talk. Yew can spit out the tongues now, if yew want."

He considered that. "First, can you tell me where this is? I am not familiar with this scene."

"Well, yew woodn't bee. Yew're a spider, aren't yew? A big one. Yew must bee from far away. This is Xanth proper."

"Xanth proper! That's where my ancestor was."

"I dew knot know about him, but yew came in on a narrative hook. I saw it drop yew here. I was so surprised that I was knot careful, and that lout caught me. Then yew rescued me. I really dew appreciate that. Most creatures woodn't have bothered."

"A narrative hook?"

"It's a device to catch someone up in a story right away. Once it hooks yew, yew can't leave the scene."

Jumper wasn't satisfied with that, so he changed the subject. "Why wouldn't someone else have bothered to help you? You seem like a nice girl, for your species."

"My species. There's the rub. Yew see, I'm knot really a girl."

"You're not? You look like one."

"From the front."

"You seem to have a nice front." She was bare, and shapely. He was remembering the descriptions handed down to the descendants by the original Jumper. Girls were supposed to have thin forelegs, thick hind legs, and fleshy cones on their torsos. She did.

"But I'm really a woodwife."

"Wood? Trees are wood. They have wives?"

"No, silly! I am made of hollow wood. See." She turned around.

Jumper stared. From the back he saw that she was indeed hollow. Her round limbs and cones were empty, as was her head. Her shaped front outside was all there was of her.

She completed her turn and faced him again. "So yew see,

I am something else. I wish I could bee a real girl, so I could make some real man happy, and not bee stalked by village louts who dew knot care what's inside as long as they can poke it from outside. But that simply is knot my nature."

"I . . . see," he said, orienting about three of his eight eyes on her. It didn't help; she remained the shell of a woman.

"And that is knot the worst of it. Com Pewter wants to make me into a Mother Board to fix his obsolescence. Because my animation is all in my wood shell. I could knot stand being shut up like that, so I'm fleeing civilization. Knot that I was ever part of it; I am an innocent woodland creature."

"I understand. I wouldn't like it either."

"But that's no concern of yewrs. Yew saved me this time, and I'll bee more careful next time. I'm really grateful. Is there any favor I can dew yew in return?"

"Can you tell me how to return to my own realm?"

She shook her head. "Yew can knot return, once yew've been hooked. Yew have to finish the narrative."

"But I was about to catch a succulent fly!"

"I'm sorry about that—what's your name?"

"Jumper."

"I'm sorry, Jumper. I'm Wenda. Wenda Woodwife, a fantasy female. I dew knot know why the narrative hook caught yew and put yew here; maybe it was just an accident. But yew're stuck in my world for the duration."

"But I'm not comfortable here!" That was an understatement, but he wasn't sure how to fill it out to full strength.

"I understand, I think. I'm knot comfortable being a fake girl; yew're knot comfortable being in an alien environment. Too bad we can knot solve each other's problems." Then she paused, looking at him. "What is that?"

"My carapace?" he asked. "I wear my skeleton on the outside. Not that I have much of one. I am mostly soft body and hard legs."

"No, that thing stuck to yewr back." She stepped forward and reached for it. It turned out to be a square paper with markings on it.

"I didn't know about that," he said, surprised.

"It's like a label, identifying yew."

"I know who I am. A lost spider."

She studied it. "I think yew had better read it, Jumper. It seems to relate to yew." She handed it back to him.

Jumper took it with one foreleg and oriented an eye on it. To his surprise he found he could read. The tongues really were versatile.

PROPHECY
A Hero unfurls the Bra & Girlls
The Good Magician will set the mission
Like the Ogre beware rogue her
Win Heart and Mind but be not blind
The Unicorn betrays the scorn
And Button Ghost unmasks the Host.

Jumper looked up. "This makes little if any sense to me. What hero? What girls? What Ogre? What Unicorn? What Ghost?"

"I dew knot know. It may bee part of yewr problem I can knot solve." She smiled. "Maybee it is part of the tangled web yew weave to confuse people."

Jumper folded the mystical note and tucked it under a fold of his carapace. "I think I could solve your problem, at least. All you need is girl clothing and someone to watch your back to make sure no one else sees it."

"Clothing! Woodwives dew knot wear clothing."

"So it would make you seem more like a real girl."

Her little mouth dropped open. "It wood, woodn't it? I never thought of that."

"Well, you're a forest creature. It shows in your speech."

She considered. "Clothing makes me think of the anti-streaking agent."

"The what?"

"It is something to put in wash water. It messes up the fauns and nymphs something awful, because then they can knot streak."

"I don't understand."

She paused, assessing his incomprehension. "It is complicated. But I might bee able to solve yewr problem, or tell yew how to. I thought it was just chance that brought me here right when yew arrived, but maybee that hook had a reason to drop yew near me. Because maybee we can help each other. What yew need to dew is go ask the Good Magician, as yewr Prophecy suggests."

"I don't believe I know him, or even where he is. Would he know the answer?"

"He knows the answer to everything. All yew have to dew is ask. Only then he makes yew pay for it with a year's service, or equivalent. So maybe that's knot for yew."

Now Jumper considered. "If the alternative is to stay here in this foreign habitat, I might be better off with that year." Then he reconsidered. "Except for one thing."

"One thing?"

"Spiders of my type live only about six months."

"But yew're much bigger now. Shouldn't yew live longer? At least in this realm? Maybee six months in yewr realm is sixty years in this one."

He wasn't sure. "Maybe so. If I knew where to find him."

"I am beginning to think that maybee we can after all help each other, as I said. I wood like to ask the Good Magician how to become a full girl instead of a half girl, and how to escape Com Pewter, who can change reality in his vicinity. But it's a dangerous trip, and there are many louts along the way. I wood never make it on my own with my innocence intact. But if I traveled with yew, no lout would bother me."

"You know the way there?"

"Yes. An enchanted path leads to it. I wood be happy to show yew."

"Then let's do it."

"Let's dew it," she agreed.